|10 TULARE PUBLIC LIBRARY

SAN JOAQUIN VALLEY LIBRARY SYSTEM

P9-DCI-338

Not Less Than Gods

BOOKS BY KAGE BAKER

The Anvil of the World
Dark Mondays
Mother Aegypt and Other Stories
The House of the Stag
The Empress of Mars
Not Less Than Gods

The Company Series

In the Garden of Iden
Sky Coyote
Mendoza in Hollywood
The Graveyard Game
Black Projects, White Knights: The Company Dossiers
The Life of the World to Come
The Children of the Company
The Machine's Child
Gods and Pawns
The Sons of Heaven

Not Less Than Gods

KAGE BAKER

TOR®

A TOM DOHERTY ASSOCIATES BOOK
NEW YORK

This is a work of fiction. All of the characters, organizations, and events portrayed in this novel are either products of the author's imagination or are used fictitiously.

NOT LESS THAN GODS

Copyright © 2010 by Kage Baker

All rights reserved.

A Tor Book
Published by Tom Doherty Associates, LLC
175 Fifth Avenue
New York, NY 10010

www.tor-forge.com

Tor® is a registered trademark of Tom Doherty Associates, LLC.

Library of Congress Cataloging-in-Publication Data

Baker, Kage.
    Not less than gods / Kage Baker.—1st ed.
        p. cm.
    "A Tom Doherty Associates book."
    ISBN 978-0-7653-1891-6
    I. Title.
    PS3552.A4313N67 2010
    813'.54—dc22

                                2009040728

First Edition: March 2010

Printed in the United States of America

0 9 8 7 6 5 4 3 2 1

In loving memory of David McDaniel (1939–1977)

Yet they who use the Word assigned,
To hearten and make whole,
Not less than Gods have served mankind,
Though vultures rend their soul.

—Rudyard Kipling, "A Recantation"

Not Less Than Gods

1824: Daughter of Elysium

Lady Amalthea R. was a trial to her father, and considered something of an adventuress by the rest of polite society. She reveled in the distinction. Having been told to go straight to hell by her enraged parent after refusing what would have been a respectable and advantageous marriage, Lady Amalthea chose instead to take a small house near Hyde Park. She was financially independent, having inherited certain sums from her late mother, and so set herself up in an establishment with her deaf and ancient nurse, Mrs. Denbigh. Attendant also were a handsome butler, a more handsome footman, a gardener so handsome he might have posed for Michelangelo, and a quite plain maid of all work.

By the time Lady Amalthea had reached her mid-twenties, she was well established as a ruined woman. The fact that she was strikingly beautiful, with the looks of a slender valkyrie, guaranteed that she never wanted for company anyway. She dabbled in politics, was given to radicalism of the deepest dye, and her bitterest regret was that she had failed to seduce Lord Byron before he decamped for the Continent. When Mary Wollstonecraft Shelley was widowed, Lady Amalthea wrote her reams of consolatory advice and insisted on hosting a dinner party in her honor when that exhausted lady returned to England.

Lady Amalthea belonged as well to several Societies, scientific, philosophical and musical especially. It chanced therefore that one smoky

evening at the end of October 1824 she made her way to the house of a
similarly notorious lady to hear an excerpt from Beethoven's new symphony, his Ninth. The entire work was scheduled for its official London
premiere the following March, but an enterprising member of the Phil-
harmonic Society of London had adapted the choral movement for two
pianofortes and four singers.

Lady Amalthea arrived as punch was being served out, and circu-
lated for a while chatting with others in her dazzling and disreputa-
ble set, as Mrs. Denbigh wandered after her like an amiable little dog.
There were young intellectuals, feminists, politicians, musicians, even
an actor or two, and one gentleman to whom her eye was particularly
drawn. He was lean, saturnine, darkly handsome, reminding her rather
of a clean-shaven Mephistopheles, and this alone would have been
enough to pique her interest in him. However, the more Lady Amalthea
saw of the gentleman, the more she was convinced she'd seen him somewhere before.

When they entered the ballroom, furnished with chairs for the per-
formance, she was pleased to note that he took his seat near hers. He
caught her eye, smiled and nodded, with a certain quizzical lift of eyebrow that made her heart race pleasantly. All thought of potential trysts
fled from Lady Amalthea, however, when she glanced down at the lyric
translation sheet she had been handed.

Schiller's sentiments charmed her, appealed to her sense of idealism.
That the beggar and the Prince might be brothers! Heroes striving toward noble conquest! A benign and starry universe in which universal
liberation waited! And then the music began . . .

Lady Amalthea sat bolt upright, spellbound. Her eyes were bright,
her lips moist, her breath came quickly. Even Mrs. Denbigh nodded along
in what she perceived to be time. When the glorious music ended, Lady
Amalthea sagged backward in her chair, panting, one hand on her bosom, quite overcome. Had the composer been present, he would most
certainly have been embraced by Lady Amalthea, and there and then
invited back to her boudoir.

Unable to confer such favor, Lady Amalthea settled for milling about afterward, excitedly discussing the symphony with her acquaintances. She made discreet inquiries as to whether the tenor or baritone might be interested in coming home with her for a cup of cocoa, only to discover that Lady Maria P. and Mrs. H. had beaten her to them; but so elevated were her spirits still, in the music's afterglow, that Lady Amalthea was yet smiling as she took her leave and swept out, Mrs. Denbigh trotting behind her.

Here, however, fate took an odd turn with Lady Amalthea. Her footman appeared, sweating and muddy, to inform her that both rear wheels had unaccountably fallen off her carriage. Even as she was registering this, a gentleman's suave voice spoke next to her ear, offering her a seat in his own conveyance. Lady Amalthea turned and came face-to-face with the dark gentleman, who bowed and kissed her hand.

He identified himself as Dr. Nennys, reminding her that they had been introduced at a supper party some months previous. Lady Amalthea was happy to accept his generous gesture on her own and Mrs. Denbigh's behalf. He gave them sips from a small vial of brandy concealed in his walking-stick, against the evening's chill, and chatted with her about Beethoven as they waited for his coach to be brought. In short order both Lady Amalthea and Mrs. Denbigh were comfortably seated in Dr. Nennys's coach. He bowed, wished them a good night, and shut the coach door. They rolled away into the darkness. Lady Amalthea remembered glimpsing a pair of All Hallows' Eve bonfires low-flickering, burning down to coals at the bottom of the drive.

And that was the last thing Lady Amalthea remembered with any clarity.

There was a confused dream, to be sure, dimly recalled afterward: she was in her private chamber with Beethoven, and he was a glorious giant, a hero, of godlike physique, profoundly amorous. Oddly enough, the act of love itself was a little chilly and awkward, even uncomfortable. There was a sense of indignity. But the music welled up and floated her away to bliss, fully orchestrated, and the soloists had the voices of angels. Lady Amalthea wept for happiness at the spirituality of it all. *Pleasure was given even to the Worm, and the Cherub stands before God . . .*

She woke, warm and rosily content, in a bed; but not her own. Lady Amalthea rolled over and stared in some confusion at the Honorable Henry B., with whom she had carried on sporadic amorous relations during the past year, though not as recently as her equally passionate relations with Lord F. or Pratt the gardener. Confusion gave way to horror as Lady Amalthea spotted the Honorable Mrs. B. lying just the other side of her husband; but Lady Amalthea's consternation was as nothing to the Honorable Henry B.'s, when he opened his eyes and saw his erstwhile mistress lying beside him, fully clothed.

Frantic inquiries and denials were hissed back and forth *sotto voce*. A discreet exit was somehow contrived, both parties white and shaking, as Mrs. B. slept on untroubled. Lady Amalthea was obliged to take a hackney coach to her own residence, where she found Mrs. Denbigh peacefully unconscious on her bed, though likewise fully clothed. When roused, and made to understand that something was amiss, Mrs. Denbigh was unable to provide any details about anything that had passed the previous evening.

So it was with some alarm, two days thereafter, that Lady Amalthea heard that Dr. Nennys had come to call upon her. She met him with trepidation well concealed, however. He greeted her with the utmost courtesy, apparently much concerned. His coachman had informed him that, upon the night of the concert, Lady Amalthea had ordered him to drive her to Lord F.'s residence and there leave her, with the request that Mrs. Denbigh should be taken on to the house by Hyde Park. Dr. Nennys wished to be assured that nothing improper had taken place. Lady Amalthea assured him that nothing had, and he took his leave.

Yet by Twelfth Night, Lady Amalthea had determined beyond all doubt that something improper had certainly taken place with *someone*, though whether with Lord F., the Honorable Henry B., or indeed Pratt the gardener was anyone's guess.

Lady Maria P. was able to provide Lady Amalthea with excellent practical advice, having been in such circumstances herself. Lady Amalthea shortly announced her departure for an extended tour of the Continent, and retired instead, under an assumed name, to a private establishment in the country. On the first of August she was delivered of a vigorous boy. Consigning him into the hands of the proprietress of the establishment, Lady Amalthea packed her bags, returned to London, and never troubled herself to think of the matter again.

1825: Adagio Molto e Cantabile

Mr. Septimus Bell was a gentleman, if of comparatively recent gentry. He was small and dapperly made, with smooth dark hair and rather fine dark eyes. He married one Dorothea Carr, a lady small and vivacious, as like him as a sister might be in appearance, and the two were as happy together as a pair of robins in one nest.

The nest they preferred was situated in London, at No. 10 Albany Crescent, a nicely furnished terrace house with a complete staff. Richardson, the butler, was a former sergeant-at-arms and kept the establishment running with military precision, so the happy couple had little more to do with their days but bill and coo.

After ten years of married bliss, however, their mutual affection had yet to produce a child. This was the only shadow on their happiness, but it loomed more darkly with each passing summer. The household staff observed that Mrs. Bell was now given to occasional weeping fits at the slightest provocation. She complained of headaches and unspecified malaise, and often sat gazing mournfully out into Albany Square, sighing whenever a governess and her charges passed the window.

Mr. Bell was at his wit's end seeking to make his wife happy. For the first time, quarrels, or something perilously near to them, could be heard emanating from the love nest upstairs. Distinguished doctors came to call at No. 10; patent nostrums arrived by post, as did a number of patent devices whose functions could only be guessed at by the scandalized household staff. In the course of time, however, all these efforts bore the desired fruit. Mrs. Bell was suddenly smiling through her still-frequent tears, and Mr. Bell stood perceptibly taller, walked with a perceptibly lighter step.

The incipient heir was formally announced to the household. Congratulations were tendered from all the staff. An expectant hush settled on No. 10, and Nature took her course.

The long-awaited day, Lammas Eve, came and stretched into night, and thence into another day, as a second doctor was called in to consult with the first. The two maids ran to and fro on their tasks, periodically reporting back to the staff downstairs. By noon of the second day they were in tears. At last they came down slowly, silent, and only patient questioning on the part of Richardson was able to elicit news of the arrival and subsequent departure of a small boy, the image of his father but blue as the Bluebird of Happiness. He had never been persuaded to take so much as one breath of mortal air.

The well-appointed nursery sat empty, while the funerary arrangements were made. The ghastly prettiness of the tiny coffin and hearse, all white silk and winking crystal beads, the little confection of a white marble gravestone selected by Mr. Bell, the avalanche of consolatory correspondence, all had their due effect on Mrs. Bell's nerves. She took to her bed and went mad. Weeping incessantly, she insisted that her child had *not* died, that the fairies had stolen it away, and implied that Mr. Bell was no manner of a man if he failed to go into Fairyland and retrieve it for her.

Mr. Bell went instead to Brook's, and remained there, gambling away a great deal of money. He had very nearly bankrupted himself, and was considering whether he ought to quarrel with a noted duelist or simply borrow a pistol and take matters into his own hands when he was approached by a fellow member.

For a brandy-sodden moment Mr. Bell thought Dr. Nennys was the Devil, dark and sleek and faintly smiling as he was; but Dr. Nennys spoke solemnly and, indeed, kindly, asserting that Mr. Bell's headlong rush to self-destruction was ill-advised. He pointed out that, sad as Mr. Bell's loss had been, countless other parents suffered bereavement daily and the ways of the Almighty were not to be questioned. He proposed, in any case, to ameliorate Mr. Bell's sorrows both familial and financial.

There was, it seemed, a child born the selfsame day as Mr. Bell's own boy, to a lady of noble blood by a lord similarly well-bred, unfortunately without benefit of clergy. A suitable home was wanted for the young person. Dr. Nennys had been authorized to seek out appropriate foster parents for him, and moreover to offer substantial monetary compensation, paid quarterly. Dr. Nennys named a certain sum, and Mr. Bell's eyes widened. It was more than enough to offset his losses at cards. Stammering, he accepted Dr. Nennys's offer. Dr. Nennys arranged to bring the infant to No. 10 that evening, at a discreetly late hour.

At midnight precisely a black coach drew up before No. 10. A black-veiled woman emerged with a bundle in her arms. Mr. Bell hurried down the walk, closely followed by Richardson. The coachman leaped down, set a trunk on the pavement, resumed his seat and drove off at some speed. The woman nodded curtly to Mr. Bell and informed him she was the infant's nursemaid, that her name was Mrs. Melpomene Lodge, that the infant was Edward Alton Fairfax, and that she would be pleased to inspect the nursery at Richardson's convenience.

The following morning Mr. Bell preceded the breakfast tray into Mrs. Bell's sickroom, bearing the infant dressed in one of their dead child's gowns. When Mr. Bell had got her to look at him, he announced that he had gone to Fairyland as she requested, and brought back their son. Mrs. Bell left off crying, astonished, and as she stared at him he set the infant in her arms. She looked down at it.

Nothing was said for an interminably long moment, in which Mr. Bell had occasion to reflect that this child bore no resemblance to the one they had buried. It was bigger, robustly pink, and had an abundance of fair hair. The only mar to its perfection was a slight bruise on the bridge of its nose. Mr. Bell held his breath, waiting for a reaction from his wife.

At last Mrs. Bell said that it had no eyelashes. Mr. Bell replied that they were certainly there; the infant was simply too fair for them to show much. She acknowledged this by pursing her lips slightly. For a while longer she continued to regard the infant, as though puzzled, and at last laid it down on the counterpane. She thanked Mr. Bell, but said she didn't think she wanted it, and might she have her breakfast tray now?

The housemaid, who had been waiting all this time with Mrs. Bell's tray, thrust it at Mr. Bell, caught up the infant and rushed from the room in tears. Aghast, Mr. Bell waited on his wife, trying to think of a way to explain that they must keep the child or face financial ruin. To his great relief, Mrs. Bell made no further reference to it, but dried her eyes and spoke calmly and coherently of small domestic matters, the first time she had done so since the death of her son.

Indeed, from that day her madness receded, until only those who had known Mrs. Bell in happier times would have said she was in any way altered. The servants remarked, amongst themselves, that she had quite a different expression in her eyes now. She was willing to tolerate the infant's presence to a certain extent, though as it grew older and obstreperously affectionate she became reserved and withdrawn, and endured its visits in tight-lipped silence. Mr. Bell, desperate to please his wife, took her away to the Continent when she was well enough to travel. In the pleasant air of Italy her spirits revived considerably. Husband and wife walked together, admired the scenery together, posed for portraits together, and were very nearly happy again.

The infant was left at No. 10 with the servants.

1826–1839: Little Lamb, Who Made Thee?

Robert Richardson had served with distinction in the 32nd Regiment of Foot, and had in fact had his left leg shot from under him at the battle of Waterloo. Invalided out of the Army, he had lived with a married sister while seeking employment. Having had some experience as a footman before joining the Army, and being possessed of an upright and dignified bearing notwithstanding his prosthetic limb, he was shortly hired as butler at No. 10 Albany Crescent. This proved satisfactory to all persons concerned.

He expressed no opinions on the irregular manner in which young Edward Fairfax (or Bell, as the infant was hastily dubbed, even though it was obvious there was no need to engage in any further charades for Mrs. Bell's benefit) had entered the household. If he felt it was a shame that Mrs. Bell never so much as inquired after the little creature, or that Mrs. Melpomene Lodge seemed too sternly efficient, more like a sergeant herself than someone intended to care for a child, Richardson kept his reservations to himself.

The below-stairs servants were more forthcoming in their judgment. While no one felt Mrs. Bell could be blamed for going mad, her lack of affection for young Edward was roundly condemned, and it was felt that Mrs. Lodge was a cold-hearted bitch who had no business minding babies. Consequently on her days out the boy was brought downstairs and tended by Cook and the parlor maids, who showered him with affection.

He was such a fine big boy, after all! Not, perhaps, the prettiest baby Cook had ever seen; his eyes were a peculiar pale blue and a bit small. On the other hand, he was good-tempered, seldom cried even when teething (which occurred very early), and suffered no infantile rashes, colds, fevers or indeed any kind of illness whatsoever. He throve on the nasty mixture Mrs. Lodge fed him, compounded of scalded cow's milk, catnip tea and certain arcane powders Mrs. Lodge did not deign to name for the rest of the staff.

In fact, Edward was more than healthy; he was remarkably intelligent. Violet, the between-stairs maid, discovered this when, at the age of eleven months, he suddenly recited back to her the entire text of "Baa, Baa, Black Sheep." She squealed in excitement and tried him on "Ring Around the Roses" and "London Bridge Is Falling Down," both of which he repeated note perfect. Violet ran and fetched Cook, who listened in disbelief and then ran and fetched Richardson. Edward was rewarded with bread and jam for his brilliance and roundly cosseted, though the below-stairs staff resolved thereafter to mind what they said around the child.

Edward's infancy passed without other incident, largely unnoticed by his adoptive parents. Richardson wondered uncomfortably whether some male oughtn't take a hand with the child, lest he warp under too much womanly influence. Signs that this might be the case were already evident, for young Edward had taken to carrying around a doll he referred to as his baby. He spent hours pretending to feed it with a spoon, or bathing it, or rocking it to sleep while he sang to it, or combing its hair. At last Richardson was moved to confront Mrs. Lodge, asking her whether she didn't feel such play was unnatural for a boy.

Mrs. Lodge had looked at him in that chilly way she had—*no more feeling than a waxwork statue*, Richardson thought to himself—and then, to his surprise, she had agreed that he was perfectly correct. The doll was confiscated forthwith and thrown out. Edward had wept inconsolably. Richardson had then overheard Mrs. Lodge telling Edward that only weak and inferior children cried. She added that he had no right to complain, as he was nothing but a bastard, no matter how well-born, and he was lucky he wasn't out in the street begging for his bread.

White with fury, Richardson had summoned Mrs. Lodge and sacked her forthwith. She had merely shrugged and decamped with her trunk, asking for no references, nor leaving any forwarding address. Her departure had provoked fresh tears in her former charge, as another piece of the only world he had ever known vanished. In vain Richardson offered his watch as a plaything. With slightly better success, he removed his prosthesis and showed Edward how it fastened to the stump of his knee. Edward then wished to know what had happened to the rest of Richardson's leg, and so Richardson told him all about the battle of Waterloo. Edward listened with wide eyes.

A governess was hired after that and duly installed in the schoolroom, but as far as Edward was concerned Richardson was his true teacher. Richardson was consulted, at any hour of the night or day, on such diverse matters as whether Robinson Crusoe had been a real man, whether the ogre Bonaparte were really dead or just shamming, and whether the holes in Jesus' hands and feet had healed over by now.

As the years rolled along, the questions tended to need answers more urgently: what, for example, was the best way to repair a hole in the plasterwork caused by a Guy Fawkes squib? How could one retrieve a tin sailboat from the bottom of the Hyde Park Serpentine? Was there any reason to be alarmed by the new and peculiar sensations experienced when inadvertently witnessing a maid in her nightdress?

Christmases came and went without so much as a card from Mr. and Mrs. Bell, who had taken to spending their winters in the south of France. Edward saved his pocket money to buy trinkets as presents for the staff, or laboriously made gifts of penwipers, or needle cases, or pasteboard boxes decorated with glued-on seashells. He took his Christmas dinner below stairs and his Twelfth Cake too, and Cook and Richardson between them always stage-managed it so that Edward never failed to get the slice with the sixpence.

But there was no concealing from the boy that other children had parents who saw them on a daily basis, rather than at intervals of four or five months. Mr. Bell did endeavor to bring the occasional present back for Edward, and generally exchanged a few polite words with him at the breakfast table, for which Edward was desperately grateful. Still, the passing years only served to emphasize his nature as a changeling: by the age of nine Edward was already as tall as Mr. Bell, resembling him in no way. One afternoon he came to Richardson and, hesitantly, asked to know what a *bastard* might be?

Having given a not altogether satisfactory answer, Richardson later lined up the household and demanded to know which of the servants had used the offending word where Master Edward could hear. One and all solemnly swore they had not. Cook then pointed out that they all knew Master Edward had an excellent memory, and only the other day had reminded her about the time she had burned the bottom out of the teakettle, which had happened when he had still been a tiny thing in long clothes.

Whether or not Master Edward remembered Mrs. Lodge, it was plain her words had had their effect upon him. As he neared his eleventh birthday the boy grew sullen and silent, more given to reckless escapades. Only Richardson's stories of the War seemed to hold his full attention. He asked Richardson how old one must be to join the Army, and whether Richardson thought a very tall boy might pass for an older one.

Lammas Eve passed, and on Lammastide a knock came at the front door of No. 10.

Richardson opened the door to behold a sleek dark man with an enigmatic smile. He asked whether the Bells were at home and, on being informed that they were in Geneva, gave his name as Dr. Nennys and asked to speak with Master Edward.

Richardson declined to permit him entrance to the house. Dr. Nennys then produced authorization unquestionably signed by Mr. Bell, eleven years and two days previous, granting Dr. Nennys authorization *in loco parentis* in all matters pertaining to his ward, Edward Alton Fairfax. Dr. Nennys also produced letters of recommendation from certain gentlemen very highly placed in certain government ministries, all certifying as to his worthiness as an educator of youth. Still somewhat reluctant, Richardson allowed him into the front hall. Dr. Nennys strode boldly past him into the drawing room.

Master Edward was summoned. Richardson stood stiffly attendant.

"So this is the boy," said Dr. Nennys, smiling as he rose to his feet. "What a splendid young man! I am delighted to make your acquaintance at last, Edward. I am Dr. William Fitzwalter Nennys, a great friend of your father."

He extended his hand to the boy, who took it wonderingly. "I'm happy to meet you, Dr. Nennys," said Edward. Dr. Nennys shook his hand firmly and then stepped back, regarding Edward with a pleased expression.

"Yes; a remarkably fine boy. And only eleven? I'd have said you were fifteen at least. Extraordinary. A boy marked for greatness, I believe. You have the look of a hero about you, Edward."

"I do, sir?" Edward stood perceptibly straighter.

"You do indeed. Now then, my boy! Your parents have arranged for you to attend school at my own establishment, Overton Hall, in Suffolk. Given the high regard I have for your father, I thought it best to come down and advise you personally."

"Overton Hall, sir?" said Richardson. "I must inform you, sir, that my master attended Harrow, and when last consulted on the matter told me that he supposed Master Edward ought to be sent there too, sir."

"He has reconsidered. Harrow is all very well in its way for common boys, I suppose, but it won't do for young Edward," said Dr. Nennys, with a dismissive wave. "Edward is a unique boy, a remarkable boy, and will do very well at Overton, I have no doubt. I look forward to personally tutoring him."

Richardson, who had long believed the worst possible thing to do to a boy was treat him as though he were the Little Lord Jesus, said: "I'm sure Master Edward has never pretended to airs or thought he was better than other boys, sir."

"Oh, really?" drawled Dr. Nennys. "Shall we set him a few maths problems? What is seventy times seventy, Edward?"

"Four thousand nine hundred, sir," said Edward promptly.

"And what is five thousand and thirty-two times six hundred and sixty-three?"

"Three million, three hundred and thirty-six thousand, two hundred and sixteen, sir," said Edward, with equal speed. Richardson turned to stare at him.

"Divided by four?"

"Eight hundred thirty-four thousand and fifty-four, sir."

"Divided by three?"

"Two hundred seventy-eight thousand and eighteen, sir."

"His answers are correct to the last figure," said Dr. Nennys, with a triumphant look at Richardson. "Though you may work out the sum with a pencil if you wish, I believe my point is made."

"Well, but he's always been good at sums," stammered Richardson.

"How many bunches of primroses appear in the wallpaper in this room, Edward?"

Edward glanced around the room once and replied, "Two thousand four hundred and seventeen, sir." He looked at Richardson a little shamefacedly. "It's only a trick, Richardson; you just count how many in a foot square—"

"But common boys wouldn't think to," said Dr. Nennys. "Overton's the place for you, Edward, I haven't the slightest doubt. Now, tell me a little about yourself! What are your aspirations, my boy?"

Richardson wondered if the boy knew what *aspirations* were, but Edward said: "I should like to be a soldier one day, sir."

Dr. Nennys's smile widened into a grin. His teeth were extraordinarily white. Richardson found it unsettling.

"A soldier! Of course. I could see that you were a brave boy; it is written in your face. We shall mold you into a perfect servant of the Crown, shall we?—and you shall defeat His Majesty's enemies."

"Oh, yes, sir, please!"

Master Edward, eyes very bright, was then dismissed, but Dr. Nennys lingered for short words with Richardson. Richardson was informed that Overton Hall had been the choice of Edward's natural father, a gentleman of some importance, and Dr. Nennys trusted no further justification was necessary to a hired servant. The date on which the next term commenced was named, and a list of school supplies was presented, to which Richardson was expected to attend. Dr. Nennys took his leave.

On the appointed day, a coach bearing Richardson and Edward drew up before the Pinford Arms. Richardson caught Edward's trunk as it was thrown down. Other boys could be seen milling around a van with the name OVERTON HALL prominently painted on its side. Richardson shook hands with Edward, told him to recollect his duty to God and the King, and pressed a half-crown of his own money on the boy. He was profoundly grateful no passengers got on for the return trip to London, and sat alone in the coach blinking away tears as far as Ipswich before he was able to master his emotions.

The boy wrote often from school, advising the household staff of his progress. He was happy and well, getting excellent marks, especially in maths; it was true, however, that he had twice been caned for fighting. He thought perhaps he might like to enter the Church, though he hastened to assure Richardson that this would not preclude his going into the Army because he could serve as a chaplain. Edward's dutiful letters to Mr. and Mrs. Bell accumulated on the dining room table, unread, for his guardians were not expected to return from Geneva until Christmas.

In the event, they never did. Mr. Bell wrote to Richardson to inform him that they had changed their plans and were going on to Italy. A fortnight later Richardson received word that their boat had capsized during a sail on the Bay of Naples. Both husband and wife were missing, presumed drowned.

Dr. Nennys himself brought Edward, red eyed and miserable, home for the funeral. He sat beside Edward for the reading of the last will and testament of Septimus Bell, which, in the event of his death and that of his beloved wife, Dorothea, left all their worldly goods to one Sibley Bell, Mr. Bell's cousin. This gentleman gladly took possession of No. 10 with all its furniture, retaining the services of the staff, but—feeling compunction, perhaps, that Edward had been left without a penny—assured the boy that he was welcome to return to No. 10 during the intervals between terms. His charity did not extend to paying Edward's continued tuition, however.

Dr. Nennys merely smiled and said he thought it might be possible to make other arrangements.

Term followed term. Edward's letters home to the servants improved in grammar and spelling, but grew briefer. Dr. Nennys was keeping him very busy with special tutoring; he was learning fencing, riding, and marksmanship. He had been told he had an extraordinary talent for calculus. Best of all, Edward had learned that his *real* father, a person of some consequence it seemed, was still alive! He was henceforth to be known as Edward Bell-*Fairfax*! Circumstances prevented Edward being acknowledged, but it was Edward's intention to make his distant parent proud with a life of heroism.

And Dr. Nennys—who was, Edward explained, a font of wisdom, a nearly godlike mentor—had intimated on many occasions that Edward was destined for greatness. It didn't matter that he was a bastard, after all. Shakespeare had written a play in which there was a character called Philip the Bastard, and he was a glorious hero and won a battle. Edward had had no messages from his august parent yet, but dared to hope that the great man might somehow contrive a discreet meeting with him.

Richardson read this aloud, smiling, and he and Cook exchanged relieved glances. The secret was out at last, and had done the boy no harm.

And then—

Edward came home for the summer holidays just after his fourteenth birthday, taller now than Richardson. He went on an outing with Richardson and Cook, spending a happy day at Gravesend. They returned to find Dr. Nennys waiting in the drawing room, his dark face impassive but his eyes glinting with suppressed anger.

Edward's father had taken an active interest in the boy at last, it seemed. He had communicated his express wish that Edward be withdrawn from Overton and enlisted in the Navy as a midshipman.

Appalled silence followed this pronouncement. At last Edward asked whether he mightn't go into the Army instead. On being informed that the arrangements had already been made and were irrevocable, Edward turned to Richardson and said that he was very sorry.

"Be so good as to leave us, Richardson, and close the doors," Dr. Nennys snapped.

Richardson glared at him but said only, "Very good, sir." He left the drawing room and drew the doors shut with a crash, after which he stood motionless on the other side, endeavoring to hear the following conversation:

"But how could he do this?" Edward's voice broke in a wail. "After all you told me about him—I thought he wanted—"

"Bell-Fairfax, I trust you will not blub like a child at the first adversity you encounter?"

"No, sir. Sorry, sir."

"I should think so. Now, listen to me. Your father has his own reasons for this decision, which neither I nor you may question. It may be that my reports of your extraordinary progress have persuaded him that you are ready *now* to begin the great work for which we have been preparing you. Your grasp of useful modern languages is excellent—we will pass over your abysmal Latin, which is unnecessary nowadays in any case—and you have begun to master your temper. What more can you learn at Overton?"

"It isn't that," said Edward, clearly struggling to speak calmly. "But I thought I might have displeased him, and I should be very sorry to."

"Bell-Fairfax, I'm quite certain that is not the case; and even if it were . . . do you remember when you thrashed that vile bully Scargill?"

"Yes, sir." Edward spoke in a small voice. "Is that it? Did he die after all?"

"No, no, my boy, and small loss if he had! Scargill will undoubtedly grow into the sort of vermin you will spend your life fighting. No. I spoke to you then of certain men, powerful men, who would have intervened to save you even if the young wretch *had* died of his injuries. Those men are watching you still. I may not tell you more at this time, but they are aware of your remarkable qualities, and they are determined you shall live to fulfill your noble destiny.

"Consider this temporary adversity a test of your resolve, a trial wherein you may prove yourself to those good men. You shall go forth into the greater school of the world!"

"I shall not disappoint them, sir," said Edward.

"I know you will not," said Dr. Nennys, and then in quite a different voice said, "Richardson! You needn't lurk out there. Come in."

Richardson opened the doors once more and stepped through into the drawing room. He beheld Edward, looking somewhat downcast, and Dr. Nennys, who still looked to be in a nasty temper.

Dr. Nennys informed Richardson that Edward was to repair to Portsmouth by the first of September, and go aboard HMS *Repulsion*. Richardson was presented with a sum of money with which to buy a sea-chest and suitable clothing for a midshipman. Dr. Nennys shook Edward's hand and took his leave, promising that they would meet again.

The money provided by Edward's remote parent was by no means generous. Coach fare to Portsmouth bit deeply into it; a night's room at the

Cock and Bottle ate up more. Edward's measurements were taken at a tailor's. The tailor then informed Richardson of the usual cost of fitting out a young gentleman in uniform.

Richardson blanched. Edward looked from one to the other uneasily. The tailor added that he did have some stock of ready-mades at a reduced price, since he was in the habit of purchasing the contents of sea-chests from the families of deceased officers. Given that the young gentleman was so unusually tall, it was entirely likely he would find something that fit him, which would save time as well as money.

They were shown the stock, a great deal of which was moth-eaten and antiquated. The tailor proudly held up a pair of knee-breeches Nelson himself might have worn. Edward looked piteously at Richardson. Richardson scowled and dug into his own purse to have two pairs of trousers new made, at least, with new linen. The cheapest of the hats was produced, an old cocked bicorn devoid of gold lace or any other distinction, and set on Edward's head; a midshipman's dirk was retrieved from a dusty boxful of them and pressed into Edward's hand.

A man's jacket was found, not too out-of-date, with a few hanging threads where its epaulets had been cut away. The sleeves were too short, but the tailor assured them he could let the cuffs out and the jacket would serve admirably, assuming the young gentleman had left off growing and the one or two moth-holes were patched.

Richardson brought the young scarecrow and his sea-chest to the *Repulsion*'s berth, where he once again shook hands and reminded Edward of his duty to his God and his Queen. He slipped most of his remaining money into Edward's pocket and turned away from his forlorn charge, hoping to catch the late coach so as to avoid paying for another night's lodging. As it was, Richardson had to do without breakfast and leave the coach at Esher, limping the rest of the way into London. Cook opened the kitchen door to him when he reached No. 10 at last, and thought he looked as though he had aged twenty years.

1847: In Adamantine Chains and Penal Fire

"I wondered if you'd turn up!"

Dr. Nennys turned at the hoarse greeting, and found himself face-to-face with the old man, staring at him across the short stretch of pavement that separated them. The other's eyes were red, his cheeks sunken in; he had shaved in haste and carelessly, leaving white chin-stubble glinting in the morning light. He stood straight, though, his spine stiffened by rage. He took a lurching step toward Dr. Nennys.

"Have you seen him yet? Have you? Eh?"

"I arrived here not five minutes ago for that very purpose," said Dr. Nennys. "Richardson, I believe?"

"You know I am, sir," said he, baring his teeth. "Have you come from his damned father? Or is *he* content to let his boy hang? Eh? So long as nobody knows the truth? That'd be convenient for him, wouldn't it? Wouldn't it, damn you?"

"Calm yourself! I came at his express wish, if you must know, to learn the truth of the matter."

"Then, sir, in God's name, *do something for him*! He didn't mutiny. The other officers will testify he never mutinied. He laid hands on a superior officer, right enough, but that captain's a madman. The men'll tell you. He was a hero, damn you, he'd been made a commander! He followed his duty as he saw it. Oh, this fucking worthless Navy—"

"Richardson, your agitation is understandable, but I will not listen to such language." Dr. Nennys's quiet voice cut through Richardson's wrath like steel. The old man halted, put his shoulders back to stand ramrod-upright.

"Sir! Very sorry, sir."

"I will do what I can for him, of course. Where is he?"

"They've still got him chained up in the *Zagreus*," said Richardson, a slight quaver coming into his voice. "In a foul little box, naked, like he was an animal. I don't think they know what to do yet. Captain South-bey's still in bed with sticking plasters all over his face. I only talked to some acting commander. There's somebody from the Admiralty expected in a day or so. Likely they'll judge him then. Please, sir—"

"Where are we?" Dr. Nennys glanced up at the inn sign above their heads. "The Keppel's Head? I'll tell you what, Richardson. You take yourself in there and have a brandy to settle your nerves. Or gin, if you prefer. Here." He drew a sovereign from his pocket and held it out to the old man.

Richardson went pale, affronted, but he took the money. "Very good, sir. Thank you, sir."

"There's a good fellow. I'll just go aboard the *Zagreus*. We'll speak later."

Dr. Nennys was obliged to display a great many documents once he had gone aboard the *Zagreus*, but he had come prepared. In the end he was escorted down into the hold by a pair of very deferential Marines, who were so considerate as to bring a chair and set it in place for him outside what looked like a cupboard door.

"Unlock it, if you please," said Dr. Nennys. "And be so good as to leave the lantern."

"Yes, sir," said the more talkative of the two. He obeyed and they took their leave. Dr. Nennys sat still a moment, observing the noisome surroundings, listening to the tidal wash against the ship's hull. Then he reached out and opened the door.

The space beyond was no more than a meter high and two meters long, slightly less than a meter deep. Edward Alton Bell-Fairfax sat within, in chains fastened to an iron bolt in the bulkhead. He peered out at the lamp, blinking, for it blinded him as thoroughly as if it had been the sun at noon.

Dr. Nennys looked closely. The hopeful boy he had remembered was gone. The young man in chains was a hulking giant, gaunt, unshaven, with bitterness and exhaustion smoldering in his pale eyes. For a moment Edward stared at Dr. Nennys, blank as a big animal. At last he turned his face away, baring long teeth.

"Bell-Fairfax," said Dr. Nennys, putting a world of sorrowful reproach into the name. "How has it come to this? You nearly killed your commanding officer."

"I ought to have killed him outright," said Edward, and his voice was now a man's voice, a dark tenor. "Since I'm to hang for it. Yes. That's my only regret, that I couldn't keep on beating his head against the deck until his skull split. D'you remember Scargill, sir, when we were at Overton? It was like that. Just exactly like that. I thought of stopping, but he was a bully, really a foul murdering little monkey in a uniform, I could see he wasn't going to give over the flogging until he'd killed Price and, and I just thought, *Well, the world will be better off without a creature like this in it.* Shame they stopped me."

"My dear boy," said Dr. Nennys, in affected tones. "And what of the noble ideals with which you entered Her Majesty's Navy?"

"What of them?" Edward grimaced. "I went in resolved to do my duty. Imagine my surprise on learning that my duty involved blowing the Chinese to fragments, and all because they had the temerity to refuse to buy British opium! But I did my duty, sir. I was commended by my captain and promoted.

"Then I was given a command and sent to patrol the Ivory Coast, and my duty there was to stop any ships attempting to transport slaves from Africa. I was so happy, sir! An inarguably moral cause in which I might serve. I was to capture slave ships and bring them in as prizes, you see?"

"And so you did," said Dr. Nennys. "Zealously. We heard great things of you, my boy."

"But it wasn't enough, sir. I couldn't stop them. Ships I brought in were merely sold, *with their cargoes of slaves*, refitted and sent back about their business. I could name you upright British merchants, Christian men all, who worked hand in glove with the Portuguese!

"So I began to set the blacks ashore, and burn the ships I took. Even this wasn't enough. I led expeditions to the barracoons where slaves were embarked. I set them free there, too. I burned the warehouses and the smithies where chains were forged. Damn me, do you know, the blacks fought to defend them? I had half a dozen black kings complain to me about the destruction of their property.

"One day a warship brought an admiral, and I was summoned aboard and made to give an account of myself. I was told my zeal was excessive. 'Where are your prizes? Principles are all very well, but business is business, don't you know?' And they took me from my duty, sir, and sent me here aboard the *Zagreus*.

"I soon saw what manner of captain I had to serve under, and what his particular pleasure was. I thought I'd seen cruelty before, sir, in the service, but I never dreamed men like Jeremiah Southbey existed. Men are *murdered* here, always under color of discipline and law. I watched my fellow officers' faces and saw that they'd do nothing, for fear and custom. And then Price broke a basin in the galley, and Southbey would've had him flogged to death for it. The rest you know.

"So I will die, sir. But as God is my witness—if He isn't blind and deaf—I could not have acted otherwise."

"Well." Dr. Nennys stroked his chin. "I am to take it, then, that you've grown disillusioned? You've seen the ways of the world, and they disgust you? The pettiness of mediocre men in office, for example? The hypocrisy of the Church?"

Edward gave a hoarse chuckle. "Well put, sir."

"And you face the gallows without fear, happy to leave such a world?"

"I do."

"Would you not rather make it a better world?"

"Were there any chance of doing so, sir, I should cheerfully devote my life to such a cause. But I've learned rather more about the nature of humanity than you meant to teach me, I fear."

Dr. Nennys smiled. "Not at all, my boy. You've learnt precisely what we wanted you to learn."

Edward's eyes burned through the shadows. "Have the kindness to explain yourself, Doctor."

"This ordeal was the last necessary lesson," said Dr. Nennys. "You've seen how futile are the efforts of second-rate politicians, and pious frauds, in improving the lot of mankind. Now then, Bell-Fairfax! You are ready to take up the great cause for which I have readied you since your boyhood—the cause for which you were born, one might say."

Edward held up his arms, displaying his chains. "And how am I to take up any cause, sir?"

"Tell me first whether you're willing."

"You know I am!"

"Then watch and listen." Dr. Nennys stood, and called to the Marine who stood guard at the companionway. "You there! Pray inform your commanding officer I'd like a word with him. And have the prisoner's sea-chest brought. He's being transferred."

Both the Sergeant of Marines and the acting captain came, and looked gravely at the written order Dr. Nennys showed them, with all its seals and signatures and countersignatures. Dr. Nennys added a few quiet words about it being the Admiralty's wish that this matter be handled with the utmost discretion.

He met with no arguments. Edward's shackles were unlocked, he was permitted to crawl from his cell—though he was still unable to stand to his full height, belowdecks—and dress himself. The Sergeant of Marines approached with a pair of handcuffs, but Dr. Nennys waved his hand dismissively.

"How shall he carry his trunk, man, wearing those? I'll take full re-sponsibility for the prisoner."

"As you like," muttered the sergeant. He avoided looking at Edward, as did the rest of the crew when Edward followed Dr. Nennys on deck and down the gangplank to the dock. From somewhere up among the rigging, however, came a cry of "Three cheers for Mr. Bell-Fairfax!"

"Who said that? Take that man's name!" cried the acting captain, but the answer was a derisive laugh, as the topmen whooped and scrambled above like monkeys. From the depths of the ship came faint calls of "hurray, hurray, hurray," and looking back Dr. Nennys saw faces peering from gunports, from the masthead platforms, even one or two wizened countenances pressed to the scuppers. Edward set his sea-trunk on his shoulder and gave them an ironic salute. He turned away from the *Zagreus* and followed Dr. Nennys ashore.

"And *that* is power," said Dr. Nennys smugly.

Rooms were taken at the Keppel's Head. Richardson quite broke down on seeing Edward; when he had recovered himself he was sent to a haberdasher's, and then to engage the services of a tailor. The tailor was duly brought and took Edward's measurements, clicking his tongue as he calculated the amount of yardage necessary to clothe Edward like a gentleman. Having been promised an extra five pounds if he worked through the night, the tailor hurried away to produce a suit of clothes. A bath was drawn; Edward emerged from it to find supper had been brought up. Richardson waited on Edward with trembling hands, until Edward bid him sit and eat.

During all this time Dr. Nennys made no reference to Edward's release, other than to allude to some great matter to be discussed at a more convenient moment. Nor were any details forthcoming until after the tailor delivered Edward's garments the next day, when Richardson was sent ahead to the new railway station with Edward's trunk carried by an obsequious porter.

"Let us walk, Bell-Fairfax," said Dr. Nennys, stepping out on the pavement. Edward stepped down beside him and Dr. Nennys tilted back his head, considering the tailor's work. All around them was the bustle of Portsmouth, the ship-chandler's agents hurrying to and fro, the sailors ashore roistering, the shouts of the workers in the refitting yards. Out of uniform, Edward faded into the background—or very nearly, allowing for the fact that he towered over every other mortal on the street by a good head.

"I have waited a great many years for this day, I may tell you," said Dr. Nennys, as they started up the Hard toward Park Road.

"And why would that be, sir?" said Edward, tipping his hat to a passing lady.

"I brought you into the world, my boy. Surely you've suspected as much? And you may have felt some shame at the irregular circumstances of your birth. Do not. There was nothing sordid or accidental about it. You were planned for, Bell-Fairfax, you were *needed*. Shall I tell you by whom?"

Edward had stopped on the pavement, staring at him, but caught up in two long strides. "Please, sir!"

"Then hear me out. A great many ages of the world ago, in a great civilization long since vanished, the most intelligent men of their nation looked about them and drew exactly the same conclusions you have drawn, in your time in the Navy. There was no shortage of valiant heroes desiring to make the world an earthly paradise, but they were continually foiled by the greed and sloth of their rulers. Science was made to serve the vanity of kings, or banned outright by superstitious priests.

"And so they came together, these good and wise men, and formed a society to work in secret for the improvement of the world. Only Science, they felt, could alleviate human suffering, by developing advances in medicine, in agriculture, in sanitation. Only a hierarchy of great intellects should guide and rule mankind.

"This hierarchy, working in the shadows over centuries, brought its nation to unparalleled prosperity and comfort. Yet its members saw all too plainly that human nature would pull their empire down. Therefore they fled, taking their arcane knowledge with them, and so survived the catastrophe to confer their benefits on other nations.

"You would recognize many names among its members, over the ages. Archimedes, for example. Heron of Alexandria! Vitruvius. Their inventions were brilliant, and yet how often did they offer their gifts, only to see the ignorant and ungrateful multitudes reject them? You may, perhaps, invent a marvelous lamp that burns without oil; but you will find the oil merchant then becomes your enemy.

"So matters stood in the last days of the Emperor Augustus. The Roman Empire was in full flower, but the signs of its decay were already too obvious to the members of the hierarchy. They convened a meeting in a house at Ostia, to determine whether they ought to continue their long struggle. Many among them despaired of ever succeeding. But even as they were about to cast their votes for dissolution, something extraordinary happened.

"A stranger entered the room. He informed them that he was one of their own members, but from an epoch far in the future. He exhorted them to continue their good work, even to expand their operations, for the day would come when they would indeed rule mankind with wisdom and benevolence! Not only would Science conquer Time and overcome its limits, it would defeat Age, Death and Illness as well. Men would live in undreamed-of comfort.

"The stranger presented them with a chest bound in silver. Within this chest, he said, was all that was needed to ensure their victory.

"Having said this, he vanished from among them like a shadow. The silver-bound chest remained on the table, however.

"The most senior member of the hierarchy opened the chest, and I need hardly tell you that his hands were trembling as he did so. Shall I tell you what he found inside?"

Edward looked around them at the commonplace world he had inhabited before this moment. The grimy street, the idlers sauntering to and fro, the rumbling wagons full of pitch or ship's biscuit bound for some dreary and interminable voyage: all of them were about to vanish, like a painted curtain rising to reveal . . .

"What was it, sir?"

"Nothing more than a folded sheet of parchment," said Dr. Nennys placidly. "Yet it was a kind of parchment they had never seen, white as the snows of Aetna. It was closely covered with written instructions. They were to go to the widow of a certain pig farmer, and give her sickly child certain medicines, in order that he might live to manhood and become one of their number. They were to invest certain sums with certain merchants. They were to make copies of every book they owned, and keep them at a certain location in the Alps. There were certain undesirable men who must be removed from office, by whatever means might be managed. And one of their number must seek out a certain woman and marry her, and produce as many heirs as possible.

"The hierarchy followed these instructions to the letter. The reasons for some of the commands became evident in short order, as their investments paid out handsomely and a fire broke out in the hierarchy's library, consuming a number of books which had fortunately been copied and secured elsewhere the week before.

"At the end of a year, the hierarchy found itself wealthier, more secure, than ever before. And then, a second list of instructions appeared in the silver-bound chest, as if by magic. The instructions were duly followed. Once again the hierarchy's fortunes rose. Exactly one year later, a third list appeared. The hierarchy perceived that their counterparts in the future had given them a lamp by which to see the way forward, while the common run of humanity continued to grope in the darkness.

"With this advantage, the hierarchy grew, and spread. We are everywhere. We survived Rome's fall. In time, da Vinci joined our ranks. So too did Roger Bacon, and John Dee. The silver-bound chest is kept in the hierarchy's headquarters, which are presently in England, I am proud to say, and the annual list of instructions continues to appear without fail.

"The list for the year 1824 required us to manage the engendering of a certain remarkable child. Need I tell you that the child walks beside me as I speak?"

Edward was silent a long moment, staring at the pavement as he walked. "A man, now," he said at last. "And very much entertained by your story. But can you prove any of this, sir?"

Dr. Nennys laughed. They had come by this time to the railway station. He waved his hand at the locomotive engine that was just pulling in, hissing steam, belching smoke as its titanic wheels revolved in their tracks. Its bright brasswork flared in the sunlight, cinders flew from it, and the earth still vibrated from the thunder of its approach.

"Here's proof, my boy! This is our work, this herald of the new age. *Technologia*, the Greeks called it. Science applied to practical purposes. We've had the knowledge to build steam engines for a thousand years. Had our people been able to work freely and in the open, Shakespeare might have ridden one of these from Stratford to London.

"Fortunately, we now have the goodwill and assistance of some of the most powerful men in the nation. It was a trifling matter to liberate you from that hell-ship! Greater wonders lie ahead, but it will take steady work to bring them into being."

"If this is true," said Edward cautiously, "then I have found my purpose at last."

"Master Edward!" Richardson appeared like a specter through a cloud of steam. "Doctor, sir. We have a first-class carriage, all neat and proper. Your trunk's already stowed, sir."

1848: Joyful, as a Hero Going to Conquest

"Here's the man."

Ludbridge peered over the top of his *Times* and saw Greene approaching him across the library. Ludbridge was surprised; Greene worked Downstairs and came up from his office about as often as a mole left its burrow. Following Greene was an extraordinarily tall young man, vaguely familiar to Ludbridge from somewhere. After watching a moment, he recollected that the man had been at the banquet for new members, sitting across from the old member who had sponsored him.

The old member had been Dr. Nennys, Ludbridge remembered now. He rather disliked Dr. Nennys. However, he smoothed out his nascent scowl and nodded civilly at Greene.

"Ludbridge."

"Greene."

"I don't know if you've been introduced to young Bell-Fairfax? Bell-Fairfax, Ludbridge."

"An honor, sir." Bell-Fairfax inclined forward in a curt military bow.

"How d'you do, sir."

"New member," said Greene. "In fact, a Residential member."

"Ah." Ludbridge came alert. There were two classes of gentlemen at Redking's Club. Public members tended to be professionals in the arts and sciences, with a few MPs and cabinet ministers among them.

Residential members, as their name implied, had rooms on the premises and tended to be gentlemen who followed no very clearly defined trade. Many of them had been in the service; few had any living relatives. They were, to a man, unmarried. Ludbridge himself was a Residential.

"And he attended your old school, as well," said Greene, with a significant look. He had just used a code phrase.

"Did he, indeed?" Ludbridge smiled. The phrase had told him that Bell-Fairfax was a member of the Gentlemen's Speculative Society, the inner circle at Redking's.

"He did. I've just been giving him a tour of the club, but I'm rather pressed for time," said Greene. "Would you mind very much taking him under your wing for a bit?"

"Not at all." Ludbridge folded up his paper and, setting it aside, rose from the depths of his chair. One of the other members frowned at them for carrying on a conversation in the library. Greene shrugged apologetically at him, and the three men walked out into the corridor.

As private clubs went, Redking's was not particularly noteworthy in appearance. It was housed in a plain brick edifice in Craig's Court; its rooms, while comfortable, were neither grand nor imposing. Nor was there anything exceptional within them to which Ludbridge might point with pride. Not, at least, in the rooms Upstairs.

Downstairs was quite another matter.

Greene led them to an inconspicuous door off the front entry hall, which, when opened, revealed a staircase. They descended together, after which Greene nodded to them and hurried away to his office.

Ludbridge turned and surveyed Bell-Fairfax critically.

"You're rather tall for the work," he said. "I assume you have other remarkable qualities?"

"I hope so, sir."

"I hope so as well. Now, do you really need a tour, or have you been down here before?"

"I haven't seen anything but the rooms Upstairs, sir."

"Hmph. Ever seen an iceberg?"

"Yes, sir."

"Nine-tenths of 'em are below the water, you know; same with Red-king's. Everything down here belongs to the Society, though—"

There was the muffled sound of an explosion, some distance down the corridor in which they stood. From below a far door, something like smoke began to curl.

"Hell," said Ludbridge, and set off down the corridor at a dead run. Bell-Fairfax passed him at perfectly amazing speed, and Ludbridge thought to himself: *The beggar's fit, at any rate.* The other reached the door first, and pounded on it.

"Hallo! Anyone in there?"

No reply but strangled coughing came, with a high-pitched shrilling noise behind it, and the sound of clawing at the door from within. Ludbridge arrived then, with several other men from rooms down the hall. Before their astonished eyes Bell-Fairfax tore the door from its hinges and cast it aside as easily as though it had been a playing card. Clouds billowed out; a man fell forward onto the carpet. Ludbridge grabbed him and backed away with him. Bell-Fairfax, meanwhile, had taken a deep breath and leaned round the door frame to peer into the room.

"No one else in there, sir!"

"Be all right," gasped the man who had been in the room. "Fans clear it out—experiment—titanium tetrachloride went wrong. My face burned?"

"Not much. You'll want the medics to have a look at you, all the same, Kirke," said Ludbridge. Bell-Fairfax, meanwhile, was watching in fascination as the chemical mist vanished into little vents, revealing a room like an alchemist's chamber, full of an extraordinary white light, with glass retorts and many-colored bottles crowded on its tables. As the room's details became visible, the shrill squealing faded and at last ceased.

They loaded Kirke onto the door and carried him down the corridor to what appeared to be a double doorway. One of the other rescuers threw the doors wide and revealed the small room beyond. It too was brightly lit, from a tiny glassed lamp in its ceiling.

"We'll take him from here," said one of the other men, catching hold of the door and backing into the cabinet. Bell-Fairfax relinquished his corner of the door and stared as the cabinet dropped away out of sight, carrying the moaning Kirke and his bearers.

"It's an ascending room," said Ludbridge. "Never seen one? Ours goes down as well. That one connects to the hospital. Full marks for getting there as quickly as you did, but you were a damned fool to pull the door off that way. If there'd been a fire in that room, the rush of air would have fanned it into a blaze."

"Yes, sir," said Bell-Fairfax. They walked on a few paces, before Ludbridge said:

"Were you in the service?"

"Yes, sir. Navy."

"Thought so. Anyone else would have answered back. What rank?"

"Commander, sir. Honorably retired, on half-pay." Bell-Fairfax smiled, coldly amused by something. Ludbridge, observing him, thought: *Arrogant. I wonder why?*

"Next time something of the sort happens, feel about the top of the door by the lintel. If it's hot, you'll know something's smoldering inside," Ludbridge continued.

"Yes, sir. Though I could tell nothing was on fire."

"Through a closed door? Very likely!"

"I'd have been able to smell the heat, sir," Bell-Fairfax replied.

"You've a keen sense of smell, have you?" Ludbridge looked up at him thoughtfully. Bell-Fairfax's nose was a long aquiline, breaking to the left. His features suggested something slightly un-English, especially with those pale unnerving eyes. Ludbridge wondered whether he might be a Slav. The strength and reflexes were remarkable too, for a man who, though solid, did not appear heavily muscled. The articulation of his arms and shoulders seemed somewhat unusual . . .

"Well, Christ knows you can run," said Ludbridge. "You may do for the job, after all. Come along; I'll show you the gymnasium. Pengrove and Hobson ought to be in there, about now."

Bell-Fairfax followed obediently enough, at first, but kept pausing to peer at the double globes set at intervals along the wall. "There's no flame," he cried at last. "These aren't gaslights!"

"No; they're de la Rue's vacuum lamps," said Ludbridge, a little impatiently. "Quite a bit brighter, as you may observe, and much more convenient. Do come along, Bell-Fairfax. I hope I shan't have to stop and explain every new thing you see."

"No, sir," said Bell-Fairfax. He quickened his stride and asked no further questions, even when they stepped into another ascending room and rode it down a floor, though he gazed intently at its little vacuum lamp. Nor did he inquire after anything they encountered on the floor below, as they walked along the corridor: not though unknown machinery hissed and rattled behind closed doors, and colored lights flared and extinguished themselves.

Within one room, clearly no bigger than a dressing-chamber, a full orchestra was apparently playing, with a strangely tinny sound. From a half-open door something small darted, and the door was flung wide as a white-coated gentleman ran out after it. He caught it up and bore it back. As he passed, it was revealed to be some sort of wheeled toy, but it turned its head and regarded Bell-Fairfax and Ludbridge with glowing eyes.

"Mechanical rats," Ludbridge muttered. "Useful for reconnaissance, if they ever perfect the damned things. Used to have all the laboratories on the floors below, but Fabrication keeps expanding into odd corners. Here we are!"

He led Bell-Fairfax into a vast room, like an indoor tennis court, well lit by the vacuum lamps. It echoed with the stamping and guttural cries of two men in fencer's gear who were presently pursuing each other up and down the floor, and with a distant splashing that suggested the proximity of bathing pools in the rooms beyond.

"Gentlemen, may I have your attention?"

The fencers stopped at once, lifting their masks as they turned.

"Hallo, Ludbridge," said the nearer of the two. He was diminutive in stature, so stocky as to resemble a beer barrel on legs. His side-whiskers were bushy to such a degree that his head appeared nearly as wide as his shoulders.

"Hallo, Ludbridge," said the other, who stood slightly taller. He pronounced the name "Ludbwidge." Fate, and heredity, had conspired to give him very little chin and a great deal of overbite. "Who's this?"

"The fourth member of our team," said Ludbridge. "Perhaps. Hobson, this is Bell-Fairfax."

"How d'you do?" Bell-Fairfax leaned down and shook hands with the beer barrel.

"Bell-Fairfax, this is Pengrove."

"Charmed, you know," said Pengrove, extending a limp hand. Hobson surveyed them and gave a short laugh.

"A nice matched set we'll be, out all together! Good God, Ludbridge, Charley and I'll look like a pair of dwarves next to *him*. Inconspicuous, eh?"

"Only if we all join the circus troupe at Astley's," said Pengrove sadly. "Delighted to meet you all the same, Bell-Fairfax. Though I must go on record as wishing to know what the hell Greene was thinking. Seven feet tall, ain't you?"

"Not quite, sir."

"Oh! Well, that makes all the difference, don't it? Seriously, Ludbridge, we'll be the most obvious set of spies imaginable."

"I know," said Ludbridge. "We're going to make it a strength."

Hobson and Pengrove were also Residentials, it transpired, and so it was possible to occupy the gymnasium fairly late in the evenings for calisthenic work, after the public members had gone home. They discovered it was best they train without an audience; the four of them lined up together in exercise singlets presented an alarming spectacle.

Somewhat less disheartening was target practice, at an indoor range some five floors beneath the club. They were given training in archery as well as in the use of minié rifles, revolvers and revolvers fitted with a curious canister over the barrel that reduced the report of the shot to a dull *pop*. Bell-Fairfax was discovered to be a crack marksman and so, against all expectation, was Pengrove. Hobson practiced diligently and brought his scores up; with grim satisfaction Ludbridge signed them off, and they began the next phase of their training.

One Mr. Tilbury from the Theatre Royal was brought in, who taught them the art of *becoming someone else*. Subtle effects with a minimal use of greasepaint were his specialty; false beards were all very well for disguises, he explained, but really they suited amateurs best. It was far more effective to invent, and then to inhabit, another being entirely. He strode up and down the room before them, and with a few changes of posture and intonation became in rapid succession a costermonger, a sailor, an elderly businessman, a young girl, a drunken peer, and a bent old hag.

And one Mr. Moore, a conjuror, was brought in, to teach them sleight-of-hand tricks. Appearance, disappearance, illusion, misdirection, and the patter that accompanied it, all could be made to serve deeper matters than vanishing coins or handkerchiefs. He showed them how.

And one Mr. Dabbs was brought in, in manacles by a stone-faced guard, and meekly taught them the art of picking pockets, with a side course in opening locks and general burglary. He assured them his methods were proof against detection; had he not been so foolish as to venture into counterfeiting, on the advice of his mother-in-law, he would have been at liberty still.

Lastly, after many weeks' study with the aforementioned gentlemen, they made the acquaintance of one Mr. Jack, who was wheeled into the gymnasium by a grinning Ludbridge.

"Good morning, all," he said. "This is your next tutor."

"Good God," said Hobson. Bell-Fairfax and Pengrove looked on, too surprised for words. "What *is* it?"

"A victim," explained Ludbridge, unfastening the straps that had held Mr. Jack on his wheeled stand. He was an automaton, the size of a man but not remarkably lifelike in appearance, dressed in a shabby suit and tall hat. Ludbridge lifted him free of the stand, with a grunt of effort, and set him on his feet. He shifted his balance at once, and stood upright.

"Oh, ha-ha," said Pengrove. "It's a chap in a mask."

"Do you really think so?" Ludbridge busied himself with rolling the stand to one side. "Shame you'll have to kill him, then, isn't it?"

"Kill him! How?"

"However you please," said Ludbridge. He gestured at the cabinet of practice blades. "Stab him, if you like. Get a pistol and shoot the beggar. Kill him with your bare hands. *If* you can."

"It's all right," said Bell-Fairfax, who had tilted his head a little on one side as he stared at the automaton. "He's not alive. He's some sort of clockwork, I think."

"Oh, don't be absurd," said Pengrove, circling it cautiously. "Look at him, standing up by himself. He's the image of Spring-heel'd Jack—"

With a whirr, the figure's head spun around like an owl's, to glare at Pengrove. Hobson chuckled and went to the cabinet for a saber.

"Just a glorified practice dummy. I'll do the honors, shall I?"

"Careful, Hobson," said Bell-Fairfax, watching the automaton with a puzzled look on his face. Pengrove, meanwhile, was entertaining it with a little dance, two steps to the left, three to the right, gradually completing his transit of the thing. Its head kept turning, following him. Hobson advanced from the opposite direction, raising his saber for a head cut.

Abruptly the head spun back round, and the thing pivoted on its heel to step clear of the blow. Its palm came out, flat, to strike Hobson in the face; at the same moment it emitted a piercing screech. Hobson went over like a fallen tree and lay there groaning, clutching his nose as it fountained blood. Bell-Fairfax and Pengrove clapped their hands over their ears, wincing until the siren scream faded.

"I say!" Pengrove lowered his hands. "It's damned intelligent, all the same."

"It is indeed," said Ludbridge, helping Hobson to his feet. "Either of you chaps care to tell me how you'll do for him?"

"Shoot the bastard," said Hobson, muffled through his handkerchief.

"I think I shall." Pengrove fetched out a pepper-pot pistol. He took careful aim at the automaton, whose head swiveled round. Its eyes were lit as from within by a hellish glare. It seemed to regard Pengrove closely and then, in the instant before he pulled the trigger, it sprang into the air. Pengrove's shot struck the far wall and broke a vacuum lamp. The automaton came down immediately in front of Pengrove, and but for Pengrove's presence of mind in throwing himself backward, it had clouted him in the same way it had attacked Hobson.

"It *is* Spring-heel'd Jack!" Pengrove cried. "Bloody hell, the lads in Fabrication must have taken him out to Limehouse for a few test runs back in '38, eh?"

The automaton, meanwhile, turned and walked back to the point from which it had started. Pengrove took aim from the floor and fired again, four rapid shots in succession. The first shot knocked the automaton's hat off. It spun around, neatly dodging the other shots, and bounded toward Pengrove. Bell-Fairfax leaped into its path and swung with his fist, punching its head, which rang like a gong.

The automaton halted, then staggered backward to its starting point. There it revolved smartly on one heel and stood motionless once more. Bell-Fairfax, meanwhile, fell to his knees, clutching his hand and giving vent to a remarkable stream of profanity.

"In the Navy, were you?" remarked Hobson, wide-eyed.

"Broken your hand?" inquired Ludbridge.

"No," said Edward, shaking it as he glared at the automaton.

"I rather think you must have, from the sound it made."

"No, sir, I did not. How does the damned thing work? It's far more complicated than a clock."

"It is that," said Ludbridge. "It contains the latest thing in gyroscopes. The ball-and-socket joints are an improved design, with gutta-percha lining and graphite lubrication. There are lenses in the eyes, opening on a sort of camera obscura in the skull. It can receive an image, analyze it, and respond in one of a number of ways. You can't hear them, but it's emitting a series of high-pitched notes, and estimating your location from the echoes—"

"I beg your pardon," said Edward. "I bloody well *can* hear them. They speed up when one of us moves."

Ludbridge stared at him a moment. "Then you have an advantage the rest of us haven't. Find a way to use it, Bell-Fairfax," he said at last.

"Very well." Edward got to his feet, clenching and opening his hand. "There; it's piping again." He feinted a couple of blows, and the automaton, appearing to watch him closely, swayed from side to side in response.

"I saw a copy of Vaucanson's Excreting Duck once," remarked Pengrove, from the floor. "Very lifelike. Wasn't anything like as dangerous. Though it did excrete rather menacingly."

"Did it?" said Edward, circling the automaton. His gaze became blank, unsmiling, and he never took his eyes from it. "Hobson, if you'd be so kind—would you walk about it in the opposite direction?"

"Confuse it, eh? Delighted." Hobson, stuffing his handkerchief in his pocket, proceeded to circle the automaton counterclockwise. It responded by rapidly turning its head back and forth, attempting to watch both men at the same time. Ludbridge folded his arms and observed them in silence.

"Ah; the piping's getting faster, and irregular. Just like a heartbeat. Now, Pengrove," said Edward, "if you'd just threaten it with the pistol?"

Pengrove rose on his elbow and waved the weapon. "I say, you! Nasty thing!" As the automaton turned to track Pengrove's movements, Edward lunged at it. It whirled around, flailing steel fists, but Edward caught it about the knees and toppled it. The automaton fell with a horrendous crash and Edward was on it at once, raining a series of blows on its throat, where a skin of canvas impregnated with gutta-percha seemed to conceal vital pipes and tubing.

The automaton's siren howled, it thrashed and spat blue flame from its mouth, and at last a shower of sparks shot out. Ignoring all these, Edward struck at it relentlessly, until its head parted company with its neck and rolled drunkenly across the floor. The light in its eyes died.

"That's quite enough," said Ludbridge, stepping forward. "Fabrication will weep when they see him. Was it really necessary to tear his head off?"

"How could we be certain we'd killed him otherwise, sir?" Edward got to his feet. He lifted his skinned knuckles to his mouth.

"Yes, but you've effectively halted your course of study until they can repair him. Note that it required all three of you to dispatch him! Even if Bell-Fairfax delivered the actual coup de grace. Let's see that hand, man."

"It isn't broken, sir, I promise you." Edward held it out. Ludbridge inspected it briefly.

"Hm! We'll let the medicos decide that. You'll come along with me to the infirmary. Pengrove, Hobson, take our headless friend down to Fabrication. You might want to join us in the hospital afterward, Hobson; get your nose seen to."

Warily the others lifted Spring-heel'd Jack's body and strapped it to the wheeled stand. The thing made no protest. Bell-Fairfax followed Ludbridge to the ascending room and they rode it down to the floor on which the hospital was located.

"There's no need to act the stoic, Bell-Fairfax," said Ludbridge. "It's a damned foolish vanity to conceal an injury. You're not the Spartan lad with the fox."

"No, sir," said Bell-Fairfax. The door before them slid open and they emerged into a room furnished with chairs, at the opposite end of which was a counter and window. Several heavily bandaged gentlemen occupied the chairs, placidly engaged in reading copies of *The Times*, *Punch* or *The Illustrated London News*. A young lady in a coif, clearly a nursing sister, was seated beyond the window, engaged in some task or other.

"Hallo, Atkinson," said Ludbridge to the nearest of the men, who raised his bandaged face. "Trouble with the eye?"

"Broke the damned infrared lens," said Atkinson grimly.

"Line of duty?"

"No. Went night-shooting in Scotland and the fool bird flew straight into my face. I shall have to be fitted with a new eye."

"Oh, hard luck! This would be, er, what? Your third?"

"Fifth," said Atkinson.

"May I be of assistance, Mr. Ludbridge?" inquired the young lady, looking up from her work.

"Yes, thank you, sister." Ludbridge took Bell-Fairfax's elbow and steered him to the window. "My friend here requires a radiograph of his right hand."

"Certainly, Mr. Ludbridge." The young lady gazed intently into a roundel of blue glass mounted in a cabinet in a brass frame, rather like a ship's porthole. Her hands moved swiftly over something like a spinet's keyboard, but with a great many more keys; instead of music being produced, glowing letters appeared and floated in the blue depths of the glass.

"The radiography room is presently unoccupied. I shall send a notice to the technician. What is the gentleman's name, please?"

"Edward Alton Bell-Fairfax," said he, with a musical quality to his voice Ludbridge hadn't noticed before. The sister looked around as if startled. Bell-Fairfax smiled at her. She returned his smile, blushing prettily, and turned back to her keyboard to cover her confusion; but the corner of the smile could still be glimpsed, just beyond the snow-white edge of her coif.

"The hand has not been fractured," announced the radiography technician. His voice came hollowly from the tiny dark room without which Ludbridge sat with Bell-Fairfax, who had thrust his arm through an aperture in the wall into a box mounted on the other side. Beyond a thick pane of glass they beheld the technician, armored in long coat quilted with lead and a goggled helmet, and a lit image on the opposite wall: an immense dark skeletal hand, rendered somewhat less fearsome by the commonplace detail of a shirt button on the wrist.

"Are you certain?" Ludbridge was incredulous. "He smashed his hand into steel."

"Quite certain," said the technician, gesturing at the image. "Bruising, yes, and minor abrasions, but no fractures. Observe the abnormally dense structure of the bones." Edward, who had been smirking rather, looked up.

"What d'you mean by *abnormal*?" he demanded. The hand in the image clenched into a skeletal fist.

"Precisely what I said," said the technician. He turned his head to regard them, with the skeletal image reflected in his goggled optics. "Note, further, the superior attachment of the lumbrical musculature. I should very much like an opportunity to study your skeleton, young man."

"I regret, sir, that I am unable to oblige you at this time," said Edward, narrowing his eyes.

"Clean bill of health, then, Deane?" Ludbridge got to his feet. "Thank you. Come along, Bell-Fairfax. We'll just have the sister apply an ointment to those knuckles, shall we? And then, I think, upstairs for a brandy."

He watched Bell-Fairfax as they rode up together in the ascending room, and thought: *He knows he differs from other men, and he doesn't like it—not for all his arrogance. Could be useful, I suppose.*

1849: Scherzo in D Minor

"I believe you're ready for a challenge, gentlemen," said Ludbridge. Bell-Fairfax, who had been pounding away at a leather punching bag, lowered his fists; Hobson and Pengrove stood back and removed their fencing masks.

"What sort of challenge?" Pengrove inquired. In reply, Ludbridge went to the vaulting-horse and, using it as an impromptu table, unrolled a map. They came crowding close to look over his shoulder.

"Simply to walk a short distance along the Strand," said Ludbridge, indicating it on the map. "Without being caught."

"Ah."

"What's the trick, Ludbridge?" asked Hobson.

"You tell me," said Ludbridge. "Or, rather, don't. You'll proceed from Trafalgar Square to Bedford Street along the Strand. There will be five spotters along the route, dressed as policemen, and they will have been furnished with detailed descriptions of the three of you. Any one of them sighting any one of you will collar you forthwith, raising a considerable hue and cry. You will be dragged away in public disgrace.

"Should one of you manage to reach Bedford Street unobserved, you will have my congratulations and the satisfaction of a job well done. Should *all three* of you accomplish this feat, you will be rewarded with an outing to Nell Gwynne's."

"I beg your pardon?" said Edward. Hobson chortled.

"An exclusive establishment," he said. "The finest in all England."

"Somewhat more than that," said Ludbridge. "It might be called Redking's sister society. Though of course it does provide comforts and refreshment for the deserving."

"Oh, I say!" cried Pengrove. Bell-Fairfax's eyes brightened.

"Are there any conditions?" he asked. Ludbridge nodded.

"You are required to traverse the Strand. You may not cut across to Chandos Place to reach the goal. You may not simply take a cab or other conveyance. On the other hand, Fabrication has been instructed to provide you with any assistance or materials you request of them. You have a week to prepare; the challenge must be met on the fifteenth. Good luck, gentlemen."

On the fifteenth, Ludbridge enjoyed a leisurely breakfast Upstairs and then went for a stroll along the Strand. In Trafalgar Square he noted the first of the spotters in police uniform, an old Residential named Valance, who nodded and tapped the brim of his hat with his truncheon by way of salute.

Omnibuses rumbled along the street, and cabs, with a brisk rattle and *clop-clop-clop* of horses' hooves echoing. Crossing-sweepers, small bush-headed children in rags, trailed their brooms as they scouted for women to whom they might offer their services. Delivery-boys hurried, journeymen laborers trudged along to their respective destinations. Traffic was held up for a moment as a shepherd drove his flock through, aiming for Smithfield, and Ludbridge scrutinized both shepherd and sheep keenly.

None were his trainees in disguise, however. Smiling at the idea, he walked along a few yards. There ahead was Roberts, another spotter, staring in suspicion at an immense dustman laboring along under a binful of ashes. Bell-Fairfax, perhaps? With Hobson concealed in the bin? Roberts stepped in front of the dustman and, peering into his face, spoke sharply; the dustman lowered his bin and said something in protest, whereat Roberts stepped back and appeared to be saying something apologetic.

A dozen yards farther on, Simnell was pacing an elderly lady in purple bombazine, the breadth of whose hooped skirts gave her the appearance of a gigantic ambulatory plum pudding. Clearly, he thought one or more compact persons might be concealed somewhere within her architecture, and was in a quandary over how to determine if this was, in fact, the case. At last, darting sideways, he smacked at her lower person with his truncheon. She stopped in her tracks and Ludbridge could hear her shrill protests even from a distance. Simnell stamped furiously at an imaginary insect, tipped his hat and appeared to be explaining his timely and chivalrous actions.

Ludbridge was distracted from this by a commotion farther back along the street. He turned, wondering at the shouts, and saw Roberts turning to stare too. And where was Valance?

"Here! Here's a constable fallen down in a faint!" an omnibus conductor was shouting. Scowling, Ludbridge ran toward the knot of people that was gathering where Valance lay stretched upon the pavement.

A couple walked in the opposite direction past him, arm in arm. Ludbridge noted the young lady, fluttering her handkerchief in front of her face, while her beau bore on with a bright fixed smile, staring forward. Every instinct Ludbridge had demanded that he turn and look at them again, but he shouldered his way through the crowd and knelt beside Valance.

"Drinking at this hour of the day!" a woman declared. "He's a disgrace."

"You never know; might be a fit," said a pedlar with a tray. "My wife's brother had them."

"Give him air, if you please," said Ludbridge. Valance was pale and sweating, semiconscious, utterly limp. Ludbridge noted the tiny dart protruding from his carotid artery, just above the collar of his uniform. He plucked it out and discarded it, shaking his head. "I believe the man is ill. He ought to be carried into a house and given brandy."

"We'll see to it, sir," said one of a pair of men in nondescript clothes.

Ludbridge, glancing up at them, recognized Burdett and Cowle, two of the porters at Redking's. Grim-faced, they lifted Valance between them and bore him away in the direction of the club. Ludbridge got to his feet, dusting off the knees of his trousers, and had just turned back to see where the young couple had got to when a fresh hue and cry came from ahead. Ludbridge ran, arriving just in time to see Roberts, in the street, trying to rise on one elbow. He groped once, ineffectually, at his neck before collapsing again.

"Here! It's another policeman fallen down!" cried the pedlar. Ludbridge dropped to his knees and pulled the telltale dart from Roberts's neck.

"What's that?" said a sharp-eyed lady's maid, her arms full of parcels. "Was that a wasp? Was he stung by a wasp? That'll do it, you know. My cousin—"

"Yes! It's wasps! A swarm of wasps! Look out, they're dangerous!" Ludbridge recognized Bell-Fairfax's voice and scrambled to his feet at once, staring around, but failed to spot him. Women began to scream and men ducked, beating the air futilely. Cursing, Ludbridge grabbed Roberts under the arms and dragged him to the curb, where he propped him against a lamppost. Ludbridge stood and scanned the crowd, wondering how someone as tall as Bell-Fairfax could hide.

"Oh! Oh! I've been bitten!" shrieked a woman some distance ahead. "Help!"

"Here's a wasp!"

"Look out! You've got one on your hat!"

"Look! Look! Another poor policeman's been stung!" It was true; Simnell was down in the street, gasping and white-faced. Ludbridge sprinted to his side, narrowly avoiding being knocked down by a hysterical female flailing about with her shawl. A tiny bit of yellow and black fluff flew from her hat brim and landed on the bricks beside Simnell. Ludbridge picked it up and examined it briefly: no more than a bit of cotton daubed with paint, cleverly tied with a couple of twists of fishing line to make it somewhat resemble a wasp.

"The bastards—," said Simnell, before falling back unconscious.

People ahead were running to and fro, yelling, and a cab-horse reared in its traces. Ludbridge dragged Simnell as far out of harm's way as he was able, and ran on to the next man on watch, Preston. He arrived as Preston fell to his knees, clutching at the side of his neck. Just beyond him walked the young couple, the woman sashaying with the merest trace of exaggeration, her escort stiffly upright.

"Did you see them?" Ludbridge shouted, pulling the tiny dart from Preston's neck. Preston raised bewildered eyes.

"Who? No—no one—" He sighed deeply and fell back, unconscious. Pulling him from the street, Ludbridge realized that all the darts had come from the south side of the Strand. He looked up at the buildings there to see whether there were not some form of scaffolding or other structure that might have served as a place of concealment, but was unable to discern any. None, at least, where someone of Bell-Fairfax's size could hide—

"Help! Wasps!"

"Look, here's *another* one bit!"

"It's the Chartists! They've gone and loosed wasps on the constabulary!"

Ludbridge glanced ahead and saw Bedford Street. With resignation he walked through the crowd and beheld young Malahyde, the fifth spotter, who had just crumpled to the pavement. He bent, flicked the dart from Malahyde's neck, and hoisted him over his shoulder as a fire brigadesman might. Making his way on to Bedford Street, he saw the three figures standing behind the railings at the Adelphi Theatre: the odd-looking young couple and a slouching man in the garments of a laborer.

As Ludbridge drew near, the laborer shrugged and stood straight, seeming thereby to gain a full twelve inches in height. He met Ludbridge's eyes and smiled. The lady lowered her handkerchief and positively grinned; her companion turned his still-fixedly-smiling head with a strange jerky motion, and raised one hand in an awkward gesture to his shirtfront. The hand lifted a small panel in the fabric of the shirt, revealing a square slot through which a second pair of eyes peered.

"Bedford Street, Ludbridge." Hobson's voice emerged from the figure's chest.

"We win, I believe," said Pengrove, in a fluting falsetto.

"Something of a Pyrrhic victory, don't you think?" Ludbridge glared at them, indicating Malahyde.

"The effect of the dart wears off quickly, sir," said Bell-Fairfax. "Kirke provided me with the drug. Our own formula, sir." Looking smug, he twirled a length of hollow cane in his fingers.

"'EXTRAORDINARY OCCURRENCE IN THE STRAND,'" Greene read aloud. "'Wasps Attack Members of the Metropolitan Police. Chartist Plot Suspected.'" He lowered *The Times* and glared across his desk at Ludbridge, Bell-Fairfax, Pengrove and Hobson.

"My fault, Greene," said Ludbridge. "I never told them that creating a distraction wasn't one of their options."

"And rightly so, because it *was* one of their options," said Greene. He considered them sourly. "Perhaps not to the extent of immobilizing five fellow members and causing a public panic that gets into the papers, but an option nonetheless. You do understand, though, don't you, gentlemen, that our organization prefers to *avoid* drawing attention to its activities, as a general rule?"

"Yes, sir," said Bell-Fairfax, and Pengrove, and Hobson.

"I am pleased to hear it. I have no doubt you will conduct yourselves with greater discretion in the future. Trusting in your good sense—" Greene reached for his pen and signed the chit Ludbridge had presented. "You shall have your treat after all."

There was in Westminster a certain dining house, long established, eminently respectable, and frequented by prominent statesmen, being so conveniently situated near Whitehall. Although its public dining room was grand and spacious, it had beside exquisitely appointed private rooms available for those gentlemen of rank willing to pay a membership premium for their exclusive use. This fact was well known and therefore other diners had no great reason to remark when certain august persons, upon presenting themselves to the headwaiter, were conducted through the door marked MEMBERS ONLY.

Had any importunate visitor opened that door without the headwaiter's permission, he would have seen beyond only a corridor with four beautifully furnished rooms opening off it. Three of them contained tables, chairs, china, crystal, cutlery, linen napery, all of the finest and most costly sort but otherwise unexceptional. The fourth room was identical to the others save for an immense wine cabinet against one wall.

"Gentlemen." The headwaiter pressed the concealed switch and the entire wine cabinet swung smoothly outward, revealing the ascending room beyond it. He bowed them in.

"How thrilling," said Pengrove, as the cabinet closed behind them. The room descended and they watched rough bricks and plaster slide past, before a new view presented itself: an elegant room, dark paneled, thickly carpeted, and rather old-fashioned were it not lit by vacuum lamps behind tinted glass shades.

Beside one of these sat a woman of a certain age. It was plain she had not chosen her chair for its advantage of lamplight; for she wore smoked goggles, and her right hand rested on a cane. She turned her face as a bell rang, signaling the arrival of visitors.

"Welcome to Nell Gwynne's, gentlemen," she said. Her accent was that of the lower classes, but she spoke quietly.

"Good evening, Mrs. Corvey," said Ludbridge. "I have brought three deserving fellows for an evening's entertainment. May I present to you Mr. Hobson, Mr. Pengrove, and Mr. Bell-Fairfax?" They murmured their compliments.

"Welcome, my dears." Mrs. Corvey set aside her cane and groped about on the tea table to her right. Finding the tea service there, she deftly poured out four cups. "Please be seated and take a little tea with us, won't you?"

"We should be delighted, Mrs. Corvey," said Ludbridge. They took seats on a long divan opposite her chair, shifting about awkwardly, and Ludbridge handed around the teacups and saucers. Hobson and Pengrove drank, as did Ludbridge; Bell-Fairfax raised his cup to his mouth and halted, staring into it with an expression of consternation.

Mrs. Corvey turned her face in his direction.

"One of you doesn't care for his tea, I perceive."

Bell-Fairfax reddened. "I . . . believe someone may have adulterated your tea, ma'am." She responded with a dry chuckle.

"How keen your senses are, sir, to be sure! But you needn't be alarmed. What's in the tea will do you no harm; indeed, it is a mild prophylactic, as is only proper."

Pengrove and Hobson lowered their cups at once, taken aback. Ludbridge smiled and drank the rest of his cupful. "I assure you, Mrs. Corvey, my recruits are clean fellows and in the best of health."

"Ah! They are Residentials, then?"

"They are."

"Then pray excuse me, my dears, but I do have the greatest regard for my young ladies, and after all one cannot be too careful, don't you think?"

"Commendable caution," agreed Ludbridge. "Drink up, gentlemen." They obeyed. Mrs. Corvey made a graceful gesture of acknowledgment.

"Let us, then, set aside all unnecessary pretense. You must understand, sirs, that all of my customers are members of the Gentlemen's Speculative Society, for even an inner circle has inner circles within itself; and even members of Parliament have been known to contract the nastiest cases of the clap imaginable. But they did not contract them in *my* establishment. Have you dined, my dears?"

"We have not, ma'am," Ludbridge replied. "I think a little light refreshment would be well received."

"A pleasure, sir." She rose to her feet and, without the aid of her cane, went straight to a side table where sat a device of some kind, brass and black wax adorned with gold. A brass trumpet was attached to it by a cord; without any feeling about she picked it up. Instead of lifting it to her ear, as they half expected, she spoke into it.

"The cold buffet for four, please, and two bottles of champagne."

"She can see!" blurted Hobson.

"Yes, sir, I see indeed," replied Mrs. Corvey, replacing the speaking-horn in its cradle. "Though not with human eyes, I must confess." She returned to her seat, composedly arranging the folds of her gown. Staring at her, they noticed now the glint of steel and crystal behind her goggles.

"Shall I tell you my story, as we wait? I was born in the workhouse, and purchased by a manufacturer of pins when I was five years of age. The work requires small hands and keen eyesight, you see. One must cut tiny lengths of wire and file one end to a point, and then hammer the other end into a suitably broad head.

"There is a considerable demand for pins, as you might imagine, and so I worked from five o'clock in the morning until nine o'clock at night, by candlelight when daylight was unavailable. By the time I was twelve I was quite blind.

"So of course I was then sold into the only work I was fit for. I worked there as one of their specialty girls until I was seventeen, I believe, and then a gentleman from your organization approached me with quite a different proposition. I entered the Society's service with a will, and submitted myself for experimental surgery; now I wear goggles to conceal the result, as my appearance is rather startling."

"I am so sorry to hear it, ma'am," said Pengrove.

"My choice," Mrs. Corvey replied, with a thin smile. "The lack of cosmetic eyes provided a certain protection from unwanted attentions, when I was still in danger of receiving any. There is also an advantage to *seeming* blind; for example, Members of Parliament are reassured to imagine that the proprietress of their favorite house would be unable to identify their faces in a court of law."

At this point there was a gentle chime and one of the panels in the wall slid open, to admit four parlor maids, respectably clad in black.

Two bore platters laden with sandwiches and savories; one bore a pair of ice-buckets containing bottles of champagne, and one bore four glasses on a tray.

"Now then!" said Mrs. Corvey. "My story wasn't a jolly one, I fear; I hope you gentlemen will oblige me by putting it from your minds and dining heartily, before we begin the introductions."

There followed a pleasant interlude in which champagne and sandwiches were handed round, and the Residentials were invited to relate the story of the challenge they had faced, which they did with a great deal of hilarity and mutual interruption. After the savories, water ices were served, lemon and ratafia flavored, amusingly molded to resemble asparagus stalks. The maids bore away the dishes and brought cigars to offer; and when the pleasant fragrance of tobacco drifted in blue clouds up to the ventilation screens, Mrs. Corvey said:

"Now then, sirs, I expect you're ready to meet the ladies."

"Yes please," said Pengrove, who had made a few exploratorily suggestive remarks to the maids and been ignored.

"A word, first," said Ludbridge, as he exhaled a plume of smoke. "Don't imagine these are common whores, gentlemen. They've been trained as carefully as you have, and to the same ends. They merely employ different means."

"A lady *may* hold a pistol to a statesman's head and demand to know his plans for war or peace, but there are far more subtle and effective means of persuading him to speak," said Mrs. Corvey.

"D'you begin to understand?" Ludbridge turned his cheroot in his fingertips. "There's a reason this place is called what it is. These are your equals, gentlemen."

"I am certain they fully comprehend," said Mrs. Corvey graciously. "And there is one other thing I should mention, my dears: you will not choose from amongst my young ladies. They will choose you, as they are extending a professional courtesy. Ah! They approach."

The rustle of skirts was heard from beyond a curtain, and the ladies of Nell Gwynne's came all together into the room.

One, at least, did not wear skirts; she wore male attire, with her cropped hair combed back sleek, and smoked her own cheroot. One wore a lady's equestrienne habit, and carried a riding crop. One was gowned in severe respectable gray, bespectacled, tapping a birch rod into her palm thoughtfully as she considered the gentlemen. Three were indistinguishable from the most well-bred society debutantes, perfectly turned out in the latest fashion in colors to suit their respective blonde, brunette and auburn hair. Another seemed an intentional parody of a fallen woman, her mouth and gown a startling red, her cheeks heavily rouged, kohl rimming her eyes.

"So these are the new boys, are they?" she remarked. Her accent was cut-crystal refined, would not have seemed out of place in Belgravia. The Residentials, who had scrambled to their feet, stared mute.

"They are. Gentlemen, permit me to introduce Herbertina Love-lock, Mrs. Otley, Miss Rendlesham, the Misses Devere, and Lady Beatrice. Girls, this is Mr. Charles Augustus Pengrove, Mr. John Frederick Hobson, and Mr. Edward Alton Bell-Fairfax."

"Stop a bit," said Pengrove. "How did you learn our Christian names?"

"I know a good many things you wouldn't expect," replied Mrs. Corvey. "Useful in my line of work, isn't it? You may have at them, girls."

Mrs. Otley, she of the riding crop, stepped forward and tapped Hobson on the chest. "This looks like a sturdy little mount. I wonder if he can gallop for long distances, or is he only fit to bear burdens?"

Hobson blushed. "I—er—I should be delighted to go for a ride, madam."

"Tch! I'll do the riding, my dear. Come along." She gave him a swat with the riding crop and led him from the room to chambers beyond. Miss Rendlesham struck Pengrove lightly with her birch rod.

"This one looks like a troublemaker, to me," she said. "I daresay you speak out of turn, don't you, boy?"

"I do!" said Pengrove, wide-eyed. "Dreadfully! My parents despair over my impertinent behavior! I'm perfectly awful, if you want the truth!"

"Oh, I do," said Miss Rendlesham. "More truth than you can imagine. Step along now, and don't dawdle, or I shall become extremely vexed with you." Grasping him by the ear, she led him out. Before the sound of their footsteps faded, those in the parlor heard the swish and smack of the birch, and a small yelp.

"And that leaves this one." Lady Beatrice, the one gowned in scarlet, circled Edward consideringly. "Dear me! How perfectly immense he is. I shouldn't wonder if it will take several of us to subdue him. What do you think, ladies?"

"Four or five of us at least!" cried the Misses Devere.

"Oh, certainly," said Herbertina Lovelock.

"Your servant, dear ladies," said Edward with a grin. "Entirely at your disposal, and I do hope I won't disappoint. But surely one of you can be spared for our poor mentor Ludbridge?"

"No, I'm remaining here," said Ludbridge placidly. He blew a smoke ring and put his hand upon Mrs. Corvey's. "Mine hostess is renowned for her excellent conversation." She gave him a fond look.

"I believe I may truly say that I am happy in my chosen employment," said Pengrove, where he sprawled on a divan in the inner parlor.

"I, too," said Bell-Fairfax, from the mound of cushions beside the fire. Hobson, who still wore a bit in his mouth, made a sound of contented agreement. Lady Beatrice rose on her elbow from where she reclined beside Bell-Fairfax and took a thoughtful pull from the mouthpiece of a hookah.

"Let's play a game, shall we?" she said, through clouds of smoke.

"Oh, do let's," said the blonde Miss Devere, clapping her hands.

"What shall we play?" said Herbertina, sitting pertly upright.

"I have a suggestion," said Pengrove. Miss Rendlesham swatted him lightly with her birch.

"*You* don't choose, silly. We shall choose. I propose . . . Utter Truth!"

"Utter Truth! Yes!" Mrs. Otley stroked Hobson between the eyes with the butt of her riding crop. Pengrove snickered.

"I don't believe I know the rules."

"They are quite simple," said Lady Beatrice. "We shall appoint a topic. Each one of you gentlemen must, in turn, speak on the chosen subject for a full minute. You must be utterly truthful, and if we suspect that you are not, we ladies have full license to punish you severely."

"But I'm an inveterate liar," cried Pengrove. Hobson made a sound eloquently affirming that he was an inveterate liar too. Bell-Fairfax narrowed his eyes, but smiled and slipped his arm around the waist of the red-haired Miss Devere.

"No gentleman would refuse a lady's challenge. Utter Truth it is! Let's play to win, shall we? Delightful as severe punishment may be, in this paradise."

"And we shall start with my Hobby-horse," said Mrs. Otley, unfastening the bit and removing it from between Hobson's teeth.

"Give him some champagne!" Herbertina went across the carpet on her knees and set a full glass to Hobson's lips. He drank thirstily.

"Ahh! Thank you. Ready and willing, ladies!"

"The topic is 'Kisses,'" said Lady Beatrice. "You are to give us the name of each lady you have ever kissed, in chronological order, and the reason you did so."

Pengrove and Bell-Fairfax chortled. Hobson scratched his head.

"Mothers, grandmothers, sisters and aunts don't count, I hope?"

"I think not," said Lady Beatrice. "Cousins, however, do."

"Here we go—" Herbertina sorted through the heap of her clothing and withdrew a pocket watch. Gazing at its face intently, she raised one finger in the air. "Aannd—go!"

"Alice Abbott," said Hobson promptly. "Barmaid at the Three Crowns, in the village outside my school. I'd been drinking lemonade and gin and gotten squiffy. She told me I was sweet and put out her lips for me to kiss. Charlotte Engadine, daughter of my mother's friend, because we were briefly engaged. Louise—Louise somebody, don't know her surname, but she was French and I was in France drinking champagne and that was all the reason I needed. Her gown was striped red and white, just like cherries and cream. Mary Holborn. She lived across the landing and mended my waistcoat when I tore it coming home squiffed. I kissed her cheek to thank her. And Mrs. Otley, of course, because— well, it was what we came here to do."

He fell silent. "That's all?" said Lady Beatrice.

"Yes."

"I put it to you, ladies: has he spoken Utter Truth?"

The women looked from one to another. "Ye-es," said Mrs. Otley. "I believe he has."

"I agree. He is acquitted." Lady Beatrice pointed like an accusatory specter at Pengrove. "Now, you, sir! Speak at once!"

Herbertina held up her watch, and Pengrove said in a breathless voice: "Arabella Minton, cousin, I was eleven and she was thirteen and she said she'd teach me a new game if we went out behind the hedge. Violet, er, never knew her last name, but she was my mother's between-stairs maid. Because, she looked so fetching with her cheeks all red from beating the carpet. Mother saw me and made me apologize. Georgina Osgood, we were at a dance and went out on the terrace to get cool and she said if I was any sort of man I'd kiss her. Didn't dance with me the rest of the evening. Bridie Wiggan, my charwoman, because—because she was fairly young and willing and I'd just had word my brother had died in Kabul and, and coupling with a woman seemed to make as much sense as anything just then. I gave her a five-pound note afterward. And Miss Rendlesham, because she told me to, but I was so very, very, *very* grateful to be told. And that's all."

"Truly?" said Lady Beatrice.

"Indeed, ma'am."

"Your verdict, ladies?"

"He told the truth," said Miss Rendlesham, and there was a general chorus of agreement.

"And our judgment is for acquittal," said Lady Beatrice. "Fortunate mortal! And now—" She turned and looked over her shoulder at Bell-Fairfax. "It is your turn. Utter Truth, and nothing else, sir."

Edward smiled. He cleared his throat, coughed into his fist and said, "Mind the watch."

"Go!"

"Doris, Bess, Janet and Mary, surnames unknown, barmaids at the Pinford Arms, because they permitted it. One Miss Grigg, of Portsmouth, because she offered and I didn't know when I'd get the chance again. Five whores in the souk of entertainments in Constantinople, whose names I never learned, because it pleased me. Edith Javier of Gibraltar, because she offered. Three whores in the souk at Alexandria, whose names I never learned either, for reasons previously given. Two whores at Hong Kong Island, names unknown, reason as before. Seven whores, names unknown, in the bazaar at Bombay, reason as before. Omolara, a negress of Benin, because she offered. Kate, Audrey and Susan, last names unknown, barmaids at the Turk's Head in Bristol, because they permitted it. The Misses Devere—excuse me, I don't know your Christian names, ladies—because they offered. Herbertina Lovelock, because she offered, if somewhat perversely. Lady Beatrice, surname unknown, because she offered."

"Oh, you bloody liar!" screamed Pengrove.

"You must be an absolute collection of venereal diseases!" said Hobson. Bell-Fairfax merely shook his head.

"Ladies, have I any least trace of the clap evident in my person?"

"He has not," said Lady Beatrice. She gave Bell-Fairfax a curious stern look, somewhat assessing. "Nor is it my opinion that he has lied."

"I certainly wouldn't have said he lied," agreed the brunette Miss Devere. "Not after the events of the last two hours." Bell-Fairfax smirked.

"I appear to be favored with a natural immunity to poxes of every variety, you see," he said. "To say nothing of an ability to, as it were, endure."

"Oh, you're a beastly freak of nature," muttered Pengrove, reclining backward into Miss Rendlesham's bosom. "And I still say you're a liar. Notwithstanding—this really is the most awfully jolly work, isn't it, chaps?"

"Though I hope you are all far too wise to assume that your real work will in any way resemble our recreation here," said Miss Rendlesham.

"Naturally," said Pengrove.

"In one respect, perhaps," said Bell-Fairfax. He sat up, bright eyed, and took the hookah's mouthpiece from Lady Beatrice. Drawing deeply, he exhaled through his nose; it made him look uncommonly like a dragon. "It will be glorious labor!"

Hobson chuckled, but Pengrove and the ladies looked dubiously at Bell-Fairfax. "How d'you suppose it'll be glorious, old man?" said Pengrove. "I rather suspect the real mission will be a deal of dirty work. Nothing like the bliss our hostesses have conferred." He waved a hand to include the ladies in the room; Lady Beatrice nodded in gracious acknowledgment.

"But the end of the work is glorious," said Bell-Fairfax. He groped for his champagne glass, and drank. His eyes shone, his face was flushed. "Think of all the sordid business attendant on birth, for example—the uncompromising animal fleshliness of it—the groaning effort of the mother—the blood and shame. Yet the result is a child, perfect in its innocence, potentially an Archimedes or a Shakespeare! Now, consider the world we strive to bring into being. Can you think of any greater purpose for our lives? Its creation may involve ugly business, even immoral business, but when we have succeeded—all mankind will be liberated from ignorance and misery at last."

"That is the general idea," said Pengrove cautiously. Bell-Fairfax's voice had taken on an oratory quality, as though he spoke from a pulpit rather than the quite different place he occupied at the moment. Pengrove felt inexplicably moved by the golden voice, to a degree greater than seemed reasonable.

"I used to imagine I could change it all myself, you know," Bell-Fairfax mused, having another pull at the hookah. "Running about with a sword in my hand . . . and the world rose over my efforts like a wave over castles in the sand, and destroyed them to the last one. Ah, but *now* . . ."

He fell silent. The ladies exchanged glances.

"One way or another, they gave us what we wanted," said Lady Beatrice quietly. "Time for judgment, sisters."

Swift as thought, the ladies produced weapons—long hat pins, daggers that had been concealed under cushions, in Herbertina's case a straight razor from the pocket of her trousers, and the end of Mrs. Otley's riding crop slipped off to reveal a poniard—and positioned them so nearly to the Residentials' vitals that even drawing a deep breath seemed unacceptably hazardous. After a frozen moment of silence, Pengrove stammered: "How have we offended, ladies?"

"Mr. Hobson," said Lady Beatrice, ignoring him. "I would lay odds your engagement was broken off because your intended perceived that you were an incipient drunkard. Am I correct in this?"

"Yes," said Hobson faintly.

"Mr. Pengrove, would it be accurate to state that you have been bullied and dominated by others all your life, and unfavorably compared with your late brother to such an extent that you joined the Gentlemen's Speculative Society to prove yourself and, perhaps, to absolve yourself by earning a hero's death?"

"I . . . suppose it would. Yes," said Pengrove.

"And you, Mr. Bell-Fairfax." Lady Beatrice looked down at him where he lay, white-faced, her blade at his throat. "Clearly you have been in the Navy, despite your absence of tattoos. You served in the late actions in China and, I think, patrolled for slavers off the coast of Africa. You have a rather high opinion of yourself, as any big splendid animal might, but there is some . . . *hollowness* . . . that you have filled with fervent faith, not in a God but in your work. I needn't ask you whether I am correct. You cunningly told us the least about yourself, in that shameless list of conquests, and yet we learned more about you than your fellow Residentials."

"Ah," said Bell-Fairfax. "I see."

"Do you? I really hope so. This is the lesson, my dears: Utter Truth is a dangerous commodity. See to what extent you have been betrayed, by a little intimacy and champagne? Had we wanted to know any more about you we'd have uncovered your lives' whole histories, with a quarter-hour's indirect questions, and you'd have been unaware you'd told us anything important at all. And had we been other than what we, in fact, are—your sister agents—we might have proceeded to make your lives very unpleasant indeed. Not to say brief." Lady Beatrice removed her knife from under Edward's chin.

"As it is, we now know more about your personal inclinations than anyone else in the world," added Herbertina, as she closed up her razor. "What would an enemy do with such information? We hope you have learned that you must *never let your guards down*. Outside this room, of course."

"Indeed, ma'am," said Hobson, grabbing for his trousers.

When they emerged into the outer parlor, red-faced and clothed once more, they found Ludbridge chatting companionably with Mrs. Corvey.

"Ah! I see the ladies have administered their customary instruction," he said.

"You bastard, why didn't you tell us it was a test?" said Hobson.

"Everything's a test," said Ludbridge, blowing a smoke ring. "You ought to have expected that, by now."

1849: What Fruit Would Spring from Such a Seed

"Which of you is to be the camera operator?" inquired Felmouth, who was the departmental head of Fabrication. Pengrove raised his hand.

"I intend to train the other two as well," said Ludbridge. "In the event of anything unexpected, you know." Felmouth sniffed.

"Very well. I don't suppose one of you has had his portrait taken by talbotype?"

"I have, sir," said Hobson.

"An inferior method compared to M. Daguerre's process, but it has the advantage of making images on paper, rather than silver; much cheaper, and far more portable, which makes it eminently suitable for your purposes."

"What is my purpose, sir?" Pengrove inquired.

"You'll pose as an amateur photographer touring the Continent," said Ludbridge.

"And this is what you'll carry about with you." Felmouth opened a cabinet and brought out a wooden box, in the front of which a brass tube was mounted. He set it on the table before them and then fetched out a tripod, a wooden case full of something that clinked, several carboys full of chemicals, a contraption of poles and canvas that was either a very large umbrella or a very small tent, and a sealed packet marked PREPARED BIBULOUS PAPER.

"Shall I have a little wagon to trundle all this about?" Pengrove inquired hopefully. "Like an itinerant portraitist?"

"No," Felmouth replied. "It's only for show. You'll need to practice setting it up and taking likenesses, and you ought to be able to develop a passable negative image, but all that will be for purposes of misdirection. The real photographic studies will be taken with *this*." He opened a cupboard and brought out a hat. It was made of straw, rather high in the crown, with a band of wide black ribbon fastened with a black button and a string to secure it to the wearer's collar.

"You're joking," said Pengrove.

"Not at all," said Felmouth, and turned the hat over to reveal a small box set inside the crown. "Here is the real camera. Our own invention, and quite unknown to the world at large. Here is the lens, you see?" He tapped the black button on the hatband. "An ingenious shutter opens and closes *behind* the lens, admitting just enough light to form an image. But not on a cumbersome plate! We have created a supersensitive paper that will take an image in a fraction of a second, as opposed to five tedious minutes." He opened a drawer and withdrew a small canister. Opening the back of the little box, he deftly fitted the canister into it and closed it up again.

"There!" He set the hat on Pengrove's head and fastened the string to Pengrove's lapel, threading it through a buttonhole. The string ended in a sort of pendant, a black beanlike thing. "To capture an image, you simply turn so that the lens in the hatband is facing it, and reach up to the lapel of your coat. Squeeze this—" Felmouth tapped the pendant. "Only once, to take the image. Twice, and the cylinder rotates to enable you to take another. You may take as many as twelve to a cylinder."

"Bloody clever," admitted Pengrove. "I don't suppose the thing could be mounted in a slightly less absurd chapeau? I shall look a perfect fool."

"That will be all to the good," said Ludbridge. "What about the transmitting gear, Felmouth?"

"Ah. Just here—" Felmouth opened another cabinet and withdrew a case, about the size of a sea-chest but beautifully bound in leather and brass. Upon its lid was printed, in gold letters:

PRESSLEY'S PATENTED MAGNETISMATOR

"Who's to be your dispatches man?" Felmouth set the case down on the table.

"I am, sir," said Hobson.

"Right. You'll have a doctor's certificate stating that you have a disorder of the nerves, and must carry this about for self-treatment. What it actually is, is an Aetheric Transmitter and Receiver. We've had them for years; quite useful in sending messages from the field. This is the latest model, and has a secondary feature of particular interest."

Felmouth opened the front of the case, which folded down to reveal a gleaming brass face, whereupon were slots, knobs, dials and switches whose use could only be guessed at until he turned one of the knobs. There was a *click*, and at once a wavering screech filled the air. Hastily Felmouth turned a dial, rotating it until the screech faded, to be replaced with a sound like combers hissing on a gravel shore, and a faint disembodied voice saying, "*. . . Kossuth is presently under house arrest at Vidin, but we have great hopes of securing his removal by stages. The Grand Turk has been most cooperative . . .* "

"Good God," said Bell-Fairfax, staring at the machine.

"Yes, shocking catastrophe there, but we did our best. You can lead a horse to water, but you can't make him drink, as they say. This is the image-encoding device, here; a little tedious to use, but really invaluable for useful intelligence. Ever so much easier than trying to smuggle drawings concealed in one's coat lining!" Felmouth looked pleased with himself.

"But . . . but where was the voice coming from?" said Hobson.

"A transmitter in Hungary, naturally," said Felmouth, with scorn. "Evesden making his weekly report, if I'm not mistaken. See here, Ludbridge, oughtn't you brief your recruits a little more thoroughly?"

"They know what they need to know," said Ludbridge. "Now, may we take the toys away and play with them?"

Felmouth closed up the Aetheric Transmitter, like a concerned parent buttoning a child into a coat. "I suppose so," he said, with a sigh. "Kindly fill out the necessary paperwork, gentlemen."

For two weeks they trained with the devices. Learning to make talbotypes involved tramping about in Hyde Park with a great deal of heavy equipment, most of which Bell-Fairfax carried. Once a suitable subject had been found, Pengrove would open the camera lens while Bell-Fairfax and Hobson set up the tiny tent, into which Pengrove would rush with the exposed plate. There he spent the next half-hour washing and rinsing his print, to emerge gagging from the chemical fumes and waving a tiny study of the Serpentine blurred with ghostlike elongations of swans.

The images taken with the hat-camera, on the other hand, were astonishingly clear and sharp, and had moreover the advantage that they could be developed at leisure, when Pengrove could set up shop in a closet and develop the images: a swan beating its wings, each feather-edge sharp as a blade, or the Duke of Wellington's statue (viewed from right and left), or less monumental riders cantering along Rotten Row. It was true that Pengrove then generally had to fling open all his windows and hang the upper half of his body out for a good half-hour, gasping for breath, but the finished prints were a marvel.

When dry, they had to be inserted into a slot in the Aetheric Transmitter, which buzzed and clicked for some ten minutes before spewing out a lengthy tape printed with strings of tiny numbers. It was Hobson's duty to open out the telegraph key and sit down for two hours' weary work transmitting the numbers. Felmouth thoughtfully sent up the results when Hobson made mistakes: the same images printed on flimsy paper, but with curious white gaps here and there, as though tiles had fallen out of a mosaic.

It was far easier to use the transmitter to send simple auditory messages. There was a speaking-horn to be screwed into the front of the case, into which Hobson spoke; there was a curious device like a pair of earmuffs, which when worn made it much easier to hear incoming messages. Hobson sat before the case hour upon hour and often well into the nights, pensively turning the dials, listening for distant voices.

Ludbridge rapped briskly at Bell-Fairfax's door. After a moment it opened a crack, and one eye peered through; then Bell-Fairfax opened the door to reveal himself shirtless, one-half of his face still well lathered with shaving soap.

"Dreadfully sorry to disturb you, but you've been set another challenge," said Ludbridge.

"Very well," said Bell-Fairfax, looking apologetic. "I'll be down in five minutes, if you'd like to go rouse Hobson and Pengrove."

"This doesn't concern them," said Ludbridge. "May I come in?"

"Of course, sir." Bell-Fairfax stood back and waved Ludbridge to a chair. Ludbridge took a seat and watched as Bell-Fairfax returned to his shaving mirror. He drew out a cigar and lit it with a lucifer. Tucking away the lucifer case in his waistcoat, he looked around the room. It was Spartan in its tidiness; he noted that Bell-Fairfax had made his own bed. A moment Ludbridge's gaze lingered on the shaving stand, with its mug of soap. A bottle of Bay Rum cologne was the only item in the room indicative of personal tastes. Ludbridge exhaled smoke, looking thoughtfully at Bell-Fairfax's bare back.

"You must have had remarkable luck in your time," he said.

"I suppose so, sir," said Bell-Fairfax, hastily toweling his face dry. He reached for the bottle of cologne, but Ludbridge stopped him with a gesture.

"Leave that; it'll be better, with what we have to do. You served in China and off Africa too, and you haven't a single scar that I can see. Yet I can't think you're a coward."

"No, sir," Bell-Fairfax replied a little coldly, reaching for his shirt. "Nor was it for want of trying. I'd have liked nothing better than to have given a limb or two in the service of the nation. But it was always the other fellow who wasn't fast enough, you see."

"The fellow you were fighting? Or the fellow serving next to you?"

"Both," said Bell-Fairfax. "May I be told the nature of the challenge, sir?"

Ludbridge drew out his lucifer case once more. Holding his fingertip across the matches, he tapped it upside down and spilled out four little slips of pink paper. He handed one to Bell-Fairfax, who pulled up his braces and took it. He examined it curiously.

"It looks like a gummed label," he said.

"It is a gummed label," said Ludbridge. "I have four photographic portraits and a list in my pocket, as well. It contains the addresses of four individuals. We're going in search of them. Your objective is to get close enough to each of the four to stick a gummed label on his back, without his knowledge."

"That oughtn't be difficult," said Bell-Fairfax, turning the label in his fingers.

"Oughtn't it?" Ludbridge collected the other three labels and handed them to Bell-Fairfax. "One of the parties involved has no idea he'll be followed today. Two have been warned against some unspecified danger, and will be wary. One will not only have been warned, he will have been furnished with a description of his stalker. You are not to know which is which."

They had been lurking, peering around the corner at the house in Bedford Square for half an hour without seeing anything more notable than a maid who came out to sweep the entryway. Bell-Fairfax put his hand in his pocket and drew out the photographic portrait, studying once again its subject: a well-dressed, florid man in middle age, with a long curved nose and a tight impatient mouth.

"This was taken with one of our own cameras," Bell-Fairfax stated, glancing sidelong at the arched doorway.

"It would appear that way," Ludbridge replied.

"By which one might infer that this man is one of our members."

"A good guess."

"And though the other three portraits appear to have been taken by the same method, they have the appearance of being taken without the subjects' knowledge. So that doesn't necessarily—damn, it's stopping!"

Bell-Fairfax was referring to a cab that had pulled up before the house. They heard the house door opening, and an irascible voice raised. The subject of the image came down the steps, closely attended by a valet and a maid, the one clutching the subject's gloves and walking-stick, the other vainly offering a cup and saucer.

"No chance here, I shouldn't think," said Ludbridge. "The servants would raise a hue and cry." Bell-Fairfax, closely watching the subject, did not reply. A last gulp of tea was taken, the gloves and stick snatched from the valet, and the subject hoisted himself into the cab. The valet leaned up and spoke to the cabman, who nodded and flicked his whip. The horse started forward, making a circuit around the central park.

"I should think you've failed," said Ludbridge.

"I shouldn't," said Bell-Fairfax, never taking his gaze from the cab. As it swung about and started down toward Tavistock Mews, he ducked around the corner and flattened himself against a wall there; Ludbridge strolled after him.

"But your only chance now is following the cab, and you've no idea where it's bound," said Ludbridge.

"I beg your pardon," said Bell-Fairfax, "I heard the valet quite clearly."

"You never," scoffed Ludbridge. Bell-Fairfax ignored him, waiting for the cab to come abreast of the mews and pass. The moment it had done so he started after it, striding at remarkable speed as it turned into Great Russell Street and then onto High Street. Ludbridge ran to catch up and trotted just behind Bell-Fairfax.

"You can't really mean to course after him the whole way!" he said. Bell-Fairfax made an impatient gesture but never looked around, staring fixedly at the cab as it rolled along before him, around the corner into Greater St. Andrews Street, through Seven Dials all the way down into St. Martin's Lane. By the time they reached Charing Cross, Ludbridge was out of breath and straining to keep up; as they rolled into Whitehall he cast a longing glance in the direction of Redking's, thinking of the bar. Bell-Fairfax continued on his long legs like an automaton, fists swinging, never slowing down, directly behind the cab.

At the Privy Gardens Ludbridge developed an agonizing stitch in his side, but he kept up the chase into Parliament Street. By the time the cab reached New Palace Yard he had to stop, gasping, staring in unbelief as Bell-Fairfax kept straight on after the cab. But it was slowing and stopping at last; Ludbridge sucked in breath and sprinted to see the outcome.

The subject of the pursuit emerged from the cab and turned back a moment, reaching in for his stick. Bell-Fairfax came from behind the cab and passed him, touching him lightly on the back as he did so. As the subject straightened up with his stick in his hand, Ludbridge saw clearly the pink gummed label on the back of his coat. Bell-Fairfax, meanwhile, had doubled back and walked toward the subject at a leisurely pace. He smiled, tipping his hat, as he passed him. The subject acknowledged him with an absent nod and went into the House of Commons.

"You young bastard," said Ludbridge, wheezing painfully.

"I should judge that he was *not* the one who had been furnished with my description," said Bell-Fairfax cheerfully.

"You're not even sweating, are you? Back to the club; I'll need a brandy before the next one. And you might want to change your suit. The next one's in Whitechapel."

In rough clothing they had requisitioned from Costuming, Ludbridge and Bell-Fairfax walked up Aldgate High Street toward Whitechapel. It was mid-morning, with bright cold sunlight in abundance; and yet the streets opening off from side to side seemed to fade back into impenetrable smoky gloom. A more than customary layer of coal-soot had lacquered the cheap lodging houses, the derelict factories and ancient timber-framed shop fronts.

Bell-Fairfax turned down Goulston Street, looking from the photographic image in his hand to each building in turn. At last he stopped before one with perhaps a slight claim to respectability, in that some effort had been made to sweep and water the front step.

"This is where he lives," he murmured.

"So it is," said Ludbridge. "What will you do now, I wonder? It's half past ten in the morning. He may still be abed in there; then again, perhaps he isn't. He may be blissfully unaware you're standing out here in plain sight, or he may be watching you and studying *your* portrait. How will you know?"

Bell-Fairfax tucked the picture into his pocket. "I shall ask," he said brightly. He went to the door and pulled on the bell. Its handle came off in his hand. He set it carefully on the door's lintel, a second before the door opened a crack.

A gaunt female peered out, and then up, at Bell-Fairfax. Her iron-gray hair stuck out from under her cap all round, like a wiry halo. "Hallo, missus," said Edward, in quite passable Cockney. "Looking for my mate Bob. He says he dosses down here. Little fellow, turned out regular foppish, nice set of viskers? Vould he be in?"

The old dame's eyes glittered. She licked her dry lips and said, "Oh, yes? No, no, he ain't in. Gone down the Ten Bells. Corner of Red Lion and Church. Right at Wentworth, left at the next corner, straight on to Church. You'll find him there now, if you make haste."

"Much obliged, missus," said Bell-Fairfax, touching his hat brim. She closed the door and he stepped down with an air of triumph. "And I proceed to the Ten Bells."

"You do," said Ludbridge, falling into step beside him as he strode away. "I wonder how often you'll have the assistance of voluble landladies?"

Bell-Fairfax shrugged. They marched on, passing now and then the denizens of Whitechapel who staggered along in mid-morning intoxication or sprawled in the alleys sleeping off the previous night's gin. And here were a ragged couple, in violent quarrel: the male drove home his argument by clouting the female soundly. She clutched her jaw and wept. Bell-Fairfax halted, turned on his heel; Ludbridge blocked him.

"Let it alone," he said quietly. "She wouldn't thank you, and you'd have to kill him to make him give over."

"Small loss to anyone," said Bell-Fairfax, glaring at the man. Ludbridge raised his eyebrows.

"Do you think so? You may be right; but, after all, what would it accomplish? She'd only find another such tomorrow. In any case, men beat their wives as often in Belgravia as here. If you were to wring the neck of every brute who deserved it, you'd be obliged to reduce the population by a third. Your duty is to change the world itself, not to mete out justice. Put your strength to better use."

Bell-Fairfax pressed his lips together and walked on.

The Ten Bells loomed out of the haze at last, uninviting premises with windows smoked very nearly opaque. Stepping across the threshold, Ludbridge blinked as his eyes sought to adjust to the gloom. Lamps burned sullenly along the wall behind the bar, affording only enough light to make out that the place was tiny and shabby. Not by any means enough light for Ludbridge to have spotted the half-brick that came sailing out of the shadows, and it had broken his nose but for Bell-Fairfax snatching it out of midair.

Ludbridge caught a glimpse of some three or four grinning shadows, coming forward with clubs in their fists, before he was grabbed and dragged backward through the door by Bell-Fairfax. "I've led us into a trap—," Bell-Fairfax muttered in disgust. Ludbridge, who did not need to be told so much, took to his heels down Church Street, with Bell-Fairfax following closely. They rounded the corner onto Brick Lane and kept running, back toward Whitechapel Road.

"I think your mate Bob was waiting for you," Ludbridge said, panting as he ran.

"He wasn't in there," said Bell-Fairfax.

"How the devil could you tell?"

"They were all older men, and taller," said Bell-Fairfax, slowing his pace. He looked over his shoulder and, satisfied that they were not pursued, stopped to let Ludbridge catch his breath. As they walked briskly on, he added: "My fault, sir. Clearly, this was the one who knew to look for me. I ought to have been more circumspect."

"I'd say so, yes," said Ludbridge.

They came into Whitechapel Road once more and headed back toward Aldgate. "And shall you give it up for a bad job, and slink back to Whitehall defeated?" Ludbridge inquired jovially.

"No, sir," said Bell-Fairfax. "I will get him."

"Really? When your quarry has clearly put the word out against you? 'Here, mates, keep your eyes open for a gent what's all of seven feet tall if he's an inch, likely to come asking for me'? I should expect half the East End is aware of you now," said Ludbridge. "You'll be lucky if those chaps from Spitalfields haven't decided to—"

He became aware that Bell-Fairfax had stiffened beside him, halting for a split second as they made their way through the crowds along the high street. He glanced over to follow his companion's cold fixed stare, and saw that Bell-Fairfax was watching a slight figure some few yards ahead of them. A young man, nattily dressed, sauntered along the pavement. From time to time he veered close to another pedestrian, jostling each gentleman or lady as though by accident, generally absolving himself with a polite murmur and a tip of the hat. It required very sharp eyes indeed (and Ludbridge had them, in daylight) to note the handkerchiefs, watches and other oddments that leaped from the jostled parties to the jostler, apparently without the agency of human fingers.

Bell-Fairfax moved forward swiftly, closing the gap until he walked a mere yard behind his quarry. He worked his way through the crowd to one side as he paced the dapper gentleman, to view him sidelong. His hand slid into his own pocket. He fell back, edged to the right, and moved in once more. Ludbridge caught the flash of the pink label as it was drawn forth, and then, with a feather-touch, Bell-Fairfax had set it on the dapper gentleman's back. Bell-Fairfax then dodged forward, between his quarry and a well-dressed woman toward whom his quarry had been sidling, and thrust her roughly to one side.

"Mind your feet, can't you?" he snarled at his quarry, and tipped his hat to the lady. "Very sorry, ma'am."

The woman, recovering herself, moved off on a new trajectory through the crowd. The dapper gentleman looked indignant; he turned around, spotted Ludbridge, and at once his expression changed to one of chagrin. He shrugged and vanished in the throng as though he had been a wisp of fog.

Bell-Fairfax, meanwhile, sidestepped back to join Ludbridge. He was scowling.

"Cut that one a little fine, didn't you?" said Ludbridge.

"May I ask why there is a common thief among our ranks?"

"Because he's not a common thief," said Ludbridge, steering them back toward Aldgate. "He's an exceedingly uncommon thief, as you must have noticed. Remarkably talented. It sometimes happens that the Society has a use for his talents. Allowing him to ply his trade is a necessary evil, I'm afraid—keeps his skills in trim. Your righteous wrath is commendable, but consider the greater good, Bell-Fairfax."

Bell-Fairfax exhaled sharply. He thrust the portrait into his pocket and drew out the next one, studying it.

"Ah," he said. "This one's at Gravesend."

Rosherville Gardens was generally reached by excursion steamer, though it was nowadays a little more fashionable to go there by railway. Smart and exclusive as the steam locomotive might be, Ludbridge and Bell-Fairfax discovered that it could not be said to be a swifter mode of transport, on account of frequent stops.

As the train idled through Greenwich, Ludbridge leaned back in his seat and considered Bell-Fairfax.

"So you served in China, did you?"

Bell-Fairfax looked up from the third portrait. "I did, sir, yes."

"You can't have been much more than a boy then. Midshipman?"

"Yes, sir." Bell-Fairfax seemed unwilling to enlarge on his reply. Ludbridge took out his cigar case, offered a cigar to Bell-Fairfax, and lit his own cigar when Bell-Fairfax declined. He puffed smoke.

"So you can't have got up to much, I suppose."

"No, sir, not much."

"I served in China too," said Ludbridge casually. "Royal Marines. What'd you think of the whole business?"

Bell-Fairfax raised his eyes, looking wary. "I didn't care for it, sir."

"I didn't either." Ludbridge blew a smoke ring. "And I served under Stransham, you know. When we were at Zhenjiang . . . there were three merchants there and, you know, they were supposed to have obliged us in a certain matter and—to make a long story short—they hadn't. So I was sent out with my men to round up the merchants' wives and concubines and children and servants. Which we did, of course. We herded them into the courtyard in front of the house we'd commandeered, and our C.O.—won't tell you his name, but he was knighted a few years ago—he brought the merchants to the window looking out over the courtyard, and he bid them look well. Then he told me to give the order to prepare to fire.

"And I did. We raised our muskets and aimed into that crowd of weeping women and squalling babies. I assumed, of course, that all we'd have to do was threaten—the Chinese are very particular about their offspring, the sons at least—and the merchants would fall to their knees, begging for a second chance to do as they'd been told.

"And that was exactly what they did. But, do you know, the C.O. gave the order to fire anyway?"

Bell-Fairfax looked steadily at Ludbridge. "And did you?"

"No." Ludbridge blew another smoke ring. "I refused a direct order. Made no difference, of course. The C.O. was set on making an example of the merchants, you see. He had me relieved of command and my men fired into the crowd, and about half the women and children died at once. Then the C.O. ordered my men to reload and shoot the rest of them.

"I was told a great deal during my dressing-down about how yellow heathens only understood that sort of cruelty, how they often did worse to their own people, how they were scarcely human anyhow. You know the sort of things we were told out there, I expect."

"I remember," said Bell-Fairfax, in a whisper.

"Well, and then my C.O. went on to make an example of me. Soldiers, themselves, only understand that sort of cruelty. I was cashiered and sent home, and spent a year in prison. When I got out, Greene came round to see me, on the Society's behalf. I was recruited and became a Residential."

Bell-Fairfax said nothing. Ludbridge took a last pull on his cigar.

"The reason is all, you see," he said meditatively. "I'd killed before; I've killed since. But that wanton slaughter, all to make a point in what was after all an unjust war . . . no, by God. I've never regretted refusing that order."

"I set fire to houses," said Bell-Fairfax, in a faraway voice. "I was serving aboard the *Repulsion*. We went ashore in the gig with Mr. Hastleigh, our lieutenant. Jermyn and Shawe and I, all midshipmen. We had kegs of oil and matches and tow and oakum, to start the fires . . . we were to creep in amongst the houses of this little village, and set them alight. They were only fishermen's huts. We were laughing, because we didn't know anything. We thought it would be some sort of grand Guy Fawkes prank.

"We followed our orders. The little huts went up in flames. People ran out of them. I saw a woman carrying a baby, with her clothing afire. I tried to help her; Mr. Hastleigh stopped me and boxed my ears. He ordered me back to the boat. We all ran . . . he told me I might have gotten us all killed, and all I could think of was that poor woman beating at her rags, and the baby screaming.

"We rowed like madmen. As we came alongside the *Repulsion*, her guns began firing on the village. We cowered in the boat, with the guns roaring out over our heads. I had to hold my hands over my ears.

"When we'd given them three or four good broadsides, we pulled up anchor and sailed out of the harbor, and sat just offshore. I heard the screaming a long while after. I could see the fires burning for hours.

"In the morning, the smoke lay heavy as fog, in big rifts. We couldn't see where the village had been, or what had happened to the people there. The captain called us before him and commended us on a job well done."

Bell-Fairfax fell silent. Ludbridge shook his head.

"Wretched business," he said. "All of it. We really must make a better world, don't you think?"

Bell-Fairfax nodded. He looked down at the third portrait once more.

Stepping down from their railway carriage, they beheld Rosherville Gardens. It was a genteel place, green and well kept, and solidly genteel folk strolled amid the trees. They admired the Greek temples and statuary, or practiced at the archery range, or lost themselves in the shrubbery maze, or took refreshments at the various pavilions provided for that purpose. All the lower middle classes were dressed in their very best and on their best behavior.

"I expect you're thinking we ought to have changed our costumes before coming," remarked Ludbridge. "Rather conspicuous, aren't we?"

"No help for it now," said Bell-Fairfax shortly. He took a last glance at the portrait. "Perhaps they'll think we're gardeners. *He* looks as though he must be a waiter. We ought to go somewhere and order tea."

"If you like," said Ludbridge. He put his hands in his pockets and strolled along beside Bell-Fairfax, who glowered rather as they made their way through the crowds of children bowling hoops and shopgirls on the arms of tailors. "You might at least attempt to look as though you're enjoying your outing. I know what it is; you're making a comparison between all these happy Britons and the memory of those poor wretched Chinese. Do you find yourself despising us all? I did, at first."

"Rubbish," Bell-Fairfax muttered.

"Ah! I see you're particularly affected. But you mustn't allow it to distract you from the job at hand, you know."

Bell-Fairfax looked at him sidelong. Ludbridge only smiled.

"One can't despise whole nations," said Bell-Fairfax, with some heat. "There are innocents everywhere."

"Really? Point to one of these smug, comfortable people and tell me which has a pure heart."

"You don't know them. Any one of them might be a saint. Shall I feel contempt for them because you use words like *smug* and *comfortable*? That's just the same as telling me the villagers didn't matter, because they were *yellow heathens*. The clever use of words to reduce living people, for whom we ought to feel compassion, to mere ciphers who can be erased to suit someone's purpose." Edward kicked savagely at a stone in the path.

Ludbridge raised his eyebrows. "Bravo," he said. An infant, who had been staggering ahead of its parents along a grassy slope, tottered and fell. Its long skirts hindered its rise, and it went rolling over and over down the slope in a whirl of white lace. Edward jumped forward and caught it, swinging it up.

"Here you are," he said, smiling into the child's eyes. The baby, too astonished to cry, stared back. "Here's a pure heart, Ludbridge. Unless you're a desperate criminal in disguise, baby? No, I didn't think so."

He returned the infant to its father, who came running down the slope after it, and looked after them a trifle wistfully as they returned to the infant's mother, who stood above them wringing her hands.

"You never know," said Ludbridge *sotto voce*. "Might grow up to be a burglar."

"Bollocks," said Bell-Fairfax.

They spotted their man carrying a tray of sandwiches and lemonade to a group of chaperoned misses. He wore a striped apron and was of average build, was in fact average in nearly every unmemorable feature of his person. A careful observer might note that his gaze darted to and fro as he performed his office, and his expression was perhaps a little uneasy; but these were the only things that marked him out in any way.

"I think we'll just go take a seat." Bell-Fairfax strode toward the dining terrace. Ludbridge followed. They sat at a little table and waited. Minutes passed, and neither their quarry nor any other waiter came to wait on them. The waiters swooped perilously near, like swallows, and off again, pouncing on empty cups and saucers and whisking them in on trays, clearing away uneaten crusts, hovering attentively at the elbows of the respectably dressed; but they did not wait on Bell-Fairfax and Ludbridge.

"Then again, it must be admitted that the attire of the common laborer does confer a kind of invisibility," said Ludbridge.

"So much the better, then," said Bell-Fairfax, and rising to his feet he marched toward his quarry, who was scrubbing melted ice cream from a tabletop. As Bell-Fairfax passed, he set the gummed label on the man's back and kept going. Ludbridge rose and walked past on the waiter's other side, deliberately pausing to catch his eye. The waiter looked up, recognized Ludbridge, and started. Ludbridge grinned at him.

"We *are* everywhere," said Ludbridge.

"Oh, bugger," said the waiter, in a peevish voice. "Was it you?"

"Not at all," said Ludbridge. "A promising apprentice. Tootle-oo."

"Spa Road Station," said Bell-Fairfax. "This is our stop, I believe."

"It would appear that way," said Ludbridge. He rose and followed Bell-Fairfax as they stepped down from their carriage onto the platform at Bermondsey. There was an overpowering reek of raw sewage in the heavy air.

"I assume that the Society has some confidence we won't catch cholera?"

"It would appear that way."

Bell-Fairfax grimaced. They made their way to Neckinger Road and, passing under the railway arches, walked on toward Jacob's Island. The red sun was fading already, obscured by shrouds of fog that drifted upriver; there was no breath of wind to stir the reeking vapor between the high leaning houses or the canals that ran behind them. "Good God," murmured Bell-Fairfax, holding his nose. "Why was there ever a spa here?"

"It wasn't like this, once," said Ludbridge imperturbably. "Tanneries and docks here now; and all the poor who work in them, living in these teetering warrens. The human filth of their privies goes straight into the canals. When they require water in which to bathe or launder their clothes, or indeed to boil their dinners or drink, they simply draw up a bucketful from the canals. They'll let it sit awhile to let the worst of the stuff precipitate down, if they're not *very* thirsty, and pour what they mean to drink off the top. Filth seeps up and oozes through the floors, and in some cases the walls. This is the shop you want for cholera and typhus, my boy."

They came to the corner of Georges Row and started down it. Bell-Fairfax halted after a few steps, shaking his head like an alarmed horse. He groped frantically for his pocket-handkerchief. "There are corpses—I can smell them—" He started to tie the handkerchief over his mouth and nose.

"That will make you rather conspicuous, won't it?" said Ludbridge. "And of course there are corpses! Dead animals floating in the water; dead men and women shuttered up in their houses. What d'you expect happens, when people live like this? March on; you've work to do."

They proceeded on their way. Whitechapel and Spitalfields had been bustling by comparison, for Bermondsey was eerily silent. Not a soul moved anywhere, no drunken quarrels could be heard; only, here and there, a ghost-white child sat motionless on a doorstep, or on an upper stairway, with its sticklike legs dangling through the railings. Rifts and veils of poisonous gases hung in the air, heaviest at ground level.

"Now, you might suppose," said Ludbridge, "that the inhabitants of Whitechapel deserved their poverty. Drunkenness, idleness and all such vices. You couldn't say the same of this place! The folk are thrifty, industrious souls, every one of them. They die like flies here, simply because they can't afford to live elsewhere. You may blush at the memory of what we did to the Chinese, but see what our own people endure in our own nation!"

"But something must be done for them," said Bell-Fairfax, in a kind of strangled gasp.

"Of course. Educate them, in order that they'll know better than to drink from the canals? But what will they drink, then? Raze the whole district to the ground? But where will they live? Move them all, men, women and children, to the countryside? And how shall they live? They work the docks because they haven't the education to do anything else. There are no easy answers, my son. And, should you discover one, you will find a host of men standing ready to call you a liar, because their continued wealth depends on everything remaining exactly as it is. Now, look sharp! You've almost missed your street."

They turned down a lane so narrow it was bridged across by the shop signs on either side. Above them the upper stories shot up black against the sky, smeared now with the red of sunset, and a deeper gloom was seeping down between the houses. Here and there a candle had been lit, burning low and blue for want of air.

"There it is," said Ludbridge, pointing at a sign: THE SHIP AGROUND. Bell-Fairfax, who was doing his best not to breathe, nodded curtly. The inn was a long gabled building, looming up out of the mud. It breathed out a fragrance of gin positively wholesome in that mephitic atmosphere. They hurried within and found their way to a dark corner.

"Aren't you going to go ask the barman if he's seen your mate Jack?" Ludbridge inquired, returning from the bar with a glass of gin in either hand. Bell-Fairfax scowled.

"I shan't make that mistake again. He lodges here; sooner or later he must come in, or go out, and I'll spot him."

"Assuming there isn't an exit round the back," said Ludbridge, taking a sip of gin.

"How can you drink anything in a place like this?" Bell-Fairfax demanded, horrified. Ludbridge chuckled.

"My dear boy, it's only gin. Strong enough to stand off pestilence, I expect, and in any case I can't imagine they wash the glasses here often. If at all."

"What's become of Jack? He wasn't down the shop this morning at all," said a man at the bar. Bell-Fairfax sat straight but did not turn to look.

"He kept in upstairs today," said the barman. "Lazy beggar! Dropped the word as he was feeling sick. More likely there's someone looking for him."

"Aren't you the lucky fellow?" remarked Ludbridge *sotto voce*.

Bell-Fairfax tossed the contents of his glass on the floor and rose to his feet. He stalked out, followed at a slight distance by Ludbridge. Once in the street Bell-Fairfax crossed to the far side—not that he gained much perspective thereby—and peered up at the windows of the upper stories. One window on the topmost floor was lit from within.

"What'll you do now?" asked Ludbridge. Without answering, Bell-Fairfax looked around. He spotted an open tenement doorway and ducked into it, vanishing into Stygian blackness. Ludbridge followed and just glimpsed Bell-Fairfax's back vanishing as he swiftly climbed a flight of steep stairs. Ludbridge pursued at his best speed, up and up and up. Each landing was illuminated a little by feeble light from under the doors, enabling Ludbridge to keep Bell-Fairfax in sight. No tenants came out to inquire who might be running upstairs at such a pace; Ludbridge supposed a general listlessness made them apathetic.

At the next landing Ludbridge spotted Bell-Fairfax silhouetted against a narrow window there. Puffing and blowing, he approached. Bell-Fairfax held up a cautionary hand. Ludbridge peered past him. They had an excellent view straight across the street, into the Ship Aground's gable windows. Two were dark, but in the third they saw a man shaving himself by the light of a candle.

"Ah! But how do you know that's your man?" said Ludbridge. Bell-Fairfax only shook his head in reply. They watched, breathless, as with infinite care the man scraped away at his upper lip. At last he put down the razor and caught up a towel to dry his face. As he tossed the towel away, both Bell-Fairfax and Ludbridge nodded sharply. It was the subject of the fourth portrait.

"He's getting himself ready to go out for the evening," Ludbridge observed in a whisper. Without a word, Bell-Fairfax turned and ran back down the staircase. By the time Ludbridge, following him, emerged into the street, Bell-Fairfax had vanished.

Taking a guess, Ludbridge limped back across to the Ship Aground and made his way down an alley that ran along one side of it. Emerging into a foul muddy yard where privies leaned with open doors, he spotted a flight of outer stairs connecting with the inn's second floor. Bell-Fairfax stood beneath them, peering upward. Ludbridge joined him.

They heard a door close; someone came pattering down the stairs, and as he descended they recognized their quarry. Bell-Fairfax stepped out and, reaching up, touched the last of the gummed labels to the back of the man's coat as he passed.

Turning at the base of the stairs, the man came face-to-face with his stalkers. As if to underscore the moment, someone lit a bright lamp within, which shone out through a window and cast a square of illumination on their pale countenances.

"Dear, dear," said the man. "Not clever enough, was I? Hallo, Ludbridge."

"Evening, Stayman," said Ludbridge. "What do you think of my recruit?"

"Damned effective." Stayman grinned at Bell-Fairfax. "Well, youngster, welcome to Jacob's Island! What d'you think of it?" He made a wide gesture taking in the filthy yard, the brimful privies, the night miasma rising from the stinking canals and ditches. "What would you give, eh, to scour places like this from the face of the earth?"

"All I have," said Bell-Fairfax.

He was silent on the long walk home—for the last train had gone and no cabs would stop for them, even after they had crossed back over the Thames. Ludbridge watched him, whistling an air as they trudged along. At last Bell-Fairfax turned to him.

"How often shall I be called upon to stick labels on people?"

"Never, I should think," said Ludbridge. Bell-Fairfax said nothing more, and after a few paces Ludbridge cleared his throat.

"You said you'd give all you have to bring the longed-for day. The price will be higher than that, you know."

"Will it?"

"Oh, yes. You will be obliged to pay out all you are, as well. All your notions of chivalry, honor, pride . . . any hope you had of winning a place for yourself in the history books. *You* won't matter, d'you understand? Only the work matters."

"It's no worse than what's expected of a soldier, after all," said Bell-Fairfax at last.

"Precisely. You're a soldier, in the subtlest of wars. And an act that would be criminal, when performed by a civilian for base purposes, is quite another thing when required of a soldier. I think you see."

Bell-Fairfax nodded. They walked on down the Strand.

1850: To Strive, to Seek, to Find

Greene reached out with his left hand, attempting to pull the globe nearer as he studied the paper on the desk in front of him. Bell-Fairfax, Pengrove and Hobson watched uncomfortably, each one wondering whether he oughtn't push the globe within Greene's reach, for as matters stood it was a good ten inches out of range. At last Ludbridge snorted and, getting up, shoved the globe on its stand toward Greene.

"For God's sake, man, mind what you're doing," he said. Greene peered over his spectacles, giving Ludbridge a severe look.

"Our Customary Informant," he said, "has advised us that Louis-Napoléon will stage a coup d'etat next year, and assume dictatorship of France."

Bell-Fairfax caught his breath. "When, sir?"

"The second of December, in point of fact."

"The anniversary of Bonaparte crowning himself Emperor!" said Bell-Fairfax. "As well as the anniversary of the battle of Austerlitz, if I'm not mistaken."

"Keen on dates, are you? Well, you're correct. He's keen on them too. The following year, on the same date, he'll end the Second Republic and found the Second Empire. This will have consequences, of course. There'll be a war."

"Are we to fight the Bonapartists in France, sir?" Bell-Fairfax sat perceptibly straighter. Pengrove and Hobson looked sidelong at him.

"No," said Greene. "We are not. We will be allied with the French against Russia." Bell-Fairfax looked stunned. Greene went on: "According to our Informant, we will fight a singularly long, bloody and badly managed war. We will win, of course, but at considerable cost."

"We'll be fighting for the *French*?"

"With them, Mr. Bell-Fairfax. May I continue without further interruption?"

"Yes, sir. Sorry, sir."

"Our Informant has pointed out that advance notice of the war presents us with certain opportunities, and has recommended a number of steps to be taken. These will profit the Society, of course, but it does seem to me that we—I speak as a mere Briton now, rather than a Society member—would benefit greatly by having superior intelligence regarding the theaters of conflict, as well.

"And there is another matter . . ." Greene looked down once more at the paper on his desk. "I can't imagine you'll run into anything where we're sending you, but orders are that all operatives should be briefed to keep their eyes open. You've heard of the Franklins, I assume?"

"What, poor old Northwest Passage Franklin?" said Pengrove.

"No!" said Ludbridge scornfully. "They're a branch of our brotherhood in Philadelphia. Founded by Dr. Benjamin Franklin. Their inventor fellow."

"So he was," said Greene. "We received a curious communication from them, the other day. There appears to have been a breach of security over there."

"That's damned bad." Ludbridge sat straight.

"They're not telling us much, of course, but what we have been able to ascertain from independent sources is that some young fool broke from their ranks and took his talents to another organization."

Ludbridge grunted as though he'd been punched. Pengrove, watching, noted that he'd gone pale. "What other organization?" Pengrove inquired.

"Exactly what we'd like to know," said Greene. "And one can't have renegades running about, after all; what are vows of silence for? So we had one of ours chase down their truant and sweat him for what we could learn. Which wasn't much; some group associated with the old Burr conspiracy plans to have a go at conquering Mexico. *Filibusters*, they call themselves. Nothing Brother Jonathan can't deal with himself, and he's welcome to. The machinery's another matter, of course.

"As far as our man was able to learn, the truant hadn't actually built anything for them yet, and we made certain nothing *will* be built. Still, we don't know how much the chap told them, nor whether he took them any plans from the Franklins. So all men in the field are being advised to look out for Americans bearing suspiciously advanced weaponry or other *technologia*."

"So noted," said Ludbridge.

"And so, back to our own game. Three young gentlemen of leisure shall set out on an extended tour of the Continent and other places of interest, which will, purely by chance, include the scenes of the coming armed conflict. They will be accompanied by an older gentleman, perhaps a tutor or uncle—Silenus to a trio of Bacchuses, if you like. The young gentlemen will appear to be prime examples of British idiots. Wastrels, dilettantes, positively the last sort of creatures anyone would suspect of intelligence-gathering."

A silence greeted his statement. At last Pengrove put up his hand.

"I think I can play an idiot, sir."

"I'm certain you can," said Greene. "And if you others feel unequal to the task, I recommend you take a walk through some of the more fashionable districts of this great city and observe the Well-Bred Imbecile promenading in his natural habitat."

"Yes, sir," said Bell-Fairfax and Pengrove, in subdued voices, and Hobson added: "Where are we to go, sir?"

"You will begin with the Holy Land," said Greene. "As for the other places on your itinerary, you are not to know them in advance. You will be informed when and as necessary. Mr. Ludbridge, you are in command; Mr. Hobson is Dispatch Officer; Mr. Pengrove, you will serve as the mission's photographic portraitist, providing us with views of certain locations. Mr. Bell-Fairfax, you are Mr. Ludbridge's second-in-command. Have you any questions?"

"I assume I'm to see Parker for funds and whatnot," said Ludbridge.

"You are. The usual arrangements have been made. You'll leave on the thirtieth."

"Right." Ludbridge got to his feet. "By your leave, then, Greene, I'll just take my young gentlemen for a walk in Mayfair. Come along, chaps."

Mr. William Jenkins operated a profitable tour service, conveying hundreds of pious Britons each year to Jerusalem and other sites of interest. The tour he was presently engaged in conducting had become a source of some discomfort to him, however. The fault lay not in the Bible students and devout pensioners who made up his list of tourists; rather in the indiscretion of the owners of the packet steamer, who (in addition to providing service for Mr. Jenkins's tour) had booked a number of more secularly minded passengers as well, who were displaying unbecoming attitudes of irreverence.

Most notorious among these were four gentlemen who shared a cabin aft. They drank a good deal, wandered the decks and attempted to engage in inappropriate conversation with females, were rebuffed, blustered, were loudly and publicly seasick, monopolized a corner of the saloon and grew riotous at whist there, stuck out their legs to trip elderly gentlemen who passed their table, complained about the fare, smoked cigars in the presence of ladies, told jokes of the most infantile and scatological nature and laughed uproariously, annoyed the steward, and in general made themselves damned nuisances—though of course Mr. Jenkins phrased it in a less offensive manner when he complained to the ship's officers, which he soon did on a daily basis.

In addition to their behavior, the quartet was visually irritating as well. One was an older gentleman, who might have preserved a certain leonine dignity had he ever been sober, but as it was his scarlet nose was the warning beacon that lit his entrance to the saloon, and advised decent passengers to gather up their knitting, Scripture commentaries or travel guides and make a hasty departure before his three students, or nephews, or whatever they might be, followed in his train.

One was a grotesquely dwarfish and whiskered individual who nevertheless managed to fit no less than five different checked patterns into his attire—trousers, waistcoat, jacket, tie, and hatband—while what could be seen of his shirtfront was a jarring lime-green. Another was as markedly tall as his companion was squat, an immense youth who made matters worse with a beaver hat that added some fourteen inches to his stature, and who was forever striking his head against beams and falling down, prompting hilarity in his friends. The third was a shrill and lisping specimen of British manhood, foppishly dressed despite his manifest lack of any feature that might be deemed pleasing or, indeed, symmetrical. He wore a ridiculous straw hat and monocle, the latter of which he dropped into his tea regularly, at which his companions roared with laughter.

It was with profound gratitude that Mr. Jenkins watched them stagger ashore at Beirut, where they vanished with their considerable baggage into a crowd of mendicants screaming for baksheesh. He very nearly forgot them over the journey across Galilee, through Nazareth, through Jerusalem, as his tourists exclaimed over the ancient villages, the camels, the palm trees, the very stones that might have known the Savior's tread (though it must be admitted some complained about the heat and the curious smell compounded of dust, donkeys and vinegar). How horrified Mr. Jenkins was, then, to spot the four oafs from the steamer in the throng at the Church of the Nativity in Bethlehem!

His own genteel tourists were scandalized to observe that the fop had set up amateur photographic equipment and was profaning the sacred premises with impromptu portraits of his friends, grinning beside the Door of Humility. Much incensed, Mr. Jenkins shepherded his tourists within, where they knelt in prayer, breathing in clouds of frankincense and myrrh from the pierced silver censers that hung above the grotto. For a moment all was peaceful contemplation.

Alas, the fop and his companions followed them in, and while it was evident they were making some attempt at silence and discretion, they nevertheless erupted in snorting guffaws at the efforts of the very tall individual to walk through the Door of Humility. At last he had to get down on his hands and knees and crawl through. The four offending gentlemen lined up together at the back of the nave, and for a while seemed awed by the holy spot. At last, however, Mr. Jenkins overheard the unmistakable *pop* of a cork being removed from a flask, and a hoarse whisper of "I say! Don't you half expect Father Christmas to be lurking somewhere about?"

This was the straw that broke the camel's back, as far as Miss Hutchings was concerned—she being the spinster daughter of a vicar who was guiding her ancient parent through the Holy Land that he might see its principal sights before he died, though his cataracts presented something of a challenge—and in fury she turned and began shouting for the authorities to evict the blasphemers.

And here was where matters took a most regrettable turn. From the narthex ran a pair of monks of the Roman Catholic persuasion. From an alcove to one side of the chancel a pair of Eastern Orthodox monks came, no less swiftly. None of them seemed to understand plain English, for some reason, but Miss Hutchings was able to make her meaning clear with gestures, and in any case the guilty parties were in the very act of setting up their photographic equipment!

The monks converged on them, uttering threats and warnings, but most unfortunately a Roman monk jostled an Eastern one. The offended party turned and shoved his fellow Christian, who promptly shoved back. He, in turn, had his beard pulled. Their co-religionists turned and attempted to part them, getting shoved themselves for their pains. One monk punched another; within seconds the fray had erupted into a full brawl, with candlesticks, silver censers and a prayer book grabbed from a tourist all conscripted as weapons.

Representatives of the C. of E. present were much distressed, save for the four gentlemen whose trespass had brought about the fracas: the fop pointed his camera at the monks and removed the lens cap, while his friends hurriedly set up a tray with flash powder, and detonated it repeatedly to bathe the scene in glaring light. They were stopped, at last, by the arrival of the Ottoman police, who were much confused but decided the matter would be best resolved by ejecting all parties from the premises. Once outside, both Miss Hutchings and Mr. Jenkins did their best to explain the matter; and, since Mr. Jenkins knew a little Turkish, they did manage to get their meaning across sufficiently for the police sergeant, or whatever his rank might have been, to look about wrathfully for the four infidels in question.

They, however, seemed to have vanished. Just arriving, unfortunately, was a party of tourists from the United States of America, grim-visaged young men in black and a clergyman of some kind, to judge from his shovel hat. These the police mistook for the errant Englishmen, and there was a great deal of shouting and a very many angry words before Mr. Jenkins was able to explain that the wrong parties had been arrested.

"I do feel rotten about blaspheming in the Manger, all the same," said Hobson. Bell-Fairfax nodded agreement. They were enjoying a late and somewhat impromptu supper in the room they had obtained at a caravanserai.

"Nothing so blasphemous as the bloody monks throttling each other over who had precedence in their shrine," said Ludbridge, deftly peeling a fig. "That'll set it off, you know. The war."

"You're joking," said Bell-Fairfax. Ludbridge shook his head. "The Roman Catholics and the Eastern Christians will go to war?"

"In the persons of their French and Russian protectors, respectively," said Ludbridge. "Whole thing a shoving match between Louis-Napoléon and the Czar, of course. As I understand it. Elbowing each other for room at the Ottoman Empire's deathbed."

"Then why are *we* involved?" demanded Bell-Fairfax.

"Shoring up the Turks, evidently. It won't do to ask too many questions, you know; best to attend to our business and let the wheels roll on above our heads—" Ludbridge was interrupted by Pengrove, who flung his door wide and entered their parlor in a haze of chemical fumes.

"Here's the pictures—turned out rather well—" He coughed explosively, doubling over. "Most of them, anyway—"

"Ah." Ludbridge took the sheaf of photographs from him. Of the two talbotypes, one was a reasonably clear study of Bell-Fairfax and Hobson lounging on either side of the Door of Humility. The other was a cloudy disaster in which only the columns of the church could be made out with any clarity; the indignant Scripture tour parties were so many semitransparent ghosts, and the battling monks were a faint blur of darkness. The photographs from Pengrove's hat-camera, on the other hand, were remarkably clear and sharp: one monk's frozen grimace as a fist impacted with his jaw, a rosary arrested in mid-lash as it sailed toward someone's nose, another monk's open mouth and rolled-back eyes testifying to the effect of the sandaled foot that had just caught him in a place monks might not be supposed to require very much but evidently needed to protect.

"And it's war," said Ludbridge, with a sigh. He selected the best of the shots and tossed it at Hobson. "There you are; run that through the encoder, and then transmit it to London. You two pack the trunks. We'll need to move on fairly quickly."

"Where are we going next?" Pengrove sat down and wiped his eyes with his pocket handkerchief.

"That would be telling," said Ludbridge, tucking the other photographs inside his coat. He reached for another fig.

1850: Now at Length We're Off for Turkey

The water of the Bosporus was softly blue, the sky a blazing blue, and
Hagia Sophia with its minarets sat like a resigned dowager under guard
by four alert sentinels. Ludbridge watched as Pengrove, leaning on the
rail, fumbled at his lapel and snapped off a shot.

"Mind you don't waste the exposures," he muttered. "Greene bloody
well knows what Constantinople looks like."

Their steamer threaded its way through the Sea of Marmara, passing
a great many British merchant vessels at anchor in the Golden Horn.
Pengrove captured their images too, in one shot showing masts like a
winter forest, with Union Jacks fluttering limply. There was an interminable wait once they had got to anchor at Pera, with minor officials who
needed to come aboard and accept bribes before anyone could be allowed to go ashore. Then there were porters to be hired before, at last,
they might set off through the streets toward their hotel. All their trunks
were carried by brawny Turkish hamals, save for the Aetheric Transmitter, which Hobson hugged to his chest as they trudged along.

He stumbled and nearly fell repeatedly, unable to tear his gaze away
from the street scene. There were veiled women in richly colored robes;
there were picturesque ruins, and fountains, and green gardens, and
jackals wandering in the very marketplaces. Pengrove somehow or
other purchased three melons without quite meaning to, and then had

to buy a raffia bag in which to carry them. After that they were pursued by street vendors waving every other item imaginable, and by the time they were climbing the steep street to their hotel Pengrove was weighted down also with a brass coffee service, four strings of beads and brass bells, a pair of slippers the wrong size and a heavy ceramic object of dubious utility. Bell-Fairfax, who had been in Constantinople before, proved better able to resist the bargain rate splendors of the Orient but consented to carry the ceramic object for Pengrove, who was nearly in tears.

"Here we are," said Ludbridge in satisfaction. They peered up at their hotel. Just beyond it they saw several flags of Imperial Russia, displayed on window standards. "Next door to the Russian Embassy. Remarkable coincidence, what?"

They were given a long echoing room, innocent of much furniture but with a splendid view of the embassy next door. The hamals set down the luggage, and as Ludbridge paid them he addressed one in Turkish. The other said something in reply, bowing; they departed.

"How shall I ship all this home?" said Pengrove, setting down his raffia bag. It fell over and a melon rolled out.

"No idea," said Hobson, flinging himself down on one of the narrow beds. "Just like the dormitory at school, what?"

"Busy yourselves," said Ludbridge. "On your feet, Hobson, and tune the transmitter."

"But it's only—" Hobson fumbled for his watch. "Only half past two. We're not scheduled to call in until six o'clock."

"And you don't want to waste the first ten minutes tuning in," said Ludbridge. "You'll need to be ready at six, not quarter past six. Tune it in and then close it up again."

"But, see here, aren't we to have the chance to see the sights a bit first?" said Pengrove. "I mean, gilded glories of old Byzantium, what? Dusky beauties smiling through the latticework of hareems? Voluptuous charmers offering their delights in the marketplace, and all that?"

Bell-Fairfax looked up from where he was methodically unpacking. "There's a very good house in Stamboul," he said seriously. "Quite clean, and they provide you with coffee and pastries downstairs. You will need to be quite specific about wanting a woman, however, or they'll bring out their boys as well. Oh! Someone's outside in the corridor." And, indeed, a second later came a discreet knock. Ludbridge opened the door to reveal a lean elderly dragoman, clean-shaven, wearing a coat and trousers in the Western manner, though he also wore a fez. He bowed to Ludbridge.

"What becomes of illusions?" said Ludbridge.

"We dispel them," said the other.

"And we are everywhere," responded Ludbridge.

"Indeed! Zosimos Polemis, at your service."

"Pleased to meet you." Ludbridge waved him in and shut the door after him. "My associates: Mr. Bell-Fairfax, Mr. Hobson, Mr. Pengrove. Gentlemen, this is one of the Magi; what you might call the Society's Oriental Branch members. Our liaison. I must commend you on your arrangements for our room, Mr. Polemis! Quite the view."

"I thought perhaps you would appreciate it," said Polemis dryly, with a smile. He walked across to the window and looked out at the Russian Embassy. "Yes. If I may point out the window of interest—" Ludbridge followed him and looked across. "That one, on the floor below, ought to reward closer attention."

"Duly noted," said Ludbridge.

"I trust you will be discreet." Polemis stepped away from the window.

"Of course, my dear fellow."

"Let me see, let me see . . . The table d'hôte in this establishment is very good; the present chef is French, and has an excellent reputation among the Europeans here. There is also a coffeehouse nearby, frequented by our members. The hotel's laundress is more than competent. If you wish to see something of the city, I can arrange for a reliable guide. Do you require servants?"

"I think not, thank you," said Ludbridge. "We're accustomed to blacking our own boots."

"You're quite sure? Our people have second-level security clearance."

"Quite sure."

"Then I may dispense with further preliminaries and advise you that a certain gentleman was receptive to our offer, and wishes to meet you."

"Excellent!" Ludbridge rubbed his hands together. "We are entirely at his disposal. Would this evening be convenient?"

"I will inquire." Mr. Polemis bowed. "Anything further?"

There was not; and so Mr. Polemis took his leave, and left them to finish unpacking.

They dined satisfactorily, though the room was somewhat crowded with a miscellany of Europeans: a party of gesturing Neapolitans, two Prussian businessmen who bolted their food and then spoke a great while over a great many cigarettes, a large French family with servants, three Bulgarians who were displeased with their meal, an Aragonese nobleman who sipped his coffee and spoke to no one save the waiter, and many others. All of them glanced over in disapproval, at various times, at the four badly behaved Englishmen who flicked knobs of butter at one another with their napkins and, when that palled, tossed rolls back and forth, as well as the occasional chicken bone.

"Don't light the lamps just yet," said Ludbridge, as they reentered their room.

"Whyever not?" Pengrove shrugged out of his dinner jacket. "I say, Bell-Fairfax, the laundress is going to have the devil of a time getting these grease stains out. You might have spared my best tie."

"Sorry," said Bell-Fairfax. Ludbridge, meanwhile, walked to his trunk. It was a large and elaborate one, of the sort that opened to reveal a cabinet with drawers. He opened it now and, squatting down before it, felt carefully about until he found a hidden catch. A hidden compartment slid out between the third and fourth drawers.

"Here we are . . ." Ludbridge reached into the compartment and withdrew what looked at first, in the darkness, like a crucifix. He carried it across the room and by the faint light from the window they could see that it was, in fact, a very small crossbow. "Come here, Bell-Fairfax."

"Yes, sir." When Bell-Fairfax reached him, in three long strides, Ludbridge handed him the crossbow and, taking care to make no sound, opened the window. Stepping back, he murmured:

"Just below us. Second window back. Look at it. D'you think you can put a bolt in the outer frame of the casement?"

Bell-Fairfax stepped up to the window and peered out. "Where it wouldn't be seen by anyone looking out?"

"Just so."

Bell-Fairfax raised the little weapon to eye level and, sighting along it awkwardly, fired a bolt no more than a half-inch long. It hit its intended target with a *bang*, sounding as though a bird had flown into the casement, and nearly buried itself in the window frame. Bell-Fairfax ducked back, and Ludbridge swiftly closed the window. "Well done! You may light the lamps now, Pengrove. Hobson, it's nearly six. You're on duty at the transmitter."

"What was the purpose of the bolt, sir?" Bell-Fairfax inquired.

"All in good time," said Ludbridge, as a knock sounded at the door. Ludbridge waited until the lamps were lit before opening it to admit Mr. Polemis, who had swathed himself in a cloak.

"He will see you now," he said quietly.

"Very good. Bell-Fairfax, you'll come along. Hobson, make your report at six precisely. Lock the door after us, please, Pengrove," said Ludbridge.

They slipped out a side entrance of the hotel and proceeded along streets black but for starlight and the occasional pool of lamplight from the windows of a house. Far down on the harbor they could see the lamps of ships at anchor, and the many dim lights of Stamboul beyond. At the end of a winding lane was a coffeehouse, from which came the clicking of backgammon counters, the rattle of dice and a low hum of conversation; a single lamp flickered above the door, casting its light on a single painted tile set in the keystone of the door's arch. The tile appeared to depict a green lion with a golden ball in its jaws.

"The side entrance," murmured Mr. Polemis. He led them around to a low door, unlit. It opened to his knock, and they hurried in; Bell-Fairfax was obliged to remove his hat and bend low in order to pass through. Up a narrow flight of stairs, then, and down a corridor. A Turk in the uniform of the palace guard stood before the door at the corridor's end, watching them closely as they approached. Mr. Polemis made a certain sign. The Turk nodded and stood aside.

They entered a room overpoweringly fragrant with the scent of coffee, no doubt emanating from the bags of beans stacked along the walls. In the center of the room was a low table surrounded by cushions. A Turkish gentleman sat at the table, unconcernedly sipping coffee.

"My lord." Mr. Polemis bowed to the ground. "The visiting English."

The gentleman lifted his head. He wore a military tunic; his beard was still dark, neatly trimmed, and his black gaze was opaque. Ludbridge bowed, motioning Bell-Fairfax to do likewise. They removed their hats. Their host did not remove his fez.

"Please, seat yourselves," said the gentleman, in perfectly accented English. "Have you dined?"

"We have, sir." Ludbridge lowered himself onto a cushion, and Bell-Fairfax followed suit somewhat awkwardly.

"Will you have coffee?"

"We should like that very much, sir."

The gentleman waved his hand. Polemis brought a coffee urn on a tray and two more cups, filling them with thick rose-scented brew. Ludbridge and Bell-Fairfax drank, and after a contemplative silence of a moment or two the gentleman continued:

"I trust your voyage was a pleasant one?"

Ludbridge replied that it had been. The conversation proceeded in the same vein for some few minutes, formal small talk of the most non-committal nature. By degrees it proceeded to the subject of hunting, and whether or not Ludbridge or Bell-Fairfax had ever attended a fox-hunt in England (they had not), and whether it was customary to kill the fox once it was caught. Ludbridge explained that the hounds generally did that, and the gentleman nodded thoughtfully and observed that it was a good thing to own hounds, when killing was necessary. And why was it necessary to hunt the fox?

Ludbridge explained that foxes were great destroyers of poultry. The gentleman nodded once more, and called for Polemis—who sat patiently by the door—to fill the coffee cups again. Another pause, while coffee was sipped and savored. The gentleman reached into his tunic and drew forth a few sheets of folded paper, and set them on the table beside Ludbridge's cup.

"These are the names of two foxes," said the gentleman. "Their observed habits and where they make their dens, also."

"Very good," said Ludbridge, tucking the papers into his coat. The gentleman looked into his coffee cup a long moment, swirling its contents around and around.

"Have you ever heard the word *tanzimat*, may I ask?"

"No, sir."

"Its meaning is very similar to your English word *reformation*. Ancient and corrupt systems dismantled, and new systems, closer I think to the will of Allah, put in place. Undeserved privileges taken from petty authorities. Bribery and perjury punished. Justice, mercy and compassion guaranteed for the poor. Nor is this all: the state made strong again by the adoption of modern arrangements, rather than a medieval bureaucracy. Our empire is manifestly weak and ill, gangrenous I might say; what will save it but the amputation of its festering limb?"

"It seems an excellent policy," said Ludbridge.

"Any wise man would say so," said the gentleman, and sighed. "But not the greedy ones who profit under the old system. Not the narrow-minded zealots who regard any change as heresy, and use their scholarly authority to condemn it. Do you see?"

"We, of all people, see!" said Bell-Fairfax heatedly. Ludbridge gave him a sidelong look.

"Kindly be indulgent of my young friend," he said. "He too is a devout believer in the need for reformation."

"Commendable," said the gentleman, with a slight bow in Bell-Fairfax's direction. "To continue: my master's father saw that the empire must reform, and worked with the Magi to begin the process. My master is a wise and gentle man, and a dutiful son moreover, for he has carried our banner forward and decreed sweeping changes in the old laws. And, of course, this has made him many enemies.

"By the grace of Allah and the vigilance of his servants, my master has narrowly avoided assassination on several occasions. Interpreting the law of the All-Merciful and Compassionate to mean that he himself must be a model of mercy and compassion, my master has declined to sign the death warrants of his would-be assassins.

"Unfortunately, while meritorious and admirable in itself, his clemency has resulted in making other conspirators bolder. So is leniency repaid."

"I perceive the difficulty," said Ludbridge.

"I was certain you would." The gentleman had another sip of his coffee. He set the cup down on the table. "My master is troubled by illness; it may well please Allah to take him into Paradise sooner rather than later, and so it is therefore important that he accomplish as much as he can in his allotted time.

"When the hour of his passing comes, and may it come a thousand years from this hour, I would not have my master's virtuous soul weighed down with any consideration of executions ordered in his own defense. I, his servant, will gladly bear the weight of any sin incurred for his safety's sake—but secretly."

"Commendable," said Ludbridge. His hand strayed to the breast of his coat a moment, and touched the bulge of folded paper there. The gentleman's eyes followed his gesture.

"I am glad that you understand," he said solemnly. "Let us speak of pleasanter matters. I was delighted to learn that our fraternity of scholars and artificers has a counterpart in England! Truly it is said that we are everywhere. I have brought something with me that might interest you."

He leaned down to a satchel he had placed under the table, and withdrew a small parcel wrapped in silk. Unwrapping it, he revealed an ancient codex bound in a frame of silver.

"This is a manuscript, formerly in the possession of the illustrious al-Jazari," he said. "His own translation of a work by a certain Greek. Your brotherhood owns the companion volume, I understand . . . this, however, was locked away, and has never been copied."

He opened it for their inspection, and turned a few pages. Ludbridge and Bell-Fairfax glimpsed an image of a chariot and horses, floating over the heads of spectators who held up their stiff hands in astonishment. Ludbridge caught his breath. "Why was it never copied?"

"The subject matter was pronounced blasphemous," the gentleman replied. "It contains detailed instructions for creating wonders—such as this iron charioteer and horses that float like clouds—but their purpose was to encourage belief in the power of false gods. Unfortunately, this consideration outweighed the fact that the science might be put to other uses that are not sinful, and so the book was kept in a library of other forbidden works, under lock and key and closely guarded. It took us years of patient work to find it.

"Of course, in this modern age in which we live, no one has any desire to build temples to Zeus. Therefore I think it will do no harm if a few fellow monotheists are allowed to copy the text and illustrations."

He closed the book and wrapped it in silk once more. "When you visit me again, the book will be available for your closer inspection."

"I look forward to the occasion," said Ludbridge.

"Excellent." The gentleman turned his empty coffee cup over and set it on the serving-tray. "Good evening to you both. Walk safely in the streets."

———

Mr. Polemis accompanied them back as far as the hotel, where he bid them good night and took his leave.

"Have we just been asked to commit murder?" Bell-Fairfax asked Ludbridge in a low voice, as they climbed the stairs.

"No indeed," said Ludbridge. He was puffing a little as they reached the landing, and paused there a moment as he fumbled in his coat for his cigar case and match safe. "Merely to assist the pasha in a couple of slightly irregular executions. Have you qualms? I was under the impression you had blooded your sword on a few occasions whilst in the Navy."

"I did. Yes."

"Consider what's at stake, then, if you like. And consider the reward."

Edward was silent as they climbed to the next landing. "With or without the reward, the task seems necessary."

"That's the way." Ludbridge lit a cigar and exhaled smoke. "You'll do well, dear boy. Quite well." They reached the door of their room and he rapped briskly on the panel. "Here, Charley, let us in! We've just had an adventure!" he called loudly.

Pengrove unlocked and opened the door to them. His eyes were wide. "So have we," he said.

"What d'you mean?" Ludbridge and Bell-Fairfax entered, and locked the door. Hobson was sitting by the Aetheric Transmitter, turning and turning the earpieces in his hands.

"I got on at six to call in, just as you told me," he said. "Got through to London easily, too. Greene says he wants your expense reports weekly, not all in one huge report from the last place on the itinerary."

"So noted," said Ludbridge. "That's not all that happened, is it?"

"No," said Hobson. "After London signed off I sat awhile practicing, you know, seeing if anyone else was talking out there. I picked up a few voices, quite far away and faint. I recognized Bainbury—he was transmitting from a ship in the North Sea. But then, as I was turning the dials, suddenly I got a conversation. Quite loud! Actually had to reduce the volume. Two men talking, and sometimes a third. They seemed to be in the same room, not transmitting to each other. They were speaking English, but they weren't English at all."

"Really? What were they?" Ludbridge sank onto a chair and tipped ash from his cigar.

"Well, one of them was a Russian," said Hobson. Ludbridge nodded. "The other one—or two—were Americans."

"Really."

"And they were—as near as I could tell, the one who did most of the talking seemed to be some sort of missionary, and the other fellow was his assistant. They weren't our people, you see! That's the strangest part. Didn't seem to understand they were speaking through a transmitter at all. And I still can't think how—"

Ludbridge held up his hand. "I can. It means the hidden transmitter we planted works admirably."

"When did we plant a hidden transmitter?" asked Pengrove.

"What did you imagine the business with the little crossbow bolt was?" said Ludbridge impatiently. "It has a remarkably tiny receiver built into it. A gift from our Informant, who has suggested that the Society can learn something to its advantage by spying on the Russians. Everything it hears is transmitted directly to the London office, for the translators. But what was Brother Jonathan discussing with the Russian Bear?"

Hobson rubbed his chin. "It was . . . well, the Americans did most of the talking. Telling the Russian about the dreadful treatment they'd witnessed the Eastern priests receiving at the hands of the Roman Catholics. How they'd taken their seminary class to see the Holy Land and everywhere they went, it was the same: the Papists having at the Eastern Orthodoxers, you know, being insolent and trampling them down and all that sort of thing."

Pengrove sniffed. "The Easterners gave as good as they got, from what we could see."

"Perhaps these fellows saw a different fistfight from the one we watched," said Hobson. "Anyhow, they went on and on about it, how it was all the Pope colluding with the French and the Jews, and what did the Czar intend to do about it?"

"What did the Russian say?"

"He seemed as though he didn't know what to say," replied Hobson. "But trying to be polite, you know. The Americans were so insistent! Saying that true Christians needed to support each other against the wicked wiles of the Pope."

"I thought most of the Americans were Catholic," said Pengrove. "All those Irish who emigrated, what? Never expected they'd turn out a lot of raving Calvinists."

"Did they identify themselves?"

"The one who did most of the talking left his calling card," said Hobson. "He'd hoped to get an audience with the Russian Ambassador. He read it out for the Russian chap. Reverend Amasa Breedlove, of the Norvell Bible College of Nashville, Tennessee. I think the other fellow's name was Jackson."

"Extraordinary," said Ludbridge. "And absurd. Had a rather exaggerated sense of his own importance, evidently. Anything else of note?"

"Not that I heard," said Hobson.

"You don't suppose these would be the filibusters we were asked to watch for?" said Bell-Fairfax. Ludbridge scowled, tugging at his beard.

"Unlikely, I should think; this chap sounds more of a religious busybody. Still . . . never hurts to pass these trifles on to London. Never know what may come of it. If nothing else, we've learned that our bolt receiver works a treat! Well done, Hobson. As for our other business: Pengrove, you'll take a stroll with Bell-Fairfax tomorrow."

"Must I wear the hat-camera?"

"I'm afraid so." Ludbridge reached inside his coat and drew out the folded papers. Opening them, he smoothed them out on his knee and studied what had been written there.

"No, no!" Pengrove cried, waving his arms at the boatman. "I need the camera too!" The boatman, who had resumed his seat, glared up at the mound of photographic paraphernalia still piled on the paving stones and shook his head. Bell-Fairfax leaned forward and said something to him in Turkish, at which he expostulated, leaning forward on his oar. At last Bell-Fairfax reached into his pocket and paid out a few more coins, and rose on the thwart to haul the rest of Pengrove's equipment into the caique himself. Muttering, the boatman backed and steered them around, and took them across to Stamboul.

"He said you had so much gear with you, it constituted another passenger," Bell-Fairfax explained.

"Horrid man," said Pengrove. "Horrid place. I don't mind telling you, this is not at all what I expected of the glorious East. Not a bit like the Arabian Nights, what?"

"You've only seen the docks, so far," said Bell-Fairfax. "What if you were a foreigner, and had heard a great deal about the power and majesty of Great Britain, and then went there and all you saw was Limehouse? Stamboul is quite picturesque."

"I suppose," said Pengrove, looking across the leaping sea at the dome of Hagia Sophia. "Did you really mean it, about that brothel?"

"Yes."

"Plump beauties with veils and beads and things?"

"Yes."

"Is it expensive?"

"No. Quite reasonable."

"Really." Pengrove set his monocle more firmly in place. "I could quite fancy a visit, you know. Do you suppose we might go there first?"

"We have a job to do, Pengrove." Bell-Fairfax looked at him askance. "Can you see yourself making a report to Ludbridge? 'Well, the first thing we did was slip off for an hour's pleasant fornication'?"

"Oh, I suppose not."

"And, in any case, you'll want to purchase some French letters first."

"Why the devil would I want a French letter?"

Bell-Fairfax stared at Pengrove. "A prophylactic sheath," he enunciated carefully. Pengrove blushed scarlet and his monocle fell out.

For several hours that morning, the inhabitants of Stamboul were treated to the sight of a pair of Englishmen lugging photographic equipment here and there about the city. The smaller of the two seemed intent on photographing his outlandishly tall friend against a variety of backgrounds: crumbling old medieval fortifications, modern artillery barracks no less crumbling, decrepit mosques, the immense warship *Mahmudiye* lying at anchor with her rigging in disarray and her hull grown with seaweed.

After each shot the taller gentleman would hurry to put up a tiny portable tent, into which his friend would vanish for several minutes. Any curious onlookers venturing close were driven back by the dreadful chemical reek. Any who remained might see the smaller man stagger forth at last, waving a paper negative image on which his tall friend had been transformed into a black-skinned ghoul with silver eyes, the sight of which caused small children and less educated adults to flee screaming.

At some point the Englishmen produced a bottle, and thereafter their behavior became somewhat disorderly, at last drawing the attention of a hostile policeman. Suspicious, he took to following the Englishmen about, fuming as they posed in a disrespectful manner before the Sublime Porte itself. When they made their wobbly way to the ostentatiously grand mansion of a local official, and seemed intent on photographing it from every possible angle, the policeman decided the pair of idiot infidels had gone too far. He descended on them in wrath, threw their camera down on its tripod, stamped on it twice for good measure, confiscated their half-empty bottle, and told them in no uncertain terms to depart. With a few dismayed cries of "Oh! I say!" they slunk away.

"And now my camera's broken," said Pengrove mournfully, holding up the brass lens tube, which had parted company with the broken box.

Bell-Fairfax had found them a quiet café in the Greek Quarter, to which they had retreated.

"We can repair it tonight," said Bell-Fairfax. "It doesn't matter, does it? Be thankful he didn't snatch off your hat and dance on that as well."

"Why that particular palace?"

"Ludbridge wanted it photographed," said Bell-Fairfax. "Entrances and exits and all. We'll need to go back, once that fellow's temper has cooled."

"Perfectly splendid palace, I must say," Pengrove said indistinctly, through a mouthful of baklava. "Everyone here seems to dwell in either marble halls or filthy little huts. No middle classes, eh? And the state of those barracks! Never heard of chamber pots, clearly."

"They aren't mentioned in the Arabian Nights, I believe," said Bell-Fairfax, lounging back in his chair.

"Ha-ha. And look at that sentry over there, look at him! You'd think his rifle was a broom, the way he's leaning on it. My word, wouldn't one of our sergeants-at-arms give him a tongue-lashing!"

"Or one of our boatswains," said Bell-Fairfax.

"No way to run an empire," said Pengrove, shaking his head. "I don't envy their sultan. Well, shall we go out and buy a melon, and loiter about eating it and throwing the rinds everywhere, as we shoot Ludbridge's palace? No point pretending to be publicly intoxicated anymore, but that ought to make us look suitably like a pair of ill-bred fools."

"Excellent thought," said Bell-Fairfax. He paid their score and together they packed the camera equipment, closing up the ruined camera in its traveling-case; then they ventured out and found a fruit vendor's stall on the far edge of the bazaar.

"Oh, my word," said Bell-Fairfax, as they approached. Pengrove followed his gaze and saw a Greek girl seated within the stall, holding her veil in place with a negligent hand, looking out boredly on the passing scene. She wore apple-green satin, trimmed with jonquil-yellow embroidery. Sloe-eyed, pale as perfect ivory, and the veil was far too thin to conceal the Byzantine beauty of her features.

"She's a picture," affirmed Pengrove.

"Indeed she is," said Bell-Fairfax. He approached her and said something in Greek, with a curious soft intonation Pengrove had never heard him use before. It was suave, it was caressing, it acted on the nervous system like notes played on a violin. The girl looked up sharply; Pengrove saw her dark eyes widen, as Bell-Fairfax gazed down into them. She stammered some kind of reply, with a rosy color coming into her face. Bell-Fairfax said something further, in the same dulcet tones. She looked desperately hopeful, glanced once over her shoulder, and then spoke in a low urgent voice.

Bell-Fairfax smiled broadly. By way of reply he reached into his inner coat pocket and withdrew a sort of flat wallet. He opened it and displayed its contents, which were not pound notes. She inspected them briefly, nodded, and rose and took his hand.

"Mind the stall a moment, Pengrove, will you? There's a good chap," said Bell-Fairfax, dropping the camera bundle and allowing himself to be led into the depths of the booth.

"But—but!" Pengrove looked around frantically, unable to believe what was happening. For some ten minutes he stood there petrified, expecting that at any moment some enraged phanariote would come storming across the bazaar asking after his daughter, or wife, or sister. Instead, the languid flow of the marketplace continued all around, in the sweltering heat. Flies buzzed. Donkeys plodded. Doves crooned sleepily. Elderly kitchen slaves bargained for onions with vegetable-stall keepers, both in such listless voices they might have been chatting in a Turkish bath.

And then, cutting like a black arrow through the dreamy Arabian Nights scene, marched a phalanx of Westerners in sober black clothing. They were led by a dignified-looking elder who wore a clerical collar and a shovel hat. They walked with purpose, looking around them severely at the indolence they beheld.

Pengrove stared at them, struck by the contrast between the men and their surroundings. A fragment of muttered conversation drifted to him:

"... don't think twice about slaves here, and white slaves to boot..."
They were American voices.

When had he heard mention of Americans in Constantinople, recently? Memory of the voices Hobson had picked up came back to him. Instinctively Pengrove's hand rose to his lapel and he captured the Americans' likenesses with the hat-camera. Then they had passed him, sprinting quickly up a flight of stairs to an upper terrace.

Pengrove was still staring after them when the Greek girl emerged from the booth, followed by Bell-Fairfax. Looking smug, he kissed her hand and then tipped his hat to her. With a radiant smile she replied effusively, showering him with compliments of some kind, and ended by seizing up a pair of melons and pressing them upon him, with many expressive, not to say suggestive, gestures. He accepted them and turned to Pengrove with a smirk. "Shall we go?"

Pengrove waited until they were a decent distance away before rounding on him. "What did you think you were playing at?" he demanded.

"I should have thought that was obvious," said Bell-Fairfax, drawing out his penknife and pausing by a wall to cut a melon into quarters.

"And what about, 'No, Pengrove, we have a job to do'? What about considering what Ludbridge would say? What about bloody *French letters?*"

"I happen to keep a ready supply of them with me at all times," said Bell-Fairfax.

"And . . . and . . . you've just been a beastly cad and seduced some virgin, instead of a brothel girl!"

"She wasn't a virgin," said Bell-Fairfax, putting a slice of melon into Pengrove's waving hand. "And I didn't seduce her. I merely asked, in the politest possible fashion, whether she would be available and she answered with enthusiasm. We had a brief pleasant encounter, entirely unobserved by anyone, and have parted on the best of terms."

"You practically mesmerized her! I saw it!"

"No such thing."

"But . . . but you're in the East, for God's sake, and there might be . . . consequences," said Pengrove, subsiding enough to take a bite of melon.

"Not with a French letter," said Bell-Fairfax calmly. "And, as I believe I mentioned, I do have some sort of natural immunity to these things."

"I never met such a brazen chap in all my life," Pengrove grumbled.

"Nonsense. If you like, I'll show you the brothel after we've finished the job."

They strolled back to the district in which the mansion stood, and found that the irate policeman had departed the scene. They wandered all along the outer garden wall, placidly eating melon as they noted the large dog that came rushing to the gate, barking furiously. They made their way around to the side of the house that faced the sea, and stood there awhile by a long low private pier, tossing pebbles and bits of melon-rind into the Bosporus. Now and again they glanced over their shoulders to note the women watching them from behind the second-story latticework.

They picked their way back to the road and observed as the master of the house returned, a strangely grubby little bureaucrat for such a magnificent residence. They raised their hats as his coach rattled past, and watched with interest as he clambered out onto the back of a servant, swearing at his majordomo for not meeting him with a cup of sherbet.

Ambling on, they observed the ancient plane tree that overhung the garden wall of the mansion next door. Bell-Fairfax, looking about first to make certain they were unobserved, made an experimental leap and caught the lowest branch of the tree. Pulling himself up through the boughs, he at once drew the attention of the large dog of that particular garden, who promptly set up such a commotion that Bell-Fairfax scrambled back down into the street and ran, speedily catching up with Pengrove, who was already running.

"Do you suppose we've been publicly stupid enough?" inquired Pengrove, when they were able to pause for breath.

"Perfectly idiotic," said Bell-Fairfax.

"Seen a way into that house?"

"Yes. Did you photograph him?"

"I did. Might we perhaps go to the brothel now?"

"Don't see why not," Bell-Fairfax replied. As he settled the bundle of equipment on his shoulder, there came an impact on the air and then the *boom* of cannon fire, the sound echoing in waves off the hillsides and steep streets.

"Are they saluting someone?" Pengrove shaded his eyes with his hand, peering out at the harbor. "There are some fancy-looking boats coming in over there. Really quite Arabian Nights, you know."

"Let's see," said Bell-Fairfax. They sprinted, pacing the big caiques in their stately progress across the Bosporus, and arrived at a white mosque with a water landing, white steps coming down to the blue water.

"Oh, *frightfully* Arabian Nights!" exclaimed Pengrove. "Look!"

Bell-Fairfax had to crane his neck to see, for the view was being rapidly blocked by the Sultan's guard, marching to line the steps of the mosque. A band accompanied them, shrilling on fifes, rattling and thundering on drums and playing, of all things, the "Turkish March" by Beethoven.

"By Jove," said Bell-Fairfax. "Here's the Sultan himself."

"I can't see!" fretted Pengrove. Bell-Fairfax picked him up bodily and pushed him up into the branches of a cypress, a little awkwardly because he was unwilling to tear his gaze from the spectacle. The caiques were splendid, gilded and carved, with canopies of gold and velvet. The most magnificent of them bumped gently against the landing now, and a number of officials stood forward to help the Sultan from the boat.

Pengrove, sprawling on his cypress branch, saw a young man in a military uniform, gold lace over silk, and his fez bore a high white cockade. His lean face was handsome, but he looked exhausted and somber as he stepped forth onto the white staircase. He smiled and nodded his thanks, nonetheless, to the vizier who hurried to open a red silk parasol over him.

Pengrove, with great presence of mind, raised his hand to his lapel and took a picture of the young man, before the parasol hid him utterly: Abdülmecid I of the House of Osman, Thirty-first Sultan of the Ottoman Empire, Caliph of Islam, sick and weary, shoulders bowed under the weight of the past but dutifully climbing the steps toward the future.

Ludbridge held the photographs up to the lamplight, sorting through them slowly. "Well done," he said. "Really first-rate. Full marks for both of you."

"You're welcome," said Pengrove, a little crossly. The carnal splendors of the mystic East had, it must be said, fulfilled all his expectations; but a superfluity of ripe melon, sweet pastries and Turkish coffee had combined badly with a choppy ride back across the Golden Horn, and a lengthy session developing the images from his camera in an airless closet had not improved matters.

Ludbridge came to one image, and peered at it. "What the hell's this?" He held up the shot of the Americans walking through the Greek Quarter.

"Oh!" Pengrove cleared his throat. "Those are some Americans I saw. One of 'em's a clergyman, you can see from his hat, and I thought—*how funny, I wonder if they're the same chaps Hobson overheard next door?* So I took their portrait. Just with the hat-camera, of course, and anyway my talbotype box had been smashed to pieces by then—which reminds me, we've got to get hold of some glue so it can be mended—"

"That's rather a coincidence," said Ludbridge, slowly turning the picture in his fingers. "Did Bell-Fairfax see them too? What did he think?"

Pengrove went red-faced. "Well, er—no, he didn't see them, he was—erm—in the back of a fruit stall at the time."

"What was he doing in the back of a fruit stall?"

"Buying melons. I suppose." Pengrove studied a fly sitting motionless on the ceiling.

"What the devil is the matter with you?" demanded Ludbridge. "You're blushing like a bloody schoolgirl."

"Well, I didn't like to ask what he was doing in the back of the stall, it was a private matter—" Pengrove cast a furtive glance at the door, hoping that Bell-Fairfax and Hobson would return from their late supper. Ludbridge's eyes narrowed.

"Was it indeed? He'd gone back there with someone, had he? Was it a boy?"

"Oh, no!" Pengrove's monocle fell out. "A female, really a very charming—"

"Well then, what in hell's got you stammering like that? Especially as I understand you both went off to his favorite brothel tonight. Though that's rather a lot of fornication in one day for a man on duty, I must say . . . so he's a ladies' man?"

"I don't like to peach on a chap," said Pengrove miserably. "And it didn't do any harm to the job, honestly, he was quite discreet and the girl didn't complain and . . . and really it was just the sort of thing a rotten bounder on a grand tour would do, which is what we were pretending to be, only . . ."

"Only what?"

"He hypnotized the girl," said Pengrove. "I think. He looked straight into her eyes and—but he wasn't doing it with his eyes, I don't think, it was his voice. Yes, it was the voice. I never heard a voice like that in my life, the way he was . . . he was *tempting* her. It made me ashamed."

Ludbridge was silent for a long while, staring out the window at the lights of Stamboul.

"Yes," he said at last. "Yes, I know what you mean. He uses that voice on women. Well." He rose to his feet and, going to his trunk, put the photographs away. "None of us are saints, I suppose. Still, we won't accomplish much if he has to fuck every pretty girl who catches his eye. I'll have to have a word with him about it."

"I've investigated our foxes," said Ludbridge. He was walking with Bell-Fairfax through the cemetery, high above the city, in the bright heat of midday; the green cypresses made welcome pools of shade, and rustled in the breeze off the Golden Horn.

"Your little pasha with the seaside palace is as nasty a piece of goods as you might find in a long summer's day. Got his office by performing certain criminal services for his betters; built his fortune pocketing bribes and other people's taxes, and extorting anyone he could get his hooks into, and the odd bit of murder of wealthy heirs. You can imagine what he stands to lose if the Sultan can enforce reforms. He's been named in connection with no less than three assassination attempts on the Sultan himself. Slipped through the noose every time, letting other men take the blame.

"Plenty of people are frightened enough of him to perjure themselves blue in the face on his behalf. Dear civilized Sultan won't pursue the matter, naturally, so the pasha's free to keep plotting."

"Then it's a moral act to execute him, sir," said Bell-Fairfax, with certainty. Ludbridge, looking at him sidelong, raised an eyebrow.

"Moral, you say. Yes, very likely. I thought we'd go across tonight."

"I've thought how it might be managed," said Bell-Fairfax, stammering a little. "There's an adjoining residence, with a big plane tree in its garden—we could climb up in its branches until we can see in through his windows, and perhaps shoot him—though there are dogs, and I'm not sure what we might do if they give the alarm—"

"Tut-tut! How d'you suppose a man my age is going to go scampering up a tree? A nice sight I'd look! We're not stealing apples, Bell-Fairfax. No, I know how it's to be managed. Pengrove's excellent photographs made it fairly obvious. A good day's work, that, by the pair of you."

"Thank you, sir." Looking away, Bell-Fairfax smiled, but Ludbridge saw it.

"Which is to say, it was a good day's work when you were attending to your *job*," said Ludbridge, in mild tones but with a hint of thunder beginning to roll. "Now, I can understand a happy little visit to the daughters of joy at the end of the day, with your work accomplished. But what the hell was this business with the Greek girl in the marketplace, eh? Who d'you think you are, bleeding Tom Jones? Damned fool thing to do, and damned disappointing as well. I'd have thought you had more self-control than that. And don't you think Pengrove ran to me and tattled on you, either! You put a fellow Resident in the position of having to try to cover up for your gross dereliction of duty. By God, son, it won't do."

Edward flinched, and stared at the path as they walked. "No, sir," he muttered.

"A man with a weakness is a danger to his comrades. You ought to know that. You were the last person I'd have suspected of losing his head here and doing something as foolish as skirt-chasing. And in Constantinople, of all places! Makes me wonder if you're fit for the job."

"Yes, sir."

"Don't 'Yes, sir' me, I want to know whether you can be trusted! Talk to me. *Why did you do it?*"

Bell-Fairfax had gone scarlet. "Habit, I suppose, sir."

"*Habit?*"

"Yes, sir. I, er, I often indulge my, er, inclinations with the fair sex."

"*Habit?* You make a habit of seducing innocent girls? And don't tell me it won't happen again, because if one thing's certain in this sorry life it's that a man with an addiction *will* do it again, whether it's drink or women or anything else. And you're already the fucking wonder of the Royal Navy, aren't you, with a list of conquests like Don Giovanni!"

Bell-Fairfax looked up, startled. "I never told you that."

"No. I learned it from the ladies at Nell Gwynne's. It was their job to tell me. Does that surprise you? It oughtn't. We can't send a man out on the kind of work you're to do if we don't know all there is to know about him. And, clearly, we don't know everything about *you*."

"Sir, on my honor, my—er—dalliances have never harmed any female. It is entirely a matter of mutual agreement. I am careful to use protection and take a great deal of trouble to be certain the girl enjoys the experience as much as I do. Where's the harm?"

"Where indeed? You're the one who's always so preoccupied with the moral side of matters."

"But what we do isn't immoral!" Bell-Fairfax said. "It's simply the satisfaction of mutual need. As pleasant as—as—having a brandy or a cigar. *Where's the harm?*"

"Perhaps in seeing a woman as nothing more than a brandy or a ci-gar," said Ludbridge quietly. "And are you certain you're always quite honest about your intentions?"

"I—what? Of course I am, sir. I have never lied to any woman."

"How d'you do it, then?"

Bell-Fairfax, puzzled by his shift in tone, stared at him. "I, er, merely exert myself to be agreeable."

"Any man does that, when he wants something badly enough. You do it with remarkable success. What do you do?"

Bell-Fairfax lowered his eyes. "Well, I greet them, and tell them they're beautiful, and that I'd very much like to, er, engage in congress with them if they are so inclined, and have they a few moments free?"

"Hmph. That'd get any other man slapped, with the girl screaming for her chaperone or a policeman."

"Well, I do have certain advantages of person, sir. And one must ex-ert oneself to be charming, after all."

"One bloody must. Sure it hasn't something to do with your tone of voice?"

Bell-Fairfax appeared to think carefully before he spoke. "The voice is important, of course. One speaks soothingly to a frightened horse or a wounded animal. Or a shipmate—Shawe had to have his foot ampu-tated, and Dr. Jameson had me sit beside him while it was being done, and I talked to him the whole while and kept him calm. And the tone is only a little different when one is trying to persuade a woman to plea-sure. And it's not nearly so difficult."

"No?"

"No, sir, because—it's not as though I was asking them to do some-thing they didn't want to do."

"Damned egotist. What happens when a girl doesn't want to sample your charms, might one ask?"

"That has never happened, sir, but if it ever did, I should promptly apologize and depart."

Ludbridge glared at him. They walked on a little way, between the graves, before he said: "Be that as it may. Henceforth what you do in

London is your own concern, but I will not have you sampling women like pastries when you're on the job, do you understand?"

"Yes, sir."

"Your continued employment depends on it, is that plain?"

"Perfectly, sir."

They walked on in silence a few yards. Bell-Fairfax, relieved that the conversation appeared to have ended, attempted to change the subject.

"Curious, all these funny stone turbans lying about. They appear to have been broken off the gravestones. Shame people are such vandals."

"It wasn't vandalism," said Ludbridge. "It was by royal decree. These were the graves of the Janissaries. D'you know what they were? An elite force of soldiers, the best the Ottomans could train. Became like the Praetorian Guard, picking and choosing sultans. At last they mutinied against the father of the present fellow, and he broke them and stripped them of honors. His punishment extended to the dead as well as the living: all the carved turbans were knocked off their monuments. Something to think about, isn't it?"

"Yes, sir."

"Let's go down to the Cadde-i Kebir. I want a drink," said Ludbridge.

There was a bar in the European Quarter run by a Sardinian, with a decent stock of brandies. After they had refreshed themselves, however, Ludbridge ordered a glass of Maraschino. The waiter brought it and set it before him. When the waiter had gone, Ludbridge lit a cigar and, settling back, told Bell-Fairfax: "Make me drink that."

"I beg your pardon?"

"I detest the stuff. Persuade me to drink it."

"But—sir—"

"Oblige me!"

Bell-Fairfax looked disconcerted. He drummed his fingers on the table a moment.

"Very well. You've ordered that liqueur; it's rather costly, it can't be as bad as all that, and you may as well drink it."

"Bosh. I could as easily throw it in the gutter. It's vile."

"It doesn't seem vile. It looks charming. Nearly colorless, in that little cut-crystal liqueur glass? You could drink it in one gulp. Think of all the care and effort that went into making it. Think of your expense report. Are you going to tell Greene you spend money on expensive drinks, only to throw them in the gutter?"

"Shan't tell him. And why should I drink something I don't like, anyway?"

"But how do you know you don't like it?"

"Had it before. Disgusting syrupy mess."

"Perhaps you had the wrong sort. Perhaps this is different. Perhaps it's wonderful, and you won't know until you try."

"Doubt it."

"Ah, but doubt implies you *don't* know, doesn't it?" Bell-Fairfax leaned forward in his chair. "And you aren't afraid to experiment, are you? I don't think you are. May I just have the glass a moment?" His voice took on a cajoling quality. He took the glass and raised it to his nose. Closing his eyes, he inhaled deeply.

"Ahhh. The cherry orchards of Dalmatia. Just a hint of the windfall fruit, beginning to ferment in its skin. A green note, like the leaves bruised by the orchard laborers gathering the cherries. Something ineffable there, unexpected, no heavy jammy sweetness at all." He opened his eyes and swirled the glass. "And yet, what body. What a crystalline film there, creeping along the rim."

Holding Ludbridge's gaze, he took a tiny sip. A long column of ash had formed on the end of Ludbridge's unsmoked cigar.

"Mm. Oh. What a buttery smoothness in the mouth. What is *that*? Violets? Peaches? Cherries, to be sure, but so subtly . . . and now, fire on the palate. And now, again, the fragrance of the green leaves in the orchard, with the sunlight burning through. And you'll never know it, if you don't taste it."

His voice had dropped, had taken on an eerie incantatory quality. His eyes remained fixed on Ludbridge's, unnaturally clear and pale, as he held forth the liqueur. *No point being a bloody fool about it*, thought

Ludbridge, taking the glass. He raised it to his lips and drank. The liqueur was exactly as Bell-Fairfax had said it would be, too, delicious, celestial, violets and green leaves and fire, utterly unlike the nasty stuff he remembered. Ludbridge drank it all and set the glass down, smiling at Bell-Fairfax with profound gratitude.

Bell-Fairfax leaned back, white and shaken. He signaled to the waiter to bring another brandy.

"That was extraordinary," said Ludbridge.

"It was dreadful," said Bell-Fairfax. "It was wrong. Is *that* what I've been doing, with women?"

"What on earth's wrong about it?" cried Ludbridge. "What you did was bloody wonderful! Here, you," he addressed the waiter who brought Bell-Fairfax's brandy. "Another Maraschino, *per favore.*"

"No. No." Bell-Fairfax grabbed his drink. He knocked it back, avoiding Ludbridge's gaze. "What are you thinking? You hated the stuff. All I did was—trick you with, with a little poetic language, and—making my voice persuasive."

"Who cares how you did it, boy? The fact remains that you can do it. This should prove damned useful!"

"No, it shouldn't," said Bell-Fairfax. "I swear to you, I never understood before. I only thought I had a certain way with girls. But it's not a fair advantage, don't you see?"

"All's fair in love and war," said Ludbridge, sprawling back in his chair. He looked closely at Bell-Fairfax, noting in a new perspective his height, his curious features, and remembering other things: his remarkable strength, the keenness of his senses, that remark the radiograph technician had made . . . "By God! What *are* you?"

Bell-Fairfax looked stricken. Realizing his mistake at once, Ludbridge went on: "It's as though you were naturally born to the work. It was a lucky day for us when Dr. Nennys brought you into Redking's, my boy."

"I swear to you, sir, I never meant anything dishonorable."

"No, no, of course you didn't. Understand me: we need men with remarkable skills. To think that voice might have been wasted on a politician or an actor! No, you'll do very well. I meant what I said about the women, of course, you do realize that?—But we'll find a much better use for your persuasive abilities. Why use them to become a second-rate Casanova when you could do some *good* in the world?"

"But how, sir?"

"Oh, we'll think of a way." The waiter brought Ludbridge's second glass of Maraschino. He lifted it in a toast and drank. It was not nearly so delicious now, he noted, and thought: *So the effect wears off. Remarkable, all the same.*

1850: For the Angel of Death Spread
His Wings on the Blast

After dinner that night, Ludbridge sat reading a back number of *Punch* while Hobson made the evening report on the Aetheric Transmitter, and Bell-Fairfax and Pengrove played Beggar-My-Neighbor. At last Ludbridge arose in an unhurried fashion. He spent a while opening and closing the drawers of his trunk, packing items in a capacious leather satchel.

"Bell-Fairfax," he said, when he had closed up the trunk, "I should change my clothing if I were you. Old trousers, nothing very closely cut. You'll be rowing some distance tonight."

"Rowing, sir? Yes, sir." Bell-Fairfax, rather subdued, put down his cards. He rose and rummaged through his own trunk for suitable trousers and a Henley shirt. Pulling on his braces over the shirt, he inquired: "Anything else, sir?"

"Got a boat-cloak?"

"Yes, sir."

"Good." Ludbridge swathed himself in what seemed to be a well-worn opera cape. "Pengrove, Hobson, this is your lucky evening; you'll get a full night's sleep. We'll likely be out most of the night."

"Where are you going?" asked Hobson.

"Hither and yon," said Ludbridge. "Come along, Bell-Fairfax."

———

It was late, the streets largely deserted, and the night was moonless. They found their way down to the waterfront hearing nothing more than the *tck-tck-tck* of a night watchman's brass-shod staff of office; waiting in a darkened doorway until he had gone past, they hurried to a spot where three or four caiques were moored. Bell-Fairfax stepped down into the nearest and reached up to take Ludbridge's satchel, grunting in surprise at how heavy it was. Ludbridge sprang nimbly down and cast off.

Bell-Fairfax took the oars and they moved out across the black night water toward Stamboul.

"Where shall we go?" murmured Bell-Fairfax.

"The house of the pasha," replied Ludbridge. "There was a boat landing in the pictures, I believe." Leaning forward, he opened his satchel and rummaged around in it by touch. A moment later he drew out a pair of goggles and bound them on.

"There!" he said in satisfaction, and drew another pair from the satchel. He handed them across to Bell-Fairfax. "Put them on, please."

Bell-Fairfax shipped the oars and obeyed him. He lifted his head, staring about him in amazement. "Night vision lenses," Ludbridge explained quietly, to forestall questions. "With a thermal filter. Ellis in Fabrication came up with them. Really very useful. Let's continue on our way, shall we?"

"You appear to be on fire," said Bell-Fairfax, groping for the oars.

"You're seeing the heat of my body," replied Ludbridge, delving into the satchel once again. He drew out what looked, in Bell-Fairfax's transfigured sight, like the black silhouette of a weapon of some kind.

"Now, *this*," Ludbridge said, "is something Bainbridge invented. The, let me see, sixth generation from his original design. Not the greatest range in the world, but within its range deuced effective." He twiddled with something on the weapon's side and for a moment Bell-Fairfax saw the heat signature of ghostly red fingerprints defining an unseen dial, before they faded. There was a *click*, and a faint high-pitched whine.

"Why is it black, when everything else is so bright?"

"Because it's freezing cold," said Ludbridge. "In fact, I had to bring it wrapped in a towel in the bottom of the satchel, and the damned thing's damp from the condensation. Something to be fixed in the seventh model, I devoutly hope. Rather a drawback when a marksman's weapon makes his hands go numb."

He made several adjustments, opening out what seemed to be a telescoping rifle barrel and fitting a squat silencing cylinder on its end. Having apparently readied it to his satisfaction, Ludbridge set it in the bottom of the caique and rubbed his hands, which now appeared quite black with cold. "Bah. Ought to have worn gloves. A lesson for you, my boy. I suppose you're wondering why the gun is freezing cold?"

"I am, yes."

"Well. What would you think of a rifle that could fire icicles?"

"I would suppose one might be useful, if it existed," said Bell-Fairfax, after a moment's contemplation. "It might be more humane. No musket balls for a surgeon to have to ferret out of a wound, because they'd melt."

"True. Never thought of that. The other advantage, you know, would be that you might shoot a man and, assuming a suitable amount of time had passed before anyone found the corpse, no one would be able to tell quite how he'd died. The icicle would melt. Stab wound, perhaps?"

Bell-Fairfax rowed steadily. "Is there such a gun?" he inquired at last.

"Of course there isn't. Even if you found a different firing mechanism—for of course the flash of gunpowder would tend to melt your ammunition—what's to keep your icicle from splintering into a thousand little fragments from the force of the shot?"

"Did Bainbridge find a way to fire a gun without powder?"

"He did. Modified one of Girandoni's Air Guns. Pre-charged pneumatic firing action. Quiet, no muzzle flash, no heat. Made it sturdier, with a cast air reservoir lined with gutta-percha. Improved the charging mechanism. The ammunition had to be muzzle-loaded pretty damned quickly but they were revolutionary improvements, really. Still shattered the icicle to bits in the firing."

"Why would it have to be a literal icicle?" said Bell-Fairfax.

"You know, that's exactly what Carstairs said? Bainbridge was frightfully annoyed with him. He'd had some vision of hunters wandering in a winter landscape, able to pluck their ammunition from any over-hanging eaves or frozen waterfalls they might pass. What convenience, when you're out after reindeer! But of course the advantages to precast musket balls of ice were obvious, once someone had pointed them out."

"Did they work?"

"They did not, as it happened. They shattered too. And, of course, where to store them? So Negri was brought in from the Refrigeration project—clever man, grandfather emigrated from Venice or one of those places, made ice creams, you know, so the family had a few trade se-crets Negri brought with him—anyway, Negri worked out a freezing-chamber loaded with ammunition, a compact self-powered unit built into the gun-stock, and I'm afraid I can't tell you how, because I under-stand very little of why it works."

"Did that solve the problem?"

"Only part of it." Ludbridge looked critically at the palms of his hands, which were once again glowing red as coals by thermal per-spective. "The ammunition kept perfectly in the refrigerated chamber, but it had yet to make it out of the rifle-barrel intact. So then Carstairs asked if it was strictly necessary to use water ice at all.

"And I'm afraid that at this point Bainbridge nearly quit the project, because he's a temperamental chap. But Greene and some of the old members had a word with him, and of course once he'd let go the idea of water ice, all manner of possibilities opened up. And, really, if the police inspector finds a corpse with what appears to be a bit of melted ice cream in the fatal wound, he can't possibly think someone's in-vented a pistol that shoots ice-cream cornets."

"The weapon shoots ice cream?"

"Don't be absurd! You can't kill someone with ice cream. Unless you choke them on it, I suppose. Though as it happened, Negri came up with a formula based on one of the old family recipes, adulterated with certain chemical ingredients. Freezes hard as rock and keeps its shape even when it thaws. Only melts when exposed to blood heat."

"And that worked?"

"No. But it nearly worked. Bainbridge experimented and discovered that if each bullet is encased in a sort of woven jacket made of—but you don't need to know what exactly, simply that it's as fine as spider-silk and dissolves when it encounters any saline liquid, such as blood, and the Society bought the formula from a chemist who was attempting to make an improved surgical suture . . . where was I?

"Ah, to be sure: this silk jacket did the trick, at last. Hiss and pop and down goes your man with a bit of something icy in a vital organ, and the coroner will search with all his might and main, but he won't find anything more than a sort of pinkish smear in a mysterious wound. Here, isn't that the mansion to starboard? Pull us up to the end of the boat-dock."

By the light of the goggles, the pasha's house glowed green against the darker green of cypress and plane trees, under a bright emerald sky scattered with stars. Distantly there were a few scarlet figures, moving here and there on the terraces of Stamboul: what must be a man leading a donkey, a staggering drunk, a prone figure asleep under a bush.

The caique bumped against the end of the boat-dock and, bracing his palms on the planks, Ludbridge levered himself up and out. Bell-Fairfax, shipping the oars once more, picked up the weapon and handed it up to him, wincing involuntarily at its chill.

"Yes, see what I mean?" Ludbridge murmured, opening out a folding tripod. "Gloves or better shielding for the ammunition locker, either one. Now, where's the hareem? . . . Ah."

"It's those rooms on the third-story terrace with all the latticework," said Bell-Fairfax. "To judge from the girls peeping out of it yesterday. But you won't be able to see much from this distance, I'm afraid."

"Reach up and feel about on the left-hand optic rim on your goggles," said Ludbridge in a preoccupied voice. "The three little buttons, there? Just touch the midmost one, lightest pressure possible, two or three times."

"Oh." Bell-Fairfax caught his breath. "Like a spyglass. Opera glasses, I mean. Good God, it's as though—"

He stopped in confusion, and Ludbridge chuckled quietly.

"Ever fancied seeing what goes on in a Turkish seraglio? What you're glimpsing there, in all that scarlet confusion behind the lattice, is the master of the house paying a visit to his concubines. Watch carefully. Certain of the patterns of movement might be familiar to you." Casting a glance over his shoulder, Ludbridge noted Bell-Fairfax's features suffused with brighter fire. He turned back and peered through his goggles.

"Of course, the ideal shot would be through the latticework, but one can't be certain of hitting a vital organ and one certainly doesn't want to hit any of the women by mistake. Still . . . might be possible . . ."

"You'll never hit him through the screen!"

"Won't I? Let's just see. It's a high-accuracy weapon, this, with very little recoil. Perhaps he'll order one of them to kneel before him, which would give me a delightfully clear shot. And a roomful of screaming women would confuse matters no end; by the time anyone saw the body in clear light, the bullet ought to have melted. Assuming the ladies screamed, of course. For all I know they'd be delighted to see the beggar unexpectedly dead—hello, what's he doing?"

For the biggest, reddest blur had detached itself from the main mass of shifting lights and moved from right to left behind the lattice. It vanished for a moment, and Ludbridge was just growling in disappointment when a door opened and the pasha, red as Mephistopheles if more rotund, stepped out on the terrace. As Ludbridge swung the barrel of the weapon and fixed the target in his sights, the scarlet figure adjusted its waistband and voided a fine arc of fiery urine over the terrace wall into the garden below.

"Thank you," said Ludbridge, and pulled the trigger.

The weapon gave a faint cough. A black spot appeared between the brighter points of the target's eyes; it fell straight backward and vanished.

Ludbridge grabbed up the weapon in his arms and more or less rolled backward off the end of the dock, into the caique. "Row for your life," he told Bell-Fairfax, who obeyed promptly. Without even rising to his knees, Ludbridge switched the weapon off, folded up the legs of the tripod, and removed the canister on the barrel. He shoved it back in the satchel.

"Something to remember, son," he said, as the first of the distant screams rang out over the black water. "In the unlikely event anyone spots us and we're pursued, and should it appear that we are in real danger of being caught or killed, I shall promptly drop the satchel over the side. The goggles will need to go, too. That's always your first concern, on any mission: *do not allow the machines to fall into enemy hands.* Clear?"

"Yes, sir," said Bell-Fairfax, gasping as he labored at the oars.

"I'd have thought that if the fellow we're looking for is a Greek, he'd be in the Greek Quarter," said Hobson. They sat at an outdoor table at a café on the Cadde-i Kebir, drinking coffee. The café was deserted, for it was only midday.

"And so he would be, if he wanted the authorities to find him," said Ludbridge. "Or anyone else, for that matter. He has a great many ene-mies."

"I have to confess, I'm not sure this is quite the thing," said Pengrove uneasily. "I mean, he's a fellow Christian, isn't he? Fighting against the oppressive Turk? And weren't we on the side of the noble Greeks against the Ottomans? Lord Byron dying in Saloniki or wherever it was for their independence, what?"

"Messolonghi," said Bell-Fairfax.

"True," said Ludbridge. "And now Greece is free, or at least the Turks aren't running the shop anymore. This chap is simply carrying on the struggle for vengeance's sake. And it doesn't make sense, does it, for him to sharpen his knife for the fellow who's trying to make the empire *less* oppressive? Heedless, I might add, of the reprisals that would fall on his own people, and the fact that the Sultan's brother—who'd take over the job in the event of anything happening to Brother Dear—is quite a bit more inclined to rule by the sword."

"There's our man," said Bell-Fairfax.

They managed to avoid all looking up at once. The person in ques-tion was the Russian, Dolgorukov, apparently a minor diplomatic aide, whom they had noted going in and out of the embassy. He strolled past the café, and went into the tobacconist's next door.

"Go," said Ludbridge.

Pengrove rose and, walking with a distinct list, wandered out of the seating area and into the tobacconist's. They heard his voice raised, petulantly asking for a pound of Latakia. He vanished into the shop. A moment later Dolgorukov emerged, and walked on—not back toward the embassy, but in the opposite direction.

"What do you say, chaps, is it time for another brandy?" said Ludbridge, lurching to his feet.

"I should say so!"

"Jolly good!" Bell-Fairfax and Hobson sprang up at once, and all together they staggered out to the street. Ludbridge and Bell-Fairfax set out after Dolgorukov, keeping him in sight, while Hobson peeled off and went into the tobacconist's after Pengrove. A moment later Hobson came out pulling Pengrove after him, with Pengrove crying, "But the chap was going to sell me a chibouk, you know!"

"Got him?" Hobson murmured.

"Beautiful full-face shot as he turned around at the counter," Pengrove replied under his breath.

They dawdled along after Ludbridge and Bell-Fairfax, who kept the Russian in sight for some four blocks. He turned down a side street at last.

"Here's a jolly bar!" cried Ludbridge, pointing at one diagonally across the intersection. With cries of "Jolly good!" and "Oh, I say!" and "Who's for a glass of raki?" they made their wobbly way across, greatly disgusting a pious dragoman who was coming in the other direction. Pengrove took several shots of the side street as they went, tracking Dolgorukov's progress.

By the time they had seated themselves at a curbside table, however, Dolgorukov was nowhere in sight.

"Bell-Fairfax, watch for him," said Ludbridge in a low voice, and Bell-Fairfax, who had taken the chair with the view, nodded.

The owner of the bar was obliged to exercise patience while waiting on the quartet of Englishmen who lounged at his best street table. He was a Corsican, and disinclined to suffer fools particularly, and these were certainly fools of the first order. First they dithered over their order, with the particularly degenerate-looking one in the straw hat asking repeatedly whether he mightn't get a Pimm's Cup. When informed that none was to be had, he seemed to feel that if he explained what was in one often enough, and loudly enough, and slowly enough, a Pimm's Cup might materialize on the table. When finally convinced that he was never going to be served a Pimm's Cup in that bar though he sat there until Doomsday, he requested a crème de violette instead and sat there pouting until it arrived.

And then the oldest of the four, who had clearly been drinking well before he entered the Corsican's establishment, began telling a number of off-color jokes, at which his compatriots roared with laughter, pounding on the table and weeping in merriment. The excessively tall Englishman had a particularly oafish guffaw. When they had laughed themselves to silence, for which all the Corsican's other customers were grateful, they grew bored and began to play some sort of tabletop game that involved knocking a crumpled ball of paper to and fro and attempting to catch it in their hats. A drink was spilled and then a glass was broken, causing the idiot in the straw hat to utter piercing cries of distress. The Corsican descended on them in fury, and they were ordered out.

"All right, did you see him come back?" Ludbridge demanded, as they walked back across the intersection.

"Yes. Don't all of you look at once. See the place with the blue door near the end of the street?" said Bell-Fairfax. "That was where he came out. He hadn't the parcel from the tobacconist's with him anymore, either. He left and walked quite quickly back toward the embassy."

Ludbridge nodded. "Right. You'll find occasion to wander down that street tomorrow. Pengrove will go with you. Get it from every angle, understand?"

"Yes, sir."

"I could fancy another drink, chaps, what do you think?" said Hobson, in a bright voice. Ludbridge gave him an assessing look.

"No," he said.

Hobson had just made the six o'clock report, and was glumly closing up the Aetheric Transmitter, when Bell-Fairfax and Pengrove came in the next evening.

"Where's Ludbridge?" Pengrove took off his hat and threw himself down on his bed.

"He went out for a coffee with the dragoman," said Hobson. "Said you were to develop your photographs as soon as you came in."

"Oh, bother Ludbridge," said Pengrove, sitting up to pull off his boots. "I'm 'most run off my legs. I'll get to them," he added peevishly, for Bell-Fairfax had picked up Pengrove's hat and removed the canister of exposures.

"It's important, or he wouldn't have asked," said Bell-Fairfax.

"It is important," said Hobson. "London's had a chap who speaks Russian listening in on the embassy. He says the Russians were *told* to aid and abet this Greek fellow. It's their refuge you chaps went sneaking around today."

"Who told them?"

"The implication is, somebody high up. Who's the Czar's foreign policy chap? Count Nessel-something?"

"Nesselrode," said Bell-Fairfax.

"Yes, possibly him. When the Greek—his name is Arvanitis, by the way—had to go into hiding after the last plot failed, Dolgorukov was the one who got him out and then sneaked him back in. He's providing him with money now. When we shadowed him yesterday, Dolgorukov was taking him a packet of banknotes."

"But what for?"

"To pay for building up another ring of conspirators, I suppose," said Bell-Fairfax. "If the Ottoman Empire goes to pieces, it leaves more room for the other powers to bustle in."

"So the Russians are sitting about like vultures waiting for an elephant to die," said Hobson. "But one of 'em's had the bright idea of paying a lion to give it the coup de grâce."

"Or like an impoverished nephew waiting for a rich uncle to snuff it, but the bloody old fool lingers on for years," said Pengrove, climbing to his feet with a sigh and taking the canister from Bell-Fairfax. "And the nephew starts thinking about things like putting arsenic in Uncle's strawberry jam. Not that *I* ever did. That was purely a figure of speech. He left everything to his college anyway."

He was shut in his closet developing the photographs, and giving vent to an occasional fit of racking coughs, when Ludbridge came in.

"Much luck?" he inquired of Bell-Fairfax, as he shrugged out of his coat.

"We went all round it getting pictures," Bell-Fairfax told him. "Every window and door, as you asked."

"Good lads. Report went out as per schedule?" Ludbridge turned to Hobson. Hobson explained what the London office had found out about the Russians. Ludbridge nodded grimly.

"Of course that's what they're doing," he said. "They want to upset the balance of power. Can't have that, can we?"

"Though it might conceivably be for the best, if the Ottomans fell," said Bell-Fairfax, hesitant.

"Only if we got to the effects sale first," said Ludbridge. "Nor we wouldn't be likely to, would we, with the Czar poised right on the other side of the Danube? And we certainly don't want the French snapping up unconsidered trifles. You can rest your conscience about this Noble Greek, by the by. Polemis brought me a great deal of information on him. Quite lavish with the blood of others, but entirely unwilling to risk a drop of his own. Much the sort of fellow who prefers to spin his plots at a safe distance and send some other patriot off to deliver the bomb."

Later, after Pengrove had brought out the pictures and dragged himself off to bed, and Hobson had gone downstairs to see if anyone in the kitchen could make him a sandwich, Ludbridge sat at their one table and studied the photographs by the light of an oil lamp. He saw a high narrow house, one of several wedged together along the street. Its stuccoed walls had bay windows on the upper floors, overhanging the street level.

"Where's the back door?"

"It's in this third picture," said Bell-Fairfax, turning the image so Ludbridge could see it. Ludbridge took up a pencil and added to the plan he was making.

"So the back door's there . . . who lives to either side, eh? Did you notice?"

"Both neighboring houses appear to be vacant, sir."

"Good. Any evidence of dogs?"

"None that we observed, sir."

"So there's a street door here . . . and a back door here . . . That's a chimney-pot of some kind, I'll lay odds there's a kitchen hereabouts." Ludbridge blocked in possible rooms on his floor plan. "But on which floor? Shouldn't be surprised if the place has a cellar, too. Well. No locks with keyholes, I see."

"No, sir. Nor are there hinges on the outside. Pengrove and I thought the doors must be bolted on the inward side. But there's a knocker here." Bell-Fairfax pointed to the photograph of the street door. "And see the window, directly above? We worked it out that when anyone visiting him knocks, he must look down through the window to see who's there, and then runs downstairs and unbars the door to let them in."

"Maybe." Ludbridge rubbed his chin. "I suppose we could station ourselves on the roof of one of the neighboring houses, arrange to have his door knocked on and shoot when he comes to the window. A bit public, though, that . . . and it may be that he's only expecting visitors at prearranged times, and would be suspicious enough not to move if a knock came unscheduled. Nor have we any idea whether he's alone in there."

"We saw no one enter or leave, sir."

"Bah. We'll need more information. Here's a possibility . . ." Ludbridge picked up the photograph showing the building front, and pointed at the vacant house next door. "That looks like a proper lock with a keyhole to me. Are you very tired, Bell-Fairfax?"

"No, sir."

"Then let's go for a little walk, shall we?" Ludbridge went to his trunk and, opening it, removed a few items and slipped them into his pockets.

The Cadde-i Kebir slept, but for one or two coffeehouses spilling yellow lamplight into the street. They crossed to the opposite curbs passing them, keeping to the shadows. Without speaking, Ludbridge drew a brandy flask from his coat and passed it to Bell-Fairfax. Bell-Fairfax had a mouthful of brandy and passed it back. Ludbridge drank too and dabbed a little on his lapels for good measure. They encountered no night watchmen who might take them for an innocent pair of inebriates, however, and quickly reached the side street opposite the Corsican's bar.

At the end of the block were the houses in question, three in a row with vacant black windows. Ludbridge spotted the blue door of the midmost house, and grunted in disapproval. There were indeed no hinges visible, nor even a doorknob.

Next door, however . . .

He drew a small cylinder from his waistcoat pocket and twisted it. The tiny vacuum lamp in the end lit up, for which Ludbridge was grateful; this particular field apparatus tended to be temperamental. It flickered slightly, even so, as he surveyed the door's hinges and then its lock in rapid succession.

"Bugger," Ludbridge whispered. He reached out, grabbed Bell-Fairfax's hand and stuck the lamp in it, and was pleased to note that the younger man understood to keep the dim pool of light hovering over the lock. Ludbridge next drew a vial of penetrating oil from his pocket, as well as a tiny apparatus with a nozzle and plunger. Deftly screwing it into the vial, he sprayed oil into the keyhole, and all around the knob and lock bolt where it met the striker plate. At last he thoroughly oiled the hinges. Slipping the vial back in his pocket, he drew out a slender case of lock picks.

A moment's work opened the lock. The door opened with a satisfying lack of noise. They slipped inside, into ammoniac darkness and silence.

"This place is infested with rats," whispered Bell-Fairfax, sounding pained. He lifted the little lamp and swung its beam about, but it failed to show them anything beyond a three-foot radius. This was enough to let them glimpse the filthy entryway, littered with fallen plaster-flakes and the evidence of rats, in which they stood. A black doorway yawned to their right; before them a staircase ascended into blackness.

Muttering something uncomplimentary about de la Rue, Ludbridge took the lamp and started up the stairs, as slowly and silently as could be managed. Thanks, perhaps, to the dank atmosphere, the staircase creaked little, though its timbers were alarmingly spongy. Ludbridge, reaching the first landing, held the lamp out as far as he might and saw nothing but more steps ascending, more dust, more fallen debris and black mold. Deciding that they had climbed far enough, he handed the lamp to Bell-Fairfax once again and took out the last of the objects he had brought with him. It was a tiny tin case, no bigger than a snuff-box.

Bell-Fairfax, watching as he opened it, glimpsed a number of small black cylinders of metal lined up on a card. They were identical to the miniature crossbow bolt presently lodged in the window frame of the Russian Embassy. Ludbridge selected one, briefly checked the number engraved on its side and, lifting it between finger and thumb, looked up at the wall adjoining the apartments next door. He waved to indicate that Bell-Fairfax ought to hold up the lamp. A moment's cursory search by its light located what he wanted: a hole left by a nail or screw, where once a lamp bracket had hung. He wedged the bolt in, twisting it to fit securely into the crumbling plaster.

"Done," he murmured, closing the case and slipping it back into his pocket. He wiped his hands and they went back down the stairs, as slowly as they had entered. Ludbridge took back the lamp at the door, shut it off and thrust it into the depths of his coat, and they crept out.

As they climbed the hotel stairs to their room they spotted Hobson, climbing slowly and deliberately ahead of them.

"Hello," said Ludbridge, with a scowl. "Lingered over your sandwich, did you?"

"Took forever to wake the foreign bugger up," said Hobson. "Sorry."

Nothing more was said until they were well inside their room, when Ludbridge went to the table where his sketch was still laid out. Grabbing up his pencil, he jotted something on a scrap of paper and handed it to Hobson.

"There. Tune to that frequency tomorrow, and listen closely. Make a note of every blessed thing you hear and write it down."

"But I don't speak Russian," said Hobson.

"You won't be listening for Russian. You'll be listening for signs of life. Footsteps, yawns, snores, anything. Note them all, with the times you hear them and whether they sound close or distant, and whether it sounds as though one or two persons are there. And if you do overhear voices, whether they're speaking Russian or Greek, switch over to London and tell them immediately."

"How long am I to listen?"

"All day."

"That'll be a bit of a bore, won't it? What, just sit there doing nothing else all day?"

"You'd damned well better," said Ludbridge, without raising his voice. "That's an order, in case I hadn't made myself sufficiently clear."

"It is a bit hard on old Johnny, you know," said Pengrove the next day, as he propped the talbotype camera on its teetering legs and removed the lens cap. He backed up a pace or two to be sure it was actually pointed at Hagia Sophia—they had mended the camera as best they could, but the brass lens tube was still canted at a slightly eccentric angle—and, turning, took an unobtrusive shot with his hat-camera. "I mean, here we are, seeing the sights, enjoying ourselves, wine and roses, olive-skinned charmers and whatnot, gorgeous vistas of Mount Olympus, et cetera, and he has to sit in a room and listen to a machine buzzing."

"He's got it dead easy," said Ludbridge. "There are a number of less pleasant things he might be obliged to do."

"That's probably true," said Pengrove, turning to get a few inconspicuous shots of the ships in the harbor. "But so far he's been out for a walk once, and sat in a bar and behaved like an imbecile. Whereas Bell-Fairfax and I have behaved like imbeciles in all sorts of wonderfully scenic places. Haven't we, Bell-Fairfax?"

"We have," said Bell-Fairfax, who was busy setting up the developing tent.

"Such as places where there are dancing girls. And it really might cheer Hobson up a great deal if we could take him for a jolly night out. There was this girl who could flip over an entire row of half-crowns using only the muscles of her—"

"A man ought to be able to do his job whether or not he's bored," said Ludbridge, with an air of finality. Bell-Fairfax caught Pengrove's eye and, just perceptibly, shook his head. Pengrove sighed. He checked his watch and, slipping it back in its pocket, replaced the lens cap. Wrestling the camera into the tent, he set to work developing the plate, and presently the sounds of splashes and coughing drifted forth.

Ludbridge and Bell-Fairfax lounged outside the tent, passing a flask between them and pretending to drink. As they loitered there, Ludbridge lowered the flask suddenly and stared at a group of tourists approaching.

"Hallo! Pengrove, here's your Americans again."

The four men were walking backward to get a better view of Hagia Sophia, and the older one in the shovel hat was pointing and talking.

". . . disgrace and a reproach to the Christian world. I'll grant you the Byzantines were a lot of decadent Greeks, but that's no excuse for the rest of us. The Russians at least . . ."

"I shouldn't wonder if that is the Reverend Amasa Breedlove," said Ludbridge under his breath. "And his Bible students, I expect."

"Odd sort of Americans," said Bell-Fairfax, watching them sidelong.

"What'd you expect them to look like?"

Bell-Fairfax shrugged. "We put in at New York once. There were all sorts, just as you might see in London. Rather more slipshod and rough, I suppose. Their accent was different."

"Well, perhaps Tennesseans and New Yorkeans speak in different accents," said Ludbridge. "And you couldn't call these fellows slipshod. Something military in their bearing, don't you think?"

Bell-Fairfax nodded. The Americans kept backing toward them.

". . . the duty of the white race to see to it that this sort of thing doesn't happen again. Now, I'll tell you what: a nation that wasn't being run by a lot of fools and cowards could come in here with a fleet of warships and set things to rights in two minutes flat," announced the reverend in the shovel hat.

"Ah," said Ludbridge. Pengrove emerged from the tent, waving his negative print of Hagia Sophia, staggering from the fumes.

"Look here, chaps, this one turned out rather well—," he croaked, holding out the negative just as one of the Americans collided with him. The man turned sharply.

"Watch yourself, sir!" he said. He swept Pengrove with a glance and contempt came into his gray eyes.

"Oh, watch your own dashed self," cried Pengrove. "Look at that, look, you've made me drop my Hagia Sophia, what? I mean, really!"

"You should have watched where you were going," said the American.

"Well, you oughtn't to have been walking backward," said Pengrove, catching his monocle as it fell out of his eye. Unhappily inspired by the Muse of Comedy, he went on: "But then I've always heard you Americans are a backward lot, eh? In fact." He jabbed the American in the ribs. "In fact, you're a nation of 'backwardsmen'! D'y'get it? Like Natty Bumppo, what?"

The American stiffened. "You force me to call you to account for this, sir."

Ludbridge and Bell-Fairfax stepped forward at once.

"Now, now, let's not be hasty—," said Ludbridge, waving his flask. He took a mouthful of brandy and exhaled on the American. "Young friend just having a bit of fun. Can't hold his liquor."

"You insulted the great nation of the United States," said the American, glaring at Pengrove. "I demand satisfaction."

"Fight a *duel*?" squeaked Pengrove, appalled. "I say, you must be joking! Haven't got a pistol, and anyhow—" The American threw open his black coat to reveal a pistol in a holster.

"Here's mine. Gentlemen, may we borrow the loan of one of yours?" His countrymen opened their coats as well, all but the clergyman. He stepped forward and laid his hand on the shoulder of the offended one.

"Jackson, I must ask you to let it be," he said. "These men are clearly drunkards. Him that draws on creatures like these stains his honor."

Bell-Fairfax started forward, but Ludbridge put out an arm and elbowed him in the chest. "That's so, Vicar, that's so, we're a little the worse for drink. Charley will apologize to the chap, won't you, Charley?"

"I'm most frightfully sorry!" said Pengrove, holding out his hand. "No intention of giving offense, old man!"

The American drew back his arm. "Dr. Breedlove, sir, I cannot let this pass."

"You will," said the clergyman, in a low and urgent voice. "He is not worth your time."

"No, I certainly ain't," said Pengrove, hurriedly stepping behind Ludbridge. The American sneered at him.

"So you're a coward? Well, Doctor, I guess you're right. Honor's satisfied."

He turned his back on Ludbridge. As they walked away, Dr. Breedlove could be heard declaring: ". . . lesson to you why the degenerate and effete races of Europe have let things get into the state they're in."

"At least we're not as bad as the French," called Pengrove. They ignored him. He bent down and picked up his talbotype negative, which had gotten stepped on. "Oh, look at that! They trampled Holy Wisdom underfoot."

"They almost trampled *you* underfoot," said Ludbridge in exaspera-
tion. He rounded on Bell-Fairfax. "And if you haven't better sense than
to respond to a bully's provocation, what bleeding use are you in this
work?"

"There is such a thing as honor, however," said Bell-Fairfax, watching the Americans go.

"Not for a man in our line of work," said Ludbridge. "Too great a
luxury. You'd have done better to wonder why a class of Bible students
went so heavily armed."

"Well, but they're Americans," said Pengrove.

"Indeed they are." Ludbridge turned and watched them striding onward. "Armed Americans with the decided intent to change the world
to suit themselves. Worrisome . . ."

Hobson was sitting upright and clear-eyed when they returned, though
he had closed up the Aetheric Transmitter.

"You're not at your post for a reason, I suppose?" said Ludbridge,
scowling at him, but Hobson stood and offered three sheets of foolscap
closely covered in writing.

"I've found out a great deal, sir. Your fellow *is* alone there, only heard
one set of footsteps tramping about for the longest time. But then, company called on him! Must have been four or five other chaps. They
brought him things—food and liquor and such."

"Russians?"

"No, sir, Greeks. And then they all sat and jabbered away in Greek
together for a good long time, and I alerted London just as you said, and
they listened in too. It's rather awful. The Sultan has a trick of slipping
out the side entrance of mosques, after he's been in to pray; leaves his
guards and his marching bands and his pashas outside. Your Arvanitis
chap thinks if they observe the Sultan's movements often enough, they'll
be able to predict which mosque he'll visit on a given day, and station
someone with a pistol where they can get off a shot at him. The translator
sent a report for you." Hobson waved the foolscap up and down.

"Well done." Ludbridge took the report and, sinking onto the edge of his bed, started to read through it. He looked up again. "You've earned yourself a good dinner. Bell-Fairfax, Pengrove, take him down and see that he eats."

"Might we go sightseeing afterward?" Bell-Fairfax inquired casually.

"If you like," said Ludbridge, immersed once more in the report.

"Thank you, sir." Bell-Fairfax smiled, and Pengrove winked broadly at Hobson and turned both thumbs up.

They returned at a late hour, quite pleased with themselves, and met Mr. Polemis coming down the stairs from their room. He looked grave, but bowed slightly to them as they passed.

Ludbridge was sitting on his bed fully clothed, smoking a cigar. He glanced up at them as they entered.

"All accounted for, I see. No duels fought, eh?"

"No, sir," said Bell-Fairfax.

"Which is not to say we did not strive mightily," said Pengrove, striking an objectionable pose. Hobson, grinning, flung himself down on his bed.

Ludbridge stubbed out his cigar in a saucer. "Full marks on the report, Hobson. Certain persons are profoundly grateful for the timely warning. Bell-Fairfax, we'll be obliged to go for a walk tomorrow evening. I'd turn in and get a decent night's sleep, were I you."

It was past nine the next evening when they set out, walking once again along the Cadde-i Kebir. They stopped in briefly at a bar and had a brandy each. In contrast to the Corsican across the way, the publican who ran this place barely noticed them, so quiet they were and seated so far back in the shadows. They had dressed in dark nondescript clothing and Bell-Fairfax carried Ludbridge's satchel, which was if anything heavier than it had been when they had gone out in the boat.

Braced, they walked on again. Bell-Fairfax looked nervously at the policeman standing sentry at the corner, for the street had been deserted on the previous occasion. Ludbridge, however, nodded to the man in silence, and received a silent nod in reply.

The side street was empty of any other waking soul. When they reached the door next to the blue one, Ludbridge put out his hand for the satchel. Opening it, he drew out the goggles and handed one pair to Bell-Fairfax. With an uneasy glance up the street at the policeman, who seemed to be paying them no attention, Bell-Fairfax donned the goggles. Ludbridge took out his case of lock picks and a moment later they were inside.

The empty room to the right now seemed lit with green phosphorescence, with red blobs along the baseboard where bold rats watched the intruders. Ludbridge pointed up the stairs and held his finger before his lips.

They climbed slowly, carefully, to the landing, and paused there to briefly inspect the planted transmitter. It was still in place. Ludbridge pointed upward again. They climbed on, up to the second landing, and rats scrambled out of their way like running coals. Walk as cautiously as they might, they could not walk in perfect silence; the upper steps groaned and creaked under their combined weight. "Damn," whispered Ludbridge.

Onward, upward, and when they gained the third landing Ludbridge looked around. He spotted the ladder that led to a trap door in the ceiling.

"Out this way, I expect." He gave an experimental tug on one of the rungs and then climbed to the trap door. After a moment's brief inspection, he held out his hand.

"Oil, please."

Bell-Fairfax rummaged in the satchel and brought out the penetrating oil. Ludbridge applied it to the trap's hinges and, handing the vial back, pushed upward. Rather than opening smoothly, the whole affair tore loose from its hinges and broke into three or four rusted fragments, which Ludbridge pushed out of the way as well as he was able. Above him, stars glowed in a green sky, and cold air flowed down against his face, astonishingly fresh and sweet after the acrid musk of the abandoned house.

He pulled himself up and through, and reached down for the satchel. Bell-Fairfax passed it up and followed him up the ladder, inhaling in a long gasp when he emerged into the night. Ludbridge got cautiously to his feet. He walked to the low edge of wall that marked where the roof of the house next door began. Stepping over, he surveyed the premises. No trap door here; only a chimney.

As quietly as he might, he went to it and peered down into its black depths, which appeared as a green well with a flare of scarlet far down. A gust of warm air rose upward from it. The chimney was not a comfortingly solid brick one in the English fashion, but a circular thing of stuccoed stone, too narrow for a man of his girth; he doubted whether even Bell-Fairfax would fit.

Sighing, Ludbridge turned and lowered himself to lie flat, in order to peer over the edge of the roof at the rear wall of the house. Far below was the green gloom of an alley, fortunately deserted. There were three sets of windows going down the wall, two to a floor, and all of them shuttered.

Ludbridge sat up, nodding to himself. He turned to Bell-Fairfax, who was just sitting down beside him.

"Bit awkward, but it can be managed. How's your head for heights?" he whispered.

"They don't frighten me, sir."

"Good. We'll go down and in. Have to see how the shutters fasten. Where's the bag?"

Bell-Fairfax offered it. Ludbridge withdrew a coil of mountaineering rope and, rising and walking to the chimney, fastened the rope around its base. He gave it a good tug to test it; then backed away a few paces. "Watch," he told Bell-Fairfax, and fastened the other end of the rope around himself. "Like this." Bell-Fairfax nodded.

Ludbridge rummaged in the satchel until he found what he wanted. It resembled a pistol with a leather strap-loop at one end. He slid the loop around his wrist and, taking hold of the rope, sat down on the roof's edge. "You'll lower the satchel after me. Then you'll come down yourself."

"Yes, sir."

Ludbridge turned and lowered himself, dangling a moment in the air before letting himself down as far as the nearest window. He braced his feet against the windowsill. Bell-Fairfax peered over the edge to watch.

Ludbridge rotated the object on the leather strap into his hand, and turned a dial on its side. Then he pressed the part corresponding to a barrel along the inner frame of the shutter, and drew it back and forth slowly. He heard the faint rattle of a catch. A moment's experimentation with the device—it was an old field tool called a Variable Magnet—and Ludbridge worked out where the catch must be. Turning the knob to increase the magnetic pull, he heard the *click* that meant the magnet had taken firm hold of the catch through the wood of the frame. Ludbridge worked it upward and suddenly the right-hand shutter swung open an inch.

Stepping from side to side, Ludbridge opened the shutters. There was no glass beyond them; instead Ludbridge saw a wooden lattice. A cursory examination revealed that it was only held in place with four glazier's pins. He turned the dial once more, increasing the magnet's pull to the maximum setting, and easily drew the four pins from the old wood. Before the lattice could go crashing inward he caught it on a crooked finger. Lowering it, he peered inside and saw an apparently empty room.

The next bit was tricky, for Ludbridge had to crouch on the windowsill as he leaned inward and set the lattice on the floor. Then he eased himself in over the sill and set the Variable Magnet on the floor beside the lattice. He was sweating as he straightened up and untied the rope. *I'm getting past this*, he thought to himself, as he tossed the end of the rope out the window. *I hope the boy's a quick study.*

The rope was swiftly drawn up and a moment later lowered again, with the satchel tied to its end. Ludbridge caught it, untied it and sent the rope back up. Bell-Fairfax descended awkwardly. The frame of the window creaked with his weight. Ludbridge, meanwhile, had pulled a Collier's revolver from the satchel.

"Get the oil again," he whispered. Bell-Fairfax fetched it from the satchel. Ludbridge gestured at the door. Bell-Fairfax oiled the hinges and lock, and a moment later stood to the side and turned the knob. The door opened in near silence. Ludbridge, holding the gun to his shoulder, stepped through quickly.

He stood on an empty landing. Before him, a staircase descended. No rats here, no smell of decay; he caught the scent of food recently prepared. Cigarette smoke, too. Leaning forward, Ludbridge peered over the railing but saw no lights.

With infinite slowness they went down the stairs. Halfway down, one of the treads creaked under their weight, and they froze and waited motionless for what seemed an hour before going on. They reached the next landing at last, where a door stood open.

Weapon ready, Ludbridge sprang into the room.

He muttered an oath. There was a narrow bed against the wall, a chair, a washstand. The bed was empty, the blanket thrown back to reveal the crimson glow of residual warmth. On the floor were a saucer, in which a cigarette smoldered still, a white-hot point of light sending up a lazy trail of coiling smoke, and the faint red thermal track of naked footprints leaving the room, unnoticed until now. Ludbridge and Bell-Fairfax stared at them in horror a moment, before following them out and across the landing. The prints led down the stairs to the next landing, glowing more brightly red in the malachite darkness as they progressed.

"He must have heard us," whispered Bell-Fairfax. Ludbridge motioned for him to be silent, and slipped past him and down the stairs, following the trail as quickly as he might. Bell-Fairfax followed close behind. Brighter, brighter, the footprints were red as spectral blood now, descending and still descending.

The tracks led them to the ground floor. Here was the front door, firmly bolted; Ludbridge breathed a sigh of relief to note the tracks did not lead to the door. Nor did they lead to the dark kitchen, where a pan of coals still fluttered with waves of white heat across its scarlet surface. They led into a room to the right, where there was a divan, chairs, a table with papers spread out on it . . . all these things Ludbridge glimpsed before registering that the tracks led to a small door at the rear of the room. He grinned. Hiding in a closet?

He went across to the door. "Get ready to drag the beggar out," he murmured to Bell-Fairfax, before pulling the door open. Without benefit of oil the door opened soundlessly, revealing . . . yet another flight of dark steps descending, marked by brilliant red footprints. *At least he's trapped in the cellar*, thought Ludbridge, and angled around to look over the stair-rail.

He saw a bloodred figure on the floor, crouched, working intently at the catches of a trap door. It was the Greek, Arvanitis.

Ludbridge jumped the rail, knocking Arvanitis to one side as he did so. Arvanitis sprang at him. He saw a blade scything up toward his face and dodged, but it grazed his scalp and the fist behind it struck his temple.

The green and scarlet world vanished for a moment, in blinding stars that flashed before Ludbridge's eyes. He dropped the revolver and grabbed his opponent's wrists, as thunder seemed to echo from the cellar walls. They grappled there a moment, straining, grunting, before Arvanitis was abruptly jerked away from him and hauled backward.

Bell-Fairfax had grabbed Arvanitis from behind and was simply holding him up. The man shouted and gnashed his teeth, attempting to slash backward with his knife. "Oh, hush, can't you?" said Ludbridge wearily, and struck the blade from his hand.

"Shoot him!"

"Rather hard to do that just now without hitting you too, and I'd have the devil of a time explaining," said Ludbridge. He picked up the revolver, reversed it in his hand and hit Arvanitis hard with the butt. Arvanitis stopped screaming and sagged, limp. "At last." Ludbridge stepped back and looked around for the knife. He found it. "Let's take him back to his bed."

Bell-Fairfax backed up the stairs, dragging the unconscious body of the Greek. Ludbridge trudged after them, though he was obliged to stop, panting for breath, at the first landing. He felt the trickle of blood down the side of his face, as the scalp wound bled.

They got to the bedroom at last. "Put him in his bed and hold him down," said Ludbridge, for Arvanitis had begun to moan and struggle feebly. Bell-Fairfax obeyed. Ludbridge raised the barrel of the revolver and forced the man's mouth open with it. As Arvanitis opened startled eyes, Ludbridge shot him.

"And that's done, thank God," said Ludbridge, in a toneless voice, as Arvanitis trembled and was still. "Put the blanket back over him."

Bell-Fairfax obeyed without a word. Ludbridge took a dead hand and placed it on Arvanitis's chest, and pressed the revolver into it. He dropped the knife on the floor beside the saucer. They walked out of the room and Ludbridge sat down on the staircase, sagging forward as he held his hand to the gash on his scalp. "Go up and look in the satchel," he told Bell-Fairfax. "There's a medical kit in a compartment in the side. Tin box painted white. Bring it down, won't you, and I can clean myself up."

"Yes, sir." Bell-Fairfax fled up the stairs. When he brought back the kit he attempted to open it himself, but Ludbridge took it away from him.

"No. You go down to the front room and collect all the papers from that table. Fold them up and bring them back."

By the time Bell-Fairfax returned with the papers, Ludbridge was squinting in pain from the styptic solution he had dabbed on his scalp, but his head was clearer. Having cleaned himself up and wadded the bloody flannels into his pocket, he got to his feet once more.

"Let's get out," he said.

At the window he packed the papers in the bag, with the medical kit and the Variable Magnet, less the pushpins. "Now," he said, "we're going to do something tricky. Going to leave his friends a sealed house. I'm going up to the roof. You'll pass the bag up to me. Then you'll secure yourself on the rope and climb out, and here's the nasty fiddly bit: you'll put that latticework back in place and shove the pushpins back in on the inside, *from the outside*." He gave them to Bell-Fairfax. "Think you can do it?"

Bell-Fairfax's goggles made it hard to read his expression, but Ludbridge thought he went pale. However, "Yes, sir," was all he said.

Once up on the roof with the satchel, Ludbridge stretched out and stared up at the stars. He ran over the events of the last hour in his mind, making notes for the inevitable report, and had not got as far as he had thought he might before Bell-Fairfax hauled himself over the edge of the roof.

"How many pins did you drop?"

"None, sir."

"What, none?"

"None, sir, I was quite careful. It wasn't as hard as all that. One had only to reach through the holes in the lattice," said Bell-Fairfax, untying the rope and coiling it up. "I was able to get the latch to fall into place once I'd closed the shutters as well."

"Aren't you the clever boy." Ludbridge sat up with a groan. "Come along then."

They crossed to the other roof and went down through the abandoned house, only pausing at the door to remove their goggles. The policeman was still standing at the corner. He looked searchingly at Ludbridge, who nodded. They walked on.

"Won't the others notice we stole their papers?" murmured Bell-Fairfax, when they were in sight of their hotel. Ludbridge shrugged.

"If they get the chance to search. They shan't, of course; the police will see to that. No doubt quite grateful for being left a plausible suicide. What the Russians will make of it, of course, is another matter."

"Ah. I see, sir."

They walked on together a few more paces, before Ludbridge looked sidelong at Bell-Fairfax and said: "Now, think how much more easily that would have gone if I could have persuaded the fellow not to struggle."

The Corsican was irritated to see the party of four Englishmen in his establishment once more. They seemed better behaved today, however, or at least subdued; the older gentleman ordered only black coffee, and the idiot with the straw hat was willing to accept a glass of raki without a word of complaint. The Corsican assumed they had hangovers, and felt that it served them right.

"Was that Mr. Polemis who came to call this morning, when we were downstairs at breakfast?" inquired Hobson. Ludbridge nodded.

"It looked as though he was taking a package away with him, when he came down," said Pengrove.

"He was." Ludbridge blew on his coffee to cool it. He glanced at Bell-Fairfax, who was watching the length of the street. By day it was anything but deserted; merchants led strings of donkeys along it, street vendors with trays wandered up and down crying their wares, Europeans promenaded, hamals toted chests and sacks of goods up from the waterfront.

"Anyone knocking on the blue door yet?"

"Not yet, sir." Bell-Fairfax turned his glass by its stem, without drinking, as he watched the street. Pengrove turned and glanced idly over his shoulder.

"Oh! I say, Bell-Fairfax, here comes your . . . er . . . lady friend."

Bell-Fairfax looked along the Cadde-i Kebir and made an involuntary sound of surprise. Ludbridge followed his gaze and saw a Greek girl in trousers and jacket of a distinctive apple-green, thinly veiled in gauze, making her way along the street. Bell-Fairfax turned red and fixed his eyes once more on the side street; but as they watched, the girl turned down it.

Ludbridge leaned a little to the side to follow her progress. The girl walked with elaborate nonchalance, impudently upright, even if years of stern admonition kept her hand automatically up to hold her veil in place. Her hair was dressed with something that glinted through the veil, ornamental pins perhaps. He was aware that, beside him, Bell-Fairfax sat perfectly immobile, watching as the girl stopped before the house with the blue door.

Ludbridge held his breath. But she did not move on; she looked quickly over her shoulder and then knocked at the door.

A long moment passed. She knocked again, and backed away two paces to look up at the windows. She stared, she craned her graceful neck back. They were too far away to see her expression, and of course it was obscured by the veil anyway, but the change in her posture was perfectly eloquent: the saucy confidence fading, the quick movements of agitation and doubt, and at last the droop in her little shoulders as it began to dawn on her that the man for whom she waited would not open the door. Her beloved? Her brother, perhaps? She paced back and forth beside the door in growing bewilderment, and at last fear.

The girl turned and bolted, finally, hastening back up to the Cadde-i Kebir. Ludbridge was too far away to see whether or not there were tears in her eyes, but he imagined that Bell-Fairfax, who sat, white-faced and rigid, at Ludbridge's elbow, could see.

A policeman emerged from a doorway as she passed and made to go after her. Another stepped forth and stopped him. They conversed a moment, with gestures, and then returned to their place of hiding.

Over the next hour or so, the rest of the story played itself out to Ludbridge's satisfaction: men would arrive at the blue door, in twos and threes, and knock furtively. Policemen would emerge from the doorways opposite like wasps from a nest, arrest them, bind them, and hurry them away. By Ludbridge's third cup of coffee, the business was finished.

"Got the whole band, I shouldn't wonder," said Ludbridge, taking out a cigar.

"Will they hang them?" said Bell-Fairfax.

"Doubt it. The inquest will rule the man committed suicide, after all. But they can hold them on suspicion of murder until then, and I expect they'll talk a great deal under interrogation." Ludbridge lit his cigar and puffed smoke.

Mr. Polemis came to their door that evening, with many a bow and a smile, and gave them to understand that his friend was tremendously pleased to loan them the curious book that had so interested them. He offered forth a cedarwood box, which when opened proved to contain

the silver-framed codex in its wrappings of silk, the al-Jazari manuscript. Mr. Polemis informed them further that he would call again on
the following evening for the manuscript. He wished them a pleasant
night and took his leave.

They waited until broad day to attempt to photograph the pages, setting up a table by the open windows. Bright as that made the room, it
wasn't bright enough; Pengrove might shift the table, and crouch as
close as he dared with Bell-Fairfax holding his hat on for him, but the
images produced were dark and obscure as though seen through a
London fog on a winter twilight.

In desperation they took the book outdoors at last, and climbed the
hill to the graveyard. There, where brilliant sunlight streamed down in
the open areas between the cypresses, they experimented with laying
the pages out on the fallen gravestone of a Janissary. Ludbridge and
Hobson patrolled while Pengrove knelt before the pages and photographed them, with Bell-Fairfax turning the pages for him. Even so,
they were unable to fend off an offended Frenchwoman, who thought
Pengrove was mocking the Muslim attitude of prayer and gave him a
severe lecture on respecting the customs of others.

But the developed pictures were glorious, as they emerged from
Pengrove's improvised darkroom that afternoon. Sharp and splendidly
legible calligraphied text, snaking across pages and under fantastic
images: flying chariots, robotic figures, elaborate hydraulic systems,
complex geared machines of unknown purpose, magnificent winged
engines. And, in the upper left background of each, the same broken
inscription on stone imploring the mercy of God upon His faithful servant, Ali Hassan somebody, who departed this earth aged sixty-two
years and was an example to all men.

1850: Young Men Should Travel, If But to Amuse

When the dragoman arrived that evening to reclaim the book, he was accompanied by a younger Greek, in a fez and civilian clothing though very upright and military in his bearing. He was introduced as Mr. Mihalakis.

"And did you find the inventions interesting?"

"We did indeed, sir," said Ludbridge. "Please convey our gratitude to your worthy friend."

"I shall. Did you particularly notice the design for the steam turbine engine?"

"I did not, particularly, no," Ludbridge admitted. "I'm quite sure our associates in Fabrication will be fascinated by it, but my men and I are mere hewers of wood and drawers of water."

Mihalakis smiled. "But I have an invitation for you from our friend, and please understand that he does not speak to you as a Turk, nor I as a Greek, when we ask whether you would like to see what *we* have done with the design?"

"The *Heron* is entirely at your disposal," said Mihalakis, as they came aboard the next day. Ludbridge looked about dubiously.

"Very nice," he said, and sincerely, for the *Heron* was a beautiful craft, long and elegant, with elaborate carvings on her bows, much brasswork chased with ornamental patterns, and what looked to be a spacious saloon and ornamented flag mast aft. Over the entrance of the saloon was painted a green lion with a gilded ball in its jaws.

Ludbridge thought the *Heron* seemed to be rather underpowered, for all her splendor. What he could see of the engine housing in the waist looked undersized, and her one smokestack was distinctly small for a boat of her size. Nor was there any paddle wheel in evidence. The overall effect was of a pleasure craft designed by an amateur, with little knowledge of what was actually required to move a steam-driven craft through the water.

Mihalakis saw his expression. He waited politely until the porters had finished loading on their trunks. When they had been paid and gone back ashore, he grinned and said: "You do not for a moment imagine this boat will reliably take you to the Crimea."

Bell-Fairfax, Pengrove and Hobson, who had had no idea what their next destination might be, looked at Ludbridge.

"No, sir, I don't," said Ludbridge.

"Understandable. Shall I show you our engine room?"

"Isn't that the engine?" Bell-Fairfax pointed at the engine housing in the waist.

"That is for show," said Mihalakis. "It rattles and hisses most convincingly, however." He led them down a companionway to the lower deck. Ludbridge descended last, and when he turned round he found the others staring; for the *Heron* had a rather deeper draft than was apparent from above, and the lower deck, extending undivided by bulkheads from bow to stern, was immense. It needed to be.

Occupying a great deal of the starboard deck was a gleaming shaft and mass of rotors in a complex of pipes, nozzles, valves and blades. Balancing this out, on the port side, was a collection of tanks of polished brass, a row of lockers, and a series of wired boxes that looked as though it was some sort of electrochemical cell array. Several laborers— Ludbridge supposed they must be engineers, though they wore no ship's uniform—were involved in loading objects into one of the lockers from a crate. The objects seemed heavy for their size, were the color of old bronze, and resembled cubes of some densely compressed material.

"The al-Jazari steam turbine," said Mihalakis, waving a hand. "Somewhat improved. A great deal more efficient than a reciprocating engine, even a multiple expansion design. It powers screw propellers. It requires neither coal nor wood, while we have the compacted fuel." He pointed to the crate of cubes.

"What's that stuff?" inquired Hobson.

"An invention of the Magi. Think of it as a more useful version of Greek Fire," said Mihalakis. "But permit me to direct your attention to the tanks. They distill fresh water from the sea. Eminently practical for a vessel powered by a steam turbine, yes?"

"I should say so," said Ludbridge. "Can you drink it as well?"

"The water? Yes. Quite unnecessary to store casks of water aboard. And she has attained speeds of up to thirty-five knots, though of course it was necessary to test her at night."

"At night?" Bell-Fairfax looked up from examining the distillation tanks. "How did you prevent her from colliding with anything?"

Mihalakis held up his index finger. "Ah! *That* is an even more remarkable device. Kindly follow me."

He ascended the companionway, and they followed him back on deck to the wheelhouse just forward of the saloon.

"We had noticed—and your people must have as well—that the aetheric waves can be distorted and even stopped by solid objects. One of our gentlemen speculated that one ought, therefore, to be able to use this effect to *locate* solid objects, and even to calculate their size and distance."

They filed into the wheelhouse. There was a plain panel before the wheel, polished teak inlaid with ivory. Mihalakis reached down and slid it back to reveal, like piano keys, a line of dials and switches. The largest dial was an octagon, eight wedge-shaped segments fitted together, with a compass set just above.

"Will you have the kindness to look aft a moment, at the ornament on the flag mast?"

Obediently, they sidled out on deck and craned their necks to see. Most flag masts terminated in a ball, or a figure of an eagle or lion. The *Heron*'s mast terminated in a sort of eight-sided box, with a mirrored disc set in each face. Within the wheelhouse, Mihalakis threw a switch. "There! Come and see, gentlemen."

They went sidling back in and observed that the octagonal dial was illuminated, as though there were a vacuum lamp behind its glass panes, but only one segment at a time lit, in a clockwise motion. "Each disc is transmitting a timed burst of aetheric waves, in sequence, one after another," said Mihalakis. "Each segment on the dial corresponds to one of the discs, and displays whatever interference the aetheric wave encounters. Watch, please."

They regarded the dial a long moment, as the light swept around its face. On the left of the dial, a clumped flare of brightness appeared, and faded, and came back as the light swept by. On the right side, only a few scattered points illuminated and faded, but remained stationary.

Pengrove was the first to catch it, looking up suddenly at the waterfront, then back at the dial. "That's Pera!" he exclaimed, pointing at the left-hand brightness. "And those, there, those are the other boats! Look!"

And now Ludbridge saw that each illuminated dot corresponded with one of the caiques anchored off the *Heron*'s port bow. More: for one of the caiques had just cast off, and was moving out into the strait, and sure enough one of the dots began to move too, a little closer to the edge of the dial with each succeeding sweep of the light.

"And this would work regardless of fog or darkness, wouldn't it?" said Bell-Fairfax.

"It would, sir."

"Bloody brilliant," said Ludbridge, and shook Mihalakis's hand.

The *Heron* cast off and moved gently away from Pera, gliding up the Bosporus as effortlessly as though she were under full sail, despite the clatter and steam of her sham engine. Bell-Fairfax stood with Pengrove and Hobson on the stern deck, watching the dome of Hagia Sophia silhouetted against a golden sunset. Constantinople dwindled, and darkened, and sank into memory at last as they entered the Black Sea. The first stars pricked through the evening sky while the steward came out to light the stern lanterns. Having done this, he bowed and said, "Gentlemen, supper is prepared. Will you go inside?"

"I shall miss Pera," said Pengrove mournfully, as they crossed the deck.

"Hallo! Perhaps I won't," he added a moment later, as he stepped into the saloon. Hobson and Bell-Fairfax stared openmouthed. Rich carpets, teak paneling inlaid everywhere with mother-of-pearl and ivory, gleaming brasswork, tapestry cushions, the whole lit by heavy silver lamps. One hung just above a low table in the Eastern fashion. The table was set out with silver dishes containing an excellent supper of roast lamb and baked mullet, as well as a great mound of saffron rice garnished with nuts and pomegranate seeds. The cook was just setting down a bowl of sliced melon as they approached.

Ludbridge and Mihalakis sat on cushions by the table, idly smoking Turkish cigarettes. "You took your time," grumbled Ludbridge. "The pilaf's getting cold."

They took places on cushions around the table, though Bell-Fairfax had to fold up his legs rather awkwardly. The supper was consumed rapidly and in virtual silence; it was only when the port had been served around, with a box of cigarettes, that Hobson ventured to say:

"I'm afraid I missed the six o'clock report."

"Quite all right," said Ludbridge. "I sent word to London over the ship's transmitter. They won't expect a full report until we've arrived."

"May we know what we're to do next?" asked Bell-Fairfax, with a cautious glance at Mihalakis.

"Oh, he's in on all our little schemes," said Ludbridge, raising his glass to Mihalakis, who saluted in kind. "We'll be gathering intelligence, as it happens. Greene's project. It may be a bit tricky, and so the Magi have kindly offered some of their personnel and equipment to assist. We'll share our information, of course."

"I fear we may find it more useful than London will," remarked Mihalakis, lighting another cigarette.

"The Magi are a different group of fellows, then?" said Pengrove.

"Your cousins, perhaps," said Mihalakis. "Sons of a long-lost brother, if you like. When Constantine took the empire east, our people went with it. The name was the Fellowship of the Green Lion then, as you are probably aware. They operated in Byzantium throughout the millennium, until her fall.

"Things were rather difficult for a long while, then, regardless of the aid they received from your people in the West, until they were contacted—with infinite caution, using ancient signs and countersigns—by the counterpart group who worked under the Ottomans. *They* were descended from a group that had worked in Egypt for many centuries. We joined forces and have operated successfully ever since, though the coming age is likely to present certain challenges."

"And your Greek and Mussulman chaps don't hate each other?" said Hobson.

"We work toward the same great day," said Mihalakis, spreading his hands. "What else matters? And each of us has reached the same private conclusion in his soul, which is that no religion will ever bring that day about. Nor will great men in power, I think. The Sultan, may he live for a thousand years, but fortunate to manage another twenty, is wellmeaning but too weak. Any real change here must come through the efforts of Fuad Pasha and the others, and even they see that the best they are likely to accomplish is to salvage a modern state from the ruins of the empire. Nations rise and fall, my friends, but we are everywhere. Only *our* work has ever lasted."

"Hear, hear," said Ludbridge, raising his glass again. Bell-Fairfax, eyes shining, held his glass aloft and drank deep.

Before the glass had been emptied, the steward entered the saloon and leaned close to murmur something in Mihalakis's ear. He frowned and rose to his feet, making his excuses, and hurried into the pilot's cabin.

"What ho," said Pengrove, looking after him. "Something amiss, I wonder?"

The cook came in and cleared the remains of the supper away. He removed the table as well, folding its legs and rolling it into a bracket against a bulkhead. Mihalakis came in as he was pulling feather mattresses from a locker, and waved him from the room.

"We have received a report from Stamboul," Mihalakis said. "There has been a singular incident. The police are searching for a group of Americans who engaged in a duel of some sort. Pistols were fired."

"Not surprised," said Ludbridge. "That lot were spoiling to shoot somebody."

"They appear to have been pursuing their slave," said Mihalakis. "The man eluded them by leaping from a quay. He never hit the water, however. He appears to have detonated a bomb in midair."

"Well, that wouldn't be a duel," said Hobson. "A duel is when two fellows have it out—"

"A bomb?" Ludbridge frowned. "What sort of a bomb?"

"Pyrethanatos, I am afraid."

"Hell," said Ludbridge, with feeling. Hobson, Pengrove and Bell-Fairfax were staring at him, and so he explained: "It's one of our formulas. Consumes in a flash. We've used it for millennia. You're quite sure?" He looked at Mihalakis, who nodded.

"The unfortunate man was reduced to dust and ashes. Samples from the water were analyzed afterward, and left no doubt he had used pyre-thanatos. There were reports that a second man was shot, in fact, but neither he nor the other parties involved could be located."

"Profoundly unfortunate," said Ludbridge. He met Mihalakis's steady gaze. "You received that warning from the Franklin group, I imagine?"

Mihalakis nodded again. "An alarm has been raised. The Magi are seeking them even now, I am informed."

"D'you want us to return to Pera, and assist? We saw the buggers, after all."

"I took a photograph of them," Pengrove volunteered.

"By God, you did!" Ludbridge's eyes brightened. "Full marks, Pengrove!"

The photograph was duly located and couriered back to Stamboul by the steward, using a steam launch. They sat up long hours, emptying the box of cigarettes before a transmission came through informing them that the picture had arrived.

"And we're to go on to Sebastopol," said Hobson, slipping off the earpieces. "Greene conferred with Fuad Pasha, and they seem to think the Magi can deal with the problem."

Ludbridge grunted. "If they say so, then. Generally these things are only resolved one way."

"You mean there have been other occasions when the . . . the *technologia* has been stolen?" said Bell-Fairfax. Ludbridge and Mihalakis exchanged glances.

"It happens, once in a great while," Ludbridge admitted. "But the less said the better, for now. We have our own job to do."

The harbor official at Sebastopol found nothing much to interest him in the steam yacht that moored and sent a Greek dragoman ashore. The fellow was deferential when he explained that he had been chartered by a party of English tourists, who expressed a wish to see the ruins of Chersonesus, perhaps make a couple of talbotype prints, and take some refreshment in the taverns. They were well-to-do and inclined to spend money, the dragoman added, and followed this remark with a substantial bribe.

The harbor official pocketed it and facilitated the permits. He then ordered his nephew, newly appointed as his assistant, out to accompany the party. Ostensibly the nephew was to be their guide, but in reality to he was to oversee their activities. The nephew, a sullen youth addressed as Noman Ismailovich, went with ill grace.

He accompanied the dragoman back to the steam launch, and stared around enviously at its accoutrements while the Englishmen dithered about packing all their photographic equipment into the shore boat.

When Noman was introduced, the Englishmen seemed to find his name funny, and babbled on about it a great deal. He demanded of the dragoman what was so amusing, and the Greek, looking rather embarrassed, hastened to assure him they were paying him a compliment by comparing him to the ancient hero Odysseus.

Noman's annoyance was not lost on the Englishmen, however, and the older man clapped him on the shoulder and said something placatory. He called out some sort of order and a moment later champagne was brought out, with a trayful of glasses. Noman gladly took a glass of champagne, and then a second when it was offered. He felt a good deal more cheerful by the time they all climbed into the shore boat and rowed across to Chersonesus.

They wandered around awhile in the ancient ruins. The absurd-looking Englishman in the straw hat set up his camera and spent an interminable amount of time getting exposures of broken columns, with the warships and fortifications guarding the harbor incidentally in the background. Noman grew bored and restive; the older Englishman observed this. He pulled out a brandy flask and offered it to Noman, with a wink. Noman had a little brandy. He had a little more. The older man shared the brandy with him but there still seemed to be a great deal remaining in the flask.

The other Englishmen grew bored too, and presently insisted they should go see something more interesting than a lot of ruins. Were there any notable sights hereabouts, they wished to know? When this was translated for him by the dragoman, Noman volunteered to show them the fortifications immediately to the west. They trudged over the fields and found the battery there nearly deserted.

A bribe to the few men on duty, as well as a bottle of brandy from the boat, won them permission to take a few photographs of the two other Englishmen clowning on the parapet battery. Noman found particularly funny the shot of the short Englishman pretending to have his head stuck in the barrel of one of the great guns there, a visual feat he accomplished by simply putting his head behind the barrel and letting perspective create the illusion for the camera. Then, of course, they had to take a number of shots of the tall Englishman trying to pull the short one free, with Fort Constantine across the harbor in the background. The older man once again shared his flask with Noman, which Noman appreciated very much, for the wind off the sea was particularly cold that day.

Noman suggested that they might go look at the fortifications on the hills to the east, though he thought it might be a good idea if the camera was left behind. The absurd one pouted at this, but the other Englishmen jeered at him and he was compelled to pack his equipment back into the boat.

After a long ramble during which Noman proudly showed the Englishmen how well Sebastopol was fortified, everyone was hot and thirsty. The older Englishman proposed that they go back and row themselves to any pleasant tavern where they might get a fortifying drink, and asked whether Noman knew of any. Noman did, and so off they went to his favorite waterfront tavern.

The rest of the day was a little hard to recollect, afterward. The English insisted on paying for all the drinks, and by the time they reeled out into the afternoon Noman felt they were perfectly splendid fellows. They rowed all around the inner harbor, up and down, and Noman entertained them by singing the filthiest songs he knew, to show them he was a man of the world and not the hapless seventeen-year-old he seemed. The Greek seemed at a loss to translate some of the lyrics, but his English friends seemed to get the meaning nonetheless, and roared with laughter.

When his voice was hoarse and his mouth dry, Noman's friend with the flask miraculously produced a fresh bottle of brandy from under the thwarts, and passed the bottle around. Noman hazily tried to remember what sort of terms his czar was on with their Queen Victoria. He had the general impression the two nations were at peace; all the same, he thought he might impress the Englishmen by showing them how very well the harbor was guarded, in case they should ever dare to attempt to invade.

Noman remembered waving farewell to his new friends as they

pulled away from the harbormaster's office, where they had thoughtfully deposited him with the rest of the brandy. He sat on the harbor
wall and watched them steam away into the sunset, and was just finishing off the last of the brandy when his uncle found him.

The next half-hour was not a happy one for Noman Ismailovich.

"Don't wanna go anyplace today," Pengrove whimpered into his pillow. "Got a wretched headache. Besides, if I have to develop the beastly
photographs I'll get beastly sick."

"You're in luck," said Ludbridge, leaning down and fixing him with a
bloodshot gaze. "Mihalakis developed them last night in the lavatory.
You wouldn't remember that, however, I expect. You were speaking in
tongues by that time. We got some fine shots of the city's defenses and
we'll get more today."

"But I'm too awfully ill, really!"

"No, you're not. A little red pepper sauce on some nice crisp toast
and you'll be good as new," Ludbridge told him.

"I very much doubt that," said Pengrove sullenly, sitting up. He
clutched his head. "You're a wicked cruel old uncle, to make a poor invalid in my condition get up. Why don't you go hector the others? Except I think Hobson died in the night," he added, looking over at the
motionless heap on the pallet to his right. "Go rouse Bell-Fairfax first,
why can't you? I'll get up after he does."

"He's already up."

Pengrove focused his eyes enough to see Bell-Fairfax half-in and half-
out of the tiny lavatory cabinet, bending down to peer into the mirror as
he shaved himself. He was only slightly green. "Morning, Pengrove."

"And you'll want a decent breakfast in you, because we've got another long walk to make today," said Ludbridge, reaching past Bell-
Fairfax to grab a wet sponge from the washbasin.

"What for? And where the deuce are we?" Pengrove pulled himself
up the bulkhead and stared out a porthole, appalled. "This isn't Sebastopol!"

He saw the entrance to a narrow harbor that cut between stony mountains, crowned on one side by a couple of ruinous towers. There wasn't a building in sight, other than the towers. "No. It's Balaklava," Ludbridge told him, throwing back blankets. He held the sponge a judicious distance above Hobson's unconscious face and gave it a good squeeze.

Hobson sat bolt upright and gave vent to an explosion of profanity.

Having navigated through the channel and found a tiny strip of harbor in the gorge beyond, they beheld houses on its muddy shore. Mooring at mid-channel, they went ashore in the boat with a capacious picnic hamper and the photographic equipment.

"What in hell are we supposed to do here?" wondered Hobson, loath to climb from the boat.

"Get ourselves horses and ride inland. There's a valley Greene particularly wants intelligence on," said Ludbridge. Bell-Fairfax vaulted from the boat and was helping their boatman drag it up on the shore when some sort of minor official in a sweat-stained uniform came running out of a sentry-box, waving his hands and shouting. Mihalakis, picking his way through the mud, spoke pleadingly. There was a great deal of back-and-forth, with the official shaking his finger under Mihalakis's nose, before Mihalakis drew himself up and said something that had the tone of a demand.

The official raised his eyebrows, affronted. He said something, then turned and marched to the most prominent building—a squarish white place, low roofed—and pounded on the front door. As he waited for someone to open it he turned and gave Mihalakis a meaningful glare, and folded his arms.

"He says we are not permitted to land here, obviously," said Mihalakis. "I told him you are foolish Britons who wish to go riding in the interior and are willing to pay. I told him if he is clever he will take your money now, because you will be disappointed when you get into the valley and see that there is nothing picturesque there. He refused anyway. I asked to speak with his superior and he said that would be the Russian governor."

A servant came to the door. The official pointed at them and spoke loudly. The servant vanished back inside.

"I don't suppose we can get them to rent us some horses, then?" said Ludbridge.

"I'm not sure this is the sort of place that has horses," said Pengrove, clutching the tripod.

"Even if this fails, I may be able to suggest—," Mihalakis was saying, when the governor himself emerged, looking harried. From the open door could be heard the ceaseless crying of a baby. The official saluted and shouted something. The governor turned to stare at them.

"Come with me, Bell-Fairfax," said Ludbridge, and started purposefully up the shore toward the governor. Mihalakis went with them. The governor began shouting back at the official, a heated declaration that resolved into "*Nyet, nyet*, nyet, *nyet*, NYET—"

"D'you speak French, Bell-Fairfax?"

"Yes, sir."

"Good." Ludbridge addressed the governor. "*Mon cher monsieur, parlez-vous Français?*"

"*Shto? Oui,*" said the governor, narrowing his eyes. He was just drawing breath for another bout of *nyet*ing when Ludbridge said to Bell-Fairfax:

"Talk to him. Persuade him to let us land and rent horses. All we want is a jolly little picnic."

"What?"

"That's an order, son."

Bell-Fairfax went a bit pale, but he stepped forward, doffed his hat and spoke to the governor in French. Ludbridge watched the governor's face first; the Russian listened, scowling, openmouthed, yet gradually the anger died from his eyes. Ludbridge glanced at Bell-Fairfax, and nearly dropped his own hat, for the change in Bell-Fairfax's countenance shook him to the soul. The normally plain and horselike features had somehow become handsome, charmingly handsome without altering a line, *no wonder the chap's a seducer!* The pale eyes shone with earnestness and good humor. Bell-Fairfax seemed to be letting the governor in on a private joke he knew would delight him. His voice was smooth, encouraging, warm, as comradely as though he'd known the man for years. Ludbridge found himself desperately longing for a glass of Maraschino.

Mihalakis had drawn back a pace, watching in disbelief. The governor, by now, was smiling and nodding. So was the official. Bell-Fairfax finished his entreaty and the governor replied at some length. He gave an order to the official, who turned and ran.

"He says there are no horses for hire, but he will loan us his own mount and the carriage and pair from his stable," Bell-Fairfax told Ludbridge, in a low voice. He turned back and continued exchanging pleasantries with the governor, as the official first brought forth a splendid bay gelding and then returned leading a pair of mares hitched to an open calèche. Mihalakis made the sign of the cross.

There was a great deal of bowing and laughter and courteous talk, as Pengrove and Hobson loaded in the photography equipment and then scrambled wide-eyed into the calèche. Ludbridge joined them there, heaving himself onto the driver's seat with an effort. Mihalakis climbed up beside him and took the reins. The governor, meanwhile, clapped Bell-Fairfax on the shoulder and presented him with the bay, saying something enthusiastic about it. Bell-Fairfax smiled, replaced his hat and tipped it to the governor, and swung up into the saddle. The governor, beaming at them, pointed inland and offered some final helpful remarks.

"Let's go," said Bell-Fairfax to Ludbridge. The suave, assured mask had dropped; he looked a little frightened at what he'd just done.

They rode along a track that led off inland, between the frowning stony sides of the gorge. Ludbridge, still wishing he had a glass of liqueur, watched Bell-Fairfax riding along beside them.

"You sit a horse rather well, for a Navy chap," he observed.

"I was taught to ride as a boy," said Bell-Fairfax.

"Your people kept horses, did they?"

"No." Bell-Fairfax colored a little, looking down at the trail, and then lifted his head with a touch of defiance. "My headmaster saw to it I had lessons. Dr. Nennys said I showed promise, and ought to be trained to ride and fight."

"Nennys was your headmaster, was he?"

"He was, sir," said Bell-Fairfax. Urging the bay to a canter, he rode ahead, scouting out the track. Ludbridge mulled that over. *So the boy was groomed for a Residential from the start. Never knew Nennys was a headmaster.* He'd never cared for Nennys, with his perpetual smirk and superior air. Nennys seemed like the last person who might take upon himself the tedious business of running a school; from a couple of re-marks he'd made at the club, he'd given the impression that he disliked children. Hardly a man to act *in loco parentis* . . .

And there had been some absurd scene at the club once, hadn't there? Some old harridan accosting Nennys practically at the club's door, screaming that he was her husband who'd deserted her? Half the club had come to the windows to stare, and of course it had been ri-diculous because the woman must have been eighty if she was a day. They'd had to send out a pair of porters to hustle her away at last. Nen-nys had laughed about his infernal charm and someone else had joked that he might be the culprit after all; he was damned well preserved for a man in his forties. And it was only much later in the evening that two or three fellows deep in after-dinner brandy had debated, in Lud-bridge's hearing, on whether Nennys were forty or fifty, or in fact (as one befuddled member insisted) nearer to seventy, because he'd been a member at least as long as old Hamley, who had died over last Christ-mas, hadn't he? . . .

Ludbridge roused himself from frankly absurd speculation and looked about him as they emerged from the defile. He saw a wide val-ley crossed by a causewayed road, east to west, and on the far side steep bluffs rising to the north and west. Nothing on the floor of the valley but vineyards, a few small orchards and a stone farmhouse or two. It all looked rather dry and hardscrabble, and distinctly unimpressive.

"Don't see any fortifications," said Hobson.

"What's Greene thinking?" said Pengrove. "What use will photographs of *this* be?"

"It isn't our place to ask," said Bell-Fairfax, as he rode alongside them again. "There's a spot off here to the left that will do for a picnic, however."

They drove across and stopped, and opened the basket. The *Heron*'s cook had put together sandwiches, or something very like them, the round flat bread of the Turks cut open and filled with slices of cold lamb; there were olives and pickles, and baklava, and a canister containing ice within which nestled a bottle of champagne. They ate in the calèche, and Bell-Fairfax in the saddle, contemplating the quiet valley.

"I suppose it could be important, you know," said Pengrove at last, through a full mouth. "I suppose that road leads to Sebastopol. Suppose you landed an army back there in the mud, and marched it out here and down to the road?"

"Bravo, son. Suppose you did?" said Ludbridge, turning back to look at him. "Beginning to think that Greene might know what he's doing, after all?"

"If anyone was trying to stop an army marching along the road, that would be the place to put guns," said Bell-Fairfax, pointing with his champagne glass at the bluffs to the north.

"I shouldn't care to be on that road if they did," said Ludbridge. Mihalakis shifted uneasily in his seat.

"Is your Mr. Greene attempting to prevent some calamity of which he has been warned?" he inquired.

"He might be," said Ludbridge.

"His efforts are commendable, but must fail," said Mihalakis, shaking his head. "We have attempted it ourselves, many times. When we received the Informant's warnings about Alexandria. When Byzantium itself fell! All our efforts to preserve it went for nothing, when the hour arrived. I think the Turks are right and our fates are immutable, whatever we may do."

"One wonders, sometimes, whether the Informant mightn't be a bit more informative," Ludbridge admitted. "But he isn't, and so we soldier on. Come along, chaps; pack up the basket and get the camera out."

And for the rest of that day they wandered up and down that valley, taking pictures and measuring distances according to a list Ludbridge had, of information Greene had particularly asked for. The causeway to the right, and the bluffs to the left, were carefully photographed, in a series of images that could be assembled later into a panorama; so were some low bluffs at the eastern end of the valley. Bell-Fairfax rode at full gallop the whole length, paralleling the road, while Ludbridge timed him on his watch and noted it down, and then rode back at a canter. The bluffs to the west were throwing long shadows when they gave it up and rode back to Balaklava at last, somewhat bewildered by the exactitude of Greene's requirements and wondering whether any of it would ever matter.

The official ran out to meet them when they came back, all good fellowship gone. He watched suspiciously as they climbed down, and grabbed the reins of the mares from Mihalakis. He demanded something, money presumably, and Mihalakis paid him. They roused the boatman, who had stretched out and gone to sleep in the boat, and returned to the *Heron*.

As they went steaming back out to the open sea, they noted a Russian naval patrol boat standing off, who signaled for them to lay to immediately. The *Heron*'s captain shouted orders into a speaking-tube, and a moment later Ludbridge heard a series of muffled thumps below, as of rolltop panels sliding down; he assumed they must be concealing the turbine and other machinery.

The *Heron* lay by obligingly, and when presently the Russian lieutenant came aboard, he found one very agitated Greek tour guide and a party of drunken Englishmen. They giggled foolishly as the Russian questioned the Greek, who explained that he had, yes, taken the Englishmen into Sebastopol on the previous day, and he wished to apologize profusely if they had behaved badly, but they drank like pigs and, really, what could he do?

The Russian demanded to know whether they had or had not taken a number of photographs of the fortifications at Sebastopol. Sheepishly, the Englishmen confessed that they had.

The Russian lieutenant then demanded to see the pictures. A weak-looking little fellow, clearly drunk as an owl, stepped forward and proffered a handful of damp negative prints. The lieutenant examined them cursorily and, on seeing that they amounted to nothing more than some landscape studies, ordered the Englishman to produce the images that had been taken the previous day at Sebastopol. When this had been translated for the Englishman, he staggered to a valise and pulled out another sheaf of talbotype negatives, which when examined did indeed contain several shots of the defenses at Sebastopol, before which the other Englishmen had seen fit to make fools of themselves in a variety of undignified poses.

The lieutenant, very stern indeed, informed them that he was confiscating the talbotypes immediately. The Englishman burst into tears, saying he was very sorry and they had only been having a bit of fun, what? The Greek dragoman had a fit of hysterics, denouncing the Britons and begging the lieutenant to arrest them, if he liked, but please not to confiscate his tour vessel.

Thoroughly repelled by all this pandemonium, the Russian lieutenant departed with the talbotypes and returned to his own vessel. He turned the pictures over to his superiors and made his report.

His superiors read it through and shook their heads in disgust at such clear evidence of rampant degeneracy among English youth. One of them found the picture of Bell-Fairfax trying to pull Hobson's head out of the cannon rather funny, however. He had a print made from the negative, and tacked it up on the wall of his office. He took it with him when he retired, and eventually it ended up tacked to a rafter in the attic of his dacha in Yalta. There it remained until 1919, when the sound of gunfire shook it loose and it drifted down, indistinguishable from a dead leaf, and was swept out with the other debris on the floor when the new owners came . . .

"I thought the blubbing was a nice touch, don't you?" Pengrove said brightly, watching the patrol boat depart. "Lent it a certain verisimilitude. The chap looked as though he wanted to kick me, and the only thing that was stopping him was fearing he'd have to clean me off his shoes."

"And now perhaps there'll be an end to complaints about carrying the bloody equipment around," said Ludbridge, looking sour. "Hobson, you'll transmit the real photographs tonight. Damn! I had hoped we might sneak inland and get some shots of Sebastopol from the rear, but it ain't likely now."

"In fact, that might still be arranged," said Mihalakis, with a smile. "Perhaps you have noticed the large basket lashed down on the rear deck?"

A black wind buffeted the balloon's gondola, whining in the cables and causing the whole affair to creak alarmingly. Ludbridge looked over the side and wished he hadn't; the *Heron* far below looked like a toy, the whipping tether and hydrogen gas line seeming ridiculously inadequate to hold the balloon secure above it. *And I've got the easy job,* he thought.

"But how in God's name do you propose to steer a kite without string?" Pengrove's terrified shriek cut through the noise of the wind. He presented an even more bizarre spectacle than was his customary wont, wearing infrared goggles with a scarf bound over his hat and tied under his chin to keep the camera firmly in place.

"It is not a kite," said Mihalakis soothingly. "It is a flying machine. The Magi have employed them successfully many, many times."

"Gentlemen, the wind is rising," said Bell-Fairfax, turning his goggled face.

"Yes. Nearly ready now," said Mihalakis, climbing into the wicker framework. Above him, the great black wings fought the gusts and tried to lift away, even folded as they were. "Mr. Pengrove, please take your seat."

Pengrove managed to get his safety line unfastened, but there his mortal form balked and refused to obey him further. He clung to the side of the gondola, staring helplessly at the sort of wickerwork bosun's chair fastened immediately behind Mihalakis's harness, and the black void beyond it. "I—chaps, I—"

Ludbridge turned his face toward Bell-Fairfax and nodded. Bell-Fairfax stooped and picked up Pengrove bodily. "Come on, old man," he said, not unkindly, and thrust Pengrove over the side and into the seat. Pengrove came to life, with a galvanic clutching spasm, catching at the harness and buckling it extraordinarily swiftly.

"Very good!" shouted Mihalakis. The goggles rendered his eyes expressionless, but his grin was wide and manic. "The levers, gentlemen!"

Ludbridge and Bell-Fairfax reached out, one to either wing, and with all their strength hauled on the levers. The wings sprang outward, unfolding with the mechanical rigor of an immense umbrella. Instantly they caught the wind, with a thunderous crack. Mihalakis leaned forward, bracing his heels against the gondola, and yanked the release pin.

The wind shot them upward and out of sight immediately, against Ludbridge's expectations. He heard Pengrove's terrified yell growing fainter as the wings ascended. Clutching his safety line, Ludbridge leaned out as far as he dared and peered upward, trying to spot them. Even with his goggles adjusted to infrared, he peered in vain for any trace of them, and for a moment his heart sank.

"There they are!" cried Bell-Fairfax, from the other side of the gondola, and a moment later Ludbridge saw the flying machine circling around from behind the balloon. Mihalakis had clearly gained control of it now. He brought it down in a long swoop, past the gondola, and Ludbridge saw a gauntleted hand raised in salute. He heard another piercing scream as the wings swung around and bore them off in the direction of the Crimean mainland; Pengrove was alive and well, clearly.

Another blast of wind rocked the gondola. Ludbridge saw whitecaps

far below, and the *Heron* laboring on the swell. He groaned and withdrew into the depths of the basket, pulling out his flask as he did so.
After a fortifying gulp he handed the flask to Bell-Fairfax and looked
up into the billowing envelope of hydrogen that was all that kept them
from a shattering plunge into icy waves. It was black, as the wings were
black, for nocturnal operations. He felt rather as though he were looking up Death's robe.

"Are you unwell, sir?" Bell-Fairfax crouched beside him and handed
back the flask.

"Simply getting too old for this sort of thing, I expect," said Ludbridge.

"I'm sure they'll be all right," said Bell-Fairfax, standing again to regard the night into which Mihalakis and Pengrove had vanished. "By
Jove, don't I envy Pengrove! Do you suppose we'll ever get flying machines for the Society?"

"That sort? I expect so," said Ludbridge, having another drink. He
put the flask away. "There's generally some exchange of useful information when we do business with the Magi."

"Are there other branches of the Society?"

"Oh, yes; there's a branch in the north, and another in the far east,
for example. Group of Chinese calling themselves the Brothers of Liu
Xin. I'm told that was one of the few successes to come out of Macart-
ney negotiating over there back last century, you know; one of our
chaps recognized a certain symbol one of their chaps had embroidered
on his robe. Something similar happened in India. Lot of branch offices
got cut off and isolated during the Dark Ages, and we're only just finding one another again. Swapping research and inventions.

"I expect the process will speed up no end now we're in the modern
age. That's where the railway and the telegraph will really come in useful."

"What a wonderful idea," said Bell-Fairfax, looking up at the stars.
"The great minds of the world all working together in one common
cause. What can stop us now?"

"Anything," said Ludbridge. "Politicians. Money. All sorts of things.

Same struggle it's always been, my boy. We fight on, all the same. This fool war of Louis-Napoléon's will be fought and over with in a few months, I'd imagine; but *our* war never ends."

Bell-Fairfax watched a star fall. "And I suppose the . . . the killing is to be expected, in a war."

"It is, yes." Ludbridge reached for his cigar case and thought better of it, looking up at the balloon with suspicion. "A mad dog must be shot, for the good of all society. So must the undesirables who keep the world ignorant and poor for their own gain, like that Turk, or the ones who keep old quarrels going for spite's sake, like that Greek.

"One learns to do the job quickly and efficiently, and that's the important thing."

They had been riding there in the wind about an hour and a half, watching the stars and discussing history, when the gale brought them the distant impact of cannon fire.

"Good God." Ludbridge swung around to stare. "Where's that?"

Bell-Fairfax pointed. "Sebastopol," he cried. They saw the red flare of distant guns, and heard a very faint *pop-pop-pop* that might have been rifle fire before the dull thunder of the big guns reached them.

"Jesus Bleeding Christ," murmured Ludbridge. He gripped the cable as the gondola swung to and fro in the gusts. They watched the eastern horizon closely, but saw no more flashes. Five minutes crawled by, and then ten, and then—

"There!" Bell-Fairfax flung out his arm. "There they come."

The black wings soared out of the night, a silhouette against the stars, growing nearer with each heartbeat. Ludbridge caught his breath as they swept by, and came back around the balloon in a steadily narrowing circle.

They heard Mihalakis cry, "Catch!" and he flung out a line with a hook on the end. Bell-Fairfax snatched it from the air and turned with it, passing it around the cables as the flying machine made its second pass around, yet closer in. Just before it came level with them, Bell-

Fairfax and Ludbridge hauled together on the rope, pulling sharply down and in, until Mihalakis's feet found the edge of the gondola. A moment he poised there, while they tied off the line; he caught the cables to steady himself as they reached out and dragged the levers down. The vast black wings closed up, the shuttered machine sagged backward and swung the gondola with it for a moment—Ludbridge heard Pengrove scream again, and noted with relief that he must not have been shot—and then the whole affair swung back.

Mihalakis vaulted free, into the gondola. Bell-Fairfax reached past him and hauled Pengrove out of the wicker seat.

"What in hell happened out there?" said Ludbridge, as Mihalakis leaned down and signaled to the crewmen waiting on deck. They set to work reeling in the tether, coiling the gas lines as they went, and the balloon began to descend.

"I got quite a lot of infrared pictures," said Pengrove, through chattering teeth. "I hope Greene appreciates them. The whole of the Woronzoff Road right up to the back of the city, with all those hills and bastions, and even the beastly marshes and the river and that bridge, the Inky-something. But the swooping was too much, you know. Stomach couldn't take it. We were over some fortification or other and I had to lean out and puke. And, er, apparently I hit someone below."

Mihalakis was shaking with laughter. "There will be stories about vomiting vampyrs now. We were well away before they started shooting, never fear."

When they were safe on deck again they went into the saloon, to find that Hobson had nodded off beside the Aetheric Transmitter, in a positive sea of yellow dispatch-sheets covered in hasty scribbling. He sat up with a snort as Ludbridge and the others entered, and grabbing up a paper thrust it at Ludbridge.

"We're to move on," he said.

They stood forlornly on the quay at Varna, watching the *Heron* steam away.

"I enjoyed that," said Pengrove. "Except for the flying machine, of course. 'And so they came to windy Thrace,' what?"

"This next part may be a trifle rough, by comparison," said Ludbridge. Pengrove gave him an incredulous look.

Bell-Fairfax managed to find a porter with a wheelbarrow, who trundled their baggage to a hotel and dumped them there, either because there were no other hotels or because he was simply unwilling to go farther. They secured a room at some expense, and hauled their trunks up a steep, narrow flight of stairs to find that furniture had not been included in the agreed-upon room price.

"Why, yes, it is a trifle rough," Hobson observed, surveying the bare chamber. The one window had a view of the wall of the house opposite.

"Look at it this way: where there are no beds, there are no bedbugs," said Ludbridge.

They spent a comparatively uncomfortable night rolled up in their coats on the floor. The next morning they found a coffeehouse where they got breakfast.

"And to what charming spot am I dragging the old talbotype box?" asked Pengrove sullenly, dipping dry pastry in his coffee.

"You aren't," said Ludbridge.

"Thank God for that, anyway."

"You're going on a rowing excursion instead."

"Oh, what fun."

Ludbridge ignored the tone in Pengrove's voice. "D'you remember the body of water you saw from the *Heron*'s deck as we were coming in, that you thought was a deep harbor? It isn't. It's a lake. Here's a map." He pulled a folded sheet of flimsy paper from his pocket, and handed it to Pengrove, who opened it. It was indeed a map, printed in violet ink, showing the long lake west of Varna. Certain locations along the lake's shore were marked with circles.

"In the event you're accosted by the authorities, drop that over the side into the water. Greene particularly wants those places photographed."

"What on earth for?"

"You're not to know. Neither am I, for that matter. You and Hobson hire a boat and row out for some good shots of those locations."

"You mean I'm to go along?" Hobson brightened. "Not spend the whole day turning pictures into thousands of tiny lines of code and transmitting the damned things?"

"Yes. You could use some fresh air and exercise. Bell-Fairfax and I will go see about arranging our transportation to the next place."

"You mean we're not stopping long in lovely Varna? Jolly good!" said Pengrove. Bell-Fairfax knitted his brows.

"But . . . sir . . . does it seem quite wise to leave our trunks in that room unattended?"

"It does if one takes precautions," said Ludbridge. He took out his watch and held it up, displaying the seal pendant from its chain. "And I did, before we left the room. In the event someone unauthorized shifts my trunk, a concealed gyroscope will trigger a single-channel transmission to this receiver on my watch chain. Then something nasty involving pyrethanatos will happen to the burglars. And that, I think, is all you need to know at this time."

"The chaps in Fabrication have spared no expense to protect your socks and singlets, Bell-Fairfax," said Pengrove. "Underwear is a sacred trust, you know."

They parted ways outside the coffeehouse. Pengrove and Hobson went off toward the western edge of the waterfront; Ludbridge led Bell-Fairfax into a remote part of the city, looking for a certain address.

"Did I hear Mihalakis correctly?" Ludbridge wondered aloud, peering along a narrow lane. "Ought to have had him tell you too, Bell-Fairfax, you've got young ears . . . It ought to be this street, but I don't see a house with a green door."

"There, sir?"

Ludbridge shaded his eyes with his hand. "By God, so it is. Come along, then."

The door in question, very far down the lane, belonged to a residence of slightly shabby gentility. Ludbridge climbed the steps, looking here and there for any kind of mark or symbol, and finding only a small ornate case vertically affixed to the right-hand doorpost about three-quarters of the way up.

He knocked anyway. A girl opened the door, clearly a servant, wiping her hands on her apron. Bell-Fairfax removed his hat. Ludbridge cleared his throat and spoke in Greek: "Er . . . what becomes of illusions?"

The girl looked bewildered. ". . . Perhaps you are here to see the rabbi?" she replied, also in Greek.

"I suppose we are, yes."

"I'll talk to them, Flora," said a young man, coming quickly to the door. He wore a skullcap and, like Mihalakis, a Western-style suit. He waited until she had gone back to the kitchen and, looking Ludbridge in the eye, said in a low voice, "We dispel illusions."

"Ah." Ludbridge exhaled. "And we are everywhere. Thank you."

"Come, please." The young man stood back and bowed them in. "You are English, I believe? From the Society?"

"We are, yes. I am Mr. Ludbridge and this is my friend, Mr. Bell-Fairfax. A Mr. Mihalakis advised us we might find assistance here."

"Ah! You must have come on the *Heron*. I am Asher Canetti. Please, gentlemen, follow me. I will take you to my father. He will do whatever he can for you."

He led them through the house and out into a back garden, at the far end of which was a stable and carriage house. A pair of horses could be glimpsed within the stable, but the doors to the carriage house were closed. A rhythmic clanging noise came from within, suggesting that the rabbi kept his own blacksmith. Asher opened one of the two broad doors. The hammering stopped at once but a certain low roaring continued.

"Babbas, we have visitors."

"I'm busy," someone replied irritably, and with a hollow and echoing voice.

"These are Green Lion visitors," said Asher. At this the door was opened from inside by another youth, wearing a blacksmith's apron over his suit. He was formidable, six feet tall and broad shouldered, with a black beard, but at present he looked a little apologetic.

"Gentlemen," said Asher, "this is my brother Mordekhay, and this—"

"Close the damn door!"

"—is our father, Rabbi Yakov Canetti," said Mordekhay, waving them inside and closing the door after them. A figure was bent over beside an immense black coach, welding with a wand from which jetted a continuous blue flame, and which was the source of the roaring noise. He wore a helmet with a visor. Mordekhay bent down beside him and shouted, "Babbas, this is Magi business!"

The figure stood, hastily beating sparks from his beard. Asher took the welding wand from him and turned a knob, extinguishing the flame at once. The rabbi pushed up the visor of the helmet and stared at them. He groped in his waistcoat pocket for a pair of spectacles and put them on. Blue-white light flared on the lenses, from a lamp hung in the rafters; glancing up at it, Ludbridge saw that it was clearly something like de la Rue's vacuum lamps, and that all along the rafters and hanging from the walls were tools and machine parts of unknown purpose.

"Excuse me," said Rabbi Canetti.

"Quite all right," said Ludbridge.

Asher introduced them. "Pleased to meet you. May I offer you a glass of tea?" said Rabbi Canetti.

"We should be very obliged to you," said Ludbridge. The rabbi started out of the carriage house, and after Asher caught his arm and Mordekhay removed the welding helmet for him, they all proceeded to a little summerhouse under a grape arbor and Asher went indoors to bespeak the tea.

"And how may we be of service to our brothers?" the rabbi inquired, when the tea had been brought and poured.

"We need to get to Silistria, on the Danube," said Ludbridge. "Perhaps you might tell us the best route?"

The rabbi stroked his beard. "That would be, hmmm, in English I think about a hundred miles. There is a diligence that goes through Bazargik that can take you there. I suppose you are not at liberty to provide me with any details?"

"Unfortunately, we are not," said Ludbridge.

"Perfectly understandable," the rabbi replied, with a wave of his hand. "Would you be able to tell me how many travelers?"

"Four. And a great deal of luggage."

Mordekhay and Asher sat upright and exchanged glances.

"That is a shame," said Mordekhay. "The diligences are small and cramped."

"And their rates are outrageous, especially if you have many trunks," said Asher. The brothers were both bright-eyed with suppressed excitement.

"Babbas, it's a good road to Bazargik!"

"Smooth and straight and not very crowded!"

"And there's no moon tonight!"

"And who knows whether there aren't highwaymen on the prowl?"

The rabbi looked at his sons and raised an eyebrow. He glanced over his shoulder at the carriage house.

"Ahem. I wonder, Mr. Ludbridge, whether you would be averse to traveling at night? If you are not . . . we may be able to save you a great deal of trouble."

"I shouldn't think we'd have any objection at all, would you, Bell-Fairfax?"

"No, sir."

"Excellent," said Rabbi Canetti, and drank down his tea. "When you have refreshed yourselves, I will show you something interesting."

"Based on the splendid Concord design, but look! Steel panels inside the walls," he was saying, fifteen minutes later, as he ran a loving hand over the coach. "And, you're thinking to yourself, plate steel? What kind of horse could draw a coach made of plate steel? Ah, but, you see, it isn't.

Doesn't need to be. My sons and I have developed a tempering process to give steel greater strength and flexibility. The panels are made of thin strap steel, woven like basketwork. They will stop a bullet at ten paces, standing still. When the carriage is moving, they are even more effective.

"And look at the suspension! Improved elliptical springs. Extra thoroughbraces. Gutta-percha blocks to absorb impact. Coach lanterns here at the front. And what provides the light? Candles? Ha! Oil lamps, you say? Not at the speeds *we* can attain. Regard this lamp." He pointed at the glowing orb mounted in the rafters. "An electrical current makes it glow, from a galvanic cell array hidden in that trunk in the corner. But look at these!" He indicated the carriage lamps gleefully. "Each one fitted with its own electrical lamp, and the rotation of the wheels charges the galvanic cell arrays concealed under the driver's box. Genius, no? My Asher's work."

"A work of genius indeed, sir," said Bell-Fairfax.

"And a self-lighting, bulletproof coach impresses, but! It has other remarkable properties, which I will demonstrate tonight," said Rabbi Canetti. Asher and Mordekhay gave him a stricken look.

"But, Babbas, we thought we would go."

"It hasn't really been road-tested, and we thought—"

"What if it breaks down? We're young men—"

"So you think I'm too old?" said the rabbi, with a dangerous light in his eyes, and both his sons turned red and looked at their shoes.

"No, Babbas," they said in meek unison.

"We will all go. That is my decision," said the rabbi. He looked at his coach and smiled again. "After all, it seats eight in comfort."

They went back to their hotel, accompanied by Mordekhay with a wheelbarrow for their trunks. Ludbridge carefully deactivated the gyroscopic alarm, and Mordekhay lifted the great trunk and swung it up on his shoulder without any difficulty; Bell-Fairfax was able to carry most of the rest of the luggage, precariously stacked, leaving Ludbridge with nothing more troublesome than a carpetbag and the Aetheric Transmitter. They left a note with the concierge for Pengrove and Hobson, and went back to the house with the green door.

Having spent a pleasant afternoon in the rabbi's parlor discussing the state of the Ottoman Empire, during which time enticing aromas began to drift from the kitchen, they at length heard a knock at the front door. Mordekhay went to answer it and returned with Pengrove and Hobson, both of whom looked windblown. When they had been introduced, Pengrove saluted Ludbridge somewhat unsteadily.

"Lake expedition accomplished, sir!"

"Quite." Ludbridge frowned at him. "Have you been drinking?"

"Well, we had to, you know, to keep from freezing out there," said Pengrove, and Hobson nodded in solemn agreement. "Took us hours and hours. We were half-dead by the time we were halfway round the lake. And three-quarters dead by the time we were three-quarters around. So of course we ought to have been entirely dead by the time we got back, only the chap who owned the boat was most awfully jolly and directed us to his brother, who has a wine shop, and he sold us the most curious brandy!"

"Made from blue plums," said Hobson, swaying a little. He was clutching a brown paper parcel to his chest.

"That would be slivovitz?" said Asher.

"To be sure!" said Pengrove, looking a little uncomfortable under the weight of Ludbridge's deepening scowl. "Well. Er. Very pleased to meet you all, and terribly sorry if we've delayed you, and if you'll just excuse Hobson and I a moment we'll go dress for dinner—"

Bell-Fairfax directed them out to the carriage house, where the trunks had been left. A few minutes later they returned in formal supper attire, redolent of peppermint.

The dish served was braised chicken in a kind of tomato sauce with hot buttered noodles, and there was a decanter of muscatel on the table. Pengrove and Hobson, however, politely declined when the bottle passed their way, at which Ludbridge was a little mollified. The meal was rounded off with a splendid cheese tart. After Flora had cleared the dishes away, Rabbi Canetti went to the window and drew the curtain aside to peer out at the evening.

"I believe we ought to set out," he said. "You might wish to dress warmly, gentlemen."

Asher and Mordekhay leaped to their feet and ran upstairs, followed at a more sedate pace by the rabbi, apparently to change their garments. Ludbridge and the others went out and, by the dim light of the stars, retrieved coats from their trunks and put them on. They were standing by the cucumber-frames, watching their breath smoking in the night air, when the back door opened and three figures in voluminous long coats—dusters, they saw—appeared, framed by lamplight. They hurried up the path to the carriage house. Ludbridge recognized the rabbi, who wore a broad-brimmed hat securely held on by a leather strap under his chin.

"Are you all ready? Good! Boys, push it out and load their trunks on. If one of you gentlemen will help me with the horses?"

Bell-Fairfax assisted him in fetching out the two horses—a handsome pair of coal-black geldings of considerable size—and they were swiftly hitched to the carriage traces, which seemed of a slightly unusual design, though it was impossible to see much in the dark. Rabbi Canetti climbed up onto the driver's box. Mordekhay ran to open the gate, while Asher held the coach door open for the Englishmen and bowed them in. He climbed in after Bell-Fairfax, pulled the door shut, and leaned back and beamed at them.

"Comfortable, no?"

"Very much so," said Ludbridge, and truthfully; for they were all sprawled at their ease in the coach's vast interior, with the exception of Bell-Fairfax, who was obliged to keep his knees drawn up. The coach jolted forward through the gate and stopped, as Mordekhay closed and locked it and then scrambled up beside his father.

"The finest leather upholstery, stuffed not with horsehair but with cotton batting, and springs in the seats, just like a sofa," said Asher, as the rabbi shouted a command and the coach began to move. "But now! Feel the smoothness of the ride!"

They set off at a brisk pace through the night. Ludbridge reflected that, had it not been for the rumble of the wheels and the jingle of harness, he might have imagined he was in a gently swaying hammock. "Extraordinary!" he said. Asher folded his hands and smiled.

"It seems like a lot of trouble to take, doesn't it, to so insulate the passengers from the jars and bumps of travel? But wait and see. In the meanwhile, let me demonstrate a few other remarkable features . . ." He reached up and adjusted something on the compartment's ceiling, and abruptly they were all bathed in the light of a vacuum lamp.

"Behold! Powered by the same source as the coach lamps. You are enabled to read or consult maps as you travel. And here . . ." He reached up and opened a vent, and turned a small knob. A jet of icy air emerged. "A system of funnels catches the rushing wind disturbed in our passage and compresses it as it directs it through tubes, and at last out this vent, lowering its temperature in the process. I will close it now, because we don't want icicles to form on such a night, but you can see how this would make travel in the summer months much more comfortable."

"Brilliant," said Hobson through chattering teeth.

"It is even possible to heat the compartment by opening *this* vent," Asher added, pointing. "But that must wait until we are well clear of Varna."

"Hmm. Steam boiler has to heat up?" speculated Ludbridge.

"No . . . I had better not say any more. I believe my father wishes to show it off himself," Asher replied. He reached up and shut off the light.

The coach sped along. For a brief while they saw the lights of Varna and, as those fell behind, the road began to climb, for they were proceeding westward into the hills. At last the road swung around to the north—Asher at this point could not resist opening a panel and displaying a compass, thermometer and clock built into the door—and the road leveled out. Here the coach slowed, pulled to the side, and stopped.

Hobson, who had fallen asleep, woke with a start. "Good God! We're not there yet, are we?"

"No," Ludbridge told him, with an interrogatory look at Asher. "Are we quite all right?"

"Perfectly," Asher said. "Would you care to see the surprise now?"

On receiving a reply in the affirmative, he drew an ordinary lantern from under the seat and lit it with a lucifer. They climbed from the coach and saw Mordekhay, brilliantly lit by the twin carriage lamps, in the act of unhitching the horses. Rabbi Canetti swung himself down from the box and pulled what appeared to be a watering-can from a compartment beside the front wheels.

"Now, gentlemen!" he cried. "You have, I hope, heard of the celebrated François Isaac de Rivaz?"

"Invented a sort of an engine, back in '07, I believe," said Ludbridge. "Not a notable success, however."

"But! My boys and I have improved on his design," said the rabbi triumphantly. He went around to the rear of the coach, where there was a squarish protrusion that Ludbridge had taken for an enclosed trunk case. When Rabbi Canetti lifted its lid, however, a gleaming mass of machinery was exposed.

"Behold, gentlemen, what I may proudly venture to claim is the first practical internal combustion engine!" the rabbi declared. "Do you see a boiler? No? That's because it doesn't need one! All the motive power comes from small explosions within these cylinders here!"

"Isn't that rather dangerous?" inquired Pengrove.

"Far less so than a boiler explosion," said Mordekhay, as he threw a saddle across the back of one of the geldings. "You simply accept that an explosion is inevitable and design *for* it rather than against it. Everything safely contained within the cylinders. Nothing to scald or shoot passengers into the air."

"All it requires is fuel," said the rabbi, tilting the can to fill a cylindrical tank on the back of the coach. "I have designed it to run on alcohol. Splendidly economical, if you simply build a still in your garden. There! And this cap is screwed down, so, and then—Mordekhay, where's the key? You didn't forget the key?"

"No, Babbas," said Mordekhay, handing the geldings' reins to Ludbridge and rolling up his cuffs. He drew an object something like a small crowbar from within his long coat.

"Good, but wait! Wait!" The rabbi went running back to the front of the coach. With Asher's help the tongue was disengaged and somehow retracted under the body of the coach. A sort of tiller was opened out from the front axle, and extended up to the driver's box. Rabbi Canetti swung himself up and grasped the tiller firmly. "Now, Mordekhay!"

"Perhaps you ought to climb back inside," said Asher, holding the lantern close as Mordekhay crouched down with the key and fitted it into a squared hole in the engine-box. Ludbridge and the others lingered, however, to watch as Mordekhay cranked the key mightily, once, twice, three times. There was a report like a gunshot and the engine roared to life, rattling and throbbing. The whole coach trembled, as though impatient. "In! Please!" cried Asher, slamming shut the lid that concealed the engine.

They needed no urging to obey now. Once inside, Asher leaned out the window. "Ready, Babbas!"

With a clank, the coach started forward under its own power. It gathered speed. Its passengers looked at one another in wild surmise, as the rabbi gave a wordless and long-drawn-out cry of joy. His cry became a wild song as they jolted on, faster and faster under the wondering stars, and behind them its counterpoint came in the hoofbeats of the horses as Mordekhay followed at a gallop.

It was plain now why such care had been taken to cushion passengers, for the rabbi's coach was easily twice as fast as any horse-drawn conveyance.

"Is it possible we'll be in Silistria tonight?" inquired Ludbridge, as they passed the lights of Bazargik.

"Possible, yes," said Asher. "It is also possible we will break down. Although I wouldn't say that where my father would hear! But we have never driven the coach for any long distance yet. Not to worry; this is why my brother follows with the horses."

"It's as though we were in our own railway car, without the need for rails," said Bell-Fairfax, unable to take his gaze from the window, where village lights appeared briefly before flashing out of sight. "What will you do when you perfect it? Will you form a corporation and build them for sale?"

"Oh, no. Can you imagine the accidents, if every household kept one of these?"

"But consider the uses to which it might be put!" Bell-Fairfax shifted in his seat. "Transport of the sick and injured, for example. It might save lives."

"It might, but I'll wager any sum you care to name that it'd kill as many as it got to a hospital, traveling around by day when people were likely to blunder into its path," said Ludbridge. "And in any case, boy, that's not the way it's done! The Society prefers to keep its inventions for its own use. I daresay the Magi are the same."

"That is our policy, yes," said Asher.

"And I'll tell you why," said Ludbridge, holding up his hand, for Bell-Fairfax had opened his mouth to protest. "As long as *we* control them, we can be sure they're being put to proper use. But suppose thieves got hold of something like this, and used it to fly from the law? And, depend upon it, they would. The railways are already bringing undesirables into towns and villages that were once beyond their reach.

"*Technologia* is a two-edged blade, my boy. When we can see that the undoubted benefits will outweigh the disadvantages to humanity, only then do we release one of our machines for public use. An idea dropped in the proper ear in one place, a laboratory funded in another, and one day everyone's got a steam engine."

"And Progress and Civilization move forward," said Bell-Fairfax stubbornly.

"And so do Dark Satanic Mills and children getting crushed in weaving machines, while some industrialist grows fat on the proceeds," said Ludbridge. "But Britain becomes an empire, which—according to our Informant—is one of the things that must happen before the great day comes."

"And our own empire must fall," said Asher sadly. "Perhaps it won't happen in our lifetimes. I hope so; the Sultan is a righteous man. But we have survived such things before."

"And we are everywhere," said Ludbridge. Bell-Fairfax folded his arms and stared out the window.

"It's getting rather chilly," remarked Pengrove.

"Ah. Let me demonstrate the heater, then—very simple device, I open a valve that brings up heated air from the engine—"

At that moment there was a sudden lurch, and the coach veered wildly from one side of the road to the other. They heard the rabbi shouting in anger. The listing coach slowed, and jolted to a stop. The noise of the engine stopped.

Asher had the door open in a half-second and had vaulted out on the road. "Babbas! What has happened?" Bell-Fairfax scrambled out after him, followed by the others. They met the rabbi coming around the side of the coach.

"We lost a wheel! I saw it roll past us. Fetch out the lantern! And where is your brother?"

"Probably he fell behind, Babbas," replied Asher, pulling out the lantern and lighting it with a lucifer. By the amber circle of light they saw that a wheel was indeed missing. Rabbi Canetti inspected the axle.

"It's all right. No cracks, nothing worn. I wonder if it was the cotter bolt?"

"Have we a replacement?"

"Of course we have!" The rabbi slapped his pockets in vain. "No! Wait! Here." He reached inside his duster and dug a handful of cotter bolts from his waistcoat pocket. "You see? We'll be all right. Clearly we must redesign the wheel hubs, however."

"Right now we'd better find the wheel." Asher lifted the lantern and peered into the darkness ahead.

"We can assist with that," said Ludbridge. He leaned in, fished a pair of thermal goggles from his satchel, and handed them to Bell-Fairfax. "It'll still be hot from the friction. Ought to show up nicely. Go and fetch it back."

"Yes, sir." Bell-Fairfax pulled on the goggles. He started off into the night.

"Asher, you had better go with him," said the rabbi.

"Oh, no need," said Ludbridge. "The goggles can detect heat. He won't need a lantern."

"No, but the wheels are specially made and quite heavy. They take two men to lift."

Ludbridge chuckled and took out his cigar case. "Still no need. He's a rather strong fellow, our Edward. Cigar?"

Rabbi Canetti accepted one gratefully. Hobson produced a flask of slivovitz and they stood in a half-circle around the wagon, passing the flask back and forth and looking up at the stars. Far to the southeast were the lights of Bazargik, and the flat farmland plain they had crossed; now they were in a region of low rolling hills and more patches of farms, obscured by thick forests.

"Will the repair take long?" inquired Pengrove.

"No, not at all. Not once my Mordekhay gets here," said Rabbi Canetti. "In fact—there! I hear hoofbeats. That must be Mordekhay now."

They listened for a long moment. "Wouldn't he be coming from the other direction?" said Hobson.

"Oh," said the rabbi, and then: "I think I'd better shut off the carriage lamps."

He hurried forward and turned a pair of switches. The blue-white beams vanished, leaving the party around the coach in stygian blackness. There was no sound now but the creaking of insects in the night, for the sound of approaching hooves had abruptly stopped. Pengrove remarked as much.

"Umph." Ludbridge chewed his cigar. "Might have turned off and gone down a lane."

They stood listening a long moment. Then, not loud but distinct, they heard the whinny of a horse. A moment later there was another.

"Imagine if that was the Americans, lying in wait like Red Indians," said Pengrove, with a nervous giggle.

"D'you get any highwaymen in these parts?" asked Ludbridge.

"Unfortunately, we do," said the rabbi uneasily. "Perhaps you had better get back in the coach. I think I mentioned that it is bulletproof—"

They heard the pounding of footsteps as someone approached them at a dead run. Bell-Fairfax reappeared abruptly, looming out of the darkness. He carried the wheel over one shoulder.

"There are horsemen ahead, under some trees," he said, gasping. "They're sitting there talking amongst themselves. I believe they're trying to decide whether or not to attack us. I had to go off into a field to get the wheel, and I came up behind them as I was trying to get back to the road." He swung the wheel down, shoved the carriage upward with one hand and slid the wheel back on its hub. The rabbi dropped his cigar in astonishment.

"How many?" demanded Ludbridge.

"May I have a cotter bolt, please?" Bell-Fairfax held out his hand. "Thank you. There are ten of them, sir. If I understood their dialect, two were arguing against attacking us, because they thought the carriage lamps were ghost-lights, but I'm afraid the others were laughing at them." He drove the cotter bolt through with a blow of his fist. "Sir, have you any pliers?"

The rabbi, still staring, remembered himself and produced a pair of pliers from one of the pockets in his duster. "But, my boy, it takes a special tool and a hammer—"

"Thank you." Bell-Fairfax took the pliers and hurriedly bent the ends of the bolt. Pengrove scrambled past him and vaulted up into the coach. "Perhaps if we start up the coach and go past them at our best speed, they won't know what—damn! We don't have the key, do we?"

"That's all right," said Pengrove, leaning out with the revolvers he had fetched from his carpetbag. He jumped down. "I should think we ought to be able to hold them off with these."

"Asher, get in the coach," said Rabbi Canetti, at the same moment Asher said, "Babbas, get in the coach."

"Perhaps both of you ought to get in the coach," said Ludbridge, drawing his own revolver from within his coat.

"No! I built this thing with defenses." Rabbi Canetti ducked under the coach and unstrapped something. He ducked back out, clutching something in his arms. Bell-Fairfax peered down the road.

"They've ridden out of the trees," he announced, and now they could hear the hooves once again. "They're on the road. They're drawing sabers."

"Sabers, is it? Ha!" The rabbi dropped to his knees, setting up a tripod to support something long and cylindrical on the roadway. "Let them dare to charge *me*. Asher, get back in the coach immediately. I won't tell you again."

"Is that a mortar?" Ludbridge knelt beside the rabbi.

"An improved design of my own," said the rabbi. "And would you be so obliging as to have your nice young golem put my disobedient son in the coach?"

"They're charging," cried Bell-Fairfax, but the thunder of approaching hoofbeats and the shrill cries made that plain. Pengrove passed him a revolver. They stood their ground, waiting for the dark mass of horsemen to come within range, and then the night was illuminated by a flash from the mortar as the rabbi pulled a lever. There was a streak of light. A blazing cloud erupted before the very hooves of the onrushing horses, who screamed and reared. Two turned and bolted, bearing their unresisting riders away with them; Ludbridge could see that two or three at least had been blown clear off the road, and there seemed to be bodies in the ditches to either side.

The others were trying to control their mounts, who were dancing wildly in the red afterglow—in fact there seemed to be particles of phosphorus or some related chemical in the smoke, for it clung to both riders and steeds like luminous paint, giving them a terrifying aspect and causing them to shy from one another. The highwaymen were choking, gagging, but one nerved himself enough to yell an order to the others and two rallied themselves sufficiently to obey.

They charged forward again. Ludbridge had just taken aim when a black figure hurtled past him, shaking the very earth with hoofbeats. It was Mordekhay on one of the black geldings, brandishing a sword and roaring imprecations. Briefly there was a clash of steel, which ended with a man's high-pitched scream. One horse, still glowing like hellfire, went charging away across the night fields, dragging its glowing rider from one stirrup. The other pair of horses were bearing their riders in the opposite direction at a gallop.

Mordekhay wheeled around and came back, sheathing his sword. Rabbi Canetti got to his feet.

"And where have you been?"

"Stoyan went lame, Babbas, and I had to leave him in Bazargik. I'm sorry. What happened?"

Rabbi Canetti explained, with admirable brevity. It being agreed upon all round that a speedy departure was called for before the highwaymen regrouped, the rabbi resumed his place on the driver's seat. The others climbed back into the coach, Mordekhay produced the key and cranked the coach into clattering life, and they resumed their journey.

It was only interrupted once more, when they ran out of fuel around four o'clock in the morning. The rabbi apologized profusely, explaining that this was the longest road trial the coach had yet had and he was still uncertain how far a tank of fuel could take them. However, Ludbridge pointed out that Hobson had providentially brought several bottles of slivovitz along in his trunk. Four of them filled the tank, and the coach surged ahead as though it greatly appreciated his sacrifice.

The east was growing light when they glimpsed the first farmer's carts carrying produce to Silistria on the Danube. To avoid exciting comment, the rabbi switched the engine off and climbed down, while Mordekhay unfolded the wagon tongue and fastened the gelding into the traces. With the conversion complete the others climbed out. The first farmer to pass them on the road wondered whether he was not seeing some sort of funeral procession: jet-black horse straining at immense jet-black coach, and an odd-looking party of men in long coats following on foot.

"What was that you called my associate, back there?" Ludbridge said quietly to the rabbi, as they trudged along side by side. "You used a word with which I'm not familiar. *Golem*, I think it was."

The rabbi nodded. He peered ahead at Bell-Fairfax, who with Mordekhay was pushing the coach to ease some of the strain on the gelding. In a low voice the rabbi replied, "The Lord made Adam from red clay, did He not? Well. Some believe that the learned and wise can also make living servants from clay. There is a legend that a certain rabbi in Prague made one such, to protect our people against persecution there.

"A golem is big, and strong, and usually obedient to the will of the rabbi who made him. But he has no voice, the golem. To give him a voice is to give him a soul, and who can say whether that ought to be done? And of course a gentile such as yourself will conclude this is all so much folklore, no?

"Still . . . if some other group of learned and wise men—such as our own brotherhood—were to develop the idea independently and create a man for their own purposes, they would most likely make him big and strong and obedient, and much more human looking than the old fellow in Prague. But they could not, I think, manage to completely disguise his true nature. And, being gentiles, they might not know that a golem shouldn't be given a soul. Won't he find it painful, when they set him about the work he is to do?

"But I don't believe you will worry much about this, since you cannot believe it to be any more than a fable." The rabbi gave Ludbridge a sidelong glance. Ludbridge, looking thoughtfully at Bell-Fairfax, merely nodded.

Fortunately for the gelding, they hadn't far to go before they entered Silistria, a pleasant city in a curve of the Danube. They found an early-opening coffeehouse, and had breakfast while Mordekhay went off to obtain a team of fresh horses. Rabbi Canetti remained awake long enough to take them down to the riverfront and introduce them to a bargeman willing to take four passengers and their luggage up the Danube; then he climbed into the back of the coach and was sound asleep before Mordekhay and Asher waved and drove back to Varna.

1850: Allegro con Brio

From Silistria to Ruschuk by barge took them most of a week, for the barge was neither steam-powered nor driven by internal combustion engine. It was mule-drawn and capable of two miles an hour at its best speed. They made themselves fairly comfortable in a spare wood-paneled cabin and watched Bulgaria slip by on one hand, and Wallachia on the other.

Pengrove had plenty of time to develop the pictures he had taken in Silistria: more fortifications, more comic posing of Hobson and Bell-Fairfax against gun emplacements, and several studies of the island in the Danube across from the city. Hobson had unlimited hours at his disposal to encode and transmit the images to London. He woke them all one night, muttering strings of numbers in his sleep, and at last screaming that the number five was trying to bite his fingers.

The bargeman had a sloe-eyed daughter, young and possessed of a certain earthy charm, but she proved disinclined to cook for them. They took to venturing ashore at villages and purchasing bread and cheese. Bell-Fairfax bought a wooden tub and soap, and so they experimented with doing their own laundry. The bargeman's daughter, who spoke neither Greek nor English, watched their efforts with amusement but seemed disinclined to assist with laundry either.

In one village they managed to purchase a deck of cards and thereafter passed the time with games of whist. The bargeman's daughter, who did not play whist, circled round them impudently, peering over their shoulders at their cards and commenting to herself in an undertone. She contrived to bump her hip into Bell-Fairfax's elbow at least once in every circuit. Pengrove and Hobson would exchange glances. Bell-Fairfax would keep his eyes resolutely on his cards. Ludbridge would watch them all with the same considered detachment with which he watched his cards.

One night, long after the lamp had been blown out, Ludbridge heard a faint tapping sound. It came from the other side of the bulkhead, just above Bell-Fairfax's bunk. The sound persisted for a while before Bell-Fairfax rose silently and stole from the cabin.

Ludbridge got out his watch and checked it, and checked it again when Bell-Fairfax returned, a full three hours later.

"Bell-Fairfax."

"Sir?"

"D'you remember what I said about being a second-rate Casanova?"

"Yes, sir."

"I trust you're not going to lie to me, Bell-Fairfax."

"No, sir."

"Then what in hell have you been doing for the last three hours?"

There was a long pause while Bell-Fairfax framed his reply. "Entertaining a lady, sir."

"Hardly a lady."

"As much of a lady as it is within her power to be, sir."

"Oh, yes, of course. I'll grant you she's the sort who might cause a bit of trouble if you scorned her. Though rather obviously you *didn't* scorn her. I expect you hardly had to use your, how did you put it? Your powers of making yourself agreeable. Did you?"

The silence that followed went on too long.

"You did," concluded Ludbridge.

"I started to, sir. I stopped myself."

"Stopped yourself! Ah, I see. And that makes it perfectly all right."

"No, sir, I understand that, sir."

"Not likely, you don't. Listen to me, you God-damned young imbecile. Whether you seduce a girl or she knocks on the wall and offers herself, *it's a complication endangering the mission*. If you'd ignored the knocking like a sensible man, she'd have been a bit pouty tomorrow but nothing worse. Now she has something to hold over you. She might go bearing tales to her father. What should we do then, eh?"

"Very sorry, sir. It won't happen again, sir."

"You bloody liar. I'll tell you what *will* happen again, until we're off this damned barge, because I'm giving you an order: you'll dance attendance on that slattern as discreetly as you possibly can without her father finding you out. You'll do whatever she wants, as often as she wants, and if you have to use your powers of persuasion to keep her happy, you will do so. In fact, you must. By the time we step ashore at Ruschuk I want that girl convinced you're a dear friend for whom she wishes nothing but the best in the regrettable but utterly necessary affairs that will part the two of you, never to meet again."

". . . But, sir, that's—it—altering her perceptions in that manner— that would be as though I'd raped her."

"Ah! *Now* he feels compunction. How very unfortunate for your conscience, Bell-Fairfax, since you henceforth have no choice in the matter. I point out that you may avoid this sort of consequence in the future by exerting your self-control."

"Yes, sir."

At the end of a week they were lean, badly laundered and eager to see the last of the barge. The bargeman's daughter waved cheerfully to Bell-Fairfax as he slunk ashore at Ruschuk, where there were both laundresses and restaurants. He endured a great many acid remarks from his companions before at last they crossed the Danube into Wallachia.

"Didn't have to report to the British Consul anywhere else," muttered Pengrove. Hobson shrugged. They were sitting in an antechamber in the consulate in Bucharest, with their trunks piled around them. Ludbridge had vanished into an inner office, upon giving a certain password to a clerk.

"Any place the Russians are, you have to be careful with your papers," Hobson said.

"Shame their revolution failed," murmured Bell-Fairfax.

"What, the Wallachians? Weren't they like our Chartists?"

"Yes, but . . . this isn't England."

"This bit of it is," said Pengrove cheerily. "Not likely to get shot by any glowering Russians or Turks in here, what? Which is more than one can say out there." He waved a hand at the window. "Occupying troops that look as though they'd just as soon open fire on each other as the revolutionaries, and a new puppet prince with the Czar's fingers twitching his strings."

"We could have kept going up the Danube," said Hobson mournfully. "We might have gone all the way to Austria. I've heard it's very pleasant in Vienna."

"Not worth spending another few weeks in the company of Konstantin the Bargeman and his charming daughter, though, what?" Pengrove elbowed Bell-Fairfax, who gave him an evil look

Hobson shuddered and shook his head. "What's the point of coming here, then? You're not to take any photographs. I saw Ludbridge's orders. 'Proceed to Bucharest HQ for further instructions,' that was all they said."

"So they did," said Ludbridge sharply, emerging from an inner office. "And now I have further instructions, and you'll know what you're to know when I damned well choose to tell you."

"Yes, sir, sorry, sir," they chorused.

"Are our passports all arranged now?" added Pengrove.

"In a manner of speaking. Get those trunks up off the floor! We've got a march ahead of us."

"Are we going to a hotel?" inquired Bell-Fairfax, hoisting Ludbridge's trunk, which was the largest.

"No," said Ludbridge. "We're going downstairs."

Staggering under their luggage, they descended a staircase, and then another, and at last, after Ludbridge flashed a pass at another clerk who unlocked a door for them, they descended a still narrower stair, and found themselves in what appeared to be the consulate's basement. "Perhaps we took a wrong turn?" said Pengrove.

"No," said Ludbridge. He opened a broom closet, which did in fact contain a broom, a mop and a bucket. He leaned down, touched a particular nail head in the side of the cabinet, and the whole closet swung back. A tunnel was revealed, descending beyond, vaulted brick painted white, and lit by a series of vacuum lamps.

"I say, one feels quite at home!" said Pengrove.

"Get in," said Ludbridge, and when they had all dragged their trunks through he stepped into the tunnel as well and carefully closed the door and cabinet behind them. "Now keep going, and kindly oblige me by picking up the pace."

They trooped along the tunnel for what seemed like miles and very likely was, with no change in the prospect before them: the same neatly painted brick walls and an endless succession of vacuum lamps overhead, around which Bell-Fairfax had to duck his head lest he strike them with the crown of his hat. Eventually, however, they heard a dim roaring sound ahead.

"That's a waterfall," said Bell-Fairfax.

"Got it in one," said Ludbridge, panting. He offered no further comment and they continued on, and within a few more minutes emerged into an immense cavern, lit by vacuum lamps suspended on cables from the ceiling. At either end there was a round opening, seemingly the mouths of cylindrical tunnels in both directions; the distance between them was spanned by a cable above, and what looked for all the world like rail tracks below. In fact, the whole of the cavern resembled a subterranean railway station, with the only out-of-place elements being the complex of turbines and roaring waterfall, some three stories high, on the other side of the tracks. A uniformed porter with a baggage cart approached them.

"May I take your bags, gentlemen?" he said, in English only slightly accented.

"Oh, *thank* you," said Hobson, nearly weeping with relief. They loaded their trunks on the cart and he wheeled it away to what was clearly a loading area, for there were other trunks and crates stacked there.

"This way," said Ludbridge, striding off to the rather surreal-looking ticket booth—handsomely ornamented with a peaked roof and ginger-bread decoration—that sat near the track.

"Something's wrong," said Bell-Fairfax. "This can't be a railway station."

"And why not, boy?"

Bell-Fairfax craned his neck, tilted his head. "There's no smell of coal. No steam. No cinders."

"Fancy that," said Ludbridge. He leaned into the ticket counter. The clerk looked up at him and smiled politely.

"What becomes of illusions?" the clerk inquired.

"We dispel them."

"And we are everywhere. Four passages?"

"Yes, please."

"Calais or Aalborg?"

"Aalborg."

"May I see your remittance card?"

"Yes, sorry," said Ludbridge, and reached into his coat for it while behind him the others exchanged glances and Pengrove mouthed in silence, *Aalborg?* Ludbridge handed over a printed card to the clerk, who punched it four times and returned it. He pulled four green tickets from a reel and passed them across his counter to Ludbridge.

"You have a wait of approximately fifteen minutes. Please be seated."

Ludbridge exhaled in relief and stepped away from the counter. "There now! If you lot had dawdled we'd have missed it, and there won't be another for a week." He passed out their tickets and led them to a row of wrought-iron benches, where they took seats.

"What kind of railway uses no coal and only has trains once a week?" asked Hobson.

"Secret ones," said Ludbridge. "And, yes, we're going to Denmark."

He said no more on the subject, but pulled out his cigar case and was soon puffing away contentedly on a cigar. Pengrove, watching him, saw the cloud of smoke about Ludbridge's head suddenly disperse, blown backward; at the same moment he felt a rush of air on his own face. He looked around and saw dropped tickets flying like autumn leaves, whirling and scattering in the torrent of air that was pouring from the circular tunnel in the southern wall of the cavern.

A moment later an extraordinary thing emerged from the tunnel. It resembled a gigantic serpent made of gleaming brass. The riveted apertures of its eyes were windows, behind whose pale-blue transparency a pair of uniformed men could be glimpsed, apparently seated at a control panel. In its grinning jaws it held a faceted jewel, which threw a brilliant beam of light forward. A single horn projected from the top of its skull, and where a disc on the top of its horn touched the overhead wire a continuous shower of blue sparks ran and fell.

Revolving wheels and the subsequent emergence of railway cars behind it made plain that this was, indeed, a locomotive engine; and yet there was no billowing smoke and only the slightest noise, a smooth humming punctuated by the faint clatter of rails.

"Ah," said Ludbridge, getting to his feet. "Five minutes early. I thought it might be. Aren't you glad you hurried when you were told? Has every boy his ticket?"

"Yes, sir," the others chorused, rather shaken. The train slowed to a stop. A door in the side of the first car opened, and a uniformed man stood within looking at them expectantly.

"Passengers to Aalborg?"

"Four, sir," called Ludbridge, and led them across the platform.

"It's a Galvanic Locomotive," he explained, as they settled into their compartment. "Powered by the turbines, which are powered by the waterfall diverted from the river. Powered by rivers all the way across Europe, actually; there are ten different turbine banks on the route. No smoke. No coaling stops. No noise to speak of. No boiler explosions. No collisions, for there's only the one train and it simply goes round and round."

"Why did we build it from Bucharest to Aalborg?" Pengrove asked. "Wouldn't, I don't know, London to Paris or Rome have been a little more useful?"

"Perhaps," said Ludbridge. "But we didn't build it. Oh, we built the railway line, no question of that; but the tunnel was the gift of our Informant. In the letter of '24, I think it was. Instructed us to dig in a certain spot and there was the tunnel, bored who knows how many ages ago, ready for our use."

"The letter of 1824?" said Bell-Fairfax, with a curious smile.

"So I'm told." Ludbridge looked up at the door. Rather than opening on the outer air, as in a steam railway carriage, it opened onto an enclosed corridor that ran the length of the train. A uniformed steward had just entered the section beside their compartment, and raised his hand to rap on the window. Hobson jumped up and opened the door.

"Sirs." The steward touched the brim of his cap. "Welcome to the Galvanic Express to Aalborg. Your luncheon menus," he added, and proffered four cards printed with descriptions of various dishes. "Will you take your meals in the restaurant car, or would you prefer to dine here?"

"In the restaurant, I think," said Ludbridge.

"Very good, sir; I shall arrange to have a table set for four. The same arrangements for dinner?"

"Yes, please."

"And will you require the services of a bootblack, barber or laundress?"

"All three, I believe."

"Very good, sir; the barber will call at eight o'clock tomorrow morning. Items to be laundered should be placed in this compartment"— the steward demonstrated a sliding panel on the left side of the door—"where they may be collected without the necessity of disturbing you, for there is a corresponding panel opening on the corridor. Boots to be cleaned should be placed in this compartment to the right. I will return in fifteen minutes to take your orders, and luncheon will be served at noon promptly in the restaurant, which is in Car Number Six. May I answer any questions?"

"Not at present, thank you," said Ludbridge. The steward bowed and left them. Directly the compartment door had shut, there were whoops of gleeful laughter from the younger Residentials. Ludbridge looked on benignly.

"Look at this!" crowed Bell-Fairfax. "Oyster patties! Tournedos of beef filets. Fricandeau of veal. Sweetbreads. Terrine de fois gras. Stuffed shoulder of lamb. Terrapin bisque. Asparagus!"

"There's a wine list on the back," said Hobson. "Oh, my sainted aunt."

"I shall wake up soon and find myself back on that beastly barge, with nothing for breakfast but a lump of cheese and a crust," said Pengrove. "Good God, fancy getting the mud of the Danube off our shoes at last! And a real laundress ironing one's smalls. Utter bliss."

"Just don't make pigs of yourselves," said Ludbridge. "It's four days to Aalborg."

"And . . . this is all some sort of ancient mining tunnel?" Bell-Fairfax peered out the window at the rock walls rolling past.

"No one knows," said Ludbridge.

"Perhaps the Romans built it," said Hobson.

"An immense circle from Denmark to France to Wallachia? Bit beyond even their engineers, I should think," said Ludbridge. "It's been speculated it's a natural geologic feature, like one of those, what-d'ye-call-'ems, lava tubes in the Sandwich Islands. I have my doubts. It's a bit odd how it's all one diameter the whole way through, and runs close to underground water sources at just the places one would need them, if one were going to run a system of galvanic water-powered turbines."

"But what could it be, then?" Bell-Fairfax lowered his menu and stared at Ludbridge. Ludbridge shrugged.

"There are rumors that our Informant—whoever he, or they, might be—built it. You heard the story about the meeting at Ostia, I suppose, when you were first recruited?"

"Some chap visited them from the future, I was told," said Hobson.

"I, too," said Pengrove.

"And I," said Bell-Fairfax.

"Well, there you are. If the Society discovers how to travel through time, at some point in the distant future—and clearly they will—then the first thing they'll do, quite sensibly, is go back into the past and guarantee that that traveler walks into that house at Ostia on that particular day, and assures the Old Members that they must carry on their good fight. And then, what *I* would do next—and clearly they have done—is send the annual letters with helpful advice and instruction, based on their foreknowledge of what is to come."

"Quite true," said Pengrove. Ludbridge leaned forward, his eyes narrowed.

"But think for a moment about what that *means*," he said. "If you had the ability to travel through time, would you stop there? I wouldn't. If you knew that the very existence of that paradise of *technologia* in which you dwelt depended on some poor benighted band of fellows struggling along through the past, wouldn't you give them all the help you could?

"I think *they* built this tunnel, for our use. If they can travel through time, is it too great a stretch of one's imagination to think that they also possess machines that can burrow through rock as easily as an earthworm burrows through loam? Who knows what they might or mightn't be able to do? You think this railway is a marvel, and yet we built it ourselves, simply employing well-known scientific principles our fellow men have been insufficiently visionary to put to use. Can you imagine the machines we'll build, centuries hence?

"There have always been stories, you know, of mysterious strangers coming to the assistance of Society members who find themselves in difficult straits. Good angels, if you will. They appear at precisely the right moment, they guide one out of danger, they miraculously happen to have money or a fast horse or whatever it is one needs—and then they vanish." Ludbridge made a sleight-of-hand gesture like a conjuror, and the stump of his cigar vanished from between his fingers.

The others stared at him, openmouthed. Bell-Fairfax in particular, he thought, looked like a child who had just been told about Father Christmas for the first time.

"Sirs?" The steward rapped politely on the compartment door. "May I take your orders now?"

"Yes, thank you." Ludbridge smiled and handed him the menu card, then produced his cigar from thin air and flicked away a bit of ash. "I'll have the terrapin bisque, poached salmon and green peas, with your best sauterne. Chaps? Tell the nice gentleman what you'll have."

They left their compartment at noon and proceeded along the corridor, past other compartments, to the restaurant car. For all that its windows looked out on black primordial rock, it was elegantly appointed and beautifully lit by vacuum lamps behind tinted shades. Each table bore a single fresh rosebud in a cut-crystal vase; a string quartet played quietly on a raised dais at the rear of the car. The steward conducted them to their table and retired; the moment they had seated themselves, waiters swept in and served their meal, departing with a bow after pouring the wine.

"If I wake from this dream now, I believe I shall throw myself in the Danube," said Pengrove, considering a spoonful of terrapin bisque.

Ludbridge chuckled. "It's real enough. Enjoy it while you can; it may well be rather more rough in the Baltic, in autumn."

"Are we going to Russia?" asked Hobson.

"You'll know when I tell you," said Ludbridge imperturbably. "Do you often discuss private matters in eating houses, may I ask?"

"Of course not, but surely—" Hobson waved a hand at the other diners in the car. There were a pair of gentlemen in fezzes at the near table, a blonde lady and gentleman—alike enough to be brother and sister—at the table just beyond, and a solitary gentleman in a military uniform seated near the string quartet. "They're our own people, what?"

"Quite true. Still, it doesn't do to get out of the habit of prudence, does it?"

"It certainly doesn't," remarked one of the gentlemen wearing a fez.

"There, you see?" Ludbridge waved his soup spoon at the man, who acknowledged him with a slight bow. "You never know who might be listening."

The Galvanic Express carried them on, gliding under Europe so smoothly there was scarcely a vibration in the wineglasses at meals. No scream of whistles, no Dopplering noise anywhere; only the clink and rattle of cutlery and the soothing music produced by the string quartet punctuated the hours.

Each evening, while they were at dinner, their compartment was converted to a dormitory by the steward, for there were ingeniously designed bunks concealed within the walls. The lavatory cabinet included a shower bath, in addition to other remarkable refinements in its fixtures. Their clothes were duly laundered, their boots cleaned, and a barber came and put them in trim—for they had all, as Pengrove expressed it, taken on the appearance of Romantic poets. A repairs technician took Pengrove's talbotype camera away and returned it the next day in nearly pristine condition, though the lens tube still bore visible dents.

Quite recent editions of the London *Times*, *Punch*, and *The Illustrated Weekly News* were available for their amusement, when they weren't playing cards. Hobson was given a considerable holiday, for the Aetheric Transmitter could not be used so far under the earth, and when he discovered there was a bar in Car No. Nine he wandered off there of an afternoon and generally returned breathing peppermint fumes. Ludbridge observed him closely, scowling, but said nothing before the others.

"And all good things come to an end," said Pengrove with a sigh, as they watched the Galvanic Express pull away from the platform. The grinning head and car after car vanished into the tunnel, bound for Calais; the last they saw of it was the fanciful leviathan's tail fitted on the end car, from which a glowing lantern hung pendant.

"So they do," said Ludbridge. "Hoist your trunks, then; we'll have a devil of a climb."

But even as they were collecting their baggage, a man approached them. He was blond bearded and ruddy, and pushed a baggage cart before him. "Mr. Ludbridge," he called. Ludbridge turned and saw him.

"What becomes of illusions?"

"We dispel them," said the man, wheeling the cart up to Ludbridge's trunk. His English was excellent.

"And we are everywhere."

"So we are. Hagen Stemme, at your service."

They shook hands and Ludbridge added: "So sorry to hear you're losing Orsted."

"Ah! So are we. Still, it has been a life well lived. The Kabinet of Wonders welcomes you to the north. Will you please to step this way? We have an ascending chamber to the inn, which is much more convenient than the stairs."

So they were spared a considerable climb, a fact they appreciated more with every minute that passed in the chamber before it finally bumped to a gentle stop. The door opened and they stepped into what appeared to be someone's bedroom, with a heavily curtained bed in one corner and old-fashioned dark paneling.

"The guest room," said Stemme, as a section of panel slid shut behind them. "You have a suite of four. Nicely arranged, is it not? No one ever sees the guests arrive."

"Where are we?" Bell-Fairfax inquired.

"The Green Lion of Aalborg," Stemme replied. "It made sense to build it over the railway station. Did you enjoy your journey?"

"Rather," said Pengrove. Stemme laughed and rolled his eyes.

"Who would go to France in a coastal packet, I ask you, when he could get there in such luxury? I will leave you to unpack. Here are your keys; when you have refreshed yourselves, come down to the private room and have a glass of akvavit."

When he had left them, Hobson inquired, "What's the Kabinet of Wonders?"

"Same as the Magi," said Ludbridge, tossing him his key. "Only not Eastern. Name goes back to the days of old King Rudolf, Holy Roman Emperor in Shakespeare's day. He was a bloody poor excuse for a king but he loved machines. Kept a whole court of inventors, astronomers, alchemists, that sort of thing. We were rather heavily involved with him—Kepler, for one—and the northern branch kept the name."

"Why didn't we try to influence him to be a better king?" asked Bell-Fairfax.

"That wasn't our job," said Ludbridge. "We might have used our influence to teach him *his* job, but what then? If he'd paid more attention to being Holy Roman Emperor, he wouldn't have spent so much money in the cause of Science. And even if we had expended a great deal of effort trying to make him a virtuous, enlightened prince in the Socratic mold, it would all have gone for nothing once he'd died and a new fellow got the throne. Men don't last, my boy. Machines do."

Having unpacked, they trooped downstairs and found themselves in the common room of a bustling waterfront inn. Autumn dusk was falling blue beyond the windows, over the cold sea, and each lamp had a halo of golden fog around it. Stemme was waiting for them, slouched in the entrance to a paneled snug, and waved them over. They saw within seats drawn up to a table, whereupon was a bottle of akvavit, glasses, and a tray of savories.

"Doubtless you are stuffed like geese from your last meal, but the cold makes for a sharp appetite," said Stemme, closing the door of the snug after them. He poured out drinks and handed them round. "To the great day!"

They drank. Stemme tossed his back like water and set his glass down, looking at them with shrewd eyes. "So, gentlemen! First, I have a message for you from London. The American Breedlove and his men were *not* apprehended; it is thought they have left Constantinople altogether, and so you are to continue to watch for them."

"Damn," said Ludbridge. "I suppose that goes for all field operatives?"

"London was quite specific that you, personally, were to look for them." Stemme shrugged. "And a message came from Constantinople: it would appear that Breedlove's group are being hunted by the Franklins. There was some unpleasantness—a death?—and apparently the dead man was one of the Franklins' party."

"Sorry to hear it," said Ludbridge. "Still, good to know they're dealing with their own embarrassment. And better to know Breedlove's people haven't got pyrethanatos."

"Was that how the Franklins' man died?" Stemme shuddered. He refilled and raised his glass. "To a dead brother, then."

They drank again and Stemme set his glass down. "Now. What may the Kabinet do for you?"

"Get us into Kronstadt Fortress," said Ludbridge.

Stemme leaned backward. "Is that a joke?"

"Unfortunately, no," said Ludbridge.

"Do you know anything about the place?"

"No. I had hoped you would brief us."

"Then let me show you Kronstadt Fortress." Stemme turned. Behind him on the wainscoting was a design of carved flowers. He pressed the center of one flower and a section of paneling on the wall opposite the door slid back, revealing a square of pure white canvas perhaps a yard across. He reached up to the pierced tin lamp that hung above the table and pulled; it slid down on a chain quite easily, with a faint ratcheting noise, and stopped at just below head height. He opened its front shutter, revealing a vacuum lamp within. From another concealed panel he drew forth a small box, which appeared to contain magic lantern slides. After sorting through them briefly he selected one and inserted it in the lantern, and turned a switch.

Instantly an image was projected on the canvas, clear and sharp: a map in the modern style, distinct as a photograph. It showed a deep narrow bay, at the end of which sat St. Petersburg. Halfway down the bay, in its center, was an island. It was marked with a small town and a fortress, the fortress having a clear aim across the water to either side of the island. As effective a defense as this was, however, it was augmented by a handful of other, smaller fortresses, squat cylinders of brick rising straight from the water, scattered across the bay to both right and left.

"To begin with, there is not one fortress of Kronstadt. There are all these," said Stemme. "You would say they are like a chain across the bay, yes? And there are other barriers you cannot see. The bay is shallow. In winter it freezes solid. But even in high summer with a boat of shallow draft, what do you suppose would happen to an enemy ship if it attempted to run the gauntlet of those forts?"

Bell-Fairfax was staring at the map in horror. "It would be madness," he cried. "Are those gun emplacements an accurate illustration?"

Stemme nodded somberly.

"Sir, it couldn't be done," Bell-Fairfax said to Ludbridge. "Nelson himself couldn't have done it. Not without being blown to pieces."

Ludbridge nodded grimly, not taking his eyes from the image. "So it would appear."

"And in any case, getting *in* is not the issue. All freighters must put in at Kronstadt to have their cargo minutely examined by corrupt officials. The concern for them is getting *out*; some have been detained there for weeks, for nothing worse than attempting to enter the country with Russian money on their persons. I do not like to think what would happen to anyone they apprehended in the act of sabotage. May I ask why it would be necessary to attempt such a thing?" said Stemme, shutting off the lamp and removing the glass slide.

"You know there's going to be a war," said Ludbridge, sitting down. He helped himself to pickled herring. Stemme nodded as he put away the glass slide.

"We have been Informed."

"It has been suggested that intelligence regarding St. Petersburg's defenses is a desirable thing."

"Has it?" Stemme pressed the button in the wainscoting, retracting both the screen and the lamp. "Only intelligence? And desirable for the Society? Or for England?"

Ludbridge chewed deliberately before he answered, and began assembling a sandwich from among the savories and dark rye on the table. "Both, I suppose. Help yourselves, you lot, this is excellent. Eat something, Bell-Fairfax, you're still white as a ghost. Here's the way of it, my friend: it is felt in certain circles that a victory for Britain is *de facto* a victory for the Society. Britain will spread, *is spreading* civilization through its colonies, all across the world. The Czar's authority serves only to advance the greater glory of the Czar; our queen's authority serves to advance the mercantile classes, which promote *technologia* in their own self-interest.

"However much we may dislike the idea of an empire, for now Britain is clearly the horse to be backed."

Stemme shook his head. "Slippery. You will be seen as taking sides out of patriotism."

"I know. I thought the same thing myself, when I received my orders. Orders are orders, however."

"Our Russian members are unlikely to see it quite that way, you know." Stemme sat and poured himself another akvavit.

"Well, they needn't concern themselves; as you've just shown us, we're unlikely to be able to do much more than report back to London that Kronstadt is impregnable." Ludbridge bit into his sandwich. He made ecstatic sounds. "Mmf! Wonderful!"

"I will pass on your compliments to the cook." Stemme relaxed a little, smiling. "Is there anything else we can do for you, since you agree that it would be foolish to attempt Kronstadt?"

Ludbridge shrugged, chewing steadily. He swallowed and said, "We could look at a few lesser sites, I suppose. Might you provide us with a boat?"

"Of course. We have a yacht, very well appointed. Where would you like to go?"

"Oh, here and there," replied Ludbridge, helping himself to the akvavit. "Finland?"

The *Orn* was a sweet craft, if completely devoid of power sources advanced or arcane. She glided down the Kattegat effortlessly, to the Copenhagen roadstead. At Copenhagen they went ashore with the talbotype and took a few humorous pictures, posing Bell-Fairfax and Hobson lying under the trees at Rosenborg Gardens, clutching akvavit bottles and shamming unconsciousness.

From Copenhagen they continued down into the Baltic and made northeast, standing out well to starboard of Bornholm, north past the Oland light. They went ashore at Gotland and posed Hobson holding his nose in front of some cottages where salt cod were hung out on lines to dry, like washing.

Still north and northeast, and through the first nasty gale of autumn; there was plenty of sea-room but even Stemme and the pilot got seasick, and Hobson and Pengrove were too miserable for description. Pengrove wasted a hat-camera shot on an image of Ludbridge and Bell-Fairfax sitting side by side on a locker, stiffly upright as dogs on point, listening to the howling wind in the shrouds with identical expressions of grim anticipation on their faces.

The *Orn* brought them through it all safely, and the next day they bore due north to the bewildering labyrinth of the Aalands. Here they threaded their way between endless little green islands, and attempted to put in at Bomarsund. A Russian official in a fast cutter refused them, and went so far as to board them and demand to see their papers. He glared at the talbotype camera and, in examining it, managed to drop and break it, with a not-quite-disguised deliberateness. He managed to conceal a smile as the forlorn Englishman in the absurd straw hat picked up the brass lens tube, which had completely parted company with the box, and looked as though he might burst into tears.

Thereafter Pengrove leaned sadly at the rail, gazing out at the vast modern fortifications and fiddling with his lapel. The Russian, having had his temper soothed by the tactful Danish captain, accepted a glass of akvavit and departed.

"It was just as well he broke the camera," Stemme told Ludbridge, as they watched the cutter sailing away. "Photographing a fortress is uncomfortably close to spying, you know."

"Well, of course, in time of war," said Ludbridge. "The case could be made, however, that timely warning helps save lives on both sides."

"That's one way of looking at it," said Stemme, with a rueful laugh. "Especially if I want to ease my conscience."

He went off to relieve the pilot at the wheel. Bell-Fairfax, who had been leaning at the rail beside them, edged closer to Ludbridge.

"We *are* spies, of course," he said in a low voice.

"Of course we are, son."

"But it was true, wasn't it, what you said about Britain spreading civilization more effectively than anyone else?"

"Yes, quite true."

Bell-Fairfax stared out at the island coastlines, slipping away aft as Stemme took them out to sea again. "Looking at all those little homesteads, I couldn't help thinking of China again."

"Ah! Good point. Damned barbaric interlude, no question of that. Still . . . one rides the horse, even though the horse seldom acts like a gentleman. As long as he is capable of carrying us to our destination, we don't look too closely at his morals."

"*We* being the Society?"

"*We* being the Society. I don't envy those members living in the Roman Empire, at its height. Think of the compromises with their consciences *they* must have had to make, eh? No, we have it a great deal easier. Any nation commits crimes, in its long career, and England's no exception. Still, progress has been made since Rome, and England's star is in the ascendant. We're lucky to be Britons."

"I would like to be proud of my country," said Bell-Fairfax quietly.

"Of course you would." Ludbridge took out a cigar and lit it. Puffing, he waved out his lucifer and went on: "And I've no doubt that when the great day comes and there are no empires any longer, but only a council of enlightened nations, England will be foremost among them. Still, you know, it doesn't really matter who rules that council. The Englishman will look at the black or Chinese and see only a fellow man, as like him as a brother. The black or Chinese will look back out of the mirror and see the same thing. That will be the day wars end, you mark my words."

They flew before another gale into Helsinki, through patches of ice-crust and under falling sleet, and presented such a wretched spectacle as they struggled ashore that the Russian harbormaster waved them into his parlor and served out vodka by the stove all around before he even asked to see their papers. His kindness extended to directing them to a hotel, whence they staggered and dried themselves.

The storm raged for two days. When it abated at last they emerged and wandered along the quays, with Pengrove busily deploying the hat-camera to photograph the shipyards and fortifications. They climbed a hill and had a splendid view of the fortress-island of Sveaborg. After purchasing supplies and sailing out of the harbor they made a slow circuit of the walls there, and Pengrove photographed them from every angle.

1850: "There Are Shades Which Will Not Vanish"

"It's just as daunting in the flesh," murmured Bell-Fairfax. They were standing at the rail of the *Orn* as she slipped through the narrow channel past Kronstadt. Before them, behind them and to either side, the multiple fortresses rose straight from the water, like so many scowling policemen blocking a road, and the water was crowded with steamers and sailing vessels flying the flags of every seafaring nation.

As a mere yacht the *Orn* was not required to put in at Kronstadt, having no cargo to declare, but a Russian pilot had come aboard and taken the wheel. A Russian customs official had come aboard with him and made them all turn out their pockets to prove that they had no Russian money in them, which would have been tantamount to admitting that they were counterfeiters trying to destroy the Russian economy. Satisfied that they were not, the official was now going through their luggage on deck.

Ludbridge, with a bland smile, opened all the false compartments of his trunk and displayed endless unsavory bundles of unwashed laundry. The Russian looked disgusted and gestured for him to close it up.

Coming to the Aetheric Transmitter, the Russian scowled at the gold letters and said something to Stemme, presumably asking what a Pressley's Patented Magnetismator might be. Stemme replied, presumably explaining. The Russian shook his head and said something else.

"Bugger," muttered Ludbridge. "What's he want?"

"He says he will have to confiscate it," said Stemme.

"Oh, I say, that won't do at all!" Hobson stepped forward, pulling his doctor's certificate from inside his coat. "Look here—have to have this for my health, what? Get the, er, nervous prostrations without it, indeed I do!" He held the certificate under the customs official's nose while Stemme hastily translated. The Russian peered at the certificate, uncomprehending. He shook his head and said something else.

"He says he thinks it is contraband."

"Contraband! What? No! Look, *this* is what happens when I can't use it!" cried Hobson, and proceeded to throw a fairly good imitation of a fit, beginning with a generalized palsy and intensifying it until he dropped to the deck, flailing about and spraying spittle. "Help! Help! Oh, my poor nerves! Oh, what shall I do?"

"Here you are, poor chap!" Bell-Fairfax fell to his knees and, opening the case, withdrew the earpieces and put them on Hobson's head, for Hobson's hat had come off in his dramatic demonstration. He reached back and turned a switch on the transmitter. Hobson went limp at once, with his tongue lolling out and an expression of beatific peace on his vacant features.

"You see?" Bell-Fairfax stood up, looking into the customs official's face. "He must have his machine. You really cannot take it from him. You understand that now, I'm sure."

Stemme translated. The Russian, staring back at Bell-Fairfax, blinked and frowned. "Is this going to work when he doesn't understand what you're saying?" said Ludbridge under his breath.

"I sincerely hope so," said Bell-Fairfax, smiling at the Russian, who said something back to Stemme.

"He says you should not take such an invalid traveling," said Stemme. Bell-Fairfax held out his hands, palms up.

"Yes, very true, but our poor friend does so want to see the magnificent city of St. Petersburg before he dies! It has long been his dearest wish, for London has nothing to compare with it."

The Russian grunted. He pulled his gaze away from Bell-Fairfax and, stepping back, prodded the transmitter with his foot. He said something.

"He says to close it up. He must seal all your luggage," said Stemme.

This, apparently, meant that they were cleared for going ashore. The pilot guided them through brackish channels and the tidal mudflats of the Neva, leaving the Gulf of Finland behind them. Low islands were passed, to port and starboard, and then abruptly the geometry of a modern city was around them on all sides, as they moored before the customs house on the battery point known as the Strelka.

Here they disembarked and were obliged to go through inspection again. Stemme and the *Orn*'s steersman bid them a pleasant farewell, having no business with the officials other than to certify that they were dropping off chartered passengers and were bound back to Denmark.

"But you will not have to wait long before your contact arrives," said Stemme in a low voice, shaking Ludbridge's hand as they emerged from the customs office. "Safe journeys, my friend. And enjoy your time in St. Petersburg! It may be a city built on the dead, but it is rationally and geometrically built on the dead."

"What did that mean?" inquired Bell-Fairfax, as they watched the *Orn* backing and filling, preparatory to putting out to sea again.

"No idea," said Ludbridge.

"Can we hire a porter?" said Pengrove, sitting down on his trunk.

"No idea," said Ludbridge, looking around. "Here, you! *Parlez-vous Français?*"

This produced a notable lack of response in those working along the waterfront, though one or two persons gave Ludbridge rather a cold look and continued on their way.

"Hallo! Don't suppose any of you lot know where a man might purchase cigars?" Ludbridge bellowed.

"I think this chap knows," observed Hobson, pointing to a Russian who was approaching them with an agitated air. He was stout and bespectacled, round and red of face.

"What becomes of illusions?" he said in English, addressing Ludbridge.

"We dispel them."

"And we are everywhere. You would be Mr. Ludbridge? Cyril Boriso-vich Nikitin, at your service."

"How d'you do?" Ludbridge shook his hand. "My associates: Mr. Hobson, Mr. Pengrove, Mr. Bell-Fairfax."

Nikitin shook hands with them, though when he came to Bell-Fairfax he had to crane his neck back to look up at him. "My God! What are you, Peter the Great? That's a compliment! He was our greatest success."

"I'm afraid he is rather tall, yes," said Ludbridge. "We're all very pleased to meet you. Might we arrange for a porter or two?"

"Immediately," said Nikitin, and after a moment's impassioned ha-rangue had convinced a porter to load their trunks onto a cart and fol-low them along the waterfront to a great building on the other side of the Strelka, facing out across another branch of the Neva. Here the porter was paid off and the baggage unloaded; Nikitin bid them wait a moment and ran inside for another handcart.

While he was gone they stared around. The vast edifice before which they stood and the equally impressive edifices across the river were all of a pastel wedding-cake prettiness, beautiful examples of Enlighten-ment architecture. Only here and there, where a gilded dome rose against the skyline, were they reminded that this was Russia. The whole effect was of lightness, spaciousness, mathematical and geometric per-fection.

"Here we go," said Nikitin breathlessly, emerging with the cart. "Load these on and we'll go into my office. I have an elevating room that will take us down to the headquarters. This is the museum. Wel-come to the Kabinet of Wonders in the Kunstkamera! Clever, yes?"

"Not entirely by chance, I imagine?"

"No, of course not, though it was harder than you'd think—His Royal Highness came to distrust us at the end, such a pity, but by that time he didn't really trust anybody. But what can one do? A czar is a czar. That was Peter the Great, young man, and I hope you won't take offense—he too was extraordinarily tall, just about your height."

"None taken, sir," said Edward, but a little stiffly nonetheless.

Nikitin led them in and through a maze of corridors to a small office. "Here we are . . . please excuse the untidiness, won't you? My dear young giant, will you be so kind as to reach up and push on that bit of crown molding? Yes! How wonderful! I always need to climb to the very top of the stepladder, myself. And . . . there."

A section of wall panel slid open 'and revealed the ascending room beyond. They followed Nikitin inside and the compartment promptly dropped with them, a smooth descent to an unknown depth.

"This is an exceptionally beautiful city," said Pengrove.

"Thank you! It's the very antithesis of a medieval warren of hovels, wouldn't you agree?"

"Oh, yes, sir. I wonder if you might explain something—I hope you won't take offense—it's simply that Mr. Stemme said something a bit puzzling—"

"Stemme? Yes, good man, Stemme. What remark was that?"

"He said this was a city built on the dead."

"And so it is." Nikitin turned and gave them a somber look. The room slid to a stop and the door opened; they stepped out into a brick-lined corridor, clean and dry, lit by vacuum lamps, but with an unmistakable smell of dankness somewhere.

"Our czar who built this city, Peter the Great, won this land from Sweden but it was nothing, a swamp, a muddy mess with only the advantage that it opened on the sea. He loved the sea, that man. And our people, which is to say the Kabinet of Wonders, had tutored him to love the modern world too. We made certain that the young boy traveled to other lands and saw how accomplished, how civilized and progressive, other countries were. He went home and, as we had meant him to do, set about dragging Old Russia out of the medieval darkness. He did many excellent things for his country, our young man. But he ruled like a medieval despot, because that was the only way any czar had ever ruled.

"This city, yes, is as beautiful as a dream. He brought in splendid minds from the finest courts of the West to design it. Then he brought in serfs, ragged and beaten slaves, and worked them to death raising its foundations from the water. It was hard to build solid land, in all these mudflats. Hard to get enough stones. The serfs died in their thousands and when they did, their bodies were thrown into the excavations, shoring up the walls.

"Come, I'll show you something." He sidestepped into a small passageway and brought them to an alcove. It opened on a dark room, and as they entered they had the impression the place was a chapel. Banks of flickering candles lit it. Before them were six tombs of dark red granite, innocent of any names or dates. On the wall above each one was a life-sized painting on a wooden panel, like an icon. Each depicted a man in scarlet robes, richly trimmed and ornamented in gold leaf. But there were no Cyrillic letters spelling out names or titles, nor were the figures staring forward like saints, nor were their hands raised to bless.

Instead, each man held in his slack hand a tool of some kind, chisel or shovel or mattock. Each man's face was individual, distinct, yet all were gray, lined and exhausted looking, and all had their eyes shut as though they slept.

"Portraits of the dead. We found them when we were digging here, hiding away our headquarters under the museum." Nikitin spoke softly. "They were perfectly preserved; they'd been thrown into anaerobic mud, so deep and so cold they never rotted. We autopsied them, we studied them, we made careful drawings of them, we learned all we could from each dead man, but of course not his name. All we could do for them was give them new burials here, with as much honor and ceremony as we could provide. And they are only six, out of the thousands we know must lie all around us.

"They are martyrs, after all, to the future we wanted to bring to Russia. We think it is good to have them here, to remind us of the human cost of our plans. Remember them, when you walk the streets in the sunlight above."

They went on past other alcoves, but here living men worked or sat in quiet discussion. All in all it was not very different from Downstairs at

Redking's. In a great vaulted room with a roaring fire at one end, Nikitin poured out vodka for them.

"To your very good health," said Ludbridge, raising his glass.

"To the great day," said Nikitin, and they drank. "Ah. We have arranged rooms at a private house for you, on Anglisky Avenue just across the river. We have a private tunnel that connects to it, very useful; no one will see you arrive. This is good, since the Third Section has been more than usually intrusive lately. Not that they are likely to interfere with you much, but it never hurts to obscure one's tracks a little, whoever one may be."

"What's the Third Section?" asked Hobson.

"Our secret police," replied Nikitin. He shook his head and poured himself another shot of vodka. Hobson held out his glass and Nikitin obliged with a refill. "The present czar was not one of our students, you see. We tutored his older brother, Alexander; same story as with Peter the Great. We laid the proper foundation but the instincts of a despot won out in the end . . . and then our man ran off and became a monk and we had little Nicholas Pavlovitch to deal with. Look how long it has taken us to get a single railway in this country!"

"I gather the present fellow is difficult to control?"

"Completely uncontrollable. A fine old reactionary throwback, ruling with an iron fist. Instituted the Third Section. Imagines himself the policeman of Europe, determined to suppress every liberal revolution anywhere.

"Of course we had men in place tutoring the Czarevich, and the man promises well, nothing like his father. But, really, sometimes we feel like a bunch of Sisyphuses down here! We roll the rock of state uphill, and every time we make a little progress the rock slips and goes rolling backward into the Dark Ages."

"Ah! But that's the very reason we've come," said Ludbridge. "We're bringing you a block and tackle, so to speak. You have an Aetheric Transmitter and Receiver set, I believe?"

"We have one, yes. There's a listening post on Zayachy Island."

"Jolly good." Ludbridge rose and went to his trunk. Opening one of the secret compartments, he drew forth a pair of boxes. One was small, perhaps a bit bigger than a deck of playing cards. The other was about the size of a cigar box.

"Now, just regard these." Ludbridge sat down at the table and passed the smaller box to Nikitin. It was plain unpainted wood, with a label printed in Russian.

"Shirt studs?" Wonderingly, Nikitin opened the box and spilled a few out on the table.

"They appear to be, yes. However! Our chaps in Fabrication simply excel in making fully functioning miniatures. Concealed within each of these studs is a transmitter. Wear one of these and your man at his post will be able to hear every word that passes your lips, if he's tuned to the proper frequency. It only remains for you to place a new valet with the Czar. Can that be arranged?"

"We ought to be able to do that much, yes."

"And then, you see, though your czar may be as unmanageable as ever, you will at least have the advantage of being privy to all of his plans. We have found this sort of thing to be profoundly useful, with our prime ministers."

"Wonderful!" Nikitin picked up one of the studs and peered at it closely.

"But here are more toys," said Ludbridge, pushing the larger box forward. It was covered in velvet and fastened with a brass clasp. "What d'you suppose these are, eh?"

"I can't guess."

Ludbridge opened the box with a flourish. "Spectacles. Each one an exact copy of the pair worn by Count Nesselrode. He's your czar's chancellor and foreign minister, yes? Wouldn't it be useful to have advance warning of every move he makes? And there are transistors built into the nosepieces, here, to make certain you do. Get a man in there to substitute one for the count's present pair. Also useful as a costume accessory for one of your politicals, if he finds himself in a position to listen in to secrets, because everything he hears while wearing them will be instantaneously transmitted back to your receiver. Mind you, you'll need to expand your listening post by some five or six fellows."

"We can do that, yes," said Nikitin in delight. He picked up a pair of the spectacles and tried them on. "Who would believe it! Look out, Karl Vasilyevich."

"And Hobson here can train your new men on the receivers," said Ludbridge. "Nor is this all. Would you like permanent transmitters installed in places, as opposed to hidden on people? Council rooms, for example? Audience chambers? We can arrange them."

"I am dazzled at your munificence," said Nikitin. He looked thoughtfully at Ludbridge. "This is an attempt to prevent the coming war, is it not?"

"Well, we very much hope to be able to lessen the catastrophe, if not prevent it altogether."

"And you think we will be able to do that, with these gifts? My friend, we will try, but there is a limit to what's possible. At least until our Alexander Nicolaevich comes to power."

"Probably true," said Ludbridge. "But a better intelligence system will, at least, put you in a better position to profit when your pupil does come to power."

"That cannot be denied," said Nikitin, his smile returning. He reached over and refilled Ludbridge's glass.

"So that's Zayachy Island," observed Hobson, peering across the river. They were walking in a public garden, and for the moment had no audience before whom to behave like imbecile tourists.

"The very place," Ludbridge said.

"Well, I can see why they've got their listening post there." Hobson pointed at the soaring needle-spire of the Peter and Paul Cathedral, rising from behind the frowning walls of the fortress of the same name. "Run a bit of wire up that and it'd improve reception no end. You could pick up bloody China from there."

"With a bit of wire?" Pengrove looked doubtful.

"With a bit of wire. Something old Felmouth showed me, before he sent us out. There's a couple of screw heads at the side of the case, and if you twist a length of copper wire round them and trail it out along a chair or something, you can enhance your signal. It worked in Constantinople."

"Was *that* why you kept moving that beastly footstool in front of my bed where I'd trip over it every time I got up?" demanded Pengrove.

"I suppose so. You'd all still be asleep and snoring, and I'd have to get up early to send the morning report."

"But, look here, I very nearly fractured a toe on three separate occasions!"

Hobson drew out his handkerchief and mimed weeping at him. Pengrove pulled off a glove and brandished it at Hobson. "How dare you mock my discomfort, you beast!"

"If you were any kind of man you'd challenge him to a duel," said Bell-Fairfax, chuckling. A few passers-by had stopped at a distance and were watching them, distinctly unimpressed with British manhood.

"Yes! I shall! Come here, you bounder, let me smite you—" Pengrove swung at Hobson with the glove. Hobson danced away laughing. Pengrove chased him round and round the statuary, giving idiotic little squeals of indignation. Ludbridge lounged back against the base of a statue and, taking out a flask, sipped brandy as he watched them. Bell-Fairfax ran, practically dragging his knuckles, and fetched a couple of longish twigs dropped by a gardener and held them out. Hobson grabbed one on his near circuit and turned to confront Pengrove, waving the twig like a rapier.

"*En garde!*"

"Will you draw steel on me? How dare you, sir, how dare you!" Pengrove hurled his glove at Hobson and grabbed the other twig. They leaped back and forth pretending to duel, and a few children had gathered to watch, laughing and pointing. Suddenly, however, Ludbridge stepped forth and grabbed each of them by their collars.

"Stop it at once," he told them, in a low voice. They looked up at him, startled.

"What d'you mean?" demanded Pengrove. He turned and followed Ludbridge's gaze with his eyes. There on the far edge of the garden were the Reverend Amasa Breedlove and the other three Americans they had seen in Constantinople, staring back at them with the same expressions of disgust on their countenances as they had worn in that city, and something more: suspicion.

"How the deuce did *they* get here?" Bell-Fairfax started forward. Ludbridge let go of Pengrove and grabbed his arm.

"Let 'em be. We know who they are, but they don't know who we are. What do you want to do, fight the War of 1812 over again and get Russian kiddies caught in the cross fire? We'll have to get them, but not here and not just now. Do you understand?"

"Yes, sir."

"Too damned much coincidence for my liking. I expect they'll be thinking the same thing. Turn around, gentlemen; let's take a walk along the riverbank. I've a fancy to go look at the museum again."

They did as Ludbridge told them. Pengrove looked back once, and saw one of the Americans—Jackson, he thought—following them at a distance, along the wide streets nearly deserted but for the occasional droshky-wagon. He mentioned as much to Ludbridge, who grunted and shrugged.

"Is he? Then I've changed my mind. Let's stroll across to the fortress over there. Perhaps we can find a tavern."

The American kept after them along the bridge, doggedly following as far as the north bank of the Neva, where they nearly lost him while making a circuit of the magazine.

"Not subtle, but persistent," said Ludbridge, as they trudged along Bolshoi Avenue. "Must be a backwoodsman. Trained by Red Indians, no doubt. I suppose you wouldn't mind slouching a trifle, Bell-Fairfax? Thank you. Now, we're going to part company. Pengrove and Hobson, perhaps you'd toddle off down the right-hand street at the next corner? Bell-Fairfax, go to the left at the following corner. This is the time to remember all those clever tricks you demonstrated in London. We'll meet back at the house this evening, shall we?"

"Yes, sir." Pengrove and Hobson nodded, and Bell-Fairfax barely stopped himself from saluting. They did as they'd been told; first Pengrove and Hobson left at the next corner, and Bell-Fairfax struck off on his own. Ludbridge continued along Bolshoi Avenue for a short distance before darting down a right-hand street and stepping into a doorway, where he watched for some few minutes before he was satisfied that the American was not following him.

He made his way to the bridge, and there encountered Bell-Fairfax hurrying across, head down. He waited until they were well across before catching up with him.

"The chap must have gone after poor old Pengrove," Ludbridge said.

"I expect he recognized him more readily," Bell-Fairfax replied.

"Where are we?" Ludbridge looked around. "There's the damned customs house again. Come along; I want to go speak with our friend Nikitin."

They found him in his office at the Kunstkamera, filling out forms. He pushed his spectacles up on the bridge of his nose and peered at them.

"Americans?" he said. "Ah, yes. You've seen them, have you? The four all in black? The ones the Franklins have warned us about."

"Even they," said Ludbridge. "We ran afoul of them in Constantinople, I'm afraid, and they recognized us."

Nikitin gestured that Bell-Fairfax should close the door. When Bell-Fairfax had obliged him, Nikitin spoke quietly:

"They were brought here this morning by a member of the diplomatic corps, and given a tour of the museum. I should explain that it is customary to do this, for any distinguished guest. They were treated as though they were some sort of informal ambassadors. I sent a runner up the tunnel to you, but you were all out when he arrived. This will curtail your activities in St. Petersburg, I fear."

"Bound to," said Ludbridge. "Public displays of idiocy, in any case. We can still assist you in setting up the transmitter system before we return to London. But what are we to do?"

"If they have the ear of the Czar, there is a limit to how much we can do," said Nikitin. "Though, thanks to your generous gifts, we can find out just what exactly they are putting *into* the Czar's ear. If they promise him something alarming such as unheard-of weapons to give him supremacy, then we will be obliged to do something quite unpleasant, I suspect. It would be charming if the Franklins would send someone to deal with them first, of course."

"Have you contacted them?"

"I sent them a communication two hours ago. No word back yet. I will let you know, of course, the moment I hear anything. In the meanwhile, you had better avoid the streets, if the Americans recognize you. Use the tunnel to come and go."

"Excellent advice." Ludbridge nodded. "Good day to you, then. Come along, Bell-Fairfax."

"Do you suppose the Americans are really seminary students?" said Bell-Fairfax, as they paced along the tunnel.

"With those pistols? Bloody unlikely," said Ludbridge. "It's not outside the realm of speculation that they might be filibusters *and* spies sent to gather intelligence on the weakness of the Ottomans, in which case the prospect of their getting hold of our devices is even more of a catastrophe. I was under the impression Brother Jonathan was too preoccupied with his own affairs to meddle much in Europe's, but you never know. What does concern me is that they seem to have hooked up with the foreign policy people. I do hope they're not some sort of unofficial olive branch to Russia from their president, what-his-name, Polk? No, it's a new chap. One of their generals."

"Zachary Taylor," said Bell-Fairfax. "Though I'm afraid he's deceased now, sir. It was in the *Times*. I believe the present gentleman in office is named Fillmore."

"Eh? In the *Times*? When?"

"I read it on the train, sir. Between Bucharest and Aalborg. Quite a new copy, too, no more than a week old."

"Well, bully for you for a sharp-eyed lad." Ludbridge scowled and groped for his cigar case. "And that would mean the government's shifted about a bit since the Bible class left their home in dear old Tennessee. Well, well. London can eavesdrop on them via the new transmitters and decide if we're required to sort it all out. Assuming the Franklins don't arrive in a timely fashion."

"But weren't these transmitters for the Kabinet of Wonders' use, sir?"

"Didn't say they weren't." Ludbridge looked sidelong at Bell-Fairfax as they hurried on. "But Greene thought it prudent that London should be able to listen in discreetly as well. Anything the Kabinet picks up on what we've planted for them London will hear too."

Bell-Fairfax stopped in his tracks a moment. "Sir, is that quite honorable?" Ludbridge stopped too and lit a cigar.

"My boy, d'you recall a conversation we had about the price of this work?" He drew in smoke, exhaled. "I believe I mentioned it was rather steep. I'm quite sure I distinctly said it would cost you your notions of honor *at least*. The work is too damned important to be obstructed by one man's sense of chivalry. Lives depend upon it, Bell-Fairfax."

"But the Kabinet are our brothers, sir!"

"So they are. And they are also good and loyal Russians—to their nation, if not their czar. They're doing their best to make it a less beastly place, but they can't be expected to hand secrets to representatives of a nation with whom theirs will soon be at war. They walk a tightrope, as do we all, between being patriotic men and servants of a greater cause. One day all this deceit won't be necessary, but for now we'll just listen in on the sly and save them the embarrassment of knowingly collaborating with Her Majesty's agents."

"It will save lives, then, sir?"

"Of course it must. If we're to salvage anything from this idiotic war, it'll be through intelligence. Come along now, son. I only hope Pengrove and Hobson have the good sense not to come straight home."

They climbed the ramp at the tunnel's end and entered the house through the concealed door in the paneling under the staircase. They were quartered in a modest residence of two stories, set far back in its thinly greened garden on Anglisky Avenue. The house was fairly new, clean, furnished comfortably but without any particular character, and the windows were heavily curtained. The site had been chosen for the emptiness of the neighborhood—striking even in St. Petersburg's nearly deserted streets—and the house purpose-built to conceal the tunnel's exit.

"Hallo?" Ludbridge called, as he stepped into the front parlor. "Pengrove? Hobson?" No one answered.

"I expect they're still circling to throw the American off," said Bell-Fairfax.

"Good," said Ludbridge. "The last thing we want just now is for one of us to have to fight a damned duel."

A clammy damp had settled in the rooms since they had left that morning, and so Bell-Fairfax lit a fire. The larder had been stocked for them; they made a tolerable meal out of black bread and dry sausage, with pickled mushrooms. They ate in silence. Ludbridge expected any moment to hear footsteps coming up the passage under the staircase. A half-hour passed, and then an hour, as the world beyond the curtained windows grew dark, and when at last a sound came it was not the one he had expected.

"What the hell was that?" Ludbridge stood up. Bell-Fairfax had tilted his head and was peering up the staircase.

"It sounded like the London signal."

"Is it six o'clock? Good God, it is," said Ludbridge, sliding his watch back into his pocket. "But we wouldn't hear the signal unless—"

Bell-Fairfax was already at the top of the staircase. Ludbridge thundered up the stairs after him. He got to the top of the stairs in time to see Bell-Fairfax standing motionless in the doorway of the room that had been allotted to Hobson. Ludbridge pushed past him.

One of the curtains had been drawn a little aside, admitting enough twilight for them to make out the Aetheric Transmitter on a table in the center of the room. It had been opened out for use, with a length of wire draped over two chairs and reaching to the window—where the curtain had clearly been parted to facilitate fastening it to a tin tack driven into the windowsill. Moreover, it had been left switched on. Tiny red and amber lights glowed through the gloom. They heard a faint crackling sound and a monotonous rhythm coming from the earpieces that had been hung on the back of a third chair. Ludbridge realized it was a voice, barely audible, patiently repeating the call phrase from London.

"That damned fool," said Ludbridge. "That damned bloody—" He seized up the earpieces and slipped them on. It took him ten minutes' worth of acknowledgments and password confirmations before London was assured that all was well and that he was, in fact, the person he claimed and under no duress, as Bell-Fairfax stood in the doorway fidgeting uneasily.

When at last Ludbridge was able to sign off, he shut down the transmitter and carefully closed it up in its case before giving vent to a stream of cold, concentrated profanity.

"I expect he set it up for convenience," said Bell-Fairfax. "And didn't think he'd be gone as long as he has been—"

"Convenience my arse," snapped Ludbridge. "The lazy little bastard! That's a direct violation of procedure. The machines are never, under any circumstances, to be left open and in operating condition unless the operator is present. You were all told that! How'd he know someone wouldn't come into the room in his absence, eh? As someone did."

"But only ourselves. It's a secure house," said Bell-Fairfax.

"Oh, is it? Just because we've been told it is? And how the hell do we know the Third Section hasn't been observing the place? How do we know they haven't infiltrated the Kabinet?"

"Is that possible?" Even in the gloom, Ludbridge could see Bell-Fairfax go pale.

"Anything's possible. And if it isn't, you still ought to be as careful as though it were. What if you were captured by an enemy and interrogated, tell me that?"

"I should die before I revealed anything."

"You'd better hope you would! And do you suppose every one of our brothers has your confidence in himself?"

Bell-Fairfax looked away. "I would like to think so, sir."

"So should I," said Ludbridge, wrenching the wire from the windowsill with a savage gesture and pulling the curtain shut. "But I'd be a fool to count on it."

They returned to the room below and kept the fire going, as another hour crept by. Which is to say, Bell-Fairfax kept the fire going, rising at intervals to throw on another shovelful of coal; Ludbridge settled into grim immobility, watching the panel under the stair with a fixed glare. The night without was as silent as though they were camped in a wilderness. In a sense they were, for the house sat at the far edge of the chill splendid city, and though out on Nevsky Avenue lanterns still gleamed and droshkies still carried revelers to and fro, the immediate district could not have been darker or more deserted when it had been empty marshland. Its few denizens huddled by their hearths or stoves, behind curtains drawn against the dank night. No human voices without, not even the cry of a night-heron from the canal.

And then, the sound of hooves, the rattle and jingle of harness, the chime of wheels on macadam, all sounding surreal and distant. Ludbridge turned toward the door. Bell-Fairfax jumped to his feet.

"They're singing," he said.

"What?" But now Ludbridge heard it too: voices raised in song, loud and out of tune. A hoarse tenor chanting something in Russian, and with it a pair of baritones warbling nonsense words.

They heard the droshky stop in front of the house. The tenor went on singing a moment longer. Someone was making an effort to shush him. Ludbridge got up, clenching his fists. Bell-Fairfax, looking miserable, went to the door.

"Don't open it yet," Ludbridge told him.

"No, sir." Bell-Fairfax stood back and waited.

The droshky creaked as passengers climbed out, and now staggering footsteps could be heard coming up the garden path. The Russian driver shouted something, presumably a fond farewell, and drove away.

"Always heard Russians were sha-shavages. Couldn't have been a nicer chap!" Hobson said loudly.

"Shhh. Shh. 'Member where we are, old man! Old Luddy won't like this at all. At all. Where's my key? Oh. Don't have a key. Oh dear."

"Open the door and pull them in," said Ludbridge.

Bell-Fairfax obeyed, grabbing a collar each and dragging them across the threshold. Ludbridge swiftly closed and bolted the door behind them. Hobson and Pengrove stood blinking on the mat, swaying slightly. Both of them reeked of alcohol. Hobson clutched a wooden crate in his arms. He grinned.

"Hallo, fellows!" he said, and hiccuped.

"Look here, I'm really awfully sorry," said Pengrove. "It took us a deucedly long time to evade the Yankee Doodle chap—and then—and then—"

"Bell-Fairfax, take the crate from him," said Ludbridge.

"No, no, tha's the only thing holdin' me up, doncherknow!" said Hobson, and demonstrated the truth of his statement by promptly collapsing the moment Bell-Fairfax relieved him of the crate. He sprawled on his back, giggling. Bell-Fairfax looked into the crate. His eyes widened.

"It's bottles of vodka, sir."

"Now, you see, I can explain that—," said Pengrove. Hobson pointed an unsteady finger at Ludbridge and guffawed.

"Y'look just like Father! Same drefful frown an' thunderous eyes!"

"See, we had to step into this shop and wait while he went past, the Yankee I mean, only it was a shop that sold liquor—an' the chap, the shopkeep I mean, he said we had to buy something if we were going to stop there—at least, I expect that was what he said, he was speakin' their confounded lingo an' an' we meant only to buy a bottle but I think he misunderstood—so anyway—"

"How many bottles are missing from the case?" Ludbridge asked Bell-Fairfax.

"Four, sir."

"But two of 'em the driver had all by himself!" Pengrove hastened to explain. "See, we had this big crate then—an' we thought we ought to hire one of their beastly open carriages, because we couldn't possibly walk home with it—only the driver, he didn't speak English either, and he ended up taking us a long way out in the country by mistake—and then he got quite cross with us, so we gave him some vodka."

"Put the case in the cabinet yonder," said Ludbridge. "Lock it, and bring me the key."

"Yes, sir."

"An' we had to drink something to keep warm, you see. An' at first the driver was quite cheerful, only then he grew melancholy and wept about something. So we had to stop while he dried his eyes. An' then he was going to go kill himself by jumping in the river, at least I think that was what he was going to do, he had to pantomime it rather—so we had to stop him, didn't we? An' we drank a bit more to be, you know, companionable and we sang to him—we sang 'Begone Dull Care.' So then he was grateful and insisted on singing one for us."

"The key, sir." Bell-Fairfax presented it to Ludbridge, who fastened it to his watch chain.

"An' then he wanted us to sing along, only of course we didn't understand the lingo again so we just sort of la-la'd at the chorus—it went on for a great many choruses. Do hope the poor chap gets home all right. I say, Ludbridge, I know we oughtn't to have done it like this but we couldn't get the chap to leave us at the—the—oh, I don't think I can say it properly. The museum place, you know. And I'm sorry about the state Johnny got himself in." Pengrove tugged at his gloves fretfully. Hobson, who had fallen asleep on the floor, began snoring.

"We will discuss it at a more convenient time," said Ludbridge. "Go to bed."

"Yes, sir." Pengrove turned sadly and climbed the stairs.

Bell-Fairfax looked down at Hobson. "Shall I carry him upstairs, sir?"

"No," said Ludbridge, turning to climb the stairs himself. "Let him sleep where he is. Serve the beggar right."

There was no explosion next morning. While they were cooking breakfast, Hobson groaned and sat up, green-faced at the smell of frying eggs. Ludbridge blandly offered him some dry toast and tea. Afterward Hobson was obliged to run out to the wash-house at the back of the premises, and returned some minutes later more gray than green. Ludbridge then invited him to go for a walk. They departed together down the tunnel. Pengrove and Bell-Fairfax played cards and waited, somewhat uneasy of mind.

"I say, I don't think it's quite fair for Johnny to get a smack with the cane, you know," said Pengrove at last.

"Ludbridge won't strike him. He'll simply talk to him," said Bell-Fairfax, shuddering. "What on earth possessed the two of you to do it?"

"Well, aren't we supposed to be behaving like idiots? And I really tried to stop him drinking quite so much. But what was I to do, take the bottle away from him? I ain't his mother. And it's what a chap is supposed to do, ain't it? Get drunk and have jolly adventures?"

"I don't believe he's feeling very jolly just now," said Bell-Fairfax. "Oh! Here they come."

Pengrove listened, but heard nothing. "That's your bloody lynx ears again. It's really not natural, old man. Oh. Wait. Here, let's look as though we're terribly preoccupied with our cards."

Ludbridge and Hobson emerged from the passage in due course, Hobson once again a fearful shade of green. Ludbridge, wreathed in a cloud of infernal smoke, took his cigar from his mouth and inspected their cards, walking behind first Pengrove and then Bell-Fairfax.

"Rotten pair of hands," he said, amiably enough. "There's a Patchesi set in the cupboard. Care to have a go? We could all play."

1850: Cruel Works of Many Wheels I View

After three or four days holed up in quarters, they were paid a visit by Nikitin and his assistant, Semyon Denisovich, who brought them a samovar and news.

"A certain Vladislav Antonovich Dolgorukov returned with the Americans from Constantinople, where he was posing as a minor functionary at our embassy there," said Nikitin, removing his spectacles and polishing them. "You may have encountered him, I think? He arranges certain matters for the foreign policy staff. Rather as you may have done, from time to time."

"I think we might have seen him," Ludbridge admitted, remembering the dark house off the Cadde-i Kebir. "Not to speak to, however."

"No, of course not. I should be rather alarmed if you had. His return is alarming in itself, because, like a sharp knife, he is only brought where he is meant to be used. A meat cleaver in the kitchen is one thing, but its presence in the parlor bears watching. If you *had* crossed Dolgorukov's path, I would be a little concerned for your safety just now. And there is another thing.

"I am afraid we have confirmation that your Americans are now honored guests of His Majesty. They presented a letter of introduction from the former president Polk himself. Evidently he wished to assure the Czar of his warm regard for Russia. Reverend Breedlove has spoken long and persuasively about the sufferings of the Orthodox Christians in the Holy Land, pleading with the Czar to come to their assistance. I am pleased to note that there has been no offer of arcane weaponry, at least.

"And the last few days they have kept two of their number at the quay by the customs house, watching every ship's crew that comes ashore. Interesting, no?"

"Interesting, yes, but if they haven't got the Franklins' machines to offer him, what does your czar want with Brother Jonathan?" said Ludbridge. "A set of heavily armed Baptists could be useful, I suppose, but I should think Russia has enough homegrown brutes in her ranks."

"His Majesty has an abiding fondness for placing spies in the great capitals of Europe," explained Nikitin. "We believe he is now considering drafting these gentlemen to be his eyes and ears in the United States. Certainly he is making much of them."

"But there aren't any great capitals in America, are there?" said Pengrove. "Lot of forests and swamps and, er, bison. And Red Indians. What do the Americans want with Russia?"

"Perhaps an ally against the powers of Europe," said Nikitin. "The two nations have certain, ah, institutions in common."

"The Americans keep slaves," said Bell-Fairfax, with loathing.

"And we keep serfs," said Nikitin, with a slight bow in his direction. "Not quite the same thing, but equally regrettable. I might add to the similarities a proudly ignorant and deeply religious peasantry, a vast uncivilized interior, and a cultural elite clustered in one city on its seacoast. Add to this a common distrust of Western Europe, and . . . I believe the situation is worth our concern."

"Hm! Perhaps you're right." Ludbridge tugged at his mustache. "We'll certainly pass the word to London. Any word back from the Franklins?"

Nikitin nodded. "They apologize for all the trouble. They lost *two* men in Constantinople, apparently, but they assure us that the filibusters know nothing about pyrethanatos or any other advanced weapons. They say they are sending someone to deal with the situation."

"I should hope so!" said Ludbridge. "Well. See what you can discover with transmitters properly placed? And how is your listening post progressing?"

"There we have better news for you! Tell them, Semyon Denisovich."

His assistant, a lean sad-eyed youth, cleared his throat. "Our Department of Fabrication has put together six new receivers, sir. We are installing them in the listening post at the cathedral this very day, and would be happy to give your technician a tour of the station in the hope that he will lend us his expertise."

"That's you, Hobson." Ludbridge turned to survey Hobson, who had been sitting listlessly by the stove. "Care to get out and about a bit?"

"I should very much like to." Hobson jumped up. "I've been so dreadfully bored, you know!"

"Well, now you've something useful to do. What about placing new transmitters for you?" Ludbridge turned back to Semyon Denisovich, but Nikitin spoke.

"That is somewhat more complicated. I am afraid that the Americans have reported you to His Majesty as possible spies. Members of the Third Section have already sought for you at the Commercial Club and all the other places frequented by the English residents. There is also the matter of whatever Dolgorukov may be up to. Since, under the circumstances, it is inadvisable for you to walk abroad by daylight . . . how well do you see in the dark?"

Ludbridge smiled. "Rather well, in fact."

"It's like a perfectly immense wedge of cheese," said Pengrove in a whisper, peering up at the War Office. They had gone around the building complex twice now, waiting for the few late-night pedestrians to wander out of earshot. At the moment they stood in the shadows of the scaffolding about the cathedral across the street.

"It's an efficient and rational design for a building on a triangular lot," said Ludbridge, watching in annoyance as an ancient crossing-sweeper toddled away down Isaac Avenue. "There! Western face of the building, Bell-Fairfax. First target?"

"Western face? Third floor, eleventh window from the left," Bell-Fairfax replied promptly.

"And of course you recall it with perfect accuracy after having looked at the chart only once," said Pengrove with resignation, taking aim with the crossbow. He fired and, a second later, they heard the tiny thud of impact as the transmitter-dart embedded itself in the wooden frame of the dark window.

"Well done," said Ludbridge.

"It's not as hard as all that," said Bell-Fairfax, defensive. "You simply convert what you see to a mathematical formula. Same as memorizing charts. I'm sure anyone could do it."

"Yes, yes, no doubt, but in the meanwhile it's exceedingly convenient that *you* can," said Ludbridge, watching the street. He handed another transmitter to Pengrove, who reloaded. "Second target?"

"Western face, second floor, third window from the right."

Pengrove took aim and fired, neatly hitting the window frame. "Next?"

"North face."

"Damn. Less cover over there. Very well, no help for it. Disguises at the ready? Go." They trudged all three toward the open square between the Admiralty building and the northern side of the War Office. The Kabinet of Wonders had provided them with laborers' garments and the gear of those squads sent out to repair the streets at night: tools and a net bag full of the curious wooden paving blocks used in certain parts of the city.

Even Nevsky Avenue was silent and deserted at this hour, lit far down by a few lanterns. No one was awake to watch them when they paused midway across the square. "Northeast face, second floor, ninth window from the right," said Bell-Fairfax.

Ludbridge gave another transmitter to Pengrove, who drew the crossbow from his pocket, loaded hastily, aimed and fired.

"Oh, good shot. Ah-ah-ah, here comes a watchman." Ludbridge opened the shutter on their dark lantern and held it low to the ground. They were all crouched over, minutely examining the paving blocks, when the watchman strode up and demanded that they identify themselves. Bell-Fairfax looked up and meekly responded, for he had been spending a few hours daily learning Russian from Semyon Denisovich.

The Russian nodded at his reply, said something in an imperative tone of voice, and pointed in the direction of Voznesensky Avenue, on the eastern side of the War Office. Bell-Fairfax dropped his eyes and nodded. The watchman set out across the square, clearly intending that they should follow him, so they did. It took him a moment of casting about on Voznesensky Avenue to find what he sought, but at last he stopped and pointed downward at a particular spot on the paving. Ludbridge shuffled close and held out the lantern. Its strip of light revealed a paving block protruding up from its fellows by a good quarter-inch.

"*Da, da!*" said Ludbridge, and Bell-Fairfax drew out a mallet. He said something further to the watchman, who walked away, apparently satisfied. Bell-Fairfax pounded the block down. The mallet-blows echoed across the wide empty street. Ludbridge fished out another transmitter and handed it to Pengrove, who reloaded.

"Target?" whispered Ludbridge.

"Eastern face? Er, third floor, first window on the right," said Bell-Fairfax. He held the mallet poised to deliver the final blow just as Pengrove fired, and the faint sound of the bolt hitting home was neatly masked by the rolling echo.

"Fortuitous," said Ludbridge, picking up the lantern once again. "Shall we toddle on?"

They landed bolts in two of the windowsills at the Admiralty, and then ventured east to the vast square dominated by the Alexander column, where they proceeded slowly along in front of the Senate building, choosing carefully among its thousands of windows to sink bolts in the frames of the three specially requested by the Kabinet.

"Any more on the list?" inquired Ludbridge, as they paused at the base of the column.

"Only two, sir," said Bell-Fairfax. "Rather difficult, however."

"Eh? Why's that?"

Bell-Fairfax pointed to the Winter Palace, looming before them on the north side of the square.

"Hell." Ludbridge rubbed his face with both hands. "They want transmitters planted in the Czar's rooms, don't they?"

"Only one, sir. They asked if we mightn't plant the other in the telegraph station on the roof."

"Oh, that'll be easy, won't it? We're not breaking and entering, I don't think."

"We won't have to, sir. The royal quarters have windows in the western face of the palace."

"Jolly good," said Pengrove, in a sepulchral voice. "Perhaps you can sing a few comic songs to distract the palace guard, Ludbridge."

They walked across to the park in front of the Admiralty, and lurked under the trees there while contemplating their targets. There was a canister-shaped turret on the northern end of the roof, clearly the telegraph station. Directly below were the windows of the royal apartments. Pengrove giggled helplessly.

"Can't do it, Ludbridge, not with this little pea-shooter."

"You're right." Ludbridge turned to Bell-Fairfax, who promptly shrugged out of his long coat. Bound to his back underneath was another crossbow, considerably bigger than the one Pengrove had been concealing in his pocket. He unfastened it, swung it over his shoulder and cranked its bow taut. Ludbridge handed him a bolt. He loaded it, took aim at the telegraph station, and fired.

"Did it hit?" Pengrove craned his neck, squinting through the night.

"Didn't hear it."

"I did," said Bell-Fairfax, holding his hand out for another bolt. Ludbridge supplied one.

"And the fearsome Czar was asleep in the royal bed," murmured Pengrove *sotto voce*, "in his imperial purple nightgown with his initials embroidered on it in gold, dreaming of, er, being driven across the frozen Neva in a chariot pulled by Turks and Frenchmen . . . when suddenly, his pleasant dreams were shattered and so was his bedroom window . . ."

"Don't make him laugh, you bloody fool," growled Ludbridge. But the bolt flew home and they heard no glass breaking.

"Hit the target, sir," said Bell-Fairfax, lowering the crossbow. "I heard it."

"Then we'd better vanish into the night," said Ludbridge. "Just in case anyone else heard it. Come along!"

They fled back along the front of the Admiralty, pausing only to strap the big crossbow back in place. Bell-Fairfax pulled his coat on over it once again, and they walked on. They were about to cross back diagonally to the church when they heard a commotion coming from the other direction, toward the Neva.

"Stand to," Ludbridge ordered.

"What is it?" whispered Pengrove. But they could hear the voices clearly now, echoing across the empty ground: men engaged in mortal struggle, fighting on the Isaakievsky Bridge. One broke free and ran; they could hear his footsteps pounding a moment, and then there was a gunshot, shockingly loud. The runner faltered, but kept on, albeit at a reduced pace. The others came after him and caught him near the base of the Bronze Horseman.

"Good God, they're the Americans," said Bell-Fairfax.

A distant cry from another quarter, now; watchmen were coming to investigate the shot. And from the base of the monument, words suddenly distinct: "Stop kicking him, boys, stop! He's no good to us if you kill him!" Even with the distortion of echoes, they recognized the voice of the Reverend Amasa Breedlove.

"Well, I guess that Prince Orlov could get a dead man to talk," said someone else, and then shouted, for their victim had pushed away from the monument and was running again, straight down the square toward Ludbridge and the others where they stood. Even dragging one leg, his speed was remarkable. His captors were prevented from following him by the arrival of watchmen from the direction of the Winter Palace. There were roared orders in Russian.

The runner dove into the shadows of the Admiralty and came face-to-face with Ludbridge and the others. He half-collapsed forward, staring at them wildly.

"Please," he gasped, clutching at his leg, which was throwing off a shower of sparks through what appeared to be a bullet wound. "I beg thee all, run for thy lives. *Opasnost'! Da?*"

Ludbridge looked at the blue-crackling wound, looked back into the American's terrified face.

"What becomes of illusions?" he said.

The American started. He grabbed at Ludbridge's lapels. "We dispel them!"

"And we are everywhere," said Ludbridge. "Bell-Fairfax, pick him up. We're going to run."

Bell-Fairfax stooped and caught the man around the knees, hoisting him in a fire brigadesman's carry and keeping his hands well away from the sparking bullet wound.

"Across to Admiralty Avenue and down, at your best speed. Now!" said Ludbridge. They ran for their lives.

Bell-Fairfax quickly outdistanced the others, vanishing ahead in the darkness just past the first canal. Ludbridge heard the angry voices behind them falling silent, which was not a comfort; if the other Americans had explained themselves to the satisfaction of the watchmen, both parties might soon come hunting them. He had dropped his lantern, but the bag of paving blocks was still swinging from his belt and swung to strike him with every step he took. Pengrove kept pace with him, sprinting easily, and when they had crossed the second canal they darted to the right and worked their way back to the house on Anglisky Avenue.

Bell-Fairfax and the American stranger were waiting for them in the shadows under the trees. A handkerchief had been tied around the hole in the American's leg; it was already scorching black where it touched. Ludbridge acknowledged them with a nod as he came staggering up the path, closely followed by Pengrove, but said no word. He knocked on the door in a prearranged signal. A moment later the door was unbolted and Hobson stood there blinking at them sleepily.

"In," said Ludbridge, pushing past him. The others followed, the American dragging his damaged leg.

"Truly thou wert sent by a careful Providence," said the American, when the door had been bolted and Ludbridge had fetched out a bottle of vodka and handed it round. He appeared to be in his middle thirties, in sober clothing of a rather provincial cut, and had a plain, unremarkable face. Only the fact that a thin trail of smoke was trickling from the hole in his leg made him in any way distinctive.

"If you like," said Ludbridge. "You're from the Franklins in Philadelphia, aren't you?"

"I am, sir," said the American. "And if Dr. Franklin saw today the peril in which the Union stands, he'd weep for shame."

"Are you the one they sent to deal with Breedlove and that lot from Tennessee?"

"I have been following them for months now," said the American, with a sigh. He rubbed his red eyes. "The only survivor of my cell. Elias Matthews, at thy service and eternally in thy debt."

"Quaker, are you?"

Matthews nodded. "A Friend," he said. "As Lucas and Harloe were, the Lord rest their souls."

"They were the other members of your cell?"

"They were," said Matthews. His face was lined with exhaustion and he needed a shave. He flinched, suddenly, and held out his wineglass for more vodka. Ludbridge topped up his glass. He drank it off in a gulp and got unsteadily to his feet. "Before I tell thee more, sir, I'd beg a moment alone for decency's sake. My leg pains me something grievous."

"Of course," said Ludbridge. "Come along, lads."

They vacated the room and closed the door. They heard a rustling, and then a faint cry of pain; another cry; a clank and a thump.

"Are you all right?"

"I'm well," replied a faint voice. Ludbridge swung the door open and they beheld Matthews slumped forward on the settee, resting his right elbow on his right leg. His left trouser leg was empty and his left leg, still wearing its boot, lay on the floor.

It looked to be a mechanical wonder, gears and wires and a ball joint at the knee, with a great deal of leather strapwork that clearly served to fasten it to his body. Three cables protruded from the top, each one terminating in a sort of aglet. Their purpose was plain, for Matthews had removed his shirt and his mechanical left arm was also visible. Similar cables emerged from its artificial shoulder-joint and were wired into a flat box Matthews wore on his lower back. The leg-cables appeared to connect there too, when the leg was being worn. The metal had been gouged into his flesh when the other Americans kicked him, and he was now a mass of swiftly purpling bruises.

"Look here, d'you want something stronger for the pain?" said Ludbridge, ignoring the fact that the others were staring at Matthews in horror. "We've got a medical kit."

Matthews shook his head. "I thank thee, brother, but I can bear it. It's not so much a discomfort of the flesh; more the *idea* of discomfort, now that the leg is off. But the leg might well have exploded and that, I thought, would be the height of bad manners before such gracious hosts." He managed a strained smile.

"Is it likely to explode now?" Pengrove eyed the leg distrustfully.

"I don't think so." Matthews leaned back, taking a deep breath. "Not now I have unconnected. There was the chance that I might have set off the bomb by accident, before I could see what harm the bullet did."

"You have a bomb in your leg?" Pengrove took a step backward.

"Of course he has," said Ludbridge. "What are we always told? *Do not allow the machines to fall into enemy hands.*"

Matthews nodded. "Before I ran slap into ye, I had thought only to find a place to die where no one else might be harmed by my holocaust."

"Poor old chap! You were spared that, anyway," said Pengrove. Matthews looked oddly at him.

"But . . . be ye members of the Kabinet of Wonders, or not?"

"No; we work for the GSS," said Ludbridge. "The London branch."

"Ah." Matthews narrowed his eyes a little. "The British. And still I am indebted to thee, sir. But canst thou direct me to the Kabinet?"

"Of course we can, my boy," said Ludbridge soothingly. "This is their safe house, after all! We'll take you straight to them in the morning, as soon as you've had a rest. For that matter, when was the last time you had a meal?"

"Two days since," said Matthews, with reluctance.

"Thought so. Bell-Fairfax, poke up the fire and open a tin of potted ham. We've got some fresh eggs and a first-rate loaf of bread. We'll fix you a good old public school fry-up, you'll see," said Ludbridge.

"Thou art too kind," said Matthews, but his mouth was watering. He swallowed hard and watched as Bell-Fairfax fetched out a skillet and fried up eggs with slices of bread and potted ham. The resultant savory mess was presented to Matthews on a plate, with toast liberally smeared with jam, and another shot of vodka. While he ate ravenously, Ludbridge indicated by gestures that Pengrove and Hobson should take themselves off to bed. Though the mechanical leg had stopped sparking, it was still giving an occasional jerk, showing an inclination to work itself across the floor like some sort of grim clockwork toy, and so Pengrove and Hobson were glad enough to leave its vicinity.

When Matthews, sated and blinking sleepily, handed off his plate at last to Bell-Fairfax, Ludbridge pulled out his cigar case.

"May I offer you a smoke, sir?"

"I thank thee, yes." Matthews took one of Ludbridge's cigars with his gloved mechanical hand—it seemed to function as smoothly as though it were his original—and accepted a light.

"That's rather a nicely designed prosthesis," said Ludbridge, waving the lucifer out. "Better than anything we've got, just at present. We can do eyes, of course, and ears, but the mechanics of a limb require a bit more work."

"They are sensitive mechanisms," said Matthews, with a rueful look at the floor where his leg had just kicked spasmodically.

"Evidently! Still, I've no doubt the Kabinet can repair that one for you. They're clever chaps."

"I look forward to meeting them," said Matthews. "I was sent to warn them of a grave danger."

"Your fellow Yankees, by any chance?"

"It may be," said Matthews, as some of his former wariness returned. "I trust I may make my report to them in the morning."

"Of course you can," said Ludbridge. "Though you should know that the Franklins have already sent out a general advisory. Oh, don't worry about the washing-up tonight, Bell-Fairfax! Pour yourself a drink and come sit with us, there's a good chap. To be truthful, we've had a few unfortunate encounters with the filibusters ourselves. They've set the bloody Third Section on us, in fact."

"I am sorry to hear it," said Matthews, but offered no further details. In the silence that followed, Bell-Fairfax pushed a chair up to the fire and took a seat by them. He helped himself to a glass of vodka and offered more to Matthews, who shook his head and set his own glass aside. Ludbridge blew a smoke ring.

"Look here," he said in a bland voice. "I know our nations aren't on the best of terms. All the same, I'll be the first to admit that George III was a bloody lunatic. The whole business was shockingly mishandled. And we're all members of one fellowship, after all! We're all working for the same great day. If you've a private report to make to the Kabinet, why then of course it must remain private. But since your countrymen have singled us out for attack, you might do us the courtesy of telling us a little about them, eh? Wouldn't you say so, Bell-Fairfax?"

"I would, sir," said Bell-Fairfax, gazing steadily into Matthews's face. "In order that we might protect ourselves, after all."

"That's true," said Matthew. He sighed. He leaned back tiredly, seeming to have resolved something in his mind. "Very well. I trust that all I tell ye shall be held in the strictest confidence? Listen not as Britons, but as brothers."

"Fair enough," said Ludbridge.

"My nation is at war within itself," said Matthews. "And it stands in peril of its very soul. One pernicious thing caused the very bell to crack that signaled our freedom from kings and tyranny. Ye know well enough what that thing is."

"Slavery," said Bell-Fairfax.

"Aye. It prances like a mocking shadow after all our solemn posturings. All the noblest ideals of Liberty that we profess remain dreams, insubstantial while the negro groans in bondage.

"We should have been, we *must be* a republic of liberty and justice for all. In that alone is our salvation, and toward that end we strive to abolish slavery. But now, a second grinning giant arises to tempt us to damnation.

"He is a doctrine asserting that it is America's *manifest destiny* to expand—by conquest. To rule over an empire, in the very name of the principles it must betray thereby. The Almighty Himself, this doctrine saith, gave America this divine right, though the tyrants of old claimed to be the Lord's anointed too.

"To this end the Indian is hunted from his native place and exterminated, but he is not the last victim of this vicious hypocrisy. Nothing less than the whole of the two continents conquered will satisfy it; and the end result will be a vast empire of white slave-holding Americans ruling plantations, living like feudal kings above the grave of that great Experiment on which our nation was founded. We would be a second Rome, greater and more damned."

Matthews was shaking with emotion. Bell-Fairfax made to pour him another drink, and this time he held out his glass. "Forgive me. I burn so with anger, I may die of it." He drank again, set his glass aside, and continued:

"This doctrine has its *filibusters* fighting in its cause." Matthews pronounced the word with a sneer of distaste.

"But how did they come to be shooting at you?" said Ludbridge.

Matthews grimaced and shook his head. "I must tell thee all, I see. One of our brothers in Philadelphia had an apprentice, whom he brought into our ranks. The said boy was gifted beyond genius. *He* devised the means by which I was given back mine arm and leg. He rose through our ranks too young, on that account. Too soon, and his pride made him foolish.

"He attended a lecture by one of these filibusters, and was filled with the fire of their ambition. He came to us and argued earnestly that we ought to be underwriting the filibusters' cause; for, he said, ought not all nations be enforced to become Christian republics like our own?

"We reasoned with him, explaining that such an argument itself betrays the spirit of our republic and denies Christ. We may, and ought, persuade other nations by our shining example, but never by force of arms. He grew angry. He broke with us; he went to the filibusters."

"Good God!" Ludbridge feigned being shocked.

Matthews nodded miserably. "We are quartered in a building Dr. Franklin himself purchased, when he founded the American branch. Mounted above the door of the inmost meeting room is an ancient emblem, given to Dr. Franklin, so it's said, by thine own branch, before the revolution began. It is the bas-relief head of a lion, enameled in green, and in its jaws it held a disc of pure gold—gold made by alchemy, we were told. More, it was whispered that the disc itself was scribed with the alchemical means for making gold, though in secret and coded phrases and an obscure alphabet.

"Before his desertion, the boy climbed up secretly and wrenched the gold disc free, and took it with him to offer to his new companions."

"Good God," repeated Ludbridge. "What a calamity. When did this happen? We can't have our secrets known, old chap!"

"It happened at the beginning of this year," said Matthews. "And our secrets will not be known. The boy is dead."

"Dead, is he? That's convenient."

Matthews scowled and reddened. "We are no murderers. He was thrown from his horse, it seems, and killed. Even so, he had had some words with the filibusters, and delivered the golden disc to them. What he revealed to them we do not certainly know; but they are now aware that we exist, and have that which would greatly further their cause, if they could lay hold of it; which is to say, the *technologia*."

"That's damned bad."

"I know." Matthews took a drag on his cigar. "Well, we managed to find their meeting place, and planted a transmitter. We learned a little of their intention to meddle here, and so a cell was put together to follow their agents and observe them—Lucas, Jenkins and I. We discovered enough to alarm us, in the Holy Land, and we knew we must find out more.

"Lucas, who was a negro, went to them and told a story of having been brought to Bethlehem by his master, who had died of fever there. He offered himself to their service if they would only pay for his passage back to the States. Well, sir, they took him, since they wanted a servant who spoke English. He traveled with them after that to Constantinople. Jenkins and I followed, and he sent us his reports with a transmitter he had concealed in a prayer book. I fear they treated him badly; he was chained in their rooms when they went out, but he endured it for the sake of the mission.

"He learned the whole of their plot, and whence they were bound. He copied their papers and dropped them through a window to Jenkins and I. We bid him escape—it was easily done, for he had a device to cut through steel. He wanted to wait until midnight, but we persuaded him to leave while they had gone out to supper, for we had booked passage on a ship to take us to this city and it was due to sail at half past eight. Would to God we had waited!

"Lucas freed himself and hurried to meet us, where we waited for him near the quay. We saw him, and called to him and waved. He ran toward us. But as he ran we heard shouts of anger, and lo! There were the filibusters, where they had come walking back from their supper. They drew their pistols and fired. Lucas was shot, and he nearly went down, clutching the prayer book that concealed his transmitter.

"When he knew they must overtake him he leaped from the quay, and in midair over the water he destroyed himself, even as I was nearly obliged to do tonight. Himself, his transmitter, and all the goods he carried went up in a rolling flame, no more than a puff of ash upon the wind."

"A good man," murmured Ludbridge. Bell-Fairfax's eyes were wide.

"The best of men," said Matthews sadly. "Jenkins and I turned to walk away, but they shot at us; we knew then they must have seen us calling to Lucas. We ran. There was a great hue and cry by that time, with the Mussulman police running from all directions to the quay. We ran in the opposite direction. The filibusters came after us still. I can run at great speed, if ungracefully, and so I thought little of it when Jenkins fell behind; but then I saw that he had fallen, and when I turned back to him I saw he had been shot too.

"I tried to pull him up, to carry him, but he bid me remember our orders, and run on; for I had all our machines, hidden on my person. It broke the heart in me but I bid him farewell, and I ran.

"For three days I hid myself, going from place to place, and on the third day I chanced to see a doorway with the sign of the green lion above it, very twin to the one in Philadelphia. I went in and sat, and presently a Mussulman came and asked what I would have. I showed him this." Matthews stripped off the glove on his right hand, revealing that he wore a signet ring bearing the lion emblem. "I said it was remarkable that his door bore the same sign. He looked grave and, speaking low, exchanged with me the words of recognition.

"He hid me in an upstairs room. I told him my story. He brought me food and coffee and promised to see if anything could be learned of Jenkins.

"Three more days I remained there, and then one morning he told me the Magi had found Jenkins dead, floating in the bay.

"They had determined, too, that the filibusters had departed for this city. I resolved to follow after, for that was my duty. The Magi attempted to convince me otherwise, but when they saw that I was resolute they paid for my passage on the steamer *Sunderland*. Hither I came, desiring to warn the Kabinet of Wonders but mindful of my likely death.

"We were delayed a week at Kronstadt, as our cargo was searched. The *Sunderland*'s captain hid me in a compartment in his cabin. This night he rowed me ashore and left me at the Strelka. I thought it an easy walk across to the Kunstkamera, where I knew the Kabinet might be found; instead three men came swiftly toward me in the dark, and I recognized the filibusters. The rest ye know."

"I'm afraid they've been waiting for you," said Ludbridge. "We ran into them in Constantinople, too. The Kabinet have had them watched since we arrived, so that's something, at least."

"But how did they know to look for me here?"

"I expect they must have taken your friend alive."

"Dear God," said Matthews, slumping.

"All's not lost," said Bell-Fairfax. "The Kabinet *are* forewarned, and you're safe now. Your friends didn't die in vain."

"But the Czar himself must be warned! There is more—"

"What more, son?" Ludbridge leaned forward. But Matthews drew himself up, shook his head.

"I think, sir, I'd better wait and make my report to the Kabinet themselves."

"Just as you like, old fellow, just as you like; but you needn't worry." Ludbridge got to his feet. "Bell-Fairfax, fetch a pillow and some blankets from upstairs and move the settee over here by the fire. Anything we ought to do about your leg, for the night, Matthews?"

There wasn't, and so it was left on the floor until morning. Ludbridge himself carried it the next day when they took Matthews through the tunnel to the Kabinet's headquarters. Matthews rode in a chair carried by Bell-Fairfax and Hobson, of which image Pengrove couldn't resist taking a photograph. When Matthews arrived, somewhat red-faced, he was promptly loaned a crutch and escorted off to a private meeting with Nikitin's senior officer while Matthews's leg was borne off in the opposite direction to the Kabinet's fabrication department.

"Meanwhile, we've good news for you," Ludbridge told Nikitin. "We got all your transmitters placed, exactly as you wanted them."

"I stand ready to assist your chaps in tuning them in," said Hobson, with a salute.

"Magnificent!" Nikitin rose from his chair. "And I would recommend you might wish to go all together to visit the cathedral today, and by tunnel. The Third Section has men searching the city, going from house to house hunting for the American. It is perhaps better that you are not in the house until they give up the hunt."

"Are they likely to break in?" Ludbridge gave Hobson a meaningful glare, but Hobson held up his hands.

"They won't find a thing if they do! I shut up the transmitter and put it away last night, all according to procedure, on my honor."

"We can send a man to wait there as caretaker until it's safe," Nikitin assured Ludbridge.

"And you can meet *my* associates," said Hobson to Ludbridge, assuming an authoritarian air and taking hold of his lapels. "Besides, there's a first-rate view of the city from the tower. You could do with a bit of fresh air and sunlight, in my considered opinion."

"Oh, we could, could we?" said Ludbridge, squinting at him. "Perhaps you're right. It would do me a world of good to see you working for once, anyway."

"Then follow me," said Hobson.

He led them along another brick tunnel under the city, which looked exactly like all the other tunnels through which they had tramped, and smelled of the same riparian dankness for much of its length. Near its far end, however, they began to catch a distinct fragrance of frankincense, which grew stronger when they climbed the stairs.

"Notice the odor of sanctity?" said Hobson, grinning. "I'm told we're right under something called an iconostasis. *The* iconostasis, apparently. Here we are!" He opened the door to reveal a low chamber, quite long. Desks were against one wall, in a row, and on each sat an apparatus of tubes, dials and wires that resembled the inner workings of the Aetheric Transmitter. Clustered around a table at the far end of the room were a half-dozen young men, talking excitedly amongst themselves. They rose to their feet when Hobson entered with the others.

"Johnny Albertovich!" The foremost, whom they recognized as Semyon Denisovich, started forward. "We are receiving on Number

Three! We heard the staff in the telegraph tower taking down messages!"

"You'll hear more than that presently," said Hobson, rubbing his hands together. "Gentlemen, may I present my fellow Englishmen? Mr. Pengrove, Mr. Ludbridge, Mr. Bell-Fairfax—he's the giant. I thought they needed an outing, don't you know. Mikhail Ilych, perhaps you'd show them the sights, while we set to work here?"

"Jolly good, sir!" A gleeful youth stepped forward. "Very pleased to make your acquaintance! Acquaintance*s*. Pardon me very much. Will you please to follow me through?" He opened a tiny door, revealing that its outward side was faced with brick veneer, and gestured out into a narrow staircase, clearly some sort of custodian's crawlway.

"Thank you. I expect you'd better remove your hat, Bell-Fairfax," said Ludbridge. Mikhail Ilych scrambled through, followed by Pengrove and, with a certain lack of dignity, Ludbridge, who had to be boosted from behind by Bell-Fairfax before he could proceed crabwise up the staircase. Bell-Fairfax was obliged to do the same, with the added discomfort of bending nearly double.

Mikhail Ilych led them on through the narrow slot in the masonry, up and around and up and around some three or four times before they emerged into the light of day, filtered as it was through the high windows above the iconostasis, which was a great structure gleaming with gold leaf below. They found themselves on a narrow iron catwalk that continued around and up, through the tower and toward the belfry. The air was close, stiflingly hot, and redolent of frankincense.

Quietly as they might, they followed Mikhail Ilych upward until at last they emerged into the belfry. They settled against the rail, gasping, grateful for the breeze; though Ludbridge noticed Mikhail Ilych glancing nervously at the carillon behind them, and checking his watch.

"Not going to be caught up here when the chimes sound, I hope?"

"No, sir, we have ten minutes," said Mikhail Ilych. He leaned over and pointed to a thin line of copper wire that ran up the wall of the tower, nearly invisible even close to and certainly unseen from below. "Regard our signal amplification wire! Even before Johnny Albertovich's gracious assistance, we could receive signals from many parts of the world. This tower has attained a height of four hundred and four feet, in English measurement. Directly above us is the clock, which is of Dutch manufacture."

"Very nice," said Ludbridge, gazing out at the city.

"I say!" Pengrove took a few shots with his hat, in rapid succession.

"There's the man," said Bell-Fairfax suddenly. Ludbridge turned his head and followed Bell-Fairfax's gaze. A man was crossing the open square below the church, bareheaded in the morning sunlight, carrying a parcel under his arm. He was easily recognized as the Russian attaché they had followed in Constantinople. What had his name been? Dolgorukov.

"Vladislav Antonovich Dolgorukov," murmured Bell-Fairfax, as though he had been reading Ludbridge's mind.

"I wonder why they all have those vitchy middle names?" said Pengrove, and took a photograph of Dolgorukov.

"It is a form of patronymic," explained Mikhail Ilych absently, staring hard at the man far below. "I think we should climb down now."

"In case he should happen to glance up at us?" Ludbridge said.

"It would not be convenient if he recognized you," Mikhail Ilych replied. "I wonder what he was doing at the prison?"

They descended the tower and went back down through the secret passage. Hobson was seated at one of the desks in the listening post, wearing a pair of earpieces and slowly twirling the knobs on the Aetheric Receiver; he looked for all the world like a burglar intent on persuading a safe to open. His trainees stood in a respectful half-circle around him, watching closely.

"Aaaand . . . here we are, we've got somebody," said Hobson. Grabbing up a pencil and a slip of paper, he noted down the position on the dial. "Here!" Slipping off the earpieces, he stood up and waved Mikhail Ilych to take his place on the bench. Mikhail Ilych sat and slipped on the earpieces. His eyes widened.

"You hear him?"

"That's Prince Orlov!"

"There you go, then, that one was . . ." Hobson consulted a list on the paper. "Transmitter Number Twenty-three. Mark its place. Now we'll just move on to the next on the list—"

"You seem to have everything well in hand," said Ludbridge. "We'll just leave you to work, shall we?"

"Yes, yes, you're dismissed," said Hobson, with an impudent wave. "Now then, Piotr Fyodorovich, take a seat . . ."

Ludbridge set off back down the tunnel, flanked by Bell-Fairfax and Pengrove. "He seems to be doing rather a good job," said Bell-Fairfax.

"Eh? Yes. Comforting to discover the boy's competent, at least."

"I should think we'll be going home soon, shouldn't we?" said Pengrove. "Once he's got them trained? It would be ever so jolly to walk down the Strand again and not have to play the fool any more than was my customary habit."

"Likely," said Ludbridge, in a preoccupied sort of way. "Did I see you taking a photograph of that Russian, Pengrove? What's his name?"

"Dolgorukov," said Bell-Fairfax.

"To be sure."

"I did, yes," said Pengrove.

"Good man," said Ludbridge. "Let's go back and pay a call on friend Nikitin, shall we?"

They found him in one of the rooms allotted to the Kabinet's fabrication department. He was standing, with some three or four others, around a table on which was Matthews's prosthetic leg. All wore shield-visors over their eyes. The leg had been opened out, one side folded back like the lid of a box, and one of Nikitin's colleagues had just removed a somewhat flattened and blackened bullet and was standing back, holding it up in a pair of surgeons' clamps. He was saying something shocked sounding in Russian.

Nikitin, noticing that the Englishmen had entered, stepped back and lifted his visor. "We disconnected the bomb! It's quite safe now. Really a remarkable piece of equipment. Would you like to see?"

"What, the bomb? No, thank you!"

"No, no, the limb!" Nikitin gestured for his colleagues to make room around the table. Ludbridge and the others stepped close. They beheld, within the opened space, a number of gears and pulleys, with a bewildering profusion of cables and wires. These filled the lower leg, but above the knee were also compartments, which when opened proved to reveal a flask of brandy, a lucifer safe, a set of lock picks, a pair of opera glasses, a magnifying glass, a tiny portable spirit-lamp, a roll of paper and a pencil, a map case, a compass, a sewing kit, a roll of bandage, fishhooks and twine, and—in two pieces, but meant to be fitted together for use—a hacksaw.

"Bloody ingenious," said Ludbridge, after inspecting it briefly. "I'd have crammed a revolver in somehow, though."

Nikitin shrugged. "The gentleman is a Quaker. I expect his creed does not permit such things. I am more intrigued by the degree of miniaturization of the servomotors here and here. Have your people anything like it?"

"No, we haven't," said Ludbridge. "Pengrove, just step close and get a few good pictures, would you? Fabrication at home will particularly want to see this. Much damage to repair?"

"The bullet hole itself will be simple to patch; but we will have to specially manufacture the wire to replace this section, and devise a better insulating substance." Nikitin poked at the ruined section with a retractor. "We shall no doubt learn a great deal."

"Saw your Dolgorukov fellow at the prison, by the way," said Ludbridge.

Nikitin dropped the retractor. His colleagues looked up.

Secure in his lower office, Nikitin went to a shelf and brought down a file box. "May I ask *precisely* where you saw him?"

Bell-Fairfax looked at Ludbridge before replying. "We were in the bell tower of the cathedral, sir, above the listening post. He appeared to be coming from the prison, we were told."

"By whom?"

"The young man who was our guide. Mikhail Ilych, I believe was the name."

"Ah." Nikitin fixed his gaze on a sealed message in a tray that was marked with what was presumably the Russian word for *Incoming*. "And this would be his report, I expect, since it is dated five minutes ago." He opened the message and glanced at it. "Yes; a diligent boy. He confirms it. But, just to be certain . . ." Nikitin opened the file box and took out a photograph. He passed it to Bell-Fairfax. "You're quite sure this is the man you saw?"

Ludbridge stepped close to Bell-Fairfax and peered at it. The subject in question was a man of perhaps forty years of age, solidly built. His features were regular and unremarkable, other than in that the whole set of them, eyes, nose and mouth taken all together, seemed too small for the breadth of his face, as though they had been squeezed together in the middle. It was enough to strike someone trained to remember faces, though not enough to make him in any way distinguishable by anyone else.

"Yes, sir, quite sure," said Bell-Fairfax, handing the photograph back to Nikitin.

"And you can trust Bell-Fairfax's eyes," said Ludbridge. Nikitin grimaced and shook his head.

"So he was visiting the Trubetskoy battery," he said. "I shall be interested to hear whether one of the prisoners is found today dead in his cell. It will look exactly like a suicide, I'm sure. I devoutly hope that is the case."

Aware that his guests were staring at him, Nikitin explained: "If someone dies in the Trubetskoy prison, then I will know why Vladislav Antonovich is in St. Petersburg, and I will not have to worry about what else might be in the wind. Perhaps it will be enough to tell you that the Third Section has a group within itself? A shadow organization. They employ certain specialists to perform tasks of which the Czar must remain quite unaware, but which are logically necessary for carrying out his orders. You know, I think, the sort of thing I mean."

Bell-Fairfax went a little red but Ludbridge nodded, without comment.

"Vladislav Antonovich is a skilled and eminently discreet member of this group, perhaps the best at what he does. He never murders; he simply arranges deaths and they happen. We had intelligence from the Magi that he was in Constantinople, and that one of his *arrangements* had gone badly wrong. To speak frankly, they praised your efficiency in the matter."

"Very kind of them," said Ludbridge, in a neutral voice.

"You didn't encounter himself directly, of course."

"No."

"Fortunate." Nikitin looked down at the file case. He slipped the photograph of Dolgorukov back in place. "Indeed. Should we happen to discover anything more about his purpose now that he has returned— such as his reasons for escorting the filibusters here—and should we wish to interfere for any reason . . . I wonder whether we might impose on your amiability so far as to ask for a similar favor from you?"

"We should be delighted to oblige, sir," said Ludbridge. "Though of course we must inform London."

"Of course," said Nikitin. He closed the file case and looked up at them. "We have very little of our own to offer other than astronomical observations, but we can give you a full schematic of the American's prosthesis."

"I am certain that would be kindly received," said Ludbridge.

They resided for the next two days in the Kabinet's underground guest quarters, which were comparatively Spartan but had the advantage of a billiards table for amusement. They saw little of Hobson, sequestered as he was with the team at the listening post, but from the little he was able to tell them when he returned at night the work was going very well indeed, and he had made firm friends among his team.

The Kabinet's man posted in the house on Anglisky Avenue duly answered the door when the Third Section came inquiring, and stood by mildly while they searched the house and found no American. It was then deemed safe for Ludbridge and crew to return.

A week of stupefying boredom followed.

Rather than spend his hours watching the rain beat the leaves from the trees in the garden, Pengrove invented a game of carpet-billiards using Black Bullet boiled sweets and a poker. He became very skilled at it, by his own account.

No actual matches were held because neither Ludbridge nor Bell-Fairfax would play with him, the one having acquired a bundle of back numbers of *The Illustrated London News* and the other having got hold of a Russian grammar with which to improve his grasp of the language. They sat in the window seat and read, and smoked, and grunted in response to his attempts to start conversations. Hobson generally returned through the tunnel from the listening post a short while after sunset, by which time it was too dark to play, and so boiled sweet billiards failed to become established as a popular parlor game.

One such spectacularly dull day dragged itself away into night, and they drew the curtains and moved to the table beside the stove, where a single lamp provided enough light to read.

Ludbridge looked up after a while, frowned, and took out his watch.

"Where the hell is Hobson? It's nearly six."

"I had the impression the chaps at the listening post were going to give him a laudatory dinner," said Pengrove. "To celebrate finishing the job, you know. They think the world of him, I gather."

"Laudatory, eh? How nice for Hobson," said Ludbridge, snapping the watch shut. "No doubt the six o'clock report will just float through the aether of its own volition, as if by magic." He rose and went upstairs to Hobson's room, muttering to himself.

Pengrove sighed. He watched Bell-Fairfax poring over the Russian grammar.

"What on earth are you doing with your eyes?" he cried after a moment.

"I beg your pardon?" Bell-Fairfax looked up, startled.

"You can't possibly be reading."

"I've been reading all week."

"But, I say, your eyes are racing back and forth like—like I don't know what. Makes me positively giddy to watch. You can't take in anything by just running your eye over the pages like that."

"That's absurd," said Bell-Fairfax, somewhat surlily. "I've been reading at a perfectly normal rate. I have committed to memory one chapter a day. Two hundred ninety-eight pages, eighty-one thousand five hundred and eight words, six thousand seven hundred and fifty-one lines."

"Really," said Pengrove, staring at him. "You've counted every punctuation mark, I suppose."

"Twenty-one thousand, two hundred and seventeen. Oh, close your mouth! Anyone could do it, if he simply applied himself."

"Just as you say, old man," said Pengrove hastily.

"It's perfectly normal," Bell-Fairfax repeated. He slammed the book shut and got up to poke up the fire in the stove. A gust of wind sent the rain drumming particularly hard against the windows, and a palpable chill seeped into the room.

"Let's put on a few more sticks, shall we?" said Pengrove, turning up his coat collar. As Bell-Fairfax obliged, he added: "I hope we can leave this beastly country before the river freezes over. Surely we've gathered all the intelligence we could."

"I don't see how we're to leave, if the Third Section are looking for us," said Bell-Fairfax. "Unless the Kabinet has a convenient tunnel that comes out in Trafalgar Square."

"Wish they'd add a new station to that Galvanic Railway," said Pengrove. "That's the way to travel, eh? Not much scenery, but, my hat! What comfort."

"What veal cutlets," said Bell Fairfax longingly, rubbing his hands together before the blaze. He shut the stove. They heard a heavy tread on the stairs.

"Hobson come in yet?" said Ludbridge, as he descended.

"Not yet, sir."

"Hmph. Well, we've got our exit arranged for us. London's sending a crew to get us out next week."

"Hurrah!" Pengrove jumped up and did a little dance of celebration.

"How will they manage? I understood the Third Section is watching all the quays," said Bell-Fairfax.

"Did I say we were leaving by boat?" said Ludbridge. He sat down, looked around irritably, and got up again. "Ought we to wait supper until the Darling of the Aetheric Waves graces us with his presence? No, we oughtn't. He'll be dining out anyway. Is there any of that smoked salmon left?"

They made a decent supper out of odds and ends from the pantry. The rain let up, and a strong wind blew the storm clouds out; a few stars soon glittered in the night, visible even through the curtains.

Two hours afterward there was still no sign of Hobson. Ludbridge went twice to peer down the tunnel, waiting for him, but each time returned to his chair with his scowl deeper. Bell-Fairfax returned to his book and Pengrove, as unobtrusively as possible, got a rag and a tin of polish from his luggage and set about cleaning his boots.

There was the clatter of iron on stone and a droshky could be heard pulling up in front of the house, full of merrymakers singing in Russian. Pengrove closed his eyes and murmured an involuntary prayer. The Almighty was not pleased to hear him, however, for Hobson's voice was clearly audible amongst the singers, and a moment later he bid them a hilarious farewell.

"Oh, no," murmured Bell-Fairfax. Ludbridge got to his feet.

The carriage rolled off into the night, taking its inebriated choir with it. Hobson's footsteps sounded loud on the paved garden path, as he staggered toward the front door.

"Blow out the lamp," said Ludbridge. Bell-Fairfax obeyed.

There was a crash and a thud as Hobson fell on the front step and collided with the door. It was followed by knocking, and Hobson's voice raised plaintively:

"I say, letta fella in! It's bloody freezing out here!"

"Open the door and pull him in," said Ludbridge. Bell-Fairfax dragged

Hobson across the threshold. Pengrove opened the door of the stove, which lit the room sufficiently to reveal Hobson, swaying and blinking, in a long fur coat.

"Now, you may think I'm drunk," he enunciated carefully, "but in realilly it was this deuced long bear-rug tangled my feet, you see, and that's why I fell down."

"Are you going to tell me you haven't been drinking?" said Ludbridge, in a deadly cold voice. Hobson rolled his eyes, as though Ludbridge had just asked the stupidest question imaginable.

"Well, of course we had *some* drinks, I mean, it was a party, what? And would have been rude not to anyway. And we had a little kvass with dinner but that's nothing, no stronger'n barley-water really, and then they ordered a bottle of port because they said that's what Englishmen drink, so I had to, didn't I? An' then I had to toast them in their drink so I had to order a bottle of the best vodka, what? What? Honor demanded it."

"And did it demand you put us all in danger by coming home in a public conveyance to the front door, instead of through the tunnel?"

Hobson puffed out his cheeks and made a scornful noise, waving his hands. "Pitch-black out there! Nobody sees. No Red Indians lurking behind the gate, I c'n assure you. Nor Bruvver Jonathan neither. We came out of the restaurant an' Igor Stepanovich said, 'Oh look, the rain's stopped,' and damme if he wasn't right, and Boris Ivanovich said, 'Let's hire a droshky an' ride around awhile under the beautiful stars!' And you couldn't say no to that, could you? But I was freezing. So we stopped a muzhik and bought his coat from him. So then we had a nice drive."

"Go to bed," said Ludbridge, clearly controlling his temper with an effort.

"Of course. Certainly." Hobson put his nose in the air in an affronted sort of way and took four steps toward the staircase before stepping on the hem of his coat and falling flat. Bell-Fairfax hastily picked him up and relieved him of the coat. Hobson proceeded on up the stairs in dignified silence, ramrod-straight but clutching the handrail as though at any moment the house might shift on its foundations and heel over to starboard.

When Hobson's bedroom door had closed, Ludbridge took out a cigar and lit it from the stove.

"May we light the lamp again?" asked Pengrove.

"Do as you like. I'm going to go walk off my temper in the tunnel," said Ludbridge. He left through the door under the stairs and both Pengrove and Bell-Fairfax drew deep breaths.

"I thought he was going to explode," said Pengrove. "Poor Johnny!"

"But we're on the job, Pengrove, and he got drunk," said Bell-Fairfax. "And what if he led the Americans here? Or the Third Section?"

"Surely they've forgot about us by now, haven't they?" said Pengrove. "We've lain low for simply ages."

"We haven't forgotten about them," said Bell-Fairfax. "And *we're on the job*. We've all got human failings, and I know the job's almost done, but none of us can afford to be careless until it is."

"I suppose," said Pengrove, but thought to himself: *We've all got human failings, have we? What would you know about human failings?*

1850: Victory Crowned Not Your Fall with Applause

Hobson did not come down for breakfast next morning, at which Pengrove and Bell-Fairfax were privately relieved. Ludbridge said nothing on the matter, sipping tea as he read a back number of *Punch*.

At about half past nine there came a timid-sounding knock at the door to the tunnel. Pengrove went to answer it and let in Semyon Denisovich, who looked rather pale.

"Cyril Borisovich requests that you come to his office at once, sirs. He has a matter of grave importance to discuss."

"Not surprised," said Ludbridge. "Pengrove, Bell-Fairfax, come along."

"Should I go wake Hobson, sir?" said Bell-Fairfax.

"I shouldn't bother," said Ludbridge. Bell-Fairfax exchanged glances with Pengrove. They rose to follow Ludbridge and Semyon Denisovich into the tunnel.

Nikitin was sitting in his subterranean office. Sheets of yellow paper, densely scribbled on, covered the desk before him. He raised a haggard face as they came in.

"My friends," he said, waving them to seats. "I am afraid your excellent gift has proven itself invaluable already."

"*Afraid*?" Ludbridge said. "Ah. You've learned something disquieting from the transmitters, I take it?"

"We have," said Nikitin. "Do you ever long for the blissful ignorance of your childhood? I think at the end of my life I shall look back and see that mine ended the day you arrived here. Make no mistake, I am terrifically grateful to you! I shudder to imagine what could have happened . . . Yes, we have learned something. A great deal. I told you there is an inner cabal within the Third Section, did I not?"

"You did. And the fellow Dolgorukov is one of them."

"He is. And I told you I was afraid he was arranging something. We know that he is, yes, arranging something in his usual manner. Three days ago a prisoner escaped from the Trubetskoy Bastion prison. It has not been formally admitted, because such things are never admitted.

"His name is Ayrat Kazbek. He is a Crimean Tatar, arrested for organizing a cell of saboteurs during the war against the Turks in 1829. He escaped and was a fugitive for a number of years, celebrated among his countrymen resident here; but our czar is implacable as the Grim Reaper when he wishes to punish, and Kazbek was recaptured at last and sent to Trubetskoy Bastion. There he remained until Dolgorukov effected his escape."

"Why would your man do that?"

"Please! He is not *our* man. The Third Section freed Kazbek for their own reasons. They are hiding him with a group they have infiltrated, Wallachians resident here who grew mutinous during the late suppressions in the Danubian principalities. They believe Dolgorukov is one of their number. They enthusiastically welcomed Kazbek as a fellow rebel."

"And so?"

"And so the Third Section now has a teeming nest of scorpions for its use. When they have done what Dolgorukov has primed them to do, they can then be arrested and blamed—with justice—and executed. All praise to the Third Section, for rooting out conspiracy!"

"What, precisely, are these people being primed to do?"

"To commit an infamous act that will provide a reason for going to war again," said Nikitin, taking off his spectacles and rubbing his face.

"And what's the point of giving them Kazbek?"

"Kazbek is the weapon with which to commit it. A devout Moslem and a crack marksman," said Nikitin. "The most famous in a hand-picked assortment of enemies of Russia. What a show trial it will be! The Czar will have perfect justification for moving against the Ottomans again."

"But the war isn't coming for another four years, what?" said Pengrove.

"The Third Section does not know that," said Nikitin, with a wretched smile. "They know only that their master would like to expand his empire as far as the Dardanelles. They imagine this will give him the perfect excuse."

"If they look to give the Czar an excuse to declare hostilities, then they cannot mean their assassin to make an attempt on his life," said Ludbridge.

"No, they do not."

"And yet, arming a marksman who has a profound hatred of the Czar guarantees he will almost certainly hit his target."

"In this case, it does, yes."

"And so his target would be . . . ?"

"The Czarevich," said Nikitin. "Alexander. Our pupil."

There was a silence. "But . . . isn't it a bad idea to kill the heir to the throne?" said Pengrove.

"Not that unusual for the Romanovs," said Ludbridge, with a grim chuckle. "They've had spare princes executed now and then."

"Sad but true. And Alexander Nikolayevich has liberal ideas," said Nikitin. "We worked hard enough to ensure he had them, and he is no longer a boy—he is past thirty. It is supposed his reforming inclinations are set in his character now. It is feared he will be weak and lenient as a ruler, like Abdülmecid. And he has three younger brothers! Certain conservative ministers feel any one of them would be preferable to the Czarevich."

"Can the Czar really consent to such a thing?" said Bell-Fairfax.

Nikitin shrugged. "He may not know, but I cannot imagine he will kill himself over the bier. Not with such a golden pretext for invading Turkey."

"So Dolgorukov invents a conspiracy, lures a few malcontents into taking part in it, and gives their assassin access to your prince," said Ludbridge. "And you'd like us to do something about the conspirators, I expect?"

"No," said Nikitin. He looked down at a piece of paper on his desk, and slowly pushed it across to Ludbridge. "We can prevent the assassination ourselves. I would like you to do something about these people instead."

Ludbridge took the paper and studied it. It was a list of names and addresses.

"These aren't Wallachian names," he said after a moment.

"No. They are Russians."

"And Dolgorukov is among them. Are they members of the Third Section, by any chance?"

"They are. They form that inner circle of which I told you."

Ludbridge raised his eyebrows. He slipped the paper inside his coat. "This is rather an extreme measure," he said.

"Extreme measures are called for." Nikitin's hands were clenched in fists on his desk. "If the Third Section are capable of this, thwarting them will not be enough. They will try again. We know there will be a war, we know Russia must lose it, and in the aftermath it *must* be our man on the throne! Who else can we trust with reconstruction?"

"You understand that if we do this for you, you will have your own war here in St. Petersburg," said Ludbridge.

"It is already a war," Nikitin said. "And more is at stake than adding a few wretched hectares of land to our dominions. We fight for Russia's soul. Will she remain a nation in bondage to a brutal despot? Or can we bring her into the sunlight of the world at last? I would die to free my country. I would certainly kill for her.

". . . At least, if I knew how to kill," he added, looking down at himself in embarrassment. "I am a mere scholar. You gentlemen, on the other hand, are soldiers."

"Courteous of you to use the word," said Ludbridge. "It sounds so much better than *assassins*. I know, I know, the purpose is all; and I have a keen appreciation of your struggle, upon my word I do.

"But we are going to commit a massacre for you. You must know that there is no way we can make this look like accidents or suicides. Your opponents will know murder has been done. They will hunt for whoever was responsible."

"But you are strangers, and will be gone," said Nikitin. "And we are now able to listen to the most private of their counsels. We will use our advantage as ruthlessly as they use theirs."

"You will have to," said Ludbridge. "Well, fair enough. Let's see . . . You do realize, this will have to be done all in the course of one night? And within the next six days. We've already had word that London's pulling us out."

Nikitin nodded. "I am confident of your skill."

"How very kind. Your people will have to do the legwork, too. We'll need photographs of the targets, of their houses, floor plans if possible, and detailed descriptions of their routines. And we'll need them tomorrow at the latest, so as to allow time to study them."

"We can obtain these things."

"We'd do it ourselves, you know, but the matter of the Yankees strutting about the city with loaded guns makes it so awkward."

For the first time since they had entered the room, Nikitin gave a genuine smile.

"The Americans may not trouble us much longer," he said. "They have been granted permission to tour the country, in the company of picked guides who would show them exactly what His Majesty wished them to see. It is possible they will leave on their tour. It is equally possible they will not leave at all. In either case, their influence will cease."

"My dear chap, you're far too subtle for me," said Ludbridge. "You'll have to speak a little more plainly."

"I am not yet at liberty to do so," said Nikitin, his smile widening. "I am disappointed that you have not asked after the health of Brother Matthews."

"I haven't, have I? Well, how is Brother Matthews?"

"Very well indeed. We ought to have a copy of his leg's schematic for you within the next three or four days. The prosthetic arm, however, is even more remarkable than the prosthetic leg. We were quite surprised to learn that it, too, contained a hidden compartment. Before he escaped from Constantinople, Brother Matthews managed to fill it with a number of documents that should prove intensely interesting to His Majesty, when they are brought to his attention."

"Really." Ludbridge looked askance at Nikitin. "I don't suppose you could make a second copy of them, before we go home?"

"Since they contain information that would startle a few gentlemen in Whitehall, I am certain a copy could be spared for England," said Nikitin demurely. "In the meanwhile, we will set our best people to obtaining that other information you require."

The next several days were as busy as the previous week had been dull. The Kabinet gathered intelligence dutifully. As soon as reports came back Ludbridge commandeered one of the Kabinet's briefing rooms and began training Bell-Fairfax and Pengrove for the enterprise at hand. Photographs of the persons whose names were on the list were brought in, each feature analyzed and committed to memory. Their addresses were likewise learned, along with maps of each neighborhood, minutely inspected with an eye to entrances, exits, probable traffic and the presence of dogs.

"None of them seem to be men of any special rank," remarked Bell-Fairfax, as they trudged back along the tunnel at the end of the second day.

"They wouldn't, would they?" said Ludbridge. "Pretty well scuttles your secrecy if you're walking about with a row of medals on your chest, don't it? You'll notice, though, that four of them are ex-servicemen, like yours truly and, for that matter, you. Number Three and Number Five are former naval cadets who failed—or seemed to—and went straight from school into perfectly dull civilian jobs. Dolgorukov himself is from an old family, even if his official position is very minor embassy staff."

"They're a bit like us, really," said Pengrove.

"Except that we don't presume to make policy," said Bell-Fairfax.

"You wouldn't put a bullet in the Prince of Wales, if it was required?" said Pengrove.

"Certainly not," said Bell-Fairfax. "It wouldn't *be* required. We're working on the right side."

"To be sure, we are," said Ludbridge. They had come to the door and he opened it and stepped through. "Bloody hell—"

The room beyond was dark, the stove cold. Ludbridge flattened himself against the wall, gesturing for the others to stay back. But there was no rush of attack; only the silence of the house. Ludbridge drew a revolver from within his coat.

"Hobson!" roared Ludbridge, and darted to one side.

There was a muffled cry upstairs, and then the sound of footsteps descending the staircase hastily. "Sorry! Sorry, fell asleep!"

"For God's sake," said Ludbridge. He re-holstered his weapon, pulled out his lucifer case and lit the lamp. Bell-Fairfax and Pengrove emerged from the tunnel. They beheld Hobson standing at the foot of the staircase, rubbing his eyes.

"What time is it?" said Hobson.

"It's only half past eight. You didn't sleep through the six o'clock report, did you?"

"No, I didn't, got some coordinates for you—" Hobson dug a slip of paper from his pocket and thrust it at Ludbridge. "That's from London. For going home."

Ludbridge took it. He sniffed the air. "Have you been drinking again?"

"I solemnly swear that I have not," said Hobson, holding up his right hand. He swayed a little as he stood, however, and the smell of alcohol was evident on his breath. Ludbridge just stared at him for a moment, then turned away.

"Bell-Fairfax, see what's in the pantry," he said shortly. "I could fancy some of that black bread with the cold chicken, if there's any left."

Pengrove laid out the weapons.

"Must we all carry knives?" he said, looking doubtfully at the service blades. They were fully a foot long excluding the hafts, almost like small swords, with a wicked serration on the lower edge of the blade and a blood channel along the upper edge. He tested the point of one and watched in dismay as a red drop appeared on his fingertip.

"We must," said Ludbridge, not looking up from the map table where he was studying the latest intelligence. "The work has to be done quietly. Garrotes first when possible, knives second and possibly used in combination, revolvers dead last. And with silencers, I need hardly add."

"Ah. And here they are," said Pengrove, locating three canisters. He set them out beside the service Colts. "What's this thing like a shortened rifle?"

"Dog gun," said Ludbridge. "Fires darts to put the nice doggies to sleep. Shame to kill a dog that was only doing its job, don't you think?"

"So we would be using that at the house by the royal stables?" Bell-Fairfax looked up.

"Yes. The one with the mastiffs."

"And . . . we're not taking Hobson then," said Pengrove, having finished the weapons sorting and noting that there were only three piles.

"No." Ludbridge took a pencil and annotated a map.

"He's quite good with a knife, you know."

"Wouldn't do him a blessed bit of good if he were drunk," said Ludbridge. "Did I mention that I found out where he's getting it?"

"No." Both Bell-Fairfax and Pengrove looked up.

"Went into the cabinet to fetch out a bottle of vodka. Poured out a shot and, lo! Like the wedding feast at Cana in reverse, it had been transmuted to water. Opened another; same thing. Someone had picked the cabinet lock and been drinking the stuff and topping up the bottles with water."

"Perhaps the fellow in the grog shop cheated us," said Pengrove.

"Wouldn't stay in business long if he got up to tricks like that, would he?"

A gloomy silence fell. "Poor Johnny," said Pengrove at last.

"Poor the rest of us! He might have led anybody to this house, coming in by the door like that. We're in the first real danger we've faced, and he chooses to go to pieces."

"He's not a coward," said Pengrove.

"Some men squeal and run when they're afraid," said Ludbridge. "Other men pretend there's nothing at all wrong and tea will be served at four as usual. If there happens to be a lion roaming the parlor, guess which fellow gets eaten?"

"Did you ask him whether he'd broken into the cabinet?" said Bell-Fairfax.

Ludbridge gave a short humorless laugh. He shook his head.

"London confirmed it should be tomorrow night," said Hobson. It was the night of the sixth day, and they had slept until noon in preparation for what they were to do.

"Good," said Ludbridge. He had cleaned, and was now loading, his revolver. "We'll be back in the morning when the job's finished; we'll want our sleep badly. If all goes well, we can sleep until the rendezvous, rouse ourselves and go straight there. Your job tonight is to pack for us, Hobson. I want everything closed up and secured. The Kabinet will ship it after us. Pengrove, I know you've carried that brass coffee service across half the globe but I must ask you whether it is really essential to your continued survival."

"I suppose we could present it to the Kabinet as a gift," said Pengrove, looking mournful as he pulled on a black wool fishing jersey.

"Good man. Ready, Bell-Fairfax?"

"Yes, sir." Bell-Fairfax had already donned his jersey and was sitting quietly by the door to the tunnel. He was very pale.

"We're preventing the murder of an innocent man, son."

"Yes, sir."

"For God and Saint George, eh?" Ludbridge holstered his revolver and stood up.

"God and Saint George." Bell-Fairfax jumped to his feet.

"Tallyho," said Pengrove.

They emerged from the other end of the tunnel into the Kabinet's rooms and made their way to the arsenal. Having signed for their weapons, they proceeded to Nikitin's office.

"Hallo?" Ludbridge looked around, stepped into the antechamber and looked there. "Not here. Well, he'll be along in a minute. Harnesses on, gentlemen."

While they were fastening on the scabbards for their knives they heard voices in the corridor without. ". . . the most frightened I have ever been in my life."

"Let us hope he does not want to see you again," said Nikitin, entering the office with Matthews. Matthews's leg had been restored to him and he walked without any noticeable limp. "If he does, we will need to produce you fairly quickly, so it is probably best you remain here until we can find you passage back to New York. Ah, gentlemen! Gerasim will be along in twenty minutes with your transport. You will perhaps be relieved to know that the Reverend Breedlove and his friends are unlikely to trouble us again."

"How's that?" Ludbridge, buckling on his scabbard, turned to peer at them. Matthews, pale and shaking, took out a handkerchief and mopped his brow.

"His Majesty the Czar has ordered their arrest."

"Bravo!"

"Brother Matthews introduced himself as a courier from President Millard Fillmore," said Nikitin, going to a cabinet and producing a bottle of vodka and two glasses. "He produced some quite damning information on the group in Tennessee. It was presented as a timely warning from a fellow head of state inspired by brotherly concern." He poured out a glass and presented it to Matthews with a bow.

"Was it really?"

"Of course not," said Nikitin cheerfully. "But our brothers in Philadelphia were quite happy to transmit everything we needed to produce a believable fake. The substance was true, mind you; the Franklins simply hadn't had time yet to advise President Fillmore about the conspiracy."

"What conspiracy?"

"Why, the grand advance of Manifest Destiny! Making a friend and ally of His Majesty is only the first step. He will go to war with Great Britain (and France too, but that is only incidental) and so the British will lose their most-favored trading status, which the great republic of the United States will be only too pleased to accept instead. Of course Russia will win the war—how could it not? We are great and powerful! And so American traders will be free to travel throughout Russia, from Arkangel'sk to Petropavlovsk. But they will be selling something more than tobacco or rum or cowhides."

"And what would that be?"

"Sedition," said Matthews. "They will be fomenting rebellion, as filibusters do. Cells will be organized to overthrow the Czar and establish a democratic republic. That succeeding—which God forbid!—they'll make a grand alliance of the great powers of the Northern Hemisphere."

"God forbid, eh?" Ludbridge fitted a silencer on his revolver. "Thought you chaps were all for democratic republics."

"Sir, I can't deny I pity any nation that groans under such a tyrant. But the guarantee held out to the rebels will be that they may keep their serfs," explained Matthews. "Consider a union of slave-holding nations. What hope has abolition, outvoted by such a majority?"

"Happily, the specter will remain insubstantial," said Nikitin, with a chuckle. "When we were graciously granted permission to withdraw, His Majesty was an interesting shade of purple and roaring, positively roaring, the orders for Reverend Breedlove's arrest."

"Well done," said Bell-Fairfax. Matthews acknowledged him with a half-bow.

"Ah, here is your driver." Nikitin turned as a man in the clothing of a muzhik entered the room. "Gerasim Fyodorovich, is the wagon ready?"

"Ready for the gentlemen now."

"Then let's not waste any time." Ludbridge took out his watch and glanced at it. "Nikitin, if all goes as planned we'll return before sunrise."

The wagon traveled ponderously along Admiralty Avenue. Its load appeared to be crates of tea; in reality they were the exteriors of crates jointed together to enclose one space. Ludbridge, Bell-Fairfax and Pengrove sat inside on a bench, jostling uncomfortably as the wagon rolled over cobbles.

"First target," said Ludbridge, pulling on his gloves. "Personally drew up the orders for the massacre of three regiments of Hungarians, after they had surrendered. First advanced the suggestion that the Czarevich would be more useful as a martyr than as the inheritor of the throne."

The wagon slowed, stopped. "Go," said Ludbridge. Bell-Fairfax pushed open the rear wall of their enclosure—it swung on hinges, like a door—and held it as Pengrove and Ludbridge scrambled out and dropped to the street. He followed them and closed the door. The wagon rolled on at once. They ducked into the shadows under a stand of trees.

They stood on pavement beside a wall, looking into the garden on the other side. Beyond the garden they recognized one of the mansions carefully photographed by the Kabinet's intelligence-gathering crew.

"Should be two mastiffs on thirty-foot chains, southwest corner of the house," prompted Ludbridge in a low voice.

"I know—" Pengrove unslung the tranquilizer rifle from his shoulder and, raising it, peered through the thermal sight. "There they are! One's lifted his head. Looking this way." He took aim and fired. There was a muffled yelp. He cocked the weapon, dropping another dart into the chamber, and aimed and fired a second time. No yelp, but a high-pitched keening whimper. Pengrove put the gun back over his shoulder. Ludbridge took out his watch and counted off sixty seconds.

"They've both fallen over, sir," said Bell-Fairfax.

"Wait for it," said Ludbridge, and went on counting a moment longer. "Right. Circling the house, from the right-hand side. Go."

Pengrove attempted to scale the wall. Bell-Fairfax picked him up and set him astride it; he swung his leg over and dropped down the other side. Ludbridge and Bell-Fairfax followed him. They strode across the garden toward the house, silent on the damp earth. Ludbridge noted uneasily that, late as the hour was, there was still a lamp burning on the ground floor, and two dimly visible above, though neither shone from the location intelligence had identified as the target's bedroom. *House full of insomniacs*, Ludbridge thought.

They passed the silent dogs and stepped up on the flagstone coping that surrounded the house. Bell-Fairfax approached the lit window—French doors, actually—with caution. A dull red glow, lamplight through drapes, and a single bright bar where the curtains failed to meet. He leaned in sidelong to peer through. He turned to Ludbridge, his face rigid with tension, and pointed.

Ludbridge came close and looked for himself. He summoned his memory of the floor plans the Kabinet had obtained. This should be the target's study. The man seated at the desk, therefore, was likely to be the target. His shaven head and build answered the target's description. He was leaning forward, writing, turning his head at regular intervals to consult something. And the door fastened with a simple catch three-quarters of the way up . . .

Pengrove had already drawn his knife and, standing on tiptoe, slid the blade through between the doors. Bell-Fairfax flattened himself against the wall on the other side, poised to move. Ludbridge hoped they remembered that the doors opened out.

Evidently they did. Pengrove slid the blade upward until the catch lifted, but he did not let it drop. Bell-Fairfax swung the left-hand door open and stepped through, drawing out the braided-wire garrote. Ludbridge followed as closely as he could, but a gout of blood had already shot out and struck the wall by the time he stepped through the curtains; the target was slumping backward against Bell-Fairfax, garroted with such force the carotids had been sliced open.

Bell-Fairfax lowered the dead man to the floor slowly, carefully, and disentangled the garrote. He leaned forward, resting his hands on his knees, taking deep breaths. Ludbridge stepped past him to glance at the papers on the desk. He grinned savagely. Grabbing up the coded message and the cipher book that lay open there, he turned and saw Pengrove staring in at the dead man, horrified. He struck Bell-Fairfax lightly on the shoulder. "Go," he muttered. Bell-Fairfax lurched upright and ran out, with Ludbridge close behind him, and Pengrove sprinted after them to the garden wall. Bell-Fairfax recollected himself sufficiently to hoist Pengrove over the wall first, and then they were all three together in the street beyond. The wagon—which had circled around and come past again—rolled on ahead a few yards away. They ran after it. Bell-Fairfax pulled the door open and they scrambled in.

"God, this is easier when you needn't attempt to conceal anything," said Ludbridge. Bell-Fairfax doubled over, gagging.

"One down, five to go, what?" said Pengrove, with a trace of hysteria in his voice. "I say, Bell-Fairfax, are you all right?"

"Of course he's all right. Aren't you, my boy?"

"Yes, sir," said Bell-Fairfax with a gasp, sitting upright.

"A damned bad fellow got what he richly deserved just now," said Ludbridge, sliding the papers and cipher book under the bench. "And the world's a better place."

"Didn't think there'd be quite so much blood, however," said Pengrove.

"There'll be more, before we've done."

At Ekaterinskaya Place the wagon stopped again, in the pool of deep shadow thrown by a tower. "Second target," said Ludbridge. "Authorized the murder of a prison guard to enable Kazbek to escape. Over the past twenty years has arranged for the murder of eight survivors-in-exile of the Decembrist uprising. Lives alone in an upstairs flat with a female servant."

They climbed down from the wagon and it rolled on. They found themselves in a somewhat less palatial neighborhood, residences above shops, but the shops sold costly wares and the residences were anything but shabby.

"There." Bell-Fairfax pointed. "Rear entrance."

The building in question was a jeweler's shop, and to its right an archway led to a courtyard behind the building. All the windows they could see were dark. They walked up the passageway quiet as cats. The yard was in utter blackness under a clouded sky, but so thoroughly had they studied the layout of the place on paper that they needed no light. As one, they turned to the left and made their way up the brick staircase that connected to the upper story.

The door at the top of the staircase was locked. Ludbridge took out a case of lock picks and worked patiently at the door until, with a faint *snick*, the lock gave. Ludbridge stood, putting the case away, and, lowering his face to Pengrove's, he whispered, "Servant."

Pengrove stared at him a moment in incomprehension before nodding and reaching into his coat. He withdrew a small bottle. Ludbridge opened the door and nodded at him.

Pengrove walked into the darkness of the flat. It was warm, and smelled of good food recently prepared. Counting doorways, he made his way to what the Kabinet's intelligence had said was the servant's bedroom. The door was standing open. With great caution he tilted past the frame to peer in.

The bed was empty.

Pengrove heard his own heart pounding loud. He turned and retraced his steps to the back entrance. Ludbridge and Bell-Fairfax looked at him expectantly, but he jerked his thumb in the direction of the servant's bedroom and shook his head. Ludbridge scowled.

"Right. In her master's bedroom, I expect. Proceed as with Target Five."

Bell-Fairfax nodded and slipped past him into the house, with Pengrove following. They made their way to the target's bedchamber.

The servant lay on the side of the bed nearest the door, turned toward her master, who lay on his back. Pengrove took a sponge from his pocket, uncorked the bottle with his teeth, and shook a little of its contents onto the sponge. He leaned over and quietly pressed the sponge against the servant's face. Her eyes shot open, her hand clutched spasmodically; then she relaxed into deeper unconsciousness.

Bell-Fairfax walked around the side of the bed, irresolute. Pengrove saw his difficulty. How to garrote a man lying on his back? At last Bell-Fairfax drew the knife and, leaning down, cut the target's throat. He wasn't quite quick enough; the target opened his eyes and managed a hoarse squawk before his mouth filled with his own blood.

Ludbridge was in the doorway at once. "What the hell happened?"

"He woke up," Bell-Fairfax said. His hands were shaking. "It's all right now."

Ludbridge took in the scene in a glance. "Next time put a pillow over the face first. He'll wake up, but he won't be able to shout. Now clean your knife on the sheet and let's go."

Moving mechanically, Bell-Fairfax obeyed and sheathed his knife. He came around the foot of the bed and bent to lift the servant in his arms.

"Bloody fool! What d'you think you're doing?" Ludbridge clenched his fists.

"We can't leave her to wake beside *that*." Bell-Fairfax walked down the hall with the girl, into her room, and put her down on her own bed. Fuming, Ludbridge waited by the door. Pengrove slipped past him down the steps, followed, a moment later, by Bell-Fairfax. Ludbridge closed the door and followed. They ran, all three, down the passage and out to where the wagon waited in the shadows.

"You're a chivalrous idiot," said Ludbridge, when they had seated themselves and the wagon rolled on.

Bell-Fairfax shook his head, as though to clear it. "Coriander. Garlic. Beets. Vodka. Red pepper. Cumin. They must have been in his last meal. His blood reeked of them."

"You're imagining it," said Ludbridge gruffly, though he suspected Bell-Fairfax hadn't imagined it at all. "Calm yourself, for God's sake."

"But you were right to move the girl," said Pengrove. "Take heart, old chap. Worse things happen at sea, what? And you certainly ought to know! You were a Navy man, with a sword and all. Thought you must have become positively inured to spilled blood in the service."

"I never killed in cold blood before," said Bell-Fairfax.

"You'll become accustomed to it," said Ludbridge. "You must, son. Suppose a surgeon had to get his blood up before he could make himself amputate for gangrene? And we're surgeons, in a way. A calm hand's needed when the stakes are high."

"Yes, sir," said Bell-Fairfax.

"You'll do better on the next one," said Ludbridge. The wagon rumbled on.

"Third target. Active in crushing the rebellion of the Poles; arranged for the poisoning of the Polish rebel heroine Emilia Plater," said Ludbridge. Bell-Fairfax's expression settled into hard lines.

"Filthy thing to do," he said.

"Just so. No squeamishness, now."

"No, sir."

"Dog at this one, Pengrove. Chained at the rear of the house, by the back gate."

The wagon stopped. They emerged into a bush, or so it seemed; their driver had pulled them up into a service alley running behind a rather grand house, paralleled by a ditch thickly screened with scrub willows. They avoided getting their boots muddy and walked to the gate at the rear of the property. They could hear the dog on the other side growling a threat, a low rolling snarl punctuated by *whuffs*. Bell-Fairfax hoisted Pengrove onto his shoulders. Pengrove rose over the fence, into the view of a momentarily astonished borzoi, who was shot with a dart before he could react. He yelped and ran away, to the length of his chain; paused a moment to lick the spot where the dart had hit him, and folded up in a heap, unconscious.

"Wait for it," said Ludbridge, counting off the seconds. "Go."

Pengrove stepped onto the fence, jumped down and opened the gate from within. Ludbridge and Bell-Fairfax entered the yard. They surveyed the imposing mansion. Immediately before them were steps going down to what must be a kitchen entrance. Lamps shone behind curtains, and there was a sound of drunken merriment.

"Servants having a party," said Ludbridge, smiling. "Very nice."

Someone began to sing, in a high pure tenor, a sweet and melancholy folk tune. His voice carried; they could still hear it when they circled around to the front of the house. Ludbridge pointed up at the balcony.

Bell-Fairfax nodded. He bent and made a stirrup of his hands for Pengrove, who swarmed up him and stood on his shoulders. He could just reach the lower edge of the balcony and pulled himself up on its rail. Uncoiling a thin rope from around his waist, he made one end fast on the balustrade and tossed the other down. As Bell-Fairfax climbed up hand over hand, Pengrove turned and went to work on the balcony door with a case of lock picks.

They entered the room. There, as they had expected, was the target in his bed, flat on his back and snoring. Pengrove glanced nervously at the open balcony, through which the servant's song was now floating, quite audible.

Bell-Fairfax advanced on the bed. Dutifully, he took a pillow and thrust it down over the target's face. The target woke at once and began fighting like a madman, clawing to throw off Bell-Fairfax, who had to lean on the target with all his weight. He groped with one hand to draw his knife, but the target nearly threw him off.

"Stab him!" Bell-Fairfax hissed. Pengrove drew his knife and advanced on the bed. He lifted the knife but did not advance farther. He began to sweat.

"What do I—where do I . . ."

The distant tenor's voice rose in tender reproach, musically tearful. In desperation, Bell-Fairfax raised his knee and drove it into the target's stomach. The target folded up, with just the same *whuff* sound the dog had made, and Bell-Fairfax threw the pillow to one side and seized him by the throat with both hands. He closed the man's throat with his thumbs, crushed and wrenched. There was an audible *crack*. The target's clawing hands dropped away. The left hand and arm flopped down over the edge of the bed.

"Oh, I'm sorry," whispered Pengrove, aghast. The tenor began another verse, rising an octave. "I'm so awfully sorry!"

Bell-Fairfax merely shook his head. "Let's get out." He dove through the window and slid down the rope. Pengrove untied the rope, dropped it, and swung his legs over. Bell-Fairfax caught him when he jumped.

"All well?" murmured Ludbridge.

"I funked it," said Pengrove.

"All well," said Bell-Fairfax. "Target struck."

Ludbridge raised his eyebrows, but said nothing as they hurried back around the side of the house. They exited through the gate. The tenor reached the end of his song at last, to general applause.

"Bell-Fairfax, I'm so awfully sorry," Pengrove repeated, when they were back in the wagon.

"It's all right."

"What happened?" said Ludbridge.

"The fellow woke up and fought. I tried to knife him, but I got in the most beastly funk. I simply froze," Pengrove babbled.

"But the kill was accomplished?"

"It was, sir." Bell-Fairfax leaned back, flexing his shoulders and rolling his neck.

"Really, I don't know what came over me—I may not have it in me to do this, Ludbridge, I'm so sorry—"

Ludbridge held up his hand. "Not all men do. Quite all right; I'd rather you realized it now and told the truth."

"I think I might manage shooting someone. It's just—stabbing—I really can't—"

"So noted. We'll all have a nice brandy when this is finished. Until then, let's do our best, shall we?"

"Yes, sir," said Pengrove sadly.

The wagon rolled only a few hundred yards this time, along the same service alley, and stopped in another patch of deeper night.

"Fourth target," said Ludbridge. "Retired from public duties. During his bureaucratic career, oversaw the forced removal from their parents of hundreds of Jewish children for conscription into the Army. Fairly high mortality rates. Had a reputation for perverse cruelty. Seconded the suggestion that the Czarevich ought to be killed."

They exited the wagon and, leaping the ditch, climbed over a wall into the garden beyond. They found themselves in a little courtyard where a fountain bubbled, water jetting from a statue of a naked youth holding up a conch shell.

"Bedroom," whispered Ludbridge, pointing up at a window. Bell-Fairfax and Pengrove craned back their heads to study it. There was no balcony. Bell-Fairfax shrugged and, stooping again to make a stirrup of his hands for Pengrove, waited while Pengrove vaulted up. Pengrove had to stand at his full height on Bell-Fairfax's shoulders to reach the window-latch. However, it opened fairly easily with the blade of his knife.

He climbed in and looked around. There was a bed, with a mound of blankets suggestive of an unconscious sleeper. Pengrove took a quick step close to confirm that there was, indeed, a man asleep in the bed. He turned back, opened the other side of the window and fastened the end of the rope around the window-mullion. A moment later Bell-Fairfax climbed through. They advanced on the bed.

Its occupant lay on his belly, both arms under the pillow. Pengrove, anxious to prove himself after the last incident, grabbed up the pillow from the other side of the bed and thrust it down on the sleeper's side-turned face. Bell-Fairfax moved in with drawn knife and, after a moment's hesitation, stabbed once in either of the man's kidneys, twisting the blade as he withdrew it. There was a muffled scream. The bed became a swamp of blood almost at once, black against the white sheets. When the man stopped moving—which he very shortly did—Pengrove removed the pillow.

"Oh, I say!" he muttered. "Wasn't this one supposed to have a beard? A-and wasn't he supposed to be an old chap?"

Bell-Fairfax, who had been cleaning his blade, came close and looked. He muttered a heartfelt oath.

Ludbridge, waiting in the garden, caught the scent of a good cigar. He ducked against the wall just as a middle-aged gentleman, placidly smoking a cigar, came strolling around the side of the house in his dressing gown and slippers.

The target—for Ludbridge recognized him from the Kabinet's photograph—sat down on the edge of the fountain. He took the cigar from his mouth, sighed, looked up and saw Ludbridge.

Ludbridge lunged forward, shoving the target backward into the basin of the fountain. The cigar went flying, scattering sparks on the footpath. Holding the target's head under water with one hand, Ludbridge pulled his knife and stabbed quickly, twice, the blade going in up under the rib cage. The target stiffened and relaxed utterly. The red ash on the end of the cigar faded out.

Bell-Fairfax, having noticed the splashing, came to the window and looked down to see Ludbridge rinsing his blade in the water. He climbed down the rope, caught Pengrove when he jumped from the window, and all three ran to the wall and got over.

"Was that him?" said Bell-Fairfax, when they were back in the wagon.

"The chap in the fountain? Yes," said Ludbridge, drying his blade on the side of his trouser-leg.

"Then we've killed an innocent man."

"Somebody else in the bed?"

"He was lying face downward," said Pengrove. "We didn't realize—"

"We've killed an innocent man!"

"My dear chap, if he was consorting with the target I doubt very much whether he was innocent," said Ludbridge. "And I don't mean mere sodomy. Nasty dogs run with other nasty dogs. In any case, it can't be helped. We got our man, which is what matters. Not likely to happen with the next target; he's a married man. You'll want the ether again, Pengrove."

"Yes, sir."

"Let's see, the next target . . . Another publicly retired fellow. Formerly an interrogator; favored torture. Owns extensive estates and on one occasion had three hundred serfs hanged over the theft of his favorite horse. They were executed in groups of ten, with the proclamation that the executions would continue until the thief confessed. When it was discovered that the horse had simply got loose and wandered away, the target was heard to observe that it was just as well, because the winter was likely to be a hard one and the serfs were likely to have starved if he hadn't hanged them first. An enthusiastic supporter of the plot to murder the Czarevich."

"This one will get what's coming to him at any rate," said Pengrove, with a sidelong glance at Bell-Fairfax.

The wagon rolled along for a great while, taking the western road out of the city. The fifth target had fled for a week's rest in the district of wealthy homes in the suburbs, between St. Petersburg and the grand palace and gardens of Peterhof. It was a full two hours before they stepped down from the wagon and found themselves in a remote country lane, standing in drifts of yellow leaves. Bare branches, black as pen-strokes, were silhouetted against the stars.

Ludbridge looked around. "There." He pointed at a house set back from the road. It was a single story dacha, though of considerable size, heavily decorated with scrollwork under its eaves.

"No climbing," said Pengrove in relief. He frowned. "No dogs?"

Bell-Fairfax lifted his head, inhaled the scents of the night. "No dogs. But it's starting to smell like morning."

"This oughtn't take long," said Ludbridge, glancing up at the westering stars. They walked toward the house through its disheveled garden, between pumpkins half-buried in a sea of gold, the fallen leaves of cherry and plum trees.

"Remember the wife," said Ludbridge, as they stepped up on the porch. Pengrove nodded and patted the pocket containing his ether bottle. "And bedroom's second doorway to the right."

Bell-Fairfax nodded. He tried the door; it was unlocked. He opened it and went in, followed by Pengrove. Ludbridge walked to the end of the porch and leaned out, looking at the night. He had badly wanted a cigar ever since the previous target, and briefly considered smoking one on the way back to the city.

There was a sudden flare in the bushes a few yards away, a red point of brightness that Ludbridge took at first for the glowing end of a lit cigar. The illusion was momentary. He realized that it was a single red leaf in a thicket, illuminated by a square of light from . . .

Ludbridge leaned over the porch rail and saw the lit window at the rear of the dacha. Someone was awake, had lit a lamp.

Within the house, Bell-Fairfax and Pengrove walked through the open door of the bedroom. There, in the great bed with its striped counterpane, lay a fond couple in early middle age, plump wife and snoring husband.

Pengrove dug in his pocket for the sponge, uncorked the bottle of ether. He had started toward the bed when Bell-Fairfax grabbed his arm. Pengrove heard, too late, the heavy tread in the hall. A bulky form appeared in the doorway, and a voice said something in a hoarse but profoundly deferential whisper—perhaps the Russian for "Master, you wished to be awakened early."

The plump wife sat up, saw Bell-Fairfax and Pengrove standing there in the shadows, and opened her mouth to scream. Terrified, Pengrove launched himself at her with the ether bottle. He stumbled over a slipper on the floor and fell, dropping the open bottle beside the bed. The wife screamed. Behind him he heard a scuffle and impact, as Bell-Fairfax charged the servant and wrestled with him.

Pengrove held his breath and dabbled in the spilled ether with the sponge. He rose on his knees and groped for the woman's face, as she screamed again and bit at his hand. There was a terrific struggle going on in the corner, with furniture smashing. He heard the bearlike servant give a mortal cry of agony, just at the moment that he gave vent to his own, for the woman had sunk her teeth into his hand. Fortunately she inhaled a good deal of ether in doing so and collapsed backward, only to reveal her husband sitting up in bed and aiming a pistol into Pengrove's face.

Pengrove dropped to the floor with a gasp, straight into clouds of ether fumes. He heard the deafening report of a pistol shot.

When next he knew anything, Pengrove was dangling head-down over Bell-Fairfax's shoulder. Yellow leaves, pretty yellow leaves like golden sovereigns, and black-currant bushes with a few berries still, close enough to reach out and pick if only Bell-Fairfax would stop marching along, though actually Pengrove didn't feel much like eating anything . . . in fact . . .

He retched, clapping his hands over his mouth.

"Pengrove's all right," he heard Ludbridge say. Pengrove watched the earth and stars shift places and found himself on his feet beside the wagon. He promptly fell against it.

"Now, let that one be a lesson," said Ludbridge. "Never let what might seem to be an easy kill fool you into complacency. If I hadn't shot the beggar, you might both have died."

"Yes, sir. Thank you, sir," said Bell-Fairfax, catching Pengrove before he fell over again and hoisting him into the wagon.

They rode back over the miles to the city, Bell-Fairfax and Pengrove lulled half-asleep by the rocking of the wagon. Ludbridge checked his watch frequently by the light of a lucifer, scowling.

"Here's another lesson," he said. "Always assume any job will take longer than you thought. It's half past four already. I do hope the fellow's a late sleeper."

"Dolgorukov?" Bell-Fairfax roused himself.

"Even he. This is the chap from Constantinople, remember? The one who puts weapons into the hands of others. He brought the Americans to Russia. He encouraged Arvanitis in the plot that made it necessary for us to take steps. He's playing the same game with Kazbek now. You might call him a tempter; has an unerring eye for finding the one fellow in a crowd who's gullible and angry enough to commit murder, and making certain he has funds and encouragement. An expert at obscuring his tracks, as well. There's never any trail evident to lead from an Arvanitis or a Kazbek to the Third Section, none at all.

"Fortunately for you, Pengrove, I retrieved your ether bottle before the last dram or so left evaporated." Ludbridge took it from his pocket and handed it off to Pengrove. "That's for the common-law wife. There's an old woman too, but she sleeps at the rear of the house and she's half-deaf."

"A housekeeper?" asked Bell-Fairfax.

"Yes, I believe so," said Ludbridge.

The wagon stopped. They swung open the door and scrambled out, horrified at what seemed to be brilliant daylight; after a moment they realized that the sun had not in fact risen, with the world still sunk in predawn gloom, but night was indisputably fled. Ludbridge pulled out his watch and checked it.

"Half past five. Oh, well, one does one's best. Let's see . . ."

The wagon had pulled into an alley, the darkest place available. They walked out to the street and Bell-Fairfax stared around. "There," he said, pointing. Ludbridge spotted the house: a two-story residence set back in its little garden, with a willow tree by the gate.

They approached and stood in the deeper gloom under the willow. "Oh, bugger," said Ludbridge. The upper floor was dark, but directly before them was a terrace upon which a pair of French doors must open, when the weather was fine. They were presently closed, but through them Ludbridge could clearly see Dolgorukov, sitting at a table and sipping from a glass of tea as he studied something—a letter? A map?

"Well, so the chap is an early riser," said Ludbridge. "We've been lucky after all. One well-placed shot ought to do it."

"I can manage it, I think," said Pengrove.

"Do you feel well enough?"

"Oh, quite." Pengrove drew his revolver, checked the silencer. He took careful aim and fired.

Three things occurred nearly simultaneously: the *pop* of the silenced report, a fracture star appearing in the third pane of the left-hand door, and Dolgorukov flinging himself backward at the last possible second.

"Jesus," said Ludbridge. They ran through the gate and across the garden, just in time to see Dolgorukov picking himself up and scrambling awkwardly into an inner room. Ludbridge kicked the door in, drawing his own revolver as they burst through all three. There was blood on the floor and a clear glimpse through into the next room, where Dolgorukov, clutching the side of his head, was shouting at two terrified women.

Ludbridge fired at him. He dodged, once more at the last possible second, and the bullet hit the younger of the women. Ludbridge, closely followed by Bell-Fairfax and Pengrove, charged into the next room in time to see Dolgorukov bolting up a flight of stairs. The two women threw themselves in front of the staircase, blocking the way, screaming imprecations at Ludbridge. He fired, killing the already-wounded wife, killing the old woman he had known must be Dolgorukov's mother, with her same broad patient face and small features.

There was a roar behind him and Bell-Fairfax raced past in a blur, leaping over the crumpled bodies of the women, bounding up the stairs after Dolgorukov. *"You damned coward—"*

Ludbridge and Pengrove heard a scream, heard smashing furniture and then—inhuman noises. Pengrove, shocked mute, was still staring at the dead women. The noises from upstairs went on for a surreally long moment, and then stopped abruptly. They heard a final *thump*, as of something hitting the floor.

"Bloody hell," said Ludbridge, shoving aside the bodies to get up the stairs. Following him, Pengrove giggled shrilly.

"It is that," he said.

Three rooms opened off the upstairs landing. Two were clearly bedrooms but the third contained a sewing machine and dressmaker's dummy, with a few bolts of cloth on a shelf. The window was standing wide open, curtains blowing in the dawn breeze. Blood was everywhere: on the curtains, on the broken deal table and chair, on the white bosom of the dummy, on the bolts of cloth. Pieces of Dolgorukov were scattered everywhere as well. His head had rolled across the room and was resting on the treadles of the sewing machine.

Bell-Fairfax, clutching his knife, had fallen to his knees in the midst of the scene of carnage. He was panting with exertion. His pale eyes were blank, his face set.

Pengrove looked into the room past Ludbridge and, turning back on the landing, doubled over and vomited.

Bell-Fairfax blinked. He looked up, saw Ludbridge. He looked around himself at the blood, at the dismembered body, and he dropped the knife. "My God," he said, in a thick voice. "Done it again."

He fumbled at his holster. "Oh, Dr. Nennys," he muttered. "How has it come to this? Never touch anyone unless your blood is as cold as the polar oceans. Worthless bastard."

He drew the revolver and set it to his temple. Ludbridge stumbled into the room and wrested the revolver from his blood-slick hand. He knelt by Bell-Fairfax.

"No, son, no," he said. "You don't have that luxury. You're not that weak. You'll do your duty, because you must. I know you."

"I don't believe you do, sir." Bell-Fairfax turned those pale eyes on him, but they were dull now, unfocused. Ludbridge thought wildly: *This is the consequence of giving a golem a soul*. He summoned all his courage and set down the gun, took Bell-Fairfax's face in his hands. He spoke rapidly.

"Yes. I know you. You were made for this work, son. I'm good at my job but you'll be better. And what's the job, boy? We're avenging angels, you and I. We wade through horrors that would kill other men, and why? *To kill the real monsters.* To stop them, because if they're not stopped the great day will never come, will it? We commit the necessary evils. We take the blood on ourselves. And we *will* pay for it in the end, yes. The job carries its own justice.

"The day will come when we'll have to sacrifice ourselves, when the job will require our lives, and we'll give our lives bravely because that'll be our duty. The score will be paid in our own blood, the balance sheet wiped clean. *But not today.* We haven't finished the job. We're soldiers, son. You're a good dutiful soldier, aren't you?"

"I hope so, sir," said Bell-Fairfax automatically.

"I know you are."

Bell-Fairfax drew a deep breath, closed his eyes. When he opened them again they were clear and sharp, the eyes of the man who had convinced Ludbridge to want a glass of Maraschino. Ludbridge felt an involuntary craving for it even now.

"My apologies, sir," said Bell-Fairfax. "I quite lost control of myself."

He picked up the gun, carefully holstered it. "We must go," said Ludbridge. Bell-Fairfax nodded. He left the room without a backward glance, Ludbridge following. Pengrove was leaning against the wall on the landing, trembling.

"All right, Pengrove?"

Pengrove nodded and fell into step with them as they descended the stairs. They passed the dead women and exited through the French doors, picking up speed as they crossed the garden and running once they were through the gate. Bell-Fairfax held the wagon door until they were all in and pulled it shut behind them. They sat in darkness, exhausted, as the wagon moved on.

They spoke little amongst themselves on the ride back. Bell-Fairfax spoke only once, when he turned to Ludbridge and said: "I truly understand now, sir, about complications."

"Eh?"

"He oughtn't to have taken a wife. He oughtn't to have lived with his mother."

When they walked up the echoing tunnel to the Kabinet's headquarters, Nikitin had not yet come in. Ludbridge sought out the arms master on duty, turned in their weapons, and asked him to let Nikitin know a report would be forthcoming later in the day. They tarried only long enough to wash their hands before going back through the tunnel that led to the house on Anglisky Avenue.

The house was dark when they stepped into the front parlor, with only a sliver of morning light coming in through the drapes.

"Hobson's not up yet, eh?" Ludbridge gave a weary chuckle. "Lazy beggar."

Bell-Fairfax lifted his head, inhaling sharply. He went to the foot of the stairs and looked up. Something in his expression made Pengrove run after him when he started up the staircase. Ludbridge followed, moved by the same impulse.

The door to Hobson's room stood open. Hobson was slumped forward at the table, snoring.

"Drunk again," said Ludbridge in disgust. He only spotted the bullet hole, with its thin trail of dried blood, when Bell-Fairfax lifted Hobson's head. "Good God!"

"Johnny!" cried Pengrove.

"But *he* hadn't done anything," said Bell-Fairfax, looking deadly pale.

"Yes, he had." Ludbridge sagged into a chair. "Came home by the front door once too often. Someone saw him. Oh, Jesus." He looked around, leaped to his feet again. "Where's the Aetheric Transmitter?"

"We will do everything we can for him," said Nikitin, as Hobson was carried away on a stretcher. "It is just possible he will regain consciousness. He may be able to tell us who did it."

"It can only have been the filibusters," said Matthews. Ludbridge looked up from the bench where he sat between Bell-Fairfax and Pengrove, who were slumped forward in grief and fatigue.

"What d'you mean? I thought they'd been arrested."

"The order was given," said Nikitin, looking embarrassed. "Unfortunately it would appear someone at court rushed to give them a timely warning. Dolgorukov, more than likely. They escaped. The Third Section has been hunting them for hours now. I had been rather pleased to hear it; I thought they might be plausibly blamed for the six executions."

"I reckon they decided they weren't going to cut and run without something to take home to their people in the States," said Matthews. He pulled up a chair and sat beside Ludbridge. "Sir, I am heartily sorry for thee and thy good friend, and for this calamity."

"Oh, *calamity*'s the word, to be sure," said Ludbridge heavily. "We're leaving in fifteen hours, and we've got to recover the transmitter somehow."

"Thou hast a bomb concealed in it, hast thou not?"

"There is one, yes."

"Ours may be detonated from a distance. What about thine?"

Ludbridge shook his head. He patted his watch chain. "If the bastards had gone after *my* gear, they'd have blown themselves to Kingdom Come, but there was no remote connection with the transmitter."

Matthews rubbed his chin. "We build a device into ours that sends a constant signal into the aether, so we may track it."

"So do we."

"Well then!" Matthews stood up. "This much at least I can do for thee, brothers. I'll find the thing, or I won't go home. Go thou and get thy rest. Brother Cyril and I will do what we may, and I promise thee better news when thou wakest."

———

When they woke, long hours later in the Kabinet's guest quarters, Nikitin himself brought them tea on a tray. "And here is news to cheer you," he said. "First, Johnny Albertovich survived his surgery and is stable. Our surgeon is guardedly optimistic."

"Thank God for that, anyway," said Pengrove. Ludbridge, methodically gulping down hot tea, merely nodded.

"Second, Brother Elias Elijavich has found your transmitter, though he has been unable to recover it for you."

"Why?"

"Because he is a Quaker," said Nikitin. "And so he cannot do what will be necessary."

He explained that, shortly after the member of the Franklins had defected to the filibusters, there had been a theft of a transmitter out of one of the listening posts in Philadelphia. The Franklins had faced the moral dilemma of detonating it and killing whoever might be near it, or leaving it in enemy hands. They found a third alternative. One resourceful brother had devised a way to locate the signal for the missing transmitter: three other transmitters had been loaded into covered wagons and driven in slow circles around the city.

"By triangulating the signal, they had located the transmitter in a boardinghouse on the bank of the—Delaware—River." Nikitin enunciated the name carefully. "They recovered the transmitter, by some extraordinary means which involved no violence, or so I am given to understand, and only a mildly criminal act. Elias Elijavich suggested we do the same.

"The boys from the listening post were entirely ready to drive wagons around St. Petersburg for a week, if necessary. They were very fond of Johnny Albertovich, you know. Fortunately they located his transmitter's signal within three hours. We went to work with a map and a set of compasses, Elias Elijavich and I. Come and see what we have found."

They followed Nikitin to one of the conference rooms. Maps were spread out on the tables, with a sheet of tracing-paper laid over the largest. Matthews stood peering down at it, as Mikhail Ilych drew on the sheet with red ink.

". . . *this* empty house on Chlebnaya Street. We have already done reconnaissance. The weeds in the garden have been trampled down; the lock on the cellar door has been broken. They must have fled there last night, after capturing the transmitter. Foolish; it is very near a police station and they are likely to be seen if they stir out, unless they are very careful. On the other hand, the police being so near will hinder anything we do. But there they remain! We think they intend to wait until nightfall, and get out of the city overland."

"Won't they try to leave by the Neva?" Matthews looked up as they entered with Nikitin. "Ah. Good evening to ye, one and all."

They returned his greeting somberly. Mikhail Illych came forward, tears in his eyes, and embraced each of them in turn.

"Johnny Albertovich was our brother," he said. "*Is* our brother, whatever happens. We will avenge this for him."

"Blood begets more blood," said Matthews quietly.

"So it does," said Ludbridge, shaking Mikhail Ilych's hand. "You let us avenge him, son. We have more experience, I suspect."

Mikhail Ilych nodded sadly. "He cannot be moved, for now; you will have to leave him with us, but I promise you, we will care for him as one of our own."

"Damned decent of you." Ludbridge coughed, looked down. "Well. As Brother Matthews said, won't the bastards try to steal a boat or something, and get away on the Neva?"

Nikitin shook his head. "They cannot, any more than you can. The river is being closely watched by the Third Section. They may think they can cross the country unseen, if they travel by night."

"And night will fall . . ." Ludbridge took his watch out, checked it. "Entirely too soon. You've got men posted, watching the place?"

"We have," said Mikhail Ilych.

"Good. Can you provide us with that wagon again, old chap?"

"And a good deal more." Nikitin bowed from the waist. "But for this moment, come and have supper. You will want a good meal in you, for this night's work."

A great deal of preparation was necessary. There was, however, time to pay a visit to Hobson's bedside in the Kabinet's infirmary, before they departed. Unrecognizable for tubes and bandages, Hobson lay still and gray as one of the dead men in the martyrs' shrine. Ludbridge shook his head. Pengrove turned away, tearful. Bell-Fairfax looked on, white and silent; as they walked away he said only, "He was an innocent."

Chlebnaya Street lay no great distance from Anglisky Avenue, in a thinly populated district of warehouses.

"They must have run to the first empty house they could find, after shooting Hobson," said Bell-Fairfax. In the darkness of the jolting wagon he was a grim shadow, with pale eyes in a pale face.

"So much the easier for us," said Ludbridge. "Though I'm not happy about the police being so nearby if things should get—how shall one put it? Theatrical."

"It's as though last night never ended," said Pengrove, with a hollow laugh. "Here we are again! The murder-fairies have magically cleaned our garments and our weapons."

"We aren't murderers," said Bell-Fairfax.

"Just as you say, old chap. The blood will spill all the same, what? And none of it will bring back Johnny."

"No," said Ludbridge. "It won't. But I invite you to consider what our world will be like, in a few years, if the Reverend Breedlove and his lads get that transmitter back to the States and take it apart. If they've any clever fellows in their ranks who can reason it out from first principles, they will. Who knows what they might extrapolate further?

"But you can be sure they'll come after the Franklins to see what else they've got that might be useful, and, with all respect to our Quaker friends, I don't give them much of a chance of holding out against a determined enemy with weapons. Then *we'll* have an enemy set on carving out a slave-holding empire, armed with our machines.

"No, I really do think we must stop them here, tonight, whatever the cost."

"We will," said Bell-Fairfax.

The wagon slowed, drew up. They emerged into a small open square at the eastern end of Chlebnaya Street. The wagon rolled away as Ludbridge looked at his watch. He tucked it away in his pocket.

"Very well. Gentlemen, do you recall the church with all the scaffolding around it, just opposite the Admiralty?"

"And the War Office," said Bell-Fairfax.

"The one with the golden dome," said Pengrove.

"That's the one. We should be on its roof no later than nine o'clock, on the highest point we can reach. Shouldn't have any difficulty climbing the scaffolding."

"On the roof?" Pengrove turned to stare at him.

"That was what I said. Bell-Fairfax, do you think you could find your way there, at need?"

"Yes, sir. It's Saint Isaac's Cathedral."

"Good. This shouldn't take long, but one never knows."

They walked up Chlebnaya Street, which was dark and seemingly deserted. As they approached, however, a shadow detached itself from a doorway and met them. It was Semyon Denisovich.

"They are still in the house," he said quietly. "They broke into the cellar, but have gone upstairs. The house belonged to the English; in a way they are burglars on your property, yes? The manager of the tallow manufactory lived there. He has since found less fragrant quarters, and so the house is used for storage."

"Is that what the stink is?" Bell-Fairfax looked disgusted. Semyon Denisovich nodded and pointed at a complex of warehouses across the canal, immediately to their right.

"That is the Tallow Depository. Your industrious merchants have filled it with barrels of grease. Rancid fat becomes candles to light the mind of the scholar, you know. Life is full of such transformations."

"So it is." Ludbridge looked thoughtfully at the house. "Are all of them in there?"

"We think so. No one has gone in or come out, but we have seen a light behind the shutters from time to time."

"How far away is the police station?"

Semyon Denisovich pointed toward the southeast. "Two streets that way."

Ludbridge nodded, never taking his eyes from the house. It was a plain wooden frame building of one story, shabby, its paint peeling. "Used for storage," he said. "Storage of tallow, by any chance?"

"Yes. There are barrels in the cellar."

"How many entrances and exits?"

"A front and back door. Two windows in each side."

"Right. How close can we get to the house without being seen?"

"Quite close. The Americans broke into the cellar easily."

"Thank you." Ludbridge shook his hand. "I'd be obliged to you if you'd pull your fellows out now. We will do what needs to be done."

"You are certain, sir?"

"Yes, thank you. Quite sure."

"Then God and all His saints go with you, sir." Semyon Denisovich bowed from the waist and walked back into the shadows.

"Pengrove?" Ludbridge turned to him. "Make your way across that lane. Position yourself where you'll have a clear shot at anyone coming out the back of the house. Be sure you mind the windows as well as the door."

"Am I to shoot anyone who emerges?"

"You are."

"To kill?"

"I should have thought that was obvious."

Pengrove nodded, tight-lipped, and slipped away into the night. Ludbridge turned to Bell-Fairfax.

"Now, my boy, we're going into the cellar."

"And up into the house to confront them, sir?"

"Good Lord, no. A chap could get killed that way," said Ludbridge, and started off for the house. Bell-Fairfax followed. They stepped over the low fence and threaded their way through the neglected garden, following the convenient wedge of obscuring shadow thrown by the house itself.

The cellar door was at the side of the house. Ludbridge squatted beside it and worked for a moment on the hinges with a vial of penetrating oil. Putting the vial away, he rose and cautiously lifted the door. It opened out with the faintest rasp.

Ludbridge pulled on his night vision goggles. After a cursory glance within he lowered himself into the cellar, motioning Bell-Fairfax to remain where he was.

The reek of tallow, in the close darkness, was stifling. A few white-hot blurs darted across the floor as rats fled from him. Ludbridge looked around. Barrels were stacked in the corner, some twenty or thirty of them, clearly leaking; the floor was a quarter-inch deep in tallow, and bootprints could clearly be seen proceeding through it toward the stairs.

Stepping cautiously, Ludbridge went to the stairs and listened.

" '. . . And they shall dwell safely therein, and shall build houses, and plant vineyards; yea, they shall dwell with confidence, when I have executed judgments upon all those that despise them round about them; and they shall know that I am the Lord their God.' There you have it, boys. That's the Lord's own promise to us. We're a great nation and we're going to be greater, because it's His will. And don't you just pity those who cross us? God Himself's going to smite them," said a voice.

"Amen. What time is it now?" a second voice inquired.

"Almost eight. Say, I can't read this damn map—," said a third voice.

"Voices! There's voices coming out of this thing!" the second voice cried.

Ludbridge turned and picked his way back through the sea of tallow. He bent and hefted the barrel nearest the window. It came free grudgingly. Gritting his teeth with effort, Ludbridge lifted it toward the cellar doorway. Bell-Fairfax, anticipating his need, drew a deep breath, leaned in and took it from him. He leaned out again, releasing his breath with a gasp, and Ludbridge followed gratefully. After closing the cellar door and sliding the broken lock back through the hasp, Ludbridge straightened up and wiped his hands on a handkerchief.

"Now then," he whispered. "Just you go to the opposite corner from Pengrove's location. Find a spot where you can watch the front door and the windows. Shoot them as they come out, and make your shots count, son."

"I will, sir." Bell-Fairfax was there one moment and gone the next, vanishing into the darkness like a ghost.

Ludbridge drew his knife and, twirling the haft between his palms, drilled first one and then another hole in the spongy wood forming the top of the barrel. He tilted it and got his arms around it. Lifting it awkwardly, he carried it around the garden, laying down a stream of liquid tallow along the side of the house and here and there splashing the house itself. At the last he drenched the wooden hand-rail by the back steps. Having emptied the barrel, Ludbridge set it down among the dry bushes and took out his handkerchief once more. He wiped his hands again and tied the handkerchief to the hand-rail.

Pulling out his lucifer safe, Ludbridge lit one and held it to the edge of the greasy handkerchief. It caught immediately. He flicked the still-burning match into the dry weeds at the side of the house and walked away.

The fire bloomed, spread, fluttered delicate shades of blue and pink in its flames before brightening to white and gold. It ran up the rail; it spread down into the weeds and advanced along the side of the house, licking up the slopped grease shining on the walls. For a long moment it was silent before some knot of pitch in the firwood boards exploded with a bang, and the flames roared out with joy.

"Fire!" shouted Ludbridge as he walked on. He made his leisurely way to the black shadow into which Bell-Fairfax had disappeared, and stepped inside just as the front door of the house opposite flew open. Bell-Fairfax raised his revolver.

A man in a black topcoat appeared in the doorway, with the Aetheric Transmitter clutched in his arms. Bell-Fairfax shot him. He fell backward through the door, an explosion of blood at his throat. There were shouts inside the house and then the front window was smashed out. There were gunshots from within. Ludbridge felt himself shoved to one side by Bell-Fairfax, just as bullets slapped into the wall behind him. He drew his own revolver and fired, aiming for the figure he spotted crouched over the dead man inside the open door. The figure rose with the Aetheric Transmitter in its arms, staggered and fell over. More movement within; someone crossed the doorway. Both Ludbridge and Bell-Fairfax fired at the moving target, but there was no way to know whether they'd hit it.

Another gunshot, from the rear of the property. Pengrove. There were no shots fired from the house after that, and it was flame shattering the windows now as the house burned merrily. The fire illuminated their hiding place, and so Ludbridge and Bell-Fairfax darted out and ran back down the street to another doorway. There were shouts now, men running from the direction of the police station.

"Oughtn't we go, sir?" said Bell-Fairfax, as Pengrove, ducking from shadow to shadow, joined them.

"Not just yet." Ludbridge turned back and watched the fire. No figures came crawling from doorways. But when would—

There was a deafening explosion and the roof blew off the back half of the house, sending flaming debris up into the night and down, clattering on the cobblestones, hissing into the canals. The fire shot up, towering under a gigantic column of smoke that blotted out the stars.

"Ah! Farewell, Aetheric Transmitter," said Bell-Fairfax.

"Felmouth won't be especially pleased, all the same. It blew at the back of the house," said Ludbridge, frowning. "That'd be your man, then, Pengrove."

"I suppose," said Pengrove. "The door opened, a man looked out and I shot him. It appeared he had something in his arms."

"So . . . first man starts out the door with the transmitter, Bell-Fairfax shoots him. That's one. Second, third and presumably fourth men break the windows and shoot at us. Not a lot of bullets for three men, especially three heavily armed Americans, were there? Second man goes over to first man and picks up the transmitter. I shot him. I saw him go down. So that's two. Third man goes over to him, I would guess to pick up the transmitter, and both Bell-Fairfax and I shoot but possibly miss. Assuming we did, and he ran to the back of the house and was stopped by Pengrove, that's three for certain. And I only heard three voices coming from above, when I went into the cellar."

They stared at the fire. Distant men were trundling a pump engine as close as they dared, running a hose into the adjacent canal.

"I don't like it," said Ludbridge. "Where's the fourth chap?"

"Right here, you limey bastard," said a voice from under the trees, some yards away. A shot rang out. An American in a black topcoat stepped into the firelight, clutching a revolver. Bell-Fairfax shot him between the eyes; he jerked backward and fell.

"Ludbridge?" Pengrove caught at his arm.

"Damn," said Ludbridge. He took a few tottering steps backward and sat down heavily on the curb, holding his stomach. Bell-Fairfax and Pengrove crouched beside him.

"Sir, I can carry you—it's not far to the safe house—," said Bell-Fairfax. Down the street by the fire, someone had noticed them, was pointing and shouting.

"No; it's nicked an artery. Renal artery, I think. Kidney too, perhaps. Bleeding to death," said Ludbridge shakily. "Job carries its own justice, you see, Bell-Fairfax? Not unexpected, after all." He pulled the goggles from around his neck, handed them to Pengrove.

"No, sir, listen to me! Look!" Bell-Fairfax pulled off his own goggles and leaned down close, staring into Ludbridge's eyes. "You *will* live! You'll die one day, but not now. Not now! It didn't really get an artery at all, that's nonsense, we'll go back and the Kabinet's surgeons will save you. You'll have a pleasant holiday somewhere restful, B-Bournemouth perhaps, and—and then—"

Ludbridge gazed back up at him, eyes wide, before giving a rusty-sounding shout of laughter. "My dear chap! You're good, but you're not *that* good!" Swiveling his eyes toward the commotion down the street, he grimaced. "Bell-Fairfax, get Pengrove out of this! Saint Isaac's. It must be nearly time . . ." He groped for his watch, sighed, and sagged forward.

With a heartbroken look, Bell-Fairfax gently leaned him backward onto the curb. Ludbridge lay staring up at the stars and smoke, his mouth open as if in wonder. Three or four men had begun to march toward them.

"We must leave him," said Bell-Fairfax, hoarse with emotion. "It's our duty."

"The silencer! The watch chain!" said Pengrove. Bell-Fairfax nodded and took them, and Ludbridge's cigar case as well. He rose to his feet. Pengrove got up too and they turned and ran. Someone from the advancing group shouted and a moment later there was the *bang* of an old-fashioned flintlock musket, but they had already dodged around a corner and a moment later were running for their lives up Offitzerskaya Street.

On and on they ran, until Pengrove's lungs burned and stars flashed before his eyes. A night watchman loomed out of a kiosk and flung his hand up before them, barking an order; Bell-Fairfax bowled him over and kept on, only doubling back to grab Pengrove, who was faltering, by the arm and pull him along. They ducked up one of the footpaths beside a canal, and crossed to the other side by a bridge. Pengrove stumbled and fell.

"Must stop a minute," he gasped, getting to his hands and knees.

"Mustn't," said Bell-Fairfax with a shake of his head, pulling him to his feet. Pengrove turned to look back over his shoulder. His eyes widened in horror.

"Good God, half the city's on fire!"

Bell-Fairfax turned, startled. They saw now a titanic column of flame, and were bewildered that one house could burn with such fury, even with a cellar full of tallow. A moment later they realized that their own, lesser blaze was burning to the left; the huge fire had sprung up just to the right.

"Bloody hell," said Pengrove. "That's the tallow warehouses. That's British property. The explosion—all the burning bits flying everywhere—" Bell-Fairfax had grabbed him again and pulled him onward before he could finish his sentence, and he ran on with renewed energy. They put another canal between themselves and the fire, as another musket shot sounded from somewhere down the street. Pengrove had lost all sense of direction by now, hurtling down one interminable street and then another, until his legs gave out on him again. He went down just as another watchman charged out in front of them. Bell-Fairfax swung, knocked the watchman flying, grabbed Pengrove and flung him over his shoulder, and ran on.

Pengrove, borne jolting along, heard more musket fire. He was able to raise his head far enough to see a mob spilling into the distant end of the street, searching for them. He saw also the city skyline backlit by the warehouse blaze, sharp as a cutout of black paper. "Oh, they'll kill us—," he gibbered.

Bell-Fairfax skidded to a stop, swung him down. "I won't let them kill you too. Climb!"

Pengrove looked up. They had reached Saint Isaac's at last, surrounded as it was with scaffolding. Bell-Fairfax caught him up again and set his feet on one of the rungs. "Pengrove, for Christ's sake!"

Hearing another musket shot, Pengrove began to scramble upward, possessed of an unreasoning anger. "I say, what do you think I am?" he muttered, as he went up hand over hand. "A bloody monkey, sir?"

"You'll be a dead one if you don't hurry," said Bell-Fairfax from above him. He reached down and pulled Pengrove up another three or four rungs. They fell together over the parapet to the lower level of the roof, just as a musket ball cracked against the scaffolding and ricocheted away.

Pengrove lay flat, gulping in breath. Bell-Fairfax rose on his knees and shouted. Pengrove rolled over and stared. A rope ladder was swinging toward them across the void. He followed it upward with his gaze. There, looming into sight, gigantic above the golden dome and underlit by the distant conflagration, was the black bulk of an airship.

Epilogue

The Evening of 1 March 1855

Pengrove gazed into his teacup. The drone of the airship's motor vibrated cup against saucer, making a pattern of concentric circles on the tea's surface. His teaspoon was skating, slowly but inevitably, toward the edge of the table. It came to the edge and danced into midair. A hand flashed out, caught it before it fell and set it beside Pengrove's saucer.

"You were an excellent field operative," said Bell-Fairfax, in his gentlest and most persuasive voice. "I thought it was the rankest injustice, to transfer you to a desk position."

Pengrove looked up sidelong before dropping his eyes again. Bell-Fairfax continued to regard him steadily.

"I asked for the job, old chap," said Pengrove. "I'm quite happy in Maps and Image Analysis. The work isn't as dull as you'd think and one does sleep soundly at night. I'm only here now because I was on the mission in '50, I suppose. Presumably someone thought I'd be useful as an advisor."

"I asked for you," said Bell-Fairfax. "You were the best man I knew for the job. And one does feel more confident with an old comrade taking care of the details. Ludbridge thought highly of you, you know."

Pengrove risked another glance at Bell-Fairfax. His eyes, pale as a winter morning sky, shone with earnest good will. The coaxing warmth of his voice summoned a host of memories. Pengrove found himself overcome with nostalgic longing for times past, when he had been a younger, happier man in a happy band of brothers. Constantinople, where he and Bell-Fairfax had played the fools so convincingly. Good old Ludbridge! Good old Hobson! . . . Ludbridge, lying in the street looking up at the cold stars. Hobson, slumped over a table with a bullet in his brain.

Pengrove shuddered and looked away, out through the brass frame of the porthole, at the stars.

"I'm gratified, but anyone might have plotted this for you. It's simply a matter of bringing you down in a park, rather than on someone's roof or in the Neva," he said.

"All the same." Bell-Fairfax smiled.

"And you're quite clear about your exit route?"

"Perfectly."

"You can hardly expect help from the Kabinet on this one, you know. They may detest the fellow, but killing their own czar is a bit much to ask them to accept."

"They'll be grateful, whatever they may say," said Bell-Fairfax, lighting a cigar. "Their man will take the throne at last. In any case, the war has dragged on long enough. Sure you wouldn't like to come along?"

Good God, thought Pengrove, *is the man lonely?* He held up his hand in refusal. "Too much blood, old chap. I can't quite reconcile our high purpose with the number of murders it seems to require."

"Necessary removals," Bell-Fairfax corrected him. "Someone must take the responsibility for them, Pengrove."

"And you seem to be quite equal to the task," said Pengrove, with a melancholy chuckle. "Quite the perfect soldier. Is this really the life you wanted, though, when you joined the Society? You were quite the idealist then. I know I envisioned a great deal more . . . philanthropy, you know. Clothing and feeding the poor. Tossing them loaves and fishes from the gondola of a flying machine. Educating them. That sort of thing, all made easier with our glorious *technologia*."

For the first time, a shadow of regret crossed Bell-Fairfax's face. "I should have preferred to serve my fellow creatures in such a manner, yes. But our duties are not always pleasant ones, are they? And I must do what is required of me."

"All the same, did you imagine for a moment that the path to the great day would be strewn with quite so many corpses?"

"I ought to have expected it," said Bell-Fairfax quietly. "I seem to be fated to the work."

Pengrove shook his head. "And then there's the question of whether we can do any real good after all. All that intelligence we gathered, wasted!"

"Not entirely."

"Oh, no? I was with Greene when we got the news about the Light Brigade. You should have seen his poor face. When I think of the hours we spent in that valley, mapping everything! How *could* they have got it wrong?"

"The finest intelligence in the world is useless if the general won't study it," said Bell-Fairfax, with a shrug. "I'm inclined to believe that direct intervention, as it were, is much more effective."

"Your present job, for example?"

"If you like."

"Well, there's no denying *you're* effective. You're getting quite a reputation amongst the Residentials, you know. That incident on the Pacific front last year, when Commodore Price so unaccountably shot himself . . . there's a rumor that was your work. It wouldn't have been, would it?"

"I am not at liberty to say," Bell-Fairfax replied. "But I can tell you he had accepted money from the Golden Circle, and deserved his miserable end."

"Golden Circle? Oh, the filibusters," said Pengrove, shaking his head. "I understood they'd shifted their interests to the Caribbean now."

"That may be the case," said Bell-Fairfax, with an opaque look. He exhaled smoke. Both men looked up as Dr. Nennys entered the saloon.

"We're at the coordinates, Bell-Fairfax."

Bell-Fairfax stood and stubbed out his cigar. "Ready, sir." He turned and extended a hand to Pengrove. "Enjoy the flight, Pengrove. Wish me luck?"

Pengrove shook his hand. "Best of luck, old chap."

"God and Saint George!" Bell-Fairfax turned and strode from the saloon, followed out by Dr. Nennys. Dr. Nennys was wearing a cloak, and the freezing blast of wind from the flight platform swirled it in theatrical flourishes.

Pengrove shivered, turning up his collar. He didn't care for Dr. Nennys. Pengrove knew a bully when he saw one. The perpetual smug smile, the patronizing attitude masking the cad underneath . . .

And he had heard a few rumors about the man lately, ugly, absurd stories that couldn't possibly be true but were chilling nonetheless. Dr. Nennys had been a member at Redking's for well over a century. Dr. Nennys never lost a duel, and always killed his opponent. Dr. Nennys had made a pact with Satan . . .

Pengrove shook his head. Fairy stories! *We live in the modern age, after all*, he thought.

The drone of the airship's engine was loud in the flight platform's cabin; both men had to raise their voices when they spoke.

"You have no qualms, my boy?" Dr. Nennys inquired, watching as Bell-Fairfax strapped on the latest version of the Ice Rifle.

"None, sir." Bell-Fairfax pulled on his goggles.

"I need hardly tell you what a proud man you have made your old headmaster," said Dr. Nennys. Bell-Fairfax smiled.

"Thank you, sir!" He saluted and, turning, stepped through the door onto the flight platform. He raised his arms as the two waiting technicians stepped forward with the harness. They fastened him in securely. Far below them, Dr. Nennys saw the grid of lights that was St. Petersburg, the bright diagonal of Nevsky Avenue, the dark winding serpent of the Neva.

"We will retrieve you at the rendezvous point in forty-eight hours," he called to Bell-Fairfax.

"Until then, sir!" Bell-Fairfax grinned at him and turned back, signaling to the technicians. They pulled the levers; Bell-Fairfax leaned forward as the wings of the flying machine unfurled. He dropped from the platform into the night. A moment later the gusts picked him up and sent him on his calculated trajectory.

Dr. Nennys stepped out on the platform, bracing himself against a strut to watch, and smiled as the thing he had made descended on black wings, over the habitations of men.